D1708287

The Eternal Masquerade

Vincent Thurman

Rev. date: 12/08/2015

To order additional copies of this book, contact:
Xlibris
1-888-795-4274
www.Xlibris.com
Orders@Xlibris.com
716341

Dedications

I would like to thank God for making all of this possible. I also want to dedicate this book to my sister Nicole D. Nance (1972-2013). Through the good times and the bad times no matter what, you will always be my little sister. I love you, & I will always miss you. Also, this book is dedicated to all the family and friends who believe in me and inspire me to write; thank you from the bottom of my heart.

Acknowledgements

I would like to thank some people who made this possible. Thanks to my wife, Nichole, for your love, support, and having faith in me to write this 2nd book. To my daughters, Amber, Montressa, Asha, and Khadijah; my nephew, Ja'von; and my two-grandsons, Zy'kise and Kyrii, I love you guys. To my family and friends, thank you for your inspiration and support. I would like to say thanks to Tina Moll for all that you've done to help me with this 2nd book. A special thanks goes to my very close friend JoAnn Brace for all your encouraging words and your voice of wisdom you gave me.

I want to say thank you to all the people who gave me encouraging words and supported me on the 1st book; that means a lot to me. Your kindness shall never go unappreciated.

Characters

Vampires
Antione Semaj (King of the Horde Coven)
Nicolette Albany (2nd command to Antione)
Erika Capri (assistant to Nicolette)
Lars Grayson (vampire muscle for Althea York)

Grey Clan
Sebastian Kane
Edmund Martin
Marcella Jacobs
Adam Mercer
Jai Li

Black Clan
Adrian Kane (Sebastian's brother)
Andre McCall
Candice Ames
Nathan Dakota

Red Clan
Alexia Kane (Sebastian's sister)
Fritz Marx (deceased)
Javier Trevor
Ethan Barclay

Witches
Estelle Craig (Jenessa's Grandmother)
Celeste Craig (Jenessa's mother deceased)

Jenessa Craig (A damphyre; genes mixed with vampire, howler, and bloodline witch)

Geneieve Fredrick (Estelle's sister, love interest of Edmund)

Persia Fredrick (Geneieve's daughter, a vampire, bloodline witch but bitten by Nathan Dakota, her ex-boyfriend)

Althea York (powerful Salem witch)

England witches
Seth Crenshall (powerful warlock from England)

Camden, Alden, and Jazmine (Seth's children)

Howlers (man-wolves)
Sasha Deren (Alpha leader, Basketball coach)

Gregory Turner

Jamal Carmichaels (Son of Karen Carmichaels, the DA)

Andrei Petrov

Additional Characters
Andree Cardan (Human with a sixth sense, he can sense and see mythical creatures of nature. Friend of Sebastian)

Hayden Nichols (an Acheri, a child vampire at the age of 7)

The Committee (Members who want to banish all mythical creatures in Haven-Crest)

1. Lindsey Dobson is the current mayor of Haven-Crest.
2. Harold Maynard and wife Susan, Fire-Chief and High School Principal, original foundering ancestors
3. Marion Burton, Chief-Doctor, an original foundering ancestor
4. Karen Carmichaels, District Attorney, an original foundering ancestor
5. Jennifer Simmons, the Judge, an original foundering ancestor
6. Sheriff Ross Michaels

Detective Karen MacRae (Lead detective for Haven-Crest Police Dept.)

Agent Monica Ambrose (with the North Carolina State Bureau of Investigations)

Xavier Michaels (Town historian and the son of Sheriff Ross Michaels)

Amy Christian (Librarian who has knowledge of deciphering symbols in ancient codes and breaking riddles)

Donna Gill (Information Systems Security/Networking Technology instructor)

Sean Rice & Susan Cease (Assistants to Donna Gill)

Deputies Liam Carter and Mark Ewing

Friends of Jenessa:
Chrisha Fleming (Montell and Felicia Fleming are Chrisha's parents)
Jai Li (Huang and Dana Li are Jai Li's parents)

News
Jewel Walker (Channel 2 News in the field reporter)
Joshua Kirkpatrick and Ashley French (Channel 2 News anchors)

Celister Howard (Town coroner)
Alonzo Quintana (Jenessa's homeroom teacher)
Rudy Trackett (Town drunk who has seen a vampire and a howler but no one believes him)
Nayda (Gypsy fortune teller)
Syngyn (Immortal vampire and howler hunter who kills for bounties (Doctor Kareem Jensyn)
Declan Toliver (the only survivor of the Unit 4 gang massacre)
Malcolm (an old friend of Edmund and Sebastian who betrayed the Grey Clan and Hutch, a rival vampire who was killed)
Medusa (Powerful voodoo witch)

The 3 mythical creatures from the map:
Shiloh Carter (Witch)
Sable (Howler)
Van Gogh (Vampire)

Introduction

Let me start by saying that Haven-Crest is one of the original towns that was set up by some of the witches who escaped from Salem. They wanted to establish a place where all witches and any mythical creatures could be safe from hunters and conservatives who were out to capture and torture them for being considered to be servants of the devil. Once they found a place of peace where they could contact each other and have fellowship, this new Covenant of witches decided to adapt and live normal lives. Some migrated south to Florida to start new lives of their own, but they still practiced their witchcraft to stay true to their purpose in life. Now, the witches who stayed in Haven-Crest felt that this would be a new home where they could start fresh and leave their past behind. They had to deal with Indians and also with outlaws trying to steal and take over the land.

On a cold December night as the howling winds blow, not a soul stirs on this frostbitten night. As fires crackle from many fireplaces within this town, an evil-hearted woman makes her way through the empty roads to her point of interest: the house of the Craigs. Roman and his pregnant wife, Estelle, are unaware of this wearisome traveler. The artic winds cut just like a knife through the woman's coat. She reaches her destination and gives a sudden hard knock at the door. Both of the residents look at each other, and Roman says, "Who could be this be at this hour?"

Estelle responds, "I don't know, but I have a very bad feeling all of sudden."

Roman walks to the front door, and suddenly there is another hard knock. Then there is old, raspy voice that says, "Roman, open the door; it's me."

Roman stands in amazement because he hasn't heard that voice in a very long time. He opens the door and he sees a figure standing there in the bitter cold with a hood draped over her face. She slowly walks in and pulls the hood back to reveal her face to Roman. "It's been a really long time since I've seen you, Roman."

He says in an easy voice. "You're right; it has been a very long time."

Roman is frozen in his tracks and partially unable to move as he sees her face. Estelle enters the room and drops her hot glass of cider on the floor. Suddenly, Althea reaches out to hug her oldest and dearest friend. When the pleasantries are out of the way, Estelle asks, "Althea, why are you here?" as curiosity has gotten the best of her.

Althea turns with a devilish grin and replies, "I'm here for the Book."

Roman and Estelle both look at each other in utter amazement.

"What book are you talking about?" Roman returns her answer with a question; she begins to look angry as if getting frustrated with Roman.

She answers, "You know what book I'm referring to. Do not play games, dear Roman. I know you were the one Lazarus gave the spell book to," says Althea.

Estelle looks at Althea and asks, "What happened to you? How did you manage to escape?"

"From the looks of it, it appears that I got a little burned at the stake if you know what I mean. As you were making your escape, some of us witches took heat so that could happen. I got really burned, but I survived. Now I want the Book because I have business to take care of," replies Althea."

"We don't have the Book, nor did Lazarus give it to me," answers Roman.

"I don't want to have to make this ugly; no one needs to get hurt," bluffs Althea.

"We can't give you the Book," answers Estelle.

"I want that Book, and I'm not leaving until I get it," threatens Althea.

Roman pushes Estelle behind him and says, "You horrible witch, you'll never see or recite any spells from the Book; I promise you that."

Althea realizes that she is outnumbered, so she tries to be cunning by saying, "Why can't we share the book? We all could profit from its power. Holding onto it isn't going to deter any other witch who comes here looking for it causing trouble. Now with us, we three could become a powerful team that no one would want to reckon with. Just share the Book with me. I have heard of the secrets it holds and spells that can be learned. Just imagine the powers we could gain together. Don't be a fool and miss this opportunity to join me with the hopes of unleashing the dark magic to rule the world."

Roman understands that this now has escalated beyond all powers of reasoning, and he knows he must rid his house and the town of Haven-Crest of this corrupt witch. Estelle has the same intentions as her husband, so she decides to make the first move before Althea can conjure any unsuspecting spells on them. Estelle reaches her hand into the bowl that's on the table, and in one quick motion throws a handful of salt on Althea, and all that can be heard is sizzling, like skin burning. She realizes that the salt has burned her own hand but hopes that it will somewhat deter Althea from her ulterior motive of getting the Book. With the salt sizzling the skin on her face and hands, Althea steps back, and suddenly the door swings open as a wintery blast of cold air rushes inside the house of Roman and Estelle. Once the wind dies down, they both see a dark figure standing in the doorway. Suffering from the burns to her face and hands, Althea yells, "Lars, help me! I can't feel my face, and it burns so bad."

Lars looks at the two witches, and immediately his features start to change. He begins breathing deeply, his fangs extend, his eyes turn a golden-black, and he starts growling and replies, "Can you make it over here by the door because I can't come in unless they invite me?"

"You can rest assured I won't invite you inside my house for anything, you hideous monster. If you want your partner out, you will just have to let her come to you," replies Roman.

Slowly, Althea crawls over to the door, and once she is outside, Lars picks her up and blurs off into the cold night. They are never heard from again. Roman slowly moves over to the door, closes it, and secures the locks. Then he turns to his wife and says, "Estelle, honey, are you alright? How's your hand? You didn't have to risk injuring yourself by throwing the salt at her, but I'm glad you did. How's the baby doing? I was hoping that things didn't get out of hand with you being pregnant; I don't want anything to hurt you or the baby. Althea was hell bent on getting the Book tonight, and I agree with the possibility of what she said about other corrupt witches coming here looking for it and putting us in danger as we try to protect the Book. I know what must be done to ensure our safety; I must follow Lazarus's orders by hiding the Book."

"We're alright, honey, and my hand will be okay after I do a healing spell on it. I figured out what she was up to, and I do believe she would have tried to hurt us, especially me in this condition. Who was that guy at the door, and what did he mean when he said he couldn't come in unless we invite him in?" replies Estelle.

Roman takes a cloth, dips it in some herbs, and wraps it on Estelle's hand. Then he recites a spell while holding her hand. He gets her a glass of cider, and they sit by the fire. Roman opens the Book of Spells and says, "To be honest, I think I may know what he is. He's called a vampire, otherwise known as a creature of the night and a servant of the devil. I remember Lazarus telling me about them. He told me that they were very rare, but in this day and time, who's to say how many there are. Well, we see that Althea has the assistance of one now, so we need to be very careful from here on out."

Estelle sips her cider and says, "I agree. I think we need to hide the Book of Spells. Why not create a map so that no one will be able to understand the words on it? We could create clues and riddles to make it hard to decipher for any mythical creature. I don't want to know where it is hidden, so don't tell me."

Roman laughs and replies, "Good idea. I'll start to work on it immediately. I see why Lazarus knew you were the best witch in the Coven. There are a couple of witches I know who can help me with this."

Roman goes over to the table and begins creating the map so that no one will be able to find the Book. For many days and nights, Roman works on all aspects of making the location very difficult to discover. Two months later on the first day of spring, Estelle gives birth to a baby girl, and they name her Celeste. In the back of Roman's mind, he knows that he must make the journey to set things in motion, so after Celeste's first birthday, Roman leaves to start his quest. While out on the quest, Roman meets a vampire named Darwin who helps him find the people he will need for the task at hand. In about six months, Roman returns home and is at ease with what he has accomplished. As the years go by, they live in peace knowing that even though at any moment, an element of evil could be lurking right outside of their front door, they have done all they can to keep the Book out of the hands of dark forces.

Chapter 1

The dark cloud that looms over the normally quiet town foreshadows the fact that some will awaken this morning to tragedy. As Jenessa awakens, she opens her eyes hoping that the events that happened last night were just a nightmarish dream. She sits up in her bed and plays back the images of what took place last night. Then she gets up and goes to check on Estelle's condition. As she walks in her room, Estelle is in her bed asleep. Jenessa walks out of the room and wonders if everything was a dream or if it really happened. Yesterday, Haven-Crest High School had a costume party for the students to raise money for the spring break trip to Myrtle Beach. Somehow there was an accident and someone died, but the sheriff's department can't find the body. Some of the witnesses there said they heard a girl scream, but no body was found and no foul play has been identified.

As for the Crenshalls, yes, there was a tragedy at their expense. The clash resulted in the death of Jazmine at the hands of a powerful witch named Estelle Craig. Camden stands at the coffin of his beloved sister. As the tears roll down his cheeks and the anger builds inside of him, he knows he must do a most hateful act to a person. He must get revenge on the woman he loves for his sister's soul. He knows in his heart this is wrong. However, he also feels he can't turn his back on his family, so what must he do? As he stands after hugging the coffin, Alden comes in and says, "I want to say I'm sorry. I know you and Jazmine were close. I tried to get father to stop, but once Estelle stripped him of his powers, he became obsessed with finding the Book and the map. I knew something like this was going to happen, but I hate that it happened to Jazmine."

Camden replies, "I've got to confront the girl I love over this business about the Book. Now I want it more than he does because we've got to bring Jazmine back. Where do we begin looking for this Book?"

Alden looks at his brother and says, "I don't know. We will have to get with Dad when he gets back."

Jamal wakes up with his body still aching, and he remembers the pain he felt last night on the way home. He reaches for the phone to call Coach Deren, and he says, "Coach, I hope I didn't wake you. I'm sorry I missed you last night, but I do want to talk to you about the changes in my body. Last night, I could hear my bones cracking and breaking, and I experienced pain like I have never felt before. What's wrong with me?"

"Get dressed and come over to my house. I can explain it to you then. I think it's about time for you to know," the coach replies.

As they hang up, Jamal hopes that Coach can give him the answers that will help him understand why his body is going through so many changes. His mom enters the room with a motherly look of concern on her face and says, "Are you okay, Jamal? I heard you in here last night moaning in pain. Is there anything you need to tell me? You know I worry about you."

Jamal replies, "Mom, I'm okay. I'm going to talk to Coach about my muscles aching; I think I was cramping because we did a lot of running yesterday."

Karen says, "By the way, how was the costume party last night? Did you have fun? Who won the cash prize?"

"It was alright. Some people had freaky costumes on though. I think the winner was the girl dressed like Lady Gaga. What have you got going on today, Mom?" replies Jamal.

"I have to be in court at nine and then get my hair done later. Let me go. I'm running late now; I'll talk to you tonight," replies Karen.

Jamal leaves headed over to the coach's house. On the way, he calls Jenessa to check on her, but all he gets is her voicemail. He leaves a message and hangs up. He stops and gets something to eat and then pulls in the coach's driveway. He gets out, walks to the front door, and rings the doorbell. Jamal hears the coach say, "Come in and shut the door."

Once inside, he walks into the kitchen and sits at the counter. The coach says, "Jamal, I'm glad you called me last night. Have you told anyone about the changes you've been going through lately?"

"Just my mom and a good friend of mine," replies Jamal.

"I need for you to be open minded with what I'm about to say. I want you to come here and stay the night so I can show you what I want you to know," says the coach.

Jamal hesitates and says, "Sure, that shouldn't be a problem; who else is coming?"

The coach replies, "There will probably be a couple of us here, but don't worry. You're ready for some conditioning, so let's go practice."

At the Li house, all is quiet; suddenly, Jai gets a hunger sensation for blood, so she sits up in the bed and looks for her bag with her flask in it. She blurs across the room to the bag and drinks all the blood in the flask. Now that the sensation has stopped, she reaches for her phone to call Jenessa and check on Estelle and says, "Hey girl, you up? I'm sorry about calling this early, but I wanted to check on Estelle."

"When I woke up this morning, I thought last night was a bad dream. I went in to check on her, but she was still sleeping," replies Jenessa.

Jai Li interrupts her and says, "Jenessa, go back in and check on her. I've got a bad feeling she may be in a sleep coma."

Jenessa jumps up and runs into Estelle's room to try and wake her up. There's no response, and then she yells for Persia to come in and help her. Persia comes in and says, "What's up? Is Auntie alright? Let me check her vitals."

Persia checks her heartbeat, pulse, and breathing. Everything feels very weak, so she turns to Jenessa and says, "I don't think Auntie is doing well. We may need to take her to a doctor to get checked out now. She could possibly be in a coma and won't wake up."

Jenessa stands in shock and then says, "Grandma doesn't believe in doctors, just her herbs to heal her. I know that sounds old school to you, but that is how she is."

"We'll just keep a check on her as the day goes on. I hate to get in your business, but what are you going to do about Camden?" asks Persia.

"Well, I don't know to be honest. This situation is far beyond our working this out now. People have been injured and even killed because Seth wants the Book so badly," replies Jenessa.

Persia frowns and says, "I see what you're saying, but you still need to talk to him. Hey, are the girls coming over today so we can hang out?"

"I guess so. Jai already called concerned about Grandma," responds Jenessa with a worried look on her face.

"Have you talked to that sexy ass Sebastian yet? Girl, he is FINE; that's who you need to be talking to. He's so cute," replies Persia.

"Sebastian's my boss, and nothing is going on there. We are just close friends who enjoy each other's company. One thing I can say about Sebastian is that he believes in loyalty to his family and friends," Jenessa explains very nonchalantly.

Persia giggles and replies, "Okay, that's my boss."

As the cousins joke around to cut the edge off of worrying about Estelle, in the back of Jenessa's mind, she knows that there is a chance she could be dying. She prays that doesn't happen.

With the top priority of finding the Book of Spells, Nicolette and Erika have assembled the best computer hacker in Haven-Crest. They have called in Donna Gill, a professor from HCU who has many degrees and certifications in System Security, Encryption, and Forensics, and her staff of top notch hackers. They all sit down with Amy and brainstorm about the riddles and codes she has discovered. Donna takes a look at the key and says, "Amy, I've read your notes, and I gather that the riddles will lead to remote locations where clues can be uncovered for the key to lead you to the map. When I hold this blue light under the key, there also appears to be information stored on it."

Donna reads the symbols, writes down what they could be, and then runs a reference check through the computer. There is so much riding on deciphering the key because that will put them in position to find the map. However, Erika and Nicolette know that working with Adrian could have deadly consequences in the end. They know he can't be trusted, but they must make a deal with the devil for right now. As Adrian comes inside of Nicolette's office, he sits down and says, "Good morning, ladies. How are you today? I see you've assembled a team to crack the riddles on the key. If there is anything I can do, please let me know."

"The same too you, Adrian. Where are your guys? Remember you said the security was 24 hour," demands Nicolette.

"Relax, don't have a cow, and yes, my guys are here and already in position," replies Adrian.

Nicolette leaves the office and heads off to her appointment. Erika says, "Adrian, this is a really big deal we have here. Don't get on her bad side by being sarcastic with her, alright?"

Adrian looks at Erika, shrugs his shoulders, and says, "I hear you; I won't blow it."

Sebastian sits laid back in his recliner thinking about Estelle. He hopes that she makes a good recovery because right now Jenessa needs her for guidance and mentoring. He tries to think of someone who could help her recover, yet no names come to mind. Suddenly, Edmund comes into the room and sees Sebastian laid back in the recliner and says, "Sebastian, what's wrong? You seem to have a major problem on your mind."

Sebastian turns and replies to his old friend, "It's Estelle. She was attacked and injured pretty badly. I checked on her last night, and it looked serious. I told Jenessa that we were coming by to check on her this morning. I offered to bite Estelle last night to help with the injuries, but she declined. She's a good woman who didn't deserve to get ambushed by Camden's father. Another thing is that she offered to give us a map to exactly where the Book that Roman hid is located."

At first, Edmund doesn't respond to his best friend; he just stares out the window. Then he turns and says, "I've known Estelle for a long time; she's a special friend to us. I would hate for her to pass on after all these centuries. We've got to do what we can for her. I know of a sorceress who could possibly help her. Let me make a call."

Edmund steps out of the room to make a call to one of his close friends to get some information. Sebastian calls Jenessa to check on Estelle. She picks up the phone and says, "Hey Sebastian, I'm glad you called. I need to talk to you; can you come over?"

Sebastian replies, "Yes, I'm coming as soon as Edmund makes a call. How's Estelle today?"

Sebastian can hear sobbing as she says, "I don't know. Its likes she's in a deep sleep and can't wake up. I don't know if she's in a coma or not. I just don't know what to do."

Sebastian tries to encourage her by saying, "Hang in there, Jenessa; you're doing a good job, and Estelle would be proud of you for not giving up on helping her recover from this injury. I have faith in you. I'll be there in a few minutes."

Jenessa hangs up and then walks in the kitchen and sits at the table with Persia. As the girls eat their breakfast, they talk about the costume party; unknown to them, someone has slipped into the house unannounced. As Estelle awakens and heads downstairs, she is greeted at the bottom of the stairs by a woman with blond hair. Estelle can sense her aura and knows she's out for her blood. Still weak, Estelle says, "Can I help you?"

The Lady in White says with a grin on her face, "Oh, Estelle, are you still injured from last night. It's a pity your powerful witchcraft hasn't healed your wounds yet. You know why I'm here, though you don't know who sent me."

Jenessa says, "Shhh, do you hear some talking? Is someone in the house besides us?"

Persia stops talking, they listen, and then she says, "Yeah, I hear some voices. Is Estelle up trying to walk around? Let's go see."

As the girls walk out of the kitchen into the den, they turn the corner, and low and behold, they see Estelle and a Lady in White standing on the stairs. The Lady in White says, "Estelle, I see you have brought backup, but while they may be witches, they can't stop me from fulfilling my mission."

Jenessa speaks up and says, "Don't hurt my grandma; she's already injured. What do you want with us? Who sent you here?"

The Lady in White grins and says, "I know she's hurt, little one, and that's the best time to strike. I was offered a deal to do this. The individual who sent me would rather remain anonymous, but you can figure it out, lover."

Estelle begins walking down the stairs, looking at the Lady in White and says, "I'm not going to hide from you. I know this is revenge for what I did to that young girl, but I didn't start this war; your partner did. I won't fight you because I know you realize that an injured witch can't use her powers until she heals."

Jenessa yells, "No! No! Grandma, stop, don't do it."

Jenessa utters a hold in place spell, but before she can get the words out, the Lady in White uses a blur movement. She blurs up the stairs and grabs Estelle by the throat. She turns and looks at girls as they stand crying and begging for Estelle's safety. As the Lady in White turns to Estelle, she looks her in the eyes and says, "This is your very last chance. Where is the Book? We know you have knowledge of its whereabouts, so the choice is yours: Your life for the Book."

Estelle looks down the stairs at Jenessa and says, "I love you; be strong because you can do it. No, I'm not giving you the Book, so kill me."

With that said, Jenessa and Persia begin yelling for her not to do it, but the Lady in White doesn't hesitate and rips out Estelle's throat with her sharp claws. As the blood drips from her hand, she licks it and says, "She has a rich bloodline, very tasty. Little one, I have a message for you. This ain't over; watch your back."

Like a puff of smoke she is gone, and the reality is setting in that Estelle, Haven-Crest's most powerful witch, is dead. The girls run over to Estelle's dead body. Jenessa holds her head in her lap and cries for her to wake up. Persia checks her vitals and looks at Jenessa, who is all to pieces. As the phoenix builds inside of her, her rage and pain comes to the forefront, and Jenessa's great power begins to emerge from inside of her. Persia sees her eyes turn yellow, and the room begins to shake from Jenessa's anger.

"What do I do without you?" Jenessa pounds onto the floor.

She thinks, "I don't want to let her go. Why did this have to happen? She's a witch for crying out loud. There must be something that can be done to save her. Who is going to help me go through my transitions as a witch or howler and a vampire? Who will I go to for love and completeness? She has to be here; she's all I have in my life, all I have to love."

"Like a star being born, you were a tiny, magnificent light, turning into a flower, starting from stem." This is special verse Estelle once told her.

Jenessa sits on the floor holding onto Estelle's lifeless body. She rubs her grandmother's hair and says, "Grandma, don't leave me," over and over.

Persia runs in the kitchen and calls 911 for an ambulance to come, and then she calls Sebastian to come over. He answers the phone and says, "Hey, Jenessa, what's up?"

Persia replies, "This is Persia. Can you come over? Estelle's dead; someone killed her."

Sebastian gasps and goes silent, and then he says, "Have you called 911?"

Persia replies, "Yes, and they are on the way."

Sebastian says, "Don't say anything; I'm on my way now."

As he hangs up the phone, he tells Edmund to drive the car over to Estelle's. He runs out of the house and does a blur movement to try to beat the police and ambulance over to Jenessa's house. Jenessa looks down at her grandmother's face and recites one of Estelle's favorite poems to her, "Ending as a bird…soaring…. back into His sky, going on to a flower, starting from stem."

As tears drop off her face onto Estelle's face, Persia comes over and hugs Jenessa and says, "Sebastian is on the way; lay her down and wash your hands. I'm going to put a sheet over her until the ambulance gets here."

Jenessa thinks, "As Estelle choked out her last word, her life ended. I saw her eyes close and her words repeated in my mind. That was the last time I will hear her talk to me. I felt so many things right then. It was just like going on a rollercoaster and at the top, riders feel like they're about to die before the drop. I felt that gut wrenching feeling in my stomach like I was going to throw up in my mouth."

Her thoughts continue, "I don't want my heart anymore; I wish my heart would have gone with Grandma." She feels guilt, hurt, sadness, and depression. However, her dominant emotions are anger and rage. Five minutes pass as she just sits there with her eyes closed. Her fists are balled up so hard that she can feel her nails piercing into her skin and blood starting to leak out."

"Jenessa," Persia says looking at her fists.

"SHUT THE HELL UP," Jenessa shouts.

Persia's eyes get wide; she grabs the bed sheet and pulls it on top of Estelle's body.

"Why? Why?" Jenessa cries.

Jenessa gets up and starts to look for something to bring her grandma back to life. A recipe or a spell that could do it; something had to work. She flips the table over and starts reading through her book but then gets angry because she can't understand anything on the pages. Why does the language have to be so hard to decipher? She starts ripping the pages up. Nothing seems real right now, nothing.

"Jenessa, calm down," Persia cries while sitting beside her.

"WHAT?" Jenessa asks.

"Calm down doing what? Calm down caring about someone I just lost?" Jenessa stares into Persia teary eyes.

"We will get through this together," Persia says while hugging Jenessa.

"I need her…I need her," Jenessa stutters looking at Estelle's still body.

"I know how you feel," Persia says as she rubs Jenessa's back, but Jenessa jerks away from Persia.

Jenessa says crying, "No you don't! No one knows what I feel like right now".

With that said, Jenessa storms out of the house into the backyard. She thinks, "Why am I feeling like this? It's as if I can't control what I'm feeling. I can't control myself." She stares up at the sky and remembers what Grandma said, "As a star being born, you were a tiny magnificent light, Going on to a flower, starting from stem, Ending as a bird…soaring…. back into His sky."

What did she mean by this? She feels another tear forming and thinks; "Here we go again." She looks down at the ground and hears pebbles crunching and footsteps that stop right before her. She looks up and sees Sebastian.

Sebastian squats down and says, "Look at me. You're going to be alright. I'm here now; pull yourself together because you can do this. The ambulance and police are on the way. Let's get the story straight. Tell them that someone broke into the house and attacked Estelle. There's no way they're going to believe you if you tell them what really happened. Afterwards, we'll discuss who and what did this to her."

Jenessa nods her head. Sebastian puts his arms around her neck, and they head into the house. Persia walks over to Sebastian and says, "Thanks, she needed someone to calm her down. I'm glad you came."

Sebastian smiles, walks Jenessa over to the couch, and says, "Can you get her a cup of water?"

As Persia walks in the kitchen to get the cup of water, the police, the ambulance, and the coroner arrive. With everyone rushing in at one time, Persia, Jenessa, and Sebastian just sit on the couch out of the way. Sheriff Michaels, Agent Ambrose, and Detective MacRae are all there and investigating the crime scene. Agent Ambrose comes over and says, "Jenessa, can I have a word with you? First, I'm sorry for your loss, I know your grandmother loved you, so I want to catch this killer and put him or her in jail. I have a couple of questions to ask. Can you tell me what happened? Did you see anything?"

Jenessa takes a deep breath and says, "I didn't see much; all I remember is that Persia and I were in the kitchen eating. We heard some voices, so we came around the corner to investigate. All I saw was the front door open and Grandma lying on the floor."

Sebastian speaks up and says, "Agent Ambrose, I know you may want to ask more questions, but you can see she's a little distressed. I would say give her a couple of days and talk to her again."

"I know. I can see she is. Please call me Monica. Will you stay with her for a while to get her to come around and help her through this ordeal? It's good to see you again, but I'm sorry it has to be under these circumstances," comments Agent Ambrose.

"Sure I will. Edmund and Marcella can handle Priceless today. It's good to see you also. I've been meaning to call you, but I've been kind of busy lately," replies Sebastian.

A few hours pass. Once the sheriff gives Celister the okay to take the body, he and his attendants load and strap up Estelle to the gurney and the head to the morgue.

Jenessa sits and watches everyone's movements, and it seems as though everything is in slow motion. She feels like she's in a trance and is numb to the pain and shock.

The deputies' words of encouragement for her loss help the healing process. Once the coroner has taken away Estelle's body, Sheriff Michaels comes over and says, "Jenessa, after Celister gets done with the autopsy, I'll call you so you can release the body to the funeral home. It'll probably be tomorrow before he's done, so please try to get some rest. Call your friends over with you tonight so you won't be alone."

Jenessa holds her head up, wipes away the tears once more, and says, "My friends are coming over tonight, so I won't be alone. Plus, my cousin Persia is here with me, and Sebastian will be checking on us. I'll be alright, sheriff; thanks for asking."

With that said, the sheriff heads back over to the crime scene at the stairs. He looks at the staircase for clues, but he sees no evidence of a struggle. He looks around the house and walks to the front door checking to see how the assailant got in the house. He writes some notes in his notepad and checks the doorknob for fingerprints. He speaks with Agent Ambrose, and they go into the kitchen. Once they are in the kitchen, he says, "I don't see anything out of the ordinary. There aren't any signs of a forced entry. There is no damage to the door or furniture or signs of a struggle on the staircase. I don't know; to me, it doesn't look like anyone broke in. Estelle may have known the individual. We'll talk to Jenessa again in a couple of days, and maybe she'll remember more then after the shock is over."

"I believe she has seen something because she in pain and hurting. We may need to talk to the cousin also. Run a check on Persia Fredrick, and see what comes back on her. She seems like a really nice girl. Nothing was stolen, so why would someone want to kill nice ole' Estelle? She never bothered anyone," replies Agent Ambrose.

They head back into the living room, and Sheriff Michaels says, "Okay, guys, let's go and give them some peace. It's been a hard day for us all, but losing her grandmother today to a horrendous crime like that has to be awful for Jenessa."

Everyone leaves the premises. Sebastian walks the police out to their cars while Persia starts to clean up the blood on the stairs. As Persia gets her cleaning bucket and squats to begin, she touches the blood and suddenly sees a vision. It is unknown to everyone else that Persia is a vampire. Her gift is that she can see visions through the physical contact with blood. By touching Estelle's blood, she sees that the map everyone is looking for is in Estelle's room. Now the challenge is finding it before anyone else beats her to it. Since she's a vampire, she wears contacts to hide her purple shaded pupils.

Now that Sebastian is back inside the house, they hear a car pull up, and it's Edmund and Jai Li. They come inside and give Jenessa their condolences; Edmund hugs Jenessa and says, "I've known your grandmother for many years, and she was one of the nicest people ever met. I'm surely going to miss her, and she will truly be missed by all her friends also. Remember, Jenessa, if you ever need anything from Sebastian or me, please don't hesitate to ask. We'll be more than glad to help you in any way we can. Estelle would have done the same for us."

Jenessa looks at Edmund and says, "Thank you, Edmund; that really means a lot, and I'm sure Grandma would have been glad to know that."

Persia says, "Mr. Martin, we appreciate your kind words, and thanks for the offer. Is there anything I can get you?"

"No, thank you, kind young lady, and what is your name?" asks Edmund.

"It's Persia Fredrick. Auntie Estelle and my mom are sisters. I'm from California, and I'm here visiting for a while," answers Persia with a show of concern on her face.

Edmund turns and says, "Sebastian, we need to go to Priceless because we have some business to discuss with the B & B Food Service."

"Okay, I almost forgot that meeting was today. Jenessa, I'll be back to check on you once I leave this meeting. Are you going to be alright? If you need me, just call," replies Sebastian.

Jenessa smiles and says, "I'll be okay. Go ahead to your meeting. I've got the girls here to look after me."

As Sebastian and Edmund leave, Jai walks over, hugs her best friend, and says, "I'm sorry to hear about Granny, but I'm not going to bring it all up. Let's just hang out and worry about that later. Who is hungry? Let's get some pizza tonight. Where is Chrisha; has anybody heard from her?"

Persia says, "Pizza sounds good to me; what about you, Jenessa?"

"That's fine with me. Somebody call Chrisha and see where she is," answers Jenessa.

Jai reaches for the phone and says, "I'll call the pizza in. Persia can go pick it up and go by and get Chrisha."

Persia gets her purse and says, "I'll go get Chrisha first and then get the pizza. Who's paying for the pizzas? I don't have any money."

Jenessa looks in her purse and gives her thirty dollars and her car keys. After Persia leaves, Jai Li says, "Jenessa, it's just you and me here, so tell me what actually happened."

Jenessa turns to her best friend, and it feels as if the words are stuck in her throat. She says, "Okay, I'll tell you, but first let me go to the bathroom. I'll be right back."

Jai Li smiles and shrugs her shoulders. Jenessa gets up and heads upstairs to the bathroom, but as she goes by Estelle's room, she stops and walks in. Her emotions are high and swirling around like a strong wind. She feels like slamming the door or kicking it down like the police do when the fugitive won't open the door.

When Jenessa walks in, she sees Estelle's bed and thinks, "I don't want to make her bed up since she last she slept in it. I want the bed to stay untouched with a little part of my grandma still with it."

Jenessa sits down the edge of the bed, running her hands against the cool silk sheets. She looks at the flowered print comforter and thinks, "This bed brings back so many memories of my grandma. No, I'm not going crazy; it's just that I loved her so."

Tears started to build up in her dark eyes. Suddenly, she feels a hand on her back and hears the words, "Child, there is no time for crying, not now, not ever."

Estelle puts her hand on Jenessa's cheek, and Jenessa wonders, "Is she alive? How?" Jenessa notices that her throat mark is gone and realizes this can't be real, at least not for long.

"I…I need you to stay Grandma, please," Jenessa cries.

"Baby, put your grief away; put it away now. You must know that what happened is my calling. The Lady in White just finished the job. I actually want to thank her for taking my pain away, finally," explains Estelle.

Jenessa cries, "Grandma are you crazy? She killed you!" She feels herself building up with anger.

"I'm going to kill her; I'm not joking," shouts Jenessa.

"Jenessa, don't turn into something you're going to regret. There are some things you're not going to be able to control. You must realize you have everything you need, no matter what," Estelle says as she tries to rationalize with Jenessa.

"Grandma, don't do this! I really need you now! THERE HAS TO BE A SPELL THAT CAN BRING YOU BACK!" Jenessa pleads.

She paces back and forth in the room and starts flipping through all the books and herb recipes.

"Baby, you must know my time is up; it was meant for me to go when I did, but you know what…. You must start fulfilling your destiny, and only you know what that is," Estelle says.

Jenessa's eyes are like a window of water droplets. The tears leak out onto dark circles underneath, and her eyes are as dark as an endless well as she cries, "What do I do without you?" while pounding her fists on the bed.

Her grandma whispers her last words, "I love you, baby. You're going to be alright because you're in good hands now."

She kisses Jenessa's forehead, and her granddaughter knows it is her spirit because she can't feel her lips. Instead, she feels the warmness of her touch. Jenessa sits there for a while valuing her grandmother's embrace for the last time. She looks out the window and sees a bird flying in the sky. She wants to be that bird right now. As she gets up and turns around, she notices Jai Li standing at the door, and Jai Li says, "Jenessa are you okay? I heard voices, and I came up to see if everything was alright. Did you see her spirit? I heard witches can do that."

"Yes, and I feel more at peace now. I feel like the fog has been lifted off my eyes. Grandma told me that there is a map I am supposed to give Sebastian, so I need to find it. Help me look for it," replies Jenessa.

As the two friends look around the room for the map, they are briefly interrupted by Chrisha calling on the phone. She says, "Hey, we are on the way, so turn the front porch light on."

Jenessa responds by saying, "Okay, I'm turning it on as we speak."

Once she hangs up the phone, Jenessa runs downstairs to switch on the front porch light. Jai Li looks through some books but sees no evidence of a map. As Jenessa comes back upstairs, she bumps into a table and knocks over a picture of Estelle and her at the beach, and a key falls to the floor. Jenessa says, "What's this? It's a key, and I'll bet it opens a safe."

The girls begin looking for a safe in the room when suddenly they're interrupted by Persia and Chrisha's return home. They leave the room, shut the door, and then head downstairs. Once downstairs, they all head to the kitchen to have some pizza and soda. At the table, they begin opening up and sharing secrets. Chrisha says, "So, we're going to tell secrets; what if we don't have any?"

"Everyone has them. We may not want to share them, but we all have them. Who's going first?" asks Jai Li.

Jenessa raises her head, looks at her friends, and speaks first. She says, "I want to go first; there's something I've wanted to tell you guys for a while now. A couple of months ago, I found out that I am part of a prophecy. What that means is my destiny has been foretold by witches from Salem. Grandma was one of the witches who escaped from Salem. She and my grandfather started a life here in Haven-Crest. She told me that I have magical entities inside of me. I can cast spells and channel mystical energy. Plus, I have vampire and howler genes inside me waiting to be unleashed."

The room goes silent, and the girls look at one another. Chrisha speaks up first and says, "I know you're just joking, right? You expect me to believe that story? I'm not gullible or even that slow."

Jai Li eats her pizza and looks at her friends from left to right. Jenessa gives her a serious look and says, "Alright, Jenessa, I get the hint. Now it's time for me to reveal my secret. The only person who knows the truth about what happened to me is Jenessa. I didn't run away; I lied because what really happened was I got turned into a vampire about three months ago. I was away doing training so I could come home and live a normal life. I now know how to control the blood hunger. I want you to understand that I won't try to attack or harm you in any way."

Chrisha looks at her two best friends, and anger starts to show on her face as she yells, "What the hell is going on?"

Jenessa sees the hurt in Chrisha's eyes, stares into her dark brown orbs, and then looks down. She remembers one time when Chrisha got so mad she punched the windows and lights out of her ex-boyfriend's car.

At first, Jai Li and Jenessa don't say anything, but one of them has to say something because it feels wrong to keep avoiding her and her questions.

"Well... we're not normal" Jenessa says as she starts looking at the ground.

"This is serious matter," Chrisha says while trying to sound and look stern.

"I-I am.... Well, you see... Sorta like" Jenessa stutters.

Her words come out like a mess. She tries to rearrange so that it doesn't sound like she's crazy.

"I'm a vampire; well, I am actually a full vampire," Jai Li finishes.

"Huh? You called me over to tell me that? You need sleep. What you're saying sounds like...I don't know," Chrisha says as she starts to get up.

"No, wait, Chrisha," Jenessa pleads. She reaches out for her hands and says, "Right now I don't need another person walking out of my life. Look, I know this doesn't make sense, but eventually it will. I really don't need for you to leave. I'm losing everyone around me. Here we go, round two of Niagara Falls," Jenessa says with a tear slipping out.

"I feel you, girl; I feel both of you, but I'm not getting into this voodoo crap. I'm a Baptist, and I've got Jesus in my life," comments Chrisha.

"It's not voodoo; it's magic, okay? I am a witch, a vampire, and a howler also," Jenessa laughs.

"Okay, you hocus pocus hairy monster with fangs," Chrisha smiles.

Chrisha always makes Jenessa smile and laugh, even when she is really down. Jenessa thinks a moment and says sarcastically, while pulling out her phone, "Thanks for my compliment."

"So...What's the status, girly?" Jai Li chimes in changing the subject.

While Jenessa watches, she can feel that Chrisha is uncomfortable and thinks, "It's not like Jai and I are going to suck her neck."

To calm her nerves, Jenessa says, "Chrisha, do you need proof of what we are to satisfy you into believing us?"

"The proof is in the pudding," Chrisha responds being sarcastic.

Jenessa decides to go first. She waves her hand and snaps her fingers, and the lights come on. Chrisha gets up and flips the switch off but they stay on. She says, "Good trick, but show me something harder, Bewitch."

Jenessa walks over to side door, out on the deck, and says, "Channel your thoughts and mediate on the power of flight, and then levitate."

Suddenly, Jenessa starts levitating in the air. As she waves her hands, magical orbs appear, and then she shoots off fireworks in the air. Jenessa waves her hands again and is back on the ground. Chrisha runs out to the deck and says, "Damn, girl, I believe you now. Why didn't you tell me you could do stuff like that? I could have handled it. We're best friends, and I can't believe you told Jai."

Jai speaks up and says, "Wait a minute; I didn't find out until a couple of days ago when I revealed myself to Jenessa."

"So, you're a vampire. Where are your fangs?" replies Chrisha.

As if on command, Jai Li moves in slow motion as her fangs extend and her eyes turn golden black. Then, slowly she changes back to Jai Li. Amazed and very easily frightened, Chrisha steps back and says, "Whoa! Damn, you know how to scare the hell out of a girl. How long have you been like that?"

Jai replies, "About three months, ever since I got kidnapped and was bitten. I've been one ever since. Don't be afraid of me because I won't hurt you."

Chrisha looks at Persia and says, "What about you; what secret do you have?"

Persia looks worried and says, "I'm a witch like Jenessa; it's in our bloodline. The secret I have is that I'm one hundred and sixteen years old. I was born in 1896, but I transitioned and still look eighteen. I use my magic from time to time, but I'd rather try to be as normal as possible."

Jenessa stands up and says, "Dag, cousin, I didn't know that you were that old. You don't look a day over sixteen, but seriously, Chrisha, you have to keep these secrets of ours between us and just us. No one can ever find out about what was said tonight."

Suddenly there's a knock at the door, and Jenessa says, "Who could that be at this hour? Who is it?"

They hear a man's voice saying, "It's me, Jamal."

Jenessa opens the door, and Jamal says, "I just heard about your grandma, and I had to come by. I hope I'm not too late."

Jenessa smiles and says, "Come in; the girls are all here."

Once inside, he hugs Jenessa and says, "I'm sorry to hear about Estelle. She was a really nice lady. Anything I can do for you?"

Jenessa smiles and says, "Just you coming by and bringing some of Ms. Karen's sweet potato pie is thanks enough. I'm glad you came. It has been kind of hard with her not being here, but with friends like you guys, I'm going to be okay."

Jamal smiles and walks in the kitchen with the other girls, and he says, "What's up, ladies? I'm glad to see you all tonight."

Persia speaks first, "Hi Jamal. I'm Persia, Jenessa's cousin, and how are you?"

Chrisha says, "Don't show him any kind of attention; it'll make his head even bigger than it already is."

As all the girls start to laugh and joke with Jamal, suddenly without warning, the front door swings open. Everyone is in awe about how the door appeared to open all by itself. As Jamal walks to the door to shut it, he sees Camden standing in the yard. Jamal walks to the door way and says, "What do you want? No one wants you here, Frenchie, so it's best that you leave now."

Camden stands there and says, "Jamal, I advise you to go back inside and tell Jenessa to come outside, please. I have no quarrel with you tonight."

Jenessa comes to the door and says, "What the hell do you want, Camden? You don't need to show your face around here after what your father did to my grandma, so get the hell out of here now before you get hurt."

"I didn't come here to fight; I came to say I'm sorry about your grandmother. I heard about it a while ago, and I came by to give my condolences. We need to talk by ourselves about this situation before it gets out of hand," Camden replies to her hostility.

Jamal yells, "Frenchie, the lady said to get the hell out of here. Why don't you give the lady some privacy? I'd hate to have to come out there and kick your ass again."

Camden utters an incantation, and before Jenessa can react, a magical force pulls Jamal out into the yard and onto the ground. As Camden looks down at Jamal, he says, "Kick whose ass? I don't think so, friend. You had better mind your damn business."

Jenessa looks at Camden, and her eyes start to turn yellow as she feels the rage building up inside of her. The clouds begin to uncover the moon, and Jamal begins to yell in agony as his bones begin cracking and making breaking noises. He stretches out on the ground, and everyone watches to see what's going on with him. Jenessa walks on the porch and says, "Camden, if you're hurting Jamal, you need to stop. I will get revenge for my grandmother and for what your family has done to me. Let Jamal go now!"

As she yells at Camden, he feels the wind pick up, and dark clouds start to form. Alden says, "Let's go; we'll have another chance at her. Now you can see that she doesn't love you because she's trying to hurt you. Let's go."

Suddenly, Camden creates a fog, and then they are gone. They rush over to Jamal to see if he is okay. He stands and says, "I'm okay. Frenchie didn't hurt me, and you can best believe that I will get his ass for this one."

Jenessa hugs him, and they all head back into the house.

Chapter 2

Once inside the house, the girls ask Jamal if is he is alright since they have just witnessed him yelling in agony and heard his bones breaking. He looks at Jenessa and says, "I'm alright; I don't know why my body has been acting like that lately."

She has a concerned look on her face and responds by saying, "You may want to get that checked out because that doesn't sound right. The main thing is that Camden didn't hurt you. He's got some nerve coming by here and acting like he's trying to show compassion. To me, he's just like his father: out for no good."

"You shouldn't even worry about Frenchie; he will get his in the end," replies Jamal.

At that very moment, Jamal's phone rings, and he excuses himself to answer. Chrisha says, "This has been one night to remember. So, let me get this straight; Camden's a witch too? Am I the only human here out of this bunch?"

Jenessa smiles and says, "The correct term for a man witch is warlock, and I guess you are the only human, which is a good thing."

They all start to laugh, and Jamal comes back into the room and says, "I'm sorry ladies; I have to cut this party short. I've got to go meet the coach tonight. He said something about a team meeting, plus it's getting late anyway. I'll call and check on you girls later."

Jamal gets his jacket and heads for the door, and Jenessa walks out on the porch and waves as he drives down the street. Back inside, Jai says, "Jen, you must be kryptonite because those two can't get enough of you."

They all laugh at Jai Li's joke, and Persia comments, "That's the Craig effect we have on men; once they get hooked, we've got them."

"What men? I ain't seen you with any man yet," Chrisha comes back sarcastically at Perisa.

They all laugh and have fun, but Jenessa is trying not to let the sorrow and hurt fester in the back of her heart. As her friends attempt to show her a good time, she has one particular thing on her mind: Camden. Is he playing mind games with her, and does he have a plan up his sleeve?

As the clouds begin to uncover their prison hold on the moon, Jamal is on his way over to Coach Deren's house for a get together, but little does he know, his reality is about to become a nightmare. About half the way there, Jamal's body begins to transition. Suddenly, the bones in his body begin to break. The cracking and the pain are nonstop, and Jamal begins to use the breathing techniques Coach Deren taught him. It usually cuts down on some of the pain, but on this night, it's not working. Jamal looks down at his hand and sees that it has popped out of joint. His fingers look as though they are getting longer. He begins to panic, so he pulls over to the shoulder of the road. Once out of the car, Jamal falls to the ground in agony and is yelling from the pain. Unseen by Jamal, a pair of eyes watch him from the bushes. After a couple of minutes of unbearable pain, Jamal gets up off the ground and continues to Coach Deren's house.

As Jamal pulls into the driveway, he notices Gregory Turner standing on the porch. Once he gets out, Gregory notices that transition has started. He walks over to Jamal and says, "Hey dude, where have you been? The coach has been looking for you. Come on; we're late. They are meeting by the bonfire."

Jamal replies, "Sorry about being late. A friend's grandmother died today. Hey, where's the coach at?"

As they walk down to the bonfire where the other teammates are gathered, Jamal notices that coach is not there, just the players. Once Gregory and Jamal reach the bonfire, the ceremony begins. Sergi calls the meeting to order and says, "Brothers, we are gathered here tonight for the joining of our newest member into the pack. We are a pack that is not governed by laws of man but by the laws of our pack. Some of you have been members for a while, and some of you are about to transition into the pack. Jamal Carmichaels, step forward; you are about to become the newest member this season. Jamal is a talented athlete and possibly a future leader of his own pack. In this chalice is an elixir that will help with your transition. We will all drink from the chalice and welcome our new brother to the pack."

As all eight members of the basketball team drink out of the chalice, Jamal hesitates, and then they start cheering him on to drink it. Once he does, his body instantly begins to change. Suddenly, the clouds begin to separate so the full moon is shown. As Jamal looks around, he begins to hear growling and clothes ripping. The elixir has begun to take effect;

his bones are breaking and cracking, and the pain is so severe that he can't recover. As he collapses to the ground, he turns to the bonfire and is shocked at what he sees. The guys on the team are morphing into wolf-like men, and they are growling and snarling. From behind, Jamal hears some growling, and he slowly turns and sees a wolf standing there as if ready to attack. He slowly turns to the bonfire, and the other wolves are circling around him and the big wolf. He tries not to make any sudden moves, and the big wolf howls and rushes in to attack. The elixir has made Jamal very dizzy. The big wolf knocks him to the ground and without hesitation, bites Jamal on the side. With his body aching in pain and the elixir making him woozy, he passes out.

As Jamal sleeps, he dreams about the events he witnessed at the bonfire. He remembers seeing his teammates turn into some kind of wolves and getting bitten on his side. Suddenly, he wakes up and looks around the room; everything is dark, like he's in a cellar. Coach Deren comes into the room and says, "Jamal, are you alright?"

Jamal tries to focus and stand up, but he has been put in chains and shackles. Jamal says, "Coach, what is this? Why the hell am I chained up like an animal? What the hell is going on here?"

The coach walks over to the window and turns and says, "Jamal, the reason you are chained up is because you have an inner beast trying to get out. I'm here to help you with that transition. Let me say that after tonight, you'll never be the same again, so as the phrase goes, out with the old and in with the new."

Coach Deren pulls back the heavy, black curtains and reveals the full moon to Jamal, and suddenly, Jamal's pupils turn red and he starts to yell in agony. The pain begins to become unbearable, and Jamal falls to the floor in the cellar. As the moon shines through the window, Jamal looks up, and his fangs extend. Jamal starts to growl and snarl like a wolf, and then his bones begin breaking and reforming in his hands and wrists. His fingers are now claws, and his face starts its transformation from human to animal.

With his clothes now ripped to shreds, Jamal comes to the end of his transformation. Though the chains and shackles have kept him from getting loose so far, from all the yanking and pulling, they are about to come out of the wall. As Coach Deren watches, he notices something odd; Jamal is the first one of the howlers he has seen fully transform into a wolf. Only alphas can do that incredible change. Also, instead of being a black or grey howler, he's a red howler. Jamal circles the room once his transformation is complete. Coach Deren stands in amazement at what Jamal has become and says, "Whoa, you are a strong one. Now that you have finished your induction into the pack, let me be the first to congratulate you. Let me say that I knew something was special about you when I met you. I could sense that you had strong howler roots and bloodline. To make your transformation complete, you need to embrace the blood of your first kill. You need to kill and drink your victim's blood in order to change at will, so go, Jamal, and enjoy your first kill."

As he looks at Coach Deren through his howler eyes with the growling and a sense of uncertainty, Jamal knows he doesn't want to kill an innocent person to satisfy the animal and blood lust that are inside of him. As hard as he tries to resist the animal urges, he can't, and the animal takes over. He dashes past Coach Deren, jumps out of the window, and runs toward the woods to fulfill his initiation into the pack.

Jamal runs about a two miles through the woods, and suddenly, he comes across a man walking down the road. He makes no sound as he observes the man and just watches him. Like a hunter stalks his prey until he's ready to shoot, Jamal studies him until he sees his opportunity to attack. As Jamal gets closer, the man is unaware he's being hunted. He suddenly hears a noise, stops, and shines his flashlight through the trees and weeds. He listens, and after he doesn't see or hear anything, he proceeds on his way home. Unseen by him, something big jumps from out of the bushes and knocks him to the ground. He reaches for the flashlight, grabs it, and shines at the object that knocked him down. To his surprise, he sees a big red wolf. The man says, "Damn, you're about the biggest wolf I've ever seen, and I've never seen a red wolf before. Please, don't kill me; I'm just trying to make it home."

The howler stands in an attack position and growls at the man. Jamal begins circling him very slowly, and he can sense fear on him. As soon as Jamal sees the man drop his hands, he rushes in for the perfect opportunity to kill him. Jamal jumps and lunges forward for his throat. The man does his best to try to fight Jamal off, but he loses the battle with the animal and his life is over in the process. Once Jamal finishes his first kill of a human and drinks the blood of this man, he feels his body start to transition again. He begins to howl, looks around, and runs off into the woods. Jamal hears another howl through the woods on this cold night. On instinct, he returns to the bonfire where it all began. As the clouds cover the full moon, Jamal begins changing back to his normal self.

Coach Deren says, "Jamal, you did well. Once you get your strength back and some rest, we'll discuss this further. Understand, you've been given this gift for a reason."

As Coach Deren looks across the lake, he sees the sun coming up on the horizon. He helps Jamal up, wraps him in a robe, and they head into his house.

As a new day begins in Haven-Crest, word has circulated about the death of Estelle, one of the town's most lovable individual. Friends and Estelle's customers begin calling to offer their condolences to Jenessa. There's a knock at the door, and Persia says, "Who is it?"

The gentleman responds, "Its Tracy, Estelle's assistant.

Persia opens the door and says, "Come in, Tracy."

He hugs Persia and asks, "Where's Jenessa? How is she handling Estelle's death? I'm still in shock; who would want to rob a nice person like Estelle?"

Persia hesitates and then replies, "She's taking it really hard, but that is to be expected. Auntie raised Jenessa since she was a baby, plus they were really close. Honestly, she's a mess. Though she puts on a strong face, I know she's hurting."

Jenessa walks into the room. Tracy walks over, hugs her, and says, "I'm sorry to hear about Estelle. She meant the world to me. If there is anything I can do, don't hesitate to ask. You know y'all are like family because family always looks out for each other, and she would want me to look after you."

As the tears begin to run down her face, she smiles and says, "Thank you, Tracy. That meant a lot. Grandma would be proud of us for being strong, and she was really proud of you. You were a great friend to her, and you meant a lot to her. Yes, she will be greatly missed. I know she's in a better place, but I really miss her."

Tracy wipes away his tears and tries to hold in his emotions, but seeing Jenessa in so much pain and heartache makes him start to cry as he says, "I was trying to be strong, but after seeing you like this, I just can't help myself."

Persia hugs Tracy again and says, "Don't hold it in; just let it go. You're crying because you love them."

Suddenly, there's another knock at the door. Persia wipes her tears away and says, "Who is it?"

"It's Alonzo Quintana, Jenessa's homeroom teacher, and my wife, Connie."

Persia opens the door and invites them in. Once inside, he says, "I came by to offer my condolences to Jenessa because I heard about what happened to her grandmother. How is she handling the tragedy? I know it must be hard on her."

Persia shakes his hand and says, "It's nice to meet you, Mr. and Mrs. Quintana. I'm Persia, Jenessa's cousin from California. Sir, she's doing as well as can be expected. She's being strong, but I know this has been devastating for her because we were here but in the kitchen when the attacker came in. I just don't understand society now. Why would someone attack a nice person like Auntie and then kill her in her own home yet not take any money or steal anything? I don't get it."

Mr. Quintana replies, "I understand what you are saying. Society has become more violent because of unemployment being cut by the governor; many people don't have money to take care of their families, so they're doing what they have to in order to survive. It's sad to say, but Estelle probably was targeted and just became an innocent victim in this tragedy."

At that moment, Jenessa walks in and says, "Hi, Mr. Quintana, how are you? I'm glad you stopped by. I see you've met my cousin, Persia."

As Mr. Quintana looks into Jenessa's eyes, he sees the hurt and anger surrounding the tragedy of her grandmother's death. He reaches out, hugs her, and says, "Jenessa, this is my wife, Connie. First, I want to say that I'm sorry for your loss, and I know she meant the world to you. When you lose someone that close, the hurt inside leaves a hole in your heart, but in time, you'll come to understand God's purpose in taking her to be with him in heaven. You have family and friends who will be here for you to help you make it through this because we love you. Is there anything I can do for you, Jenessa? I brought you one of Connie's delicious sweet potato pies."

With tears in her eyes, she replies, "Mr. Quintana, thank you for coming. Your being here is more than enough, and thank you for the pie. I enjoy being in your class, and I really think you are one of the best teachers we have at school."

He grins and says, "Jenessa, you are one of my smartest students, and I see a lot of potential inside of you. Always remember this: Don't let this tragedy become your crutch. I know it hurts now, but time will heal this and you will rise up and become a stronger individual as a result."

Jenessa smiles, and then there's a knock at the door. She excuses herself, walks to the door, and says, "Who is it?"

"It's Sheriff Michaels, Jenessa," replies the sheriff.

She opens the door to invite the sheriff in, and once he's inside the house, he says, "Good morning, Jenessa. How are you doing? Are you holding up pretty good? I stopped by to see if you want to ride to the morgue because we need you to come identify Estelle's body so you can release it to the funeral home if you're up to it."

Jenessa replies, "It's no problem, Sheriff; I can do that now. Persia can stay and take care of things until I get back. Let me get my coat."

Jenessa walks over to Persia to inform her where she is going, and then she gets her coat. As she is leaving, she runs into Mayor Dobson and his wife, Carla, outside. The mayor reaches out to hug her and says, "Good morning, Jenessa, how are you doing? I'm truly sorry to hear about your grandmother, Estelle. What happened to her was a tragedy. You know we're going to do everything in our power to arrest the criminal who did this to her. Good morning, to you too, sheriff. Are you about to leave; did we come at a bad time?"

Jenessa hugs them both and says, "Thank you for coming by, mayor, and I'm doing pretty well. It's good to see you again, ma'am. I'm taking it one day at a time; I know grandma would tell me the same thing. Yes, I'm on my way to the morgue so I can identify and release the body for the funeral home, but I'll be back. My cousin, Persia, is in the house, and I won't be gone long."

The sheriff responds, "Good morning to you too, Mayor Dobson, and good morning to you also, ma'am. We won't be gone long."

Once Jenessa and the sheriff get in the car and head down the street, the sheriff says, "Jenessa, I know this must be really hard for you to embrace at a young age. It's a lot to handle losing both your grandmother and your mother. Your grandmother was a well-known person in the community, and everyone loved her. I knew your mother when we were in school many years ago. She was a very beautiful girl back then, and we were good friends. I was devastated when I heard that she was killed in an animal attack. You were a baby at the time."

Jenessa responds, "My grandmother told me that you were a nice man, and I didn't realize that everyone loved her like this. I really miss her, and I know that everyone else will too."

Sheriff Michaels turns and looks at Jenessa and says, "Jenessa, what I'm about to say I'm going to tell you because I'm pretty sure the same applies to you. I knew Estelle was a witch, but I never said anything to anyone about it. She helped out with some of the investigations in the vampires' and howlers' departments. She helped us got rid of a vampire, and she killed a howler also. A few people knew her secret, so we never involved her in the Committee business."

Jenessa sits in shock and then turns and says, "Yes, I am a witch like my grandmother, and I know Haven-Crest has many dark secrets from what she told me."

The sheriff replies, "You seem to know a lot about Haven-Crest history. If you weren't so young, I would offer to bring you into the Committee. Your grandmother used to be a member, but she stepped down to take care of you so you wouldn't be brought into that type of environment."

As they pull into morgue parking lot, Jenessa is just in amazement about what the sheriff has just said about Estelle. As they get out of the car and head inside, they are greeted by Celister. He says, "Good morning, y'all, how are you doing this morning? Jenessa, I'm sorry to hear about Estelle. She was a really nice woman. Hang in there; everything is going to be alright. If you need anything, just let me know. You can go in and view the body, and then I can get you to sign these papers so I can release the body to the funeral home. When you're ready, you can go ahead to room one, and I'll give you some privacy."

Jenessa responds by saying, "Good morning to you too, Celister, and thank you for your offer."

Jenessa walks by the two gentlemen headed to room one to see Estelle's body. Once she opens the door and walks in, she has the sinking feeling that hits her in the bottom of her stomach. It's cold in the examining room. Jenessa walks slowly to the table, and then she stares at the sheet draped over Estelle. As she hesitates, she knows she can't be afraid of Estelle on her deathbed. Jenessa takes a deep breath and pulls back the sheet to see Estelle's face. Estelle looks like she's taking a nap; her face is so calm and peaceful. Jenessa takes her hand, rubs Estelle's hair, and says, "Grandma, I told myself I wasn't going to cry, but I can't hold back the tears. I'm sorry, Grandma; I hate that the Lady in White ripped out your throat. I should have done something to help. With all this power, surely I could have stopped her somehow. Why didn't you let me kill her? I miss you so much. I went into your room and sat on your bed, and I saw visions of our conservations. Without you, Grandma, what direction do I go in now? What do I do? All I can think about is getting revenge. I know that's not what you taught me. Also, I know that kind of thinking pulls me into black magic, but you were killed for no reason, trying to protect me from Seth. I never knew so many people thought a lot of you. Many people have been coming by to pay their respects and offer condolences. Grandma, I love you."

Jenessa lays her head down and cries on Estelle's dead body. All of a sudden, she hears Estelle's voice. As she raises her head, Estelle says, "Why are you crying, child? I'm still here. I may not be with you in body, but I am here in spirit to guide you. You are not on this journey alone; we are here for you. I knew this day was coming, so I didn't want you to do something that you would regret in years to come by trying to save me. You have people around you who are there to help you when you need them. Trust in your heart that they won't lead you astray. Watch out for Seth because he is trying to get revenge for his daughter's death through you. Jenessa, I love you too, now and forever."

Jenessa gathers herself and looks at Estelle one more time. She pulls the sheet back over her grandmother's face and then walks out of the room. She opens the door, walks up to Celister, and says, "I'm ready to release her to the funeral home."

Celister responds, "I'll call Derrick at Morrison's Funeral Home to come pick up the body and get the arrangements set up with you. Now, if I can get you to sign these papers, then you will be free to go."

As Jenessa signs the papers, Celister hands her one of his business cards and says, "If you need anything, call me."

Jenessa replies, "Thank you for everything you've done for my Grandma."

The sheriff says, "Okay, now that Estelle's body has been put into good hands, let me take you back home. See you later, Celister."

The sheriff and Jenessa walk outside, get in the car, and head back to her house. The sheriff turns and says, "I know it must have been hard to look at someone you're used to seeing every day here in the morgue. Your grandmother would be proud of you, especially about how you've been handling this whole situation."

Jenessa smiles and says, "Thank you, sheriff; that makes me feel really good."

The sheriff replies, "There are some things I want to ask you about the attack. When we did our investigation of the house, we found no evidence of a struggle or a break-in. We have no reason to suspect that anyone would want to harm Estelle. Be honest and tell me what actually happened that day. Did you see who did it? What do you know about Jazmine Crenshall? We have reason to believe that she's been murdered. We received reports that she was at the costume party, and no one has seen her since. Her father hasn't filed a missing person's report on her. We just heard through anonymous sources."

Jenessa looks at Sheriff Michaels. She hesitates and gets a gut feeling not to tell the truth, so she says, "Sheriff, I heard someone talking to her. When we came in the room to see who it was, all we saw was Grandma lying on the floor with her throat ripped out, and the front door was open. I really didn't see anything; all I heard was a voice. As far as Jazmine is concerned, I haven't seen her since the party. I didn't know she was missing. If I hear anything, I'll let you know."

The sheriff replies, "Whose voice? Was it a man or a woman?"

Jenessa looks up at the sheriff and says, "It was a…. man's voice."

The sheriff replies, "That's not a lot to go on. I think it could have been a mythical creature that did this. I know someone I can talk to about this, so don't worry about it."

As they pull into Jenessa's driveway, the sheriff puts the car in park and says, "If you need anything, don't hesitate to call. You've got my number. I'll be by later to check on you."

Jenessa looks at the sheriff and says, "Thanks, sheriff. I appreciate everything you've done for me, and thanks for the talk. I'll see you later."

Jenessa gets out of the police car and heads into the house. Once inside, she's greeted by a lot of friends and Estelle's customers. She smiles as she realizes that her grandmother was a person of stature in Haven-Crest. One thing on her mind is the fact that her grandma never told her anything about being a member of the Committee. What is the Committee? She thinks, "I'll ask Sebastian; he probably knows about it."

Jenessa takes off her coat, hangs it on the coat rack, and begins mingling with the guests. There's a knock, and as Jenessa walks toward the door, she gets a bad feeling. As she opens it, to her surprise, a relative she is very uneasy about has arrived. It's Aunt Genie, Persia's mother.

Genie smiles and says, "Lord, Jenessa, honey I'm glad to see you. I'm so sorry about Estelle. I know you must be devastated about her death. I should have called my sister more than I did, but I'm here now, and that's what counts. Where is my Persia? Jenessa, don't worry; we are family. We stick to together, and no matter what tragedy may arise, we hold each other together."

As they hug each other, Jenessa wonders what tricks she may have up her sleeve. Estelle told her that "If Genie is real nice and polite, watch out because that means she's up to something no-good, so keep an eye on her."

After they hug, Jenessa says, "Aunt Genie, I'm glad you're here. It's good to see you. I haven't seen you in a long time. I'm sorry it's under these circumstances though. I've been holding up pretty good and trying to be strong for Grandma. Persia is around here somewhere. I know she'll be glad to see you."

Principal Maynard comes over to Jenessa to offer her condolences and says, "Jenessa, honey, I'm sorry to hear about your grandmother. She was a wonderful lady. I got the best herbal tea from her store to help me sleep. I'm really going to miss her."

As Jenessa watches her begin to cry and walk away, she is amazed at the effect Estelle had on these townspeople. Some of them are crying like they were family, even though Estelle was their friend. As time goes by, it's late into the afternoon. Friends and church members have come and gone. Jenessa, Persia, and Chrisha are cleaning up the house. Jenessa says, "Thanks, guys, for helping me clean up. I appreciate all your help and support. I don't think I could have done this without you. Right now is when I need you the most. Has anybody seen Jai?"

Persia responds, "I haven't seen her. That's what family does; we help and look out for one another. We're here because we love you, Jenessa, but the real question is: What are we going to do with all this food?"

Chapter 3

Camden has become vulnerable to Seth; with the loss of Jazmine, Seth knows that Camden could be the one who turns the tides for them. Seth sees the hurt in his eyes and senses the emotional ties he has to Jenessa, so now he works carefully to paint the perfect picture to get Camden on his side. Seth goes into the cellar to see Camden kneeling beside Jazmine's coffin, and Seth says, "Son, I know you miss her, and I'm sorry I can't bring her back yet. Believe me, once we get the Book, we can do it. Then things can go back to the way they were before Jazmine was killed by Estelle."

Camden turns, looks at father with tears in his eyes, and says, "Dad, we lost Jaz because you wouldn't stop trying to retrieve this Book. Look at what the Book has cost us; you have no powers, and Jaz is dead. How much must we lose for you to understand that this Book has become your obsession? I believe you care about finding this Book more than loving your family. I lost the woman I love because of your quest. You did deceitful things behind my back to Jenessa and Estelle. I see you've formed an allegiance with Alexia, a vampire, and is she the one who murdered Estelle for you."

Seth stares at his son and says, "I don't need to explain anything to you about what I do. By any means necessary is the rule I live by now. She is helping us eliminate the competition to get the book. Yeah, Estelle's blood may be on my hands, but soon I will have my powers back and it will all wash away."

Camden shakes his head and walks back upstairs.

A few days go by, and the town of Haven-Crest is still in mourning the death of Estelle Craig. As Jenessa prepares for her funeral, knowing that this is the last time she'll see her beloved grandmother, her emotions are full; she's hurt and feels left behind. Her mother died when she was a baby from trying to protect her, and now her grandmother is also gone due her trying to protect her. Jenessa gets up out of her bed and opens the

27

door to Estelle's room. Once inside, she sits on the bed and ponders a lot of information she has gathered over the last few days. As Jenessa meditates, she slips into a trance. While in the trance, she is at the crossroads again, looking at the souls making the journey to the other side. Unsure of her surroundings, she is greeted by Lazarus, and he says, "Jenessa, why are you here? It's dangerous for you to keep coming here because the more you come; the more spirits look for ways to come back on your side. What do you need?"

Jenessa looks at Lazarus and says, "I'm looking for my grandmother. I know I'm not supposed to be here, but I need to know where she hid the map. Lazarus, I feel like I'm lost in a cloudy forest, and I can't find my way out. I yell, but no one hears me and no one answers. Where do I go from here? I know this is a turning point, but what do I do now?"

Lazarus replies, "Jenessa, the answer to that question is for you to solve it on your own. You have to follow your heart and trust that someone will show you the guidance that you seek."

As Lazarus touches Jenessa's arm, she awakens from the dream to the sound of Persia's voice.

"Jenessa, what are you doing in here? Get up and start getting yourself ready for the funeral in a couple of hours. Momma has already cooked breakfast, so come get something to eat."

As Jenessa gets up off the bed, she looks in the mirror and sees Estelle's face. Persia stares at Jenessa and says, "Are you alright? Please pull it together. Come on; let's go eat."

While the cousins exit the room and head downstairs to eat breakfast, Jenessa's thoughts are of the conversation with Lazarus. Who is the person she can trust? She clears her thoughts and prepares herself for the funeral later on in the afternoon.

As Sebastian and Edmund sit at the breakfast table drinking coffee, they have a meeting of the minds. Edmund says, "Sebastian, are you attending the funeral for Estelle?"

Sebastian sips his cup of coffee and replies, "Yes, we need to go to pay our respects to our dear friend."

Before Edmund can answer, Jai Li comes into the room and sits at the table. Sebastian says, "What's up, Jai; can we help you?"

Jai Li replies, "We need to talk."

"Talk about what?" asks Sebastian.

Jai Li says, "Jenessa needs our help. I'm worried about her. She's obsessed about finding out who attacked Estelle. She told me that Estelle told her to be careful of her Aunt Genie. As people were coming by to pay their respects, I noticed Genie doing a lot of talking to her and whispering in her ear. I feel she could be trying to brainwash her."

Edmund responds, "Jai, thanks for bringing this to our attention. We'll keep an eye on Jenessa and Genie. She could be trying to play on her sympathy and take advantage of this whole ordeal. I know her; she has a motive, but we just have to get Jenessa to see her for what she is."

Sebastian stands and says, "There are just a few hours left before the funeral. Let's go ahead and get dressed so we can show up early and talk to Jenessa. Where are Marcella and Adam so we can all leave together?"

Edmund replies, "Marcella hasn't arrived yet, and Adam is in the back ordering flowers and catering some food from Priceless to take over to Jenessa's house for the setup."

Sebastian says, "Edmund, I almost forgot about all that. I'm glad you thought of it. Once Marcella gets here, we can leave for Jenessa's house."

Jai Li replies, "I don't know what to say. You guys sure do take care of people in this town. My folks are going, so I'll go with them and see you there."

As Jai Li leaves the mansion, she receives a call from Chrisha. She says, "What's up; where are you at? Your mom said you ran out for a minute. Are we coming in with the family so we can be there for Jenessa? I'm worried about her; she has held up pretty good, but I hope she don't breakdown with all that grief she has been bottling up."

Jai Li replies, "I had to run an errand, but I'm on the way home so I can get dressed. You are right; I'm worried about Jenessa too. I think she'll hold it together for the funeral, but I think she has a lot of grief she has to let off. Well, Persia has been there so far to help her cope, but since today is the funeral, it may be another story. Let me go; I'll see you at the funeral."

The two friends hang up; worried about their best friend, with hopes that everything is well with Jenessa. Jai Li reaches in her bag for her flask to get a drink of blood to calm her nerves because she feels a hunger urge coming on. The blood soothes her vampire urges, and now she can go home and get ready for the funeral.

As Jamal is in his room getting dressed, he thinks about Jenessa and wonders how she's going to handle the grief. Karen comes in and says, "Jamal, how's Jenessa been holding up since Estelle's death? I know she must be devastated. My heart goes out to her for being so strong."

Jamal replies, "Mom, Jenessa's been doing pretty good. I've been by there a couple of times to check on her. I called her last night, and Persia said she was asleep."

Karen's curiosity is raised, and she replies, "Who is Persia?"

"That's Jenessa's cousin from California. Estelle and her mother are sisters. Persia's been here staying for a while," replies Jamal.

Karen has a nosey look on her face and says, "As long as I've known Estelle, she's never said she had a sister. They must not be close."

Jamal replies, "Mom, I don't know. All I know is she's here for her sister's funeral. You'll meet her later at the funeral and reception. I'm glad we're going together."

Karen replies, "You look rather handsome in your black suit. Let me finish getting dressed so we can leave in about 10 minutes."

At the church, people are starting to gather. Some came early to get a seat, knowing that the church will be full due to Estelle knowing a lot of people in Haven-Crest. Many people came by her Herbal Store to buy herbs and home remedies to make them feel better. With so much speculation, people are chattering, so rumors are circulating about the cause of Estelle's death. No one really knows the actual truth. Regardless of what people may say, Haven-Crest residents loved Estelle Craig for being the most humble and lovable mother figure in the town; she loved everyone. The funeral home staff arrives at the church to set up the body so the funeral can start soon. The attendants bring the flowers and casket to the front of the church.

Genie walks into Jenessa's room and says, "It's getting close to one o'clock. Are you about ready? The driver will be here in a few minutes. I don't want you to think I'm rushing you, but I'm here to give you some support. If you need anything or someone to talk to, you can talk to me. I want you to know that I'm very proud of the way you are handling this situation. It shows me how well my sister raised you."

With a look of concern, Jenessa replies by saying, "Genie, I appreciate that comment. To be honest, Grandma never talked about you a lot. She told me that you two had a disagreement that resulted in y'all not communicating for quite a while. I don't want you to think that no one wants you around, but I know you're here to show your sister that no matter what kept you from being close, love can bring you two together one more time."

As Jenessa hugs her Aunt Genie, she still has that feeling that she can't trust her. Persia walks in the room and says, "Hey, what did I miss, a family moment? The funeral car is here. Are we the only ones riding in the limo? Where are the other family members?"

Jenessa turns and says, "The rest of the family will be at the church, so I guess it's just us three."

Suddenly, there's a knock at the front door. Persia yells, "I'll get it. Who is it?"

As she opens the door, she is surprised by who's standing in the doorway. She says, "How may I help you?"

The visitor standing on the other side of the door responds by saying, "Hello, young lady, and how are you? Is Jenessa home by chance? I heard about Estelle, and I came by to offer my condolences on her loss."

Persia looks at the elderly lady with much concern. She gets an unsure vibe about what her intentions could be. She says, "It has been really hard accepting the fact that Auntie is not here with us anymore. We really miss her. How did you know Auntie? Were you a customer?"

The elderly lady responds by saying, "Well, Persia, first let me say that I've known the Craigs for a long time. I used to be good friends with Estelle, but we had a falling out and we never saw eye-to-eye ever again."

With a shocked look on her face, Persia looks at the elderly lady and says, "How do you know my name? I've never seen you before in my life. What else about us do you know?"

The elderly lady laughs and says, "Persia, your mother is Genevieve, and ….."

"That's enough, Althea. What the hell do you want? Why the hell are you here anyway?" says Genie as she walks into the room.

As Althea stands at the front door, she gives Genie a devilish smirk and says, "I heard that Estelle was murdered, and I wanted to stop by and offer my condolences to Jenessa. By the way, is she here?"

Suddenly, Jenesssa walks into the room and says, "Is someone asking about me? Is that you, Althea?"

Althea responds by saying, "Yes, Jenessa, I stopped by so I could offer you my condolences for the loss of your grandmother and talk you about some things that Estelle had if you were interested in selling them."

Jenessa looks at Althea and responds by saying, "I'm sorry, but I don't think I'll be selling anything of my grandmother's at this time."

Althea takes Jenessa's comment personally and proceeds to get angry. She stares at Jenessa and says, "You know what I want, so let's not play games. Just give me what I want, and I'll be on my way. I know you are the prophecy, and, Genie, I know your powers are not as great as mine. I notice that Estelle has a spell to keep me from entering into your house, but that doesn't mean I can't still get what I want. Let's not make this unpleasant; just give me the ……."

Suddenly, a voice interrupts by saying, "Althea, it's been a really long time since I've seen you. Where's your partner, Lars? I'm going to say this one time, so take heed to my warning. Leave now, before this gets out of hand, Althea."

As Althea turns around, she sees that Sebastian has extended his fangs and his eyes have turned golden-black. Edmund grabs him to try to keep Sebastian from attacking Althea. She smiles and says, "My, my, my, you have become the protector over this town that hates mythical creatures, or are you protecting Jenessa hoping that she gives you the map to find the Book? Either way, I'm going to get what I want. Don't worry, Sebastian, Lars will find you."

As Althea moves slowly off the porch by the vampires and witches, she knows that she won't survive, so Althea plays mind games to get to her safety by saying, "I've been searching for this Book for many decades. I know that Estelle had knowledge of the whereabouts, but she played dumb like she didn't know. My last message to you all is: Rest assured I will be back. Jenessa, I will not rest until I have that Book."

Like a puff of smoke, Althea is gone. Sebastian and Edmund slowly turn back into human-form. They step up to the porch, and Persia says, "Well, hello handsome. My, don't you gentlemen look very nice in suits? Come in. Are you gentlemen escorting us lovely ladies to the funeral because we would love some strong men on our arms?"

Sebastian and Edmund come inside the house. Sebastian replies, "Persia, thank you for that compliment. You look really nice on this sad occasion. We just stopped by to see if there is anything we can do before the funeral."

Once inside, Edmund says, "I wonder what rock Althea crawled out from under. You can best believe that she will be back, and someone will probably get hurt, so, ladies, be careful and watch your backs."

Jenessa says, "Forgive me for being rude. Aunt Genie, this is Sebastian and Edmund. They own Priceless. Fellas, this is Grandma's sister, Aunt Genie."

Edmund speaks up by saying, "It's nice to meet you, Genie. As long as we've known Estelle, she's never mentioned that she had a sister, and you are gorgeous."

Edmund gives her a peck on the back of her hand. She blushes and says, "My, you are very handsome yourself, Edmund. You sure know how to flatter the ladies. If I didn't know any better, I would believe that you're trying to charm an old lady like me."

Sebastian responds by saying, "Ladies, let me tell you that Althea means trouble when she comes around. If she came by months ago to see Estelle, then she had a devious plan up her sleeve. If she's here, that means Lars is not too far behind. He is her vampire bodyguard, so please be careful from now on out, and definitely keep your eyes open."

Edmund smiles at Genie. The limo driver knocks at the front door and then says, "I'm here to take the Craig family to the church. Is everyone ready so we can leave and be on time?"

Sebastian turns to look at the ladies and says, "Is everyone ready to go? Jenessa, do you want us to ride with you to the church?"

She smiles at her boss and replies, "Yes, I would be honored to have you escort us to the funeral. I know Grandma would have loved that."

As everyone starts walking outside to the limo, the gentlemen let the ladies get in the car first, and then they get in. The driver shuts the door, and they proceed to the church. Once they arrive, they can see all the friends and family gathered outside to pay their respects to Estelle. Jenessa looks out the window and says, "Wow, there are a lot of people here. It looks like the whole town of Haven-Crest is here for Grandma. This means a lot to me that these people really cared about her."

Genie puts on a fake smile and says, "I know Estelle would have loved that all these people are showing her this much attention. I agree with you, Jenessa; these townspeople really love Estelle. She will be sorely missed."

As the driver pulls up to the front of the church, Edmund says, "Is everyone ready? Let's give Estelle a fond goodbye and show her how much we loved her, like the rest of the town."

Chapter 4

The driver gets out and opens the limo door and the Craig family and friends get out ready for the funeral. The funeral director lines up the family according to the way they will be coming into the church. As the choir begins singing one of Estelle's favorite church songs, the family walks in to view Estelle's body one more time. There's a lot of crying from family members and friends as different people walk by and see Estelle lying in the coffin. Jenessa is holding onto Sebastian as they come in the church, leaning on him for strength and comfort during this time of sorrow. Once they get to their seats, Sebastian reaches into his coat pocket for a handkerchief to give to Jenessa to wipe the tears off her face.

As she wipes the tears, she turns and looks around the church at all the different people who have come to Estelle's funeral. She sees her friend Jai Li and her family and Chrisha and her family. Jenessa sees a couple of teachers from school and begins to feel strengthened from the support of people who care about her. As Jenessa continues to look around, she can't believe that Camden is standing in the back of the church. She stands and makes sure her eyes are not playing tricks on her. Since she is standing, people begin to wonder if she is alright.

Sebastian whispers and says, "Are you okay? What's wrong? You might want to have a seat because the service is about to begin."

Jenessa replies, "I thought I saw something. I'm just making sure I'm not going crazy. I thought I saw Camden standing in the back of the church."

She can't locate Camden again, so she sits down and the funeral begins. The Reverend Eddie Williams stands at the podium. He takes a deep breath and says, "After the choir gives us one more selection, the eulogy will be delivered by Reverend Carl Wardrett."

34

The choir sings, "The Reason Why We Sing" by Kirk Franklin. The family and friends are moved by the powerful selection. Suddenly, Jenessa begins to hear a voice calling her. She slowly turns her head and looks around the room. Jenessa spots Althea, and her eyes widen. Althea looks back at Jenessa with a smirk on her face. The voice is says, "Jenessa, I know you can hear me. You know what I want."

Jenessa tries to drown out the voice, but it's not working. The harder she concentrates, the more Althea attacks her defenses. Reverend Wardrett stands up, looks at Jenessa, and says, "I'm not here to talk about the life of Estelle Craig. I'm here to get you to understand how much Estelle Craig loved this town of Haven-Crest. Sweetheart, you may feel that you are alone, but you're not. As a community, we are here for you. Your Grandmother Estelle was one of the most wonderful individuals I've ever met. We've had many long conversations at her Herbal Store. As a dear friend, I will miss her terribly. I know this is a very difficult time for you. You have lost two people who were very close to you in your very young life, but God won't lead you into darkness. He will show you the light so you can prosper. Estelle was loved by many people in this town. She has done so much to help a lot of people who couldn't afford food for Thanksgiving, and for those of you who couldn't get your kids gifts for Christmas, she gave you money and never asked for anything in return. Jenessa, never doubt that we loved your Grandmother."

At that moment, Jenessa hears the voice more intensely. She tries hard, but she can't drown out the voice of Althea that has been haunting her. Many patrons and family members look at Jenessa as she has leaned forward in her seat and is holding her head. Suddenly, Jenessa says really loudly, "Leave me alone; why you don't stop?"

She stands up and runs out of the church. The ground begins to shake, and the church rumbles. The congregation begins to get scared and thinks it's an earthquake. Sebastian runs out behind Jenessa. The sheriff stands and says, "Everybody remain calm; it's going to be alright. I think it's all over now. Is anyone hurt? Does anybody need medical attention?"

As people begin to become calm and quiet down, some get up off the floor and make sure no one has injuries. The deputies and Agent Ambrose are spot checking many people.

Once outside, Sebastian walks up to Jenessa and says, "What's going on? Are you okay? Tell me what's wrong with you? Your powers created a small earthquake once you stood up."

Jenessa walks up to Sebastian with tears in her eyes and says, "I don't know what's going on. I keep hearing Althea's voice inside my head asking me where the Book is. It feels like she's probing my mind."

Sebastian shows concern and says, "I can understand what you're saying, but you have to be careful that you don't hurt anyone in the process. I know it's hard to concentrate to drown out the sounds and voices that have much power, but we have to be cautious, Jenessa. I came outside to help you pull yourself together before we go back in."

At that very moment, the church doors open up, and Jamal comes outside. He walks down to Jenessa, hugs her, and says, "Are you okay? I was worried about you, so I came to check on you. I know this is a lot to endure with Mrs. Estelle gone, but remember that I'm here if you need me. I know I haven't been around, but I've been going through some issues myself. What are you doing later? I'll come by and we can talk."

Sebastian says, "Jenessa, are you ready to go back inside the church?"

Jenessa smiles at Jamal and says, "Thanks for coming out here and checking on me. You really have changed. You look different. It would mean a lot to me if you did stop by later so we can talk."

Jenessa holds Sebastian by the arm, and they proceed to go back inside the church. Jamal stands there and just watches Sebastian. Suddenly, he begins to growl. Unknown to Jamal, Sebastian can hear the growling. He stops, turns, and looks at Jamal. He says nothing but heads inside the church. Once inside, Reverend Wardrett comes over to Jenessa and says, "Is everything alright? I know funerals can be very emotional and sometimes overwhelming, but, we're going to make it through this, Jenessa. You've got people here who care about you and want to help you."

Reverend Wardrett holds her hands to give her strength. He smiles and turns to the congregation and says, "Everyone, Jenessa is alright. Let's all have a seat so we can continue with the service for Estelle. While the choir gives us another selection, we can get back to our seats."

People begin to move back to their seats. Some walk by and offer Jenessa words of encouragement and support. She smiles and says, "Thank you; I appreciate all your support."

Reverend Wardrett finishes up the funeral by saying, "In closing, I just want to say that I hope the person who killed one of our most beloved mothers has a conscience and turns himself or herself into the sheriff's department. This shows how severe society has become, but faith in God will get us through these troubled times. We share love for one another; Haven-Crest bands together to support it's fallen. We will miss you, Estelle."

The funeral director comes to the front of the casket and lowers the top. Then, the pallbearers stand and come to the casket to help with the sealing of the locks. The flower girls all stand and begin walking and picking up flowers to take to the grave in the church cemetery. Members of the congregation all stand, and once the funeral director starts pushing the casket down the aisle, the family stands and follows Rev. Wardrett out of the church heading toward the cemetery. Some family members are crying because this is Estelle's last ride before the graveside services. Members of the hospitality committee head downstairs to set up the food for the reception. The pallbearers load Estelle's body into the hearse as Rev. Wardrett leads the family and friends to the graveside tribute. Once there, Rev. Wardrett hands the roses to close family members and says, "We are gathered here for those who have known Estelle Craig, a mother, grandmother, family member, and friend. We will miss you, but now you are going on to become a member of God's family. Even though your death was sudden, God knew it was time for you to come home; rest assured we will all cherish your memory and your legacy for the things you've done for this town of Haven-Crest, so ashes to ashes and dust to dust, may the power of God's love guide you on your journey into God's eternal kingdom."

Rev. Wardrette reaches down, picks up a handful of dirt, and sifts it onto the casket as he says his goodbye to Estelle. Jenessa walks up first, stands over the casket with tears in her eyes, and says, "Grandma, I'm going to miss you dearly. I know that I have a purpose to fulfill, and I won't let you down. I love you with all my heart because you raised me into the woman I have become. Mom is there waiting for you, so you both can keep an eye on me. Until we see each other again, I love you."

Then she drops her rose onto the casket. Genie comes up next with tears in her eyes and says, "Stelle, I hate to see you in this casket. I know we should have made up and worked things out. When I talked to you on the phone a couple of months back, I should have said, "I'm sorry," and worked at building our families together. I promise you I will look after Jenessa and make you proud of the Craig family. I will miss you, and I love you, big sis." She drops her rose and walks away. Persia drops her rose and says, "I miss you, and I appreciate everything you've done for me. I love you."

As other family members drop roses and make last rite comments, they head to the dining hall of the church where they are having the reception. Sebastian and Edmund have catered the event. As family and friends talk about the good times they had with Estelle, some share laughs and a few tears while others mourn and reminisce about a wonderful woman. Jenessa is the center of attention as she receives cards of sympathy and hugs from dear customers and friends of Estelle. Jai Li and Chrisha come over to their best friend, and Jai Li says, "You did really well today. Granny would be really proud of you. I know this is a difficult time for you, but my parents said if you need anything, don't hesitate to ask. Do you want me to come over tonight?"

Jenessa smiles and replies by saying, "It's good to have friends like you two. Tell your parents thanks for the offers, and I appreciate everything that they have done for me. If you want to come over tonight, it's okay with me. Aunt Genie is still there; she's alright. Let me tell you something. Guess who wants to come see me later on tonight?"

Jai Li and Chrisha both stare at Jenessa, and Chrisha says, "Who? Don't tell me it's Camden."

Jenessa laughs and says, "Girl, no, it's Jamal. He said he needs to talk to me about something tonight."

They all start to laugh, and Persia comes over and says, "What's up? Glad to see you guys. Are you coming over tonight?"

Jai Li replies, "Probably. Is your Mommy letting you hang out with us tonight, or are you on curfew."

As the girls start to laugh at Persia, she says, "Oh, I guess I'm the butt of the jokes today. If I didn't like you guys, I would probably get mad."

With Jai still laughing, she says, "Persia, you know I'm just joking with you. Of course, we are hanging out tonight. What's on the menu?"

Chrisha sits her cup on the table and says, "I say let's watch a scary movie and have girl talk."

All of the friends agree. Then Jai Li's parents signal for her to come over, and she says, "Hey, I've got to go, but I'll be over later. I'll call you guys."

As she begins to walk away, she walks past Jamal and gets a very weird feeling and smells an unpleasant scent. She stops, looks at Jamal, and says, "Jamal, do you smell that? What's that odor?"

Jamal doesn't respond at first, but then he says, "What's up, to you too Jai? No, I don't smell anything. What am I supposed to smell?"

Jai stands with an unusual look on her face and says, "It smells like an animal is in here. You don't smell that?"

Jamal doesn't appreciate the comment. He turns his head, looks around the room, and then he says, "If my senses were as keen as yours, I probably would smell that animal too. If you know what I mean."

Jai Li's eyes get really big when Jamal makes that remark. Jamal stands up and walks over to Jenessa's table. Thoughts begin racing through Jai Li's mind about what Jamal said. She thinks, "What does he know? Does he know I'm a vampire? Why didn't he smell that animal scent?"

She turns and looks back at Jamal but just disregards the thoughts all together. Her father says, "How is Jenessa doing? Are you ready to go? I have to go in by the office to pick up some papers to work on."

Jai replies, "She's doing alright; I'm going over to her house later to hang out with her. Yeah, I'm ready to go."

As Sebastian fixes himself a plate of food, Agent Ambrose walks over and says, "Why can't a nice girl have a handsome gentleman give her a call? I hope you're going to say you lost my number or you've been busy at the restaurant lately."

Sebastian blushes, smiles, and then he says, "How have you been doing, Monica? The answer to your question is: No I haven't lost your number, and yes, I've been busy at Priceless helping out Edmund. Plus we're in the process of adding on to the building. You look very nice outside of your police uniform I always see you in. Your looking like this makes me want to reconsider and give you a call later to see if we can get some drinks."

Agent Ambrose blushes, smiles, and shyly replies, "Like I said before, you sure know how to sweet talk a lady. I would love to get drinks later; I can meet you at Priceless at about eight."

Sebastian realizes he is getting caught up in the moment. He touches her hand and replies, "Since I've returned to Haven-Crest, you are by far the most beautiful woman I've seen. I adore the attention you are showing me, and I find it very flattering. I would like to return the favor by saying that any man should appreciate a sexy woman like you by his side, and the possibilities of a lifetime of love I see you have to offer just make me realize that I need to stop putting work foremost and enjoy the beautiful flowers that are right in front of me."

With that said, Agent Ambrose is smitten by the charms of Sebastian. As she bats her eyes, but she doesn't know quite how to respond to all of that. She shows Sebastian her sexy smirk and says, "If we weren't in front of all these people, I would show you how a beautiful woman responds to a handsome man's cry for attention."

At that very moment, Marcella interrupts by saying, "Excuse me, Sebastian, we're running out of ice in the cooler for the drinks."

Sebastian replies by saying, "Oh, I'll go get some more ice. Tell Edmund I'll be back in a few minutes."

Agent Ambrose is all dreamy eyed as she looks at Marcella and says, "He's one of the best catches in Haven-Crest. I envy you; I would give up my SBI job for a man like him."

Marcella's horns begin to show, and she says, "Sebastian is one of my dearest and closest friends. We've known each other for years, and anyone who tries to hurt him will have to deal with me."

Agent Ambrose gives Marcella the stare down and says, "Should I take this as a threat? I have no intentions of hurting Sebastian. Just remember, don't let the badge fool you."

Agent Ambrose walks away and heads over to Sheriff Michaels. She sits down and says, "Ross, I just had the most unusual conversation with Marcella. What do you know about her? What is her connection to Sebastian?"

Sheriff Michaels smiles at Agent Ambrose and says, "Do I sense a cat-fight? Do you think that Marcella is jealous of you? Far as I can remember, she's always worked with Sebastian and Edmund. She could be some relation to one of them. I see you have become fond of young Sebastian."

Agent Ambrose smiles and says, "We're meeting for drinks later on, and I hope that nothing happens to mess this up."

After a few hours, the crowd starts to get smaller and smaller. The ones who are left begin clean up church and move furniture back. Some of the guys from Priceless handle the cleanup details. Close friends of Estelle, Juan and Carla with their daughter Rachel, come over to Jenessa, and Juan says, "Jenessa, we are so sorry for your loss. Your grandmother did a lot for us. She was more than a friend; she was family. She wanted me to give you this because this is to help you on your journey."

Juan hands Jenessa a box that has been wrapped in black paper with a bow. She takes the card off the top and reads it. It says, "Honey, this will help you find what you're destined to do and what you will become. The journey will take you away from Haven-Crest where your powers will grow and you will gain knowledge to accomplish amazing feats."

Jenessa stands, reaches out, and hugs Juan and his family. She smiles and says, "Thank you."

As the presenters of the package exit the room, Chrisha walks over to Jenessa and says, "Who were they? What's in the box?"

With a puzzled look on her face, Jenessa responds by saying, "I don't know, but I'll open it later. Are you coming over now or later?"

Chrsiha replies, "I can come now, and Persia can take me home later to get some clothes." Are you ready?"

Jennesa and Chrisha walk over to Genie, and Jenessa says, "I'm ready to go because I know some people may stop by the house to pay their respects, and the girls are coming over tonight."

Genie puts her arm around Jenessa's shoulders and says, "Okay, I'm ready if you are. What's in the box?"

The chauffeur steps up and says, "Ladies are you ready to go? May I take the box?"

Jenessa shakes her head, and they all head outside to the limo. Once they are outside, Mayor Dobson comes over to Jenessa and says, "Hi, Jenessa; on behalf of the whole town of Haven-Crest, we are sorry for your loss. Let me say that I have the help of the HCPD and SBI working to solve this case. Rest assured, sweetheart, that we will find and arrest this culprit."

Genie speaks first and says, "Thank you, mayor that means a lot. We have faith in the Haven-Crest police. All the love and respect that the town has been showing for Estelle shows us she really did mean the world to everyone."

Mrs. Dobson replies by saying, "Excuse me for asking, but who are you?"

Genie turns her attention over to Mrs. Dobson and says, "I'm Genevieve, Estelle's younger sister. I left Haven-Crest many years ago for the big cities and bright lights of California."

With a smirk on her face, Mrs. Dobson replies by saying, "Estelle never told us she had a younger sister. Jenessa, honey, if you need anything, please don't hesitate to call on us."

The mayor and his wife hug Jenessa, and they walk toward the limo to get in to head home.

Chapter 5

At the Crenshall house, Camden is squatting on the floor. He has three candles lit with a witches' grim war open on the floor inside the pentagram which he has drawn. The sole purpose of this séance is to see if he can contact his deceased sister, Jazmine. Since her death, Camden has been tampering with the dark side of black magic. He's trying to summon the mystic energies to help him talk to his sister. Suddenly, the door opens up, and Alden says, "Cam, what are you doing? You are messing with some very dark magic. I'm worried about you. Dad seems like he's not concerned about what you're doing. We've seen what the effects of black magic can do to someone."

Camden turns, looks at his twin brother, and says, "I'm doing what I got to do to bring our dead sister back. That means with or without your help, I'm going to contact her. Where is father?"

With a concerned look on his face, Alden replies, "He's not home from work yet."

Suddenly, the flames from the candles begin to glow brightly. The lights in the room start to flicker and get dim. As Camden and his brother stand in amazement at the events that are happening right in from of them, the room grows dark. Without a word being said, they see an image in white. The image that they see begins to take on the form of a young girl in white. Camden looks at his brother and says, "I don't believe what I'm seeing. Could that be Jazmine?"

Alden seems lost for words and doesn't reply. He's just standing in amazement. Camden takes a step forward and says, "Jaz, is that you? Jaz, can you hear me?"

Suddenly, the image in white hovers in thin air, and in a soft voice, the image says, "Cam, it's me, Jaz. I can sense your pain. Why are you messing with black magic when you know what can happen with this type of power?"

Camden stands in front of the image of his sister and says, "Jaz, I'm trying everything in my power to bring you back. I miss you so much; I don't understand why this happened to you. I go to your casket every day and pray for a way for me to bring you back. I think I know a way to do that: the Book of Spells."

Jazmine replies, "I met someone on this other side who may be able to help us get a head start on the quest. Find a witch named Almyra; she is the way to the Book."

Camden responds by saying, "Father has partnered with a vampire to give us some more muscle in finding the Book. He even avenged your death; he had Estelle killed by our new ally. Her funeral was today. Jenessa hates me now because of what happened to her grandmother, but I hate her because of what Estelle did to you. This incantation I've conjured should be able to give you the ability to stay on both sides."

Alden and Camden realize what must be done in order for their sister to be reborn; they must find the Book of Spells first. Suddenly, there's a knock at the door. Seth comes into the room, and like a puff of smoke, Jazmine is gone. Seth says, "Who were you talking to in here? I thought I heard a girl's voice."

Alden speaks first and says, "Dad, Cam did a spell, and we were able to talk to Jaz. She says we need to find a witch named Almyra. She is the key to finding the Book."

Seth has a concerned look on his face and replies, "I miss her. Did you tell her that we're doing everything we can to bring her back? Our new ally is checking out some things as we speak."

Camden turns, looks at his father, and says, "Who is this ally who is supposed to be helping us out now, and what's in it for her? Does she want the Book or something to benefit her?"

Seth replies in a calm tone by saying, "Son, calm down. You can never have enough allies in a situation like this. A lot of people other than us want the Book and what the Book can do to prosper their desires. With stakes this high, you never know where a good ally might come in handy."

With that said, Seth and Alden walk into another room, leaving Camden in his room to continue reading in his black magic journal. Once they are out of sight, Seth says, "I see Camden has had a change of heart. He's more determined than either of us to find the Book in order to bring back Jaz, but we still have to monitor the magic he's experimenting with because black magic is one of the most influential types of magic out there. One can get enticed by what the incantations can do to enhance powers, so let's hope that he doesn't get corrupted."

Alden looks at his father, nods his head, and says, "I understand what you're saying. I've noticed a lot of changes in his attitude and his actions about certain things. Now, Dad, think about this; what if by him being able communicate with Jaz on the hereafter plane, she is somehow influencing Cam to reach out to the black magic for enticement? That could make things a lot worse for us if this is what's going on. I'll keep an eye on him."

After Alden finishes his conversation with his father, he heads back into the room with Camden and practices incantations on some spells. Seth heads to his study and makes a call to his ally.

At Coach Deren's house, he has called a meeting of his players. Jamal is the last one to get to the urgent meeting. Once Jamal has a seat, the coach says, "I know you're probably wondering why I've called you here. I'm going to get straight to the point because we don't keep secrets from one another in this pack. We've been offered a proposition to ally with one of our mortal enemies, the vampire. I know that I've told you never trust vampires because they will turn on you and in the process, try to kill you. An opportunity has presented itself to us, if we help an old vampire friend of mine find the Book of Spells. In return, he has gracefully offered to grant us two spells. I decided that I would present this proposal to the pack before I give him an answer."

Jamal, still new to idea of being a howler, sits back and monitors his fellow teammates rally behind their leader. Greg turns and says, "Jamal, what's the matter? This is time for a celebration. If we get the two spells, we can make this pack more dominant and become the most feared pack in the world."

Jamal looks at his friend, not knowing what to say or how to react to what the coach just presented to the pack. Without thinking, Jamal says, "If we help this vampire, how do we know he's going to live up to his part of the deal if he finds it?"

Coach Deren turns and answers Jamal by saying, "Jamal, don't worry; my friend won't stick us like that. We have been friends for a long time. Now, the next order of business is the person we need to monitor; her name is Jenessa Craig."

Once Coach Deren says Jenessa's name, Jamal almost has a heart attack. He tries to keep a straight face by not letting anyone know that he knows her personally. Greg turns and says, "Hey, Jamal, do you know that girl? Didn't she go to Haven-Crest High with you?"

Before Jamal can answer Greg, he feels his adrenaline and body temperature rising and starts feeling sweaty. He responds kind of slowly by saying, "Yeah, I know her. Her grandmother just died. So why do we need to monitor her? She isn't a vampire."

Coach Deren smiles and says, "No, Jamal, I didn't say she was. I just said we need to just keep eyes on her and check out who is coming and going. That's all."

Coach Deren gives Jamal an under-eyed look. Not really knowing how to comment on the response, he says, "Did you know your classmate is possibly a witch? I heard her grandmother was a powerful witch from Salem. She supposedly stripped Seth Crenshall, a wizard from England, of his powers, so we're monitoring her to see if she is the prophecy."

With all this talk of witches and prophecies, Jamal shakes his head in disbelief about what he's hearing. The question running through his mind is: "Do I tell Jenessa about what's going on, or do I not say anything?" His thoughts get interrupted by Coach Deren's last comment, "We are not to give ourselves away, so stay at a distance. No one is to harm or bother Jenessa either, and most of all, Jamal, stay away from her until this assignment is over."

Jamal says nothing and just shakes his head. He realizes that this is a loyalty decision he must make, yet knows that he must do the right thing by the woman he still loves.

At that very moment, the mysterious ally of Coach Deren reveals himself to the howler pack. Coach Deren says, "Fellas, I'd like to introduce Adrian Kane, our vampire ally."

With a devilish grin, Adrian says, "Good afternoon, fellas; I want to say that I know you've always heard vampires are not allies and that they are the sworn enemies of howlers. All of that is not true; your coach and I have been friends for a long time. Howlers and vampires can coexist, work together, and plot to take over the world. You can all be at ease that I won't try to deceive you or the coach. I plan to split the take fifty-fifty."

Jamal sits and watches what to him seems to be a deception on behalf of the vampire. Relying on his gut feeling, something doesn't seem right, but Jamal just goes along with the plan for right now.

It's about seven-thirty on the grandfather clock, which stands in the hallway of Sebastian's mansion. Edmund comes into the study, opens up his laptop, and then begins to do payroll for the employees. Sebastian comes in and says, "Hey, what are you doing?"

Edmund smiles and responds, "Working on this week's payroll, but the question is: Where are you going tonight dressed so sharp?"

Sebastian blushes and replies, "I'm going to have a very interesting drink with a very sexy lady if that's alright with you."

Edmund replies with a nonchalant look on his face, "Be very careful; Agent Ambrose is not a fool. She plays that helpless "I don't know anything about vampires" card very well. Overall, enjoy yourself because you deserve it."

Sebastian walks over to the bar, pours a drink, and says, "You know I appreciate you always looking out for me, watching my back, and making sure that nothing bad happens to the Clan. Edmund, you do a lot. Thanks, now, with that said, let me say that I know Monica has an agenda; she is trying to search for something, or should I say, trying to find out about vampires. Trust me, Edmund, I've got my eyes on her; let me go so I won't be late."

Sebastian walks out of the house and gets into his car. When his cell phone rings, he answers and says, "What's up, Jenessa? You kind of caught me at a bad time right now. I'll stop by when I get done, and we'll talk about this then."

Sebastian hangs up and heads toward Priceless. While driving to meet Monica, he thinks about what her motive could be. "Could she really like me, or is she trying to get information out of me? What has Fritz told her about the Clan? Does she have feelings for me?" Sebastian stops over rationalizing about Monica's ulterior motives and thinks, "Like Edmund said, enjoy myself." Once he pulls into the parking lot, he gets out and heads inside. He comes through the kitchen and heads to his office. He sits at this desk and surveys the restaurant looking for Monica, when he spots her, he stands and grabs the bouquet of flowers her has for her and heads to the bar.

Sebastian stands at the end of the bar watching Agent Ambrose. She takes a sip of her drink, turns her head and smiles at Sebastian. He walks down to the bar and says, "Hi Monica, you look incredible. I am so glad we are having a drink together. These flowers are for the most gorgeous lady in the restaurant tonight. Do you want to stay at the bar, or would you like a nice quiet table?"

Monica blushes at Sebastian's compliment. She takes a sip of her drink and says, "Sebastian, you look very handsome. Thank you! I love flowers, and it's been a long time since I had a very damn sexy man give me some. Are you sure we could get a table? It looks mighty full in here tonight."

Sebastian laughs, and says, "I know the owner, and it shouldn't be a problem. Let's get this table I already had set up for us."

Sebastian, being a true gentleman, pulls her chair out for her, and they have a seat. Monica smiles and says, "Let me be honest by saying that I've been looking forward to this for quite some time. Once I gave you my number, I was really hoping that you would call me, but better late than never. I'm a little nervous, but I think we are going to have a good time."

Sebastian laughs and says, "I didn't know that you really wanted me to call you, but I'm glad you made the first move. Couldn't you tell that I'm out of the game? I saw the hints you were throwing at me, but I was lost in the game by not reacting to them. Don't feel bad. I'm nervous too; you are the first lady I've been on a date with in a very long time. I think we both need to calm down and take it slow. Well, let me start the night off by asking, why an extremely sexy woman would want to do SBI work."

Agent Ambrose looks into Sebastian's green eyes and says, "My father was a DC cop, and I guess I wanted to be like him. He was my hero, and the community loved him. One night he was coming home from work and stopped at the store. There was robbery, and he got shot. Since then, I've dedicated my life to being a good investigator like him. I know that may sound kind of corny, but that's the way I was raised."

Sebastian shows his human compassion by saying, "Trust me, Monica, that doesn't sound corny, and believe me when I say this: Your father would be really proud of you if he could see you now. So, what does a SBI investigator do?"

Monica is flattered by the show of interest by Sebastian as he asks personal questions. She smiles and then says, "I investigate unexplained murders and sudden disappearances, so I was sent here to investigate the mysterious death of the two teenagers a few months back. I was assigned to be a special investigator to help the sheriff for a while. To be honest, I'm glad I'm still here. Now, enough about me tell me one thing: How is it that a very handsome guy like you doesn't have a girlfriend? Are you one of those guys who is afraid of commitment?"

Sebastian then shows a concerned look on his face and says, "You are very funny. I'm not afraid of commitment to a woman. I'm being very open about myself to you. I was in a relationship, and my partner died. It took me a while to really get over that, so I'm just cautious about getting close to women. However, sometimes one has to make exceptions and give romance a second try. Well, so far I am very intrigued by what I see sitting in front of me, and I am definitely enjoying being with you."

As Monica and Sebastian sit at the secluded table for two and throw lightly innocent hints at each other, both of them begin to realize that there is a connection building between them. Sebastian says, "Time surely flies when you are having fun. I wish this night would never end. Let's take a drive to somewhere more private."

Monica is flattered by Sebastian's comment and says, "I agree. I hate for this night to end also. I would love to take a ride with you. Are you ready?"

Sebastian reaches for her hand, and they head out of Priceless to his car. He opens the door, and they leave the parking lot.

Jenessa receives a text from Jamal about not coming over. She responds to the text, and Jai Li says, "I can tell by the look on your face that he's not coming. That's okay; you've got us to keep you company. Have you opened the box you got at the reception yet?"

Jenessa sets her phone down on the counter and says, "No, I haven't opened it up yet. Where is the box so we can do it now?"

Persia and the other girlfriends help Jenessa look for the box. Chrisha comes in the room with box with the bow on it and says, "Hey, I have it. Jenessa, you can open it up now."

They all huddle up around the kitchen table while they wait for Jenessa to open the box. She unties the bow, takes the top off, and reaches inside the box; to her surprise, she pulls out a rolled up piece of stiff paper. As Jenessa unrolls the stiff paper, she is surprised to see that it's the map she's been looking for. Thoughts begin running through her mind as to why Estelle left her the map. As everyone takes a look at the map, Jai Li says, "Can anyone decipher any of these symbols on it? I wonder what language this is written in."

Genie comes into the kitchen and says, "What going on? I'm not going to intrude on your girls' night. I'm just getting a soda from the fridge. What is that you are looking at?"

Persia responds to her mother by saying, "Momma, it looks like this may be a map, but it's written in some kind of code."

Genie comes to the table and to her surprise, she see the map that she has been wanting for quite some time laying on the kitchen table. She takes a good look at it and says, "Now, we need to get this map deciphered and find out what it means. Who is someone we can confide in with what we have here now?"

Jai Li speaks up by saying, "I think we need to call Sebastian or Edmund about this; they will know what to do."

Jenessa turns to her best friend and says, "You're right; we have been wondering where the map could have been. Now we can get a head start on Adrian in finding the Book. Yeah, call him."

Jai Li dials her covenant leader to inform him of what they have been given. To her surprise, the voicemail comes on. Somewhat caught off guard that Sebastian didn't answer his phone, she calmly responds to everyone by saying, "Uh, he didn't pick up; I wonder if everything is alright. I'll just call Edmund instead and see what he says."

Jai Li then calls Edmund. He picks up and says, "Hello, Jai, how can I help you?"

Jai Li replies, "Hey, we tried calling Sebastian, but he didn't pick up. The reason I'm calling is because someone gave Jenessa the map we have been looking for from Estelle. You can come over and check it out if you like. It has some type of ancient writings on it."

Edmund goes quiet, and then he says, "I'm speechless right now. This is the break we need; yeah, I'm on the way over. Well, Sebastian is out on a date tonight, but I'll leave him a message to meet us at Jenessa's."

Jai can't believe what she just heard, and she replies, "Edmund, did you say Sebastian was out on a date? I hate to be nosey, but with whom?"

Edmund replies by saying, "Jai Li you know we don't put vampire business out amongst people. That's breaking one of our codes of ethics."

Jai Li sighs and says, "I understand, so I'll see you in a little while."

As they end their phone call, Edmund tries to reach Sebastian by texting him, "Meet us at Jenessa's when you get chance." Once Edmund presses send, he gets his jacket and begins walking to the door. Suddenly, his phone goes off and he answers, "Hello, this Edmund, I'm on the way."

He hangs up, reaches for his keys, and heads out the door.

Chapter 6

As Edmund drives toward the urgent meeting for the Committee, he begins wondering what the meeting could be about. Has the newbie vampire Declan found out about Jai Li, or has Simon found a mythical creature to torture for the Committee? With that thought, Edmund pulls behind the building. He goes inside, enters through the metal door, and takes his seat next to other members of the Committee. Sheriff Michaels looks around the room, and then starts the urgent meeting by saying, "The reason I called this meeting is because we found another dead body tonight down by Moon Crest Lake. One of my deputies was making rounds and noticed the victim lying on top of the picnic table. The victim is a homeless man who was living in the area. There were bite marks on the side of the neck. We took care of the situation before any news reporters tried to break this story. Now my question is: What are we going to do about this? Could this have been done by that newbie vampire, Declan?"

Simon Ye takes a deep breath and then replies, "It may be possible that it could have been him, but it may be that another vampire has come here to Haven-Crest. I'll send my men to find Declan and bring him in."

Mayor Dobson folds his arms and comments by saying, "Hell yes, we need to find that boy. If he is starting trouble and still killing people in town, then we need to get rid of him."

Simon interrupts by saying, "Sir, don't worry. We will have him brought in the next couple of days so we can talk to him."

The sheriff puts his hands on the table, and then he replies, "I will keep my men investigating the area for clues."

Fire Chief Maynard stands up, clears his throat, and says, "Can I have the floor? Recently we had a murder of one of our most beloved and former members of the Committee, Estelle Craig. That is one murder I feel we need to try and solve for the town as well as for the family. We all knew that Estelle was a witch, but she never used her powers to hurt. She only helped the unfortunate people in Haven-Crest. I know this is wrong, but if we can't find the actual killer, then someone will have to take the fall for the slaying of her."

None of the members say a word. Everyone looks at the sheriff, and he says, "Now, wait; let's think about this. We would be breaking a lot of laws by doing that. Let's just give it a little time. We'll solve the case."

Dr. Barton raises his hand to speak. He stands and says to his fellow members, "Members, I'm acknowledging the Committee by informing you all that I am hiring another doctor for the hospital. The top candidate is Kareem Jensyn, and he comes highly recommended. He would be a good edition for the hospital. I'm giving Dr. Jensyn a second interview for the position in the next couple of days, so hopefully everything will go well."

Mayor Dobson stands, look around the room, and says, "Where is Agent Ambrose? Did anyone text her about the urgent meeting?"

Sheriff Michael's answers, "Agent Ambrose took the day off, so I'll inform her tomorrow about the situations at hand that must be taken care of."

Judge Simmons dismisses the meeting, and members begin heading out of the Town Hall to their separate lives once again. Sheriff Michaels texts Agent Ambrose "To call 911."

At that very moment, Sebastian is taking a drive to a special place to spend some time alone with Agent Ambrose. She receives a text from the sheriff. She reads it and puts the phone back in her purse. Sebastian turns and asks, "Is everything alright? Was that text important?"

She smiles at Sebastian and says, "It's nothing major; it can wait until in the morning. I'm not going to let anything spoil this evening."

As the soft music plays through the car radio, Agent Ambrose is wondering what Sebastian has in store. Suddenly, Sebastian begins driving up the hill to a sectioned-off cliff where there is a great view of the whole town. He leaves the engine running, looks at Monica, and says, "I wanted to bring you here because it's somewhere we can be alone. I want to show you one of the most exquisite sights you will ever see."

They get out of the car, shut the doors, and walk to the front of the car. With the music still playing, they look at the full moon with no clouds in the sky. Monica turns to Sebastian and says, "I agree with you. This is by far a very beautiful and romantic spot. I would love to have a picnic here. Now, why have you brought me here? I hope to take advantage of an alcohol soaked SBI agent tonight."

As Monica laughs at her joke, Sebastian looks into her eyes and says, "When I was young, I used to ride my bike here all the time, stare at the full moon, and realize how good it made me feel. Whenever I come back to watch the full moon, I realize everything is more beautiful under the moonlight."

Monica turns to look at Sebastian. Suddenly, they begin to kiss very passionately. Sebastian stops first and says, "I think we need to stop. I feel we are moving too fast. I don't want you think I'm taking advantage of you because you've been drinking."

Monica reaches out for Sebastian, and she replies, "Don't feel that way. I don't want you to stop. I am a grown woman, and I have wanted to do this ever since I met you."

They continued to kiss. Then they touch each other, and suddenly Monica starts ripping Sebastian's shirt off. Then she scratches his chest. He yells, "Ouch, wait, wait Monica, let's not do this right here. Let go to somewhere more private where we can finish this. Wow, your fingernails are sharp."

She smiles and says, "Let's go back to my hotel."

They get back into the car, and Sebastian hurries over to Monica's hotel room. Once there, she says, "Open up the bottle of champagne while I slip into something more comfortable."

She shuts the door to her bedroom, and Sebastian pops the cork on the champagne bottle. After about a couple of minutes, she comes out in a sexy, sheer cream negligee and high heels. She stands in the doorway so the lights can reflect off of her curvy body. Sebastian stands, walks over to her with a glass of champagne, they toast, and drink it all up. She grabs Sebastian again, shoves him on the couch, and begins to lower herself to him. She finishes ripping his shirt open, and then she says, "What happened to your scratches? They're gone. I don't get it. The only way those marks could be gone is if you are a…. vampire."

Sebastian does a blur movement, grabs Monica, a pushes her to the wall. She tries to scratch him again, so he holds her hands. His eyes turn golden-black and fangs extend. He looks at her jugular vein in her throat. With his fangs extended, he bites her in the neck. With blood on his face, he says in a deep voice, "I had a feeling that you were setting me up, trying to see if I was a vampire, but after tonight, all of that is going to change. Look into my eyes; you won't remember anything about me being a vampire. You will still have a crush on me as usual, but you will forget everything else."

Monica has a dazed and confused look on her face for a few moments. She can't remember anything since the restaurant. She still has the alcohol in her system, but she still has desire on her mind. She grabs Sebastian very passionately, pulls him on to her, and they begin kissing once again.

As clothes begin to fly off on the floor, Monica has one thing on her mind: Sebastian taking her and having unforgettable sex with her. Sebastian looks into her sexy eyes and responds to her undying affection. They stop, panting very heavily, and Monica says, "Sebastian, do you want to take this into the bedroom?"

Before Sebastian can answer her, his phone rings, and he reaches on the table and answers by saying, "Hey, what's up, Jai? I'm kind of busy at the moment; can Edmund handle that until I can get there? Okay, I'll be there in a little while."

Once he hangs up, Monica says, "Don't tell me you've got to go. What about us? When can we finish what we've started?"

Sebastian smiles, starts putting his clothes back on, and says, "Yeah, I've got something very important to take care of. I don't want to tell you a lie, but we can get back together real soon and finish what we've started."

He gives Monica a goodbye kiss and heads for the door. Once outside, he realizes that he can't see her again because she could really complicate things for the Clan. He gets in his car and heads toward Jenessa's house.

After doing some research on the internet on black magic, Camden believes that he may have found someone who can help him. He talked to a friend who gave him a phone number to call. He received a text to meet his friend at ten at Sheetz. Once Camden gets there, he goes inside to buy a soda and gets back into his car. He waits another thirty minutes, and then he gets the text, "I'm here."

Suddenly, there's a tap at his car window. Camden turns, opens the door, and they get in. Camden says, "I hope you've got good news for me."

His friend Chelsea says, "Yes, my uncle gave directions to her house. He called and told her we were coming. Are you sure you want to do this?"

Camden responds very quickly by saying, "Yes, I am. This is something that I need to do in order to bring back my sister and get revenge on Jenessa Craig."

Camden and Chelsea back out of the Sheetz parking lot and head to meet the Voodoo priestess Medusa. Once they get on I-85 headed north, Chelsea says, "Camden from what my uncle told me, once you see Medusa and she does what you want, you will never be the same again. Have you really thought about what you're about to do?"

Camden turns and says, "I've talked to my sister, and Jaz says this is something that I must do in order to get revenge. I hope that this will put me in the right direction to find the Book."

After about a thirty minute ride, they arrive in a dark, swampy looking area in an area called Essex, a dark, mysterious section of Haven-Crest. A lot of people in the area know what this woman of the dark mystical arts can do. Medusa is her name; she's an older black lady with long dreadlocks that look like snakes. She originally is from a Haitian village called Zambezi and is knowledgeable about a very harmful type of magic called Necromancy. She chants and practices incantation spells she calls Black Necro where she chants to spirits in hopes of gaining knowledge of the future and getting them to do favors for her. In some instances, she has even worn some items of clothing that once were owned by the spirits. As she awaits the arrival of Camden, she stirs in her cauldron and begins her chant for a spirit for Camden.

Finally, Camden and Chelsea pull into Medusa's muddy driveway. They see the candlelit small cottage set back in the woods. Once they get out, they look at each other to see who is going to take the lead to the front door. Once on the porch, Camden knocks, and an old, crackly voice says, "Come in, I've been waiting for you."

The old front door moves open very slowly, and the lights from the candles shine through the opening. Camden moves very slowly inside the cottage, and then Chelsea follows right behind him. In a scared voice, Camden says, "M… Ma'am, I'm Camden, and I'm here for your help. From what I was told, you have the power and knowledge to assist me in whatever dark magic I may need. Money is no object. No matter what the price is, I will pay greatly for your services."

Medusa stops stirring in her big cauldron; she turns and answers in a raspy voice by saying, "Young boy, what you are requesting to be done is very dangerous. It's not the money; it's more about you being able to understand and handle the dark forces that you are releasing. The Black Nerco you wish to learn about involves more than chanting. It requires you to give your soul and embrace the dark spirit. I want you to know that once you embrace the dark magic, you will never be the same again."

Camden takes a deep breath and responds ever so slowly, "I understand what you are saying, and yes, this is what I want."

Medusa walks over to her conjuring area; she pours salt into a shape of a pentagram on the floor, and then she lights the chanting candles. Camden takes off his jacket, and Medusa summons him to the pentagram. She makes one more plea to him before the ceremony begins by saying, "Once you come inside this pentagram, there's no turning back. Now, I need the article of clothing from your sister so we can chant to her dark spirit. I need for you to drink this elixir so that it will be able enhance your senses to embrace the magic of the dark side. Take your place here."

Medusa takes the bloody shirt from Camden, and then she embraces the shirt against her body as if she's drawing dark forces from it. She closes her eyes and begins to chant a Black Nerco spell, and suddenly,

Jazmine's spirit appears, hovering outside the pentagram. Camden stands inside astonished by what he sees, ready for Medusa to begin. Medusa gets her Witch's Spell Book and opens it to her chanting spells. She raises her hands and says, "Camden, as I open the gate for her spirit to appear on this side, you must offer your soul for the dark magic. Now, release your soul by saying, "Oh father, and lord of the dark forces that bless us with his power, grant me the power and knowledge that I seek to become one. I give to you my soul as an offering to be in your kingdom amongst the great and powerful."

Camden repeats the chant, picks up the ritual items, and readies himself for the end results. Medusa reaches her hand inside a bowl of white powder and quickly throws the dust at the candle. The flames make a WHOOSHING sound and then grow brighter and higher. As Camden stares at his spirited sister, he wonders if giving his soul to bring back his dead sister is paying the ultimate price for family. Medusa reaches for her dagger and instructs Camden to hold out his hand so she can sacrifice some of his blood for the ritual. He follows orders. As the blood drips into the chalice, Camden begins to feel his soul and mind being overwhelmed with so much anger and pain. He can feel the joining of his sister Jazmine to his inner soul. He yells in agony and kneels to the floor. Camden can feel the pain and all his sister has endured since her death over a month ago. The cottage begins shaking as if it's about to come tumbling down, and spirits are moaning and flying around the room. Jazmine's and Camden's souls are merging into one as Camden embraces the dark chanting. All Camden can understand is revenge. Once the fusion is complete, the flames from the candles get smaller. Medusa walks to the edge of the pentagram, touches Camden's head, and suddenly, to their horror, Camden begins to growl like a demon possesses his body. Medusa smiles and says, "Camden, can you hear me?"

There's a pause as they watch Camden raise his head up. His pupils are white, and he responds in a low voice, "We can hear you loud and clear. We appreciate everything you have done for us tonight. Your services will not be forgotten."

Camden reaches into his pocket, pulls out a roll of money, and hands it to Medusa. She takes the money and stuffs it in her pocket. She says, "Camden, before we go any further, you must acknowledge that you have embraced the Black Nerco. You can now draw dark magic from Jazmine's spirit inside of you, but be warned that the more you draw upon this dark magic and use it, the more your soul will be enticed into the powers of hell."

Chelsea stands over in the corner in complete horror at what she has just witnessed. She feels afraid and really does not know what to do or to say. She comes out from the shadows and says, "Camden, are you alright? Oh, my God, I can't believe what I just saw."

Medusa sets the bowl on the table and walks back to Camden in the pentagram; she looks at the person who stands before her in awe and folds her arms and says, "Camden, before I remove the pentagram, remember your side of the bargain; you don't know me or what things I do."

Camden looks at Medusa with a smile on his face as though he is about to be release from his magical prison. He winks at Chelsea and says "This is what I came here for, and I can never repay you enough for what you've done."

Medusa removes the salt from the pentagram and Camden steps out. Medusa says, "You may leave and never to return to my swampy bottom."

Camden reaches for his jacket, and Chelsea walks behind him as they head out of the door to Camden's car. Once inside, she says nothing but just watches Camden all the way up I-85 back to Haven-Crest. After about a thirty minute ride to the Sheetz parking lot, Camden smiles at Chelsea and says, "I want to show you my gratitude for introducing me to Medusa."

He leans over and gives Chelsea a kiss on the lips. She is caught off guard at first but responds back to his affection; then suddenly, she begins to feel her body draining of life energy. She's unable to yell or fight off what her so-called friend is doing to her. Camden leans back to his side of the car, and Chelsea's lifeless body sits in the front passenger seat. He drives her to a remote spot deep in the woods and hides the evidence. After about thirty minutes, Camden drives slowly out of the woods and heads back home with a newfound outlook on what his responsibilities are.

Sebastian pulls up in front of Jenessa's house, gets out, and goes inside. Everyone is crowded around the table, looking at the map. Once inside, Sebastian says, "Hey, there must be something very good on the table to have everyone crowded around like that. Mind if I take a look too?"

Jenessa and Chrisha slide over so Sebastian can stand at the table. He notices the ancient writings on the map. Sebastian understands that now with Estelle's map, they have a good chance of solving the riddles and tries to see if he can understand the symbols and the text on the map. There's a knock at the front door; everyone looks at each other, and Sebastian says, "Since I'm the only man here, I guess that leaves me to protect you beautiful ladies and open the door."

Sebastian walks to the door and says, "Who is it?"

The voice replies, "It's me Edmund; open the door."

Sebastian opens the door, and Edmund responds by saying, "I'm glad you're here. I have someone who may be able to read the symbols on the map. This is …."

Sebastian interrupts with a growl in his voice by saying, "I know who this is. Why is Malcolm here?"

Edmund tries to calm Sebastian down by saying, "He can read those symbols on the map. We need him before Adrian or anyone else can get ahold of him."

Sebastian says nothing; he just walks toward the table, and then Edmund brings Malcolm over. Malcolm says, "Can I touch the map? I can feel the symbols; I understand some of the text on it. Maybe it can help you on your quest."

As Malcolm rubs his hands over the map, he feels the symbols, and suddenly, he jerks his hands backs and says, "From what I am interpreting, this Book you seek has been cursed. In order for you to succeed in this quest, you must first solve this ancient inscription and then decipher the names of the people in order to find the keys and understand how to find where the Book is located."

Edmund touches Malcolm's hands and says, "I can see what you are seeing. Someone get some paper to write this down."

Persia, Jai Li, and Chrisha look for paper to write down the encrypted message. Sebastian says nothing; he turns and walks outside on the back porch. He looks up in the sky, and he tries to regain his composure. The screen door opens up as Jenessa comes outside and says, "What's up with you? Are you having a bad night? What's the problem between you and Malcolm?"

Sebastian can feel his blood bubbling in his veins. He turns, and then his eyes change to golden black and his fangs extend. He says, "You're right; I had a really bad night, and now it looks like it's becoming a nightmare. Malcolm and I have a history. I lost a dear friend on account of Malcolm. I guess when I saw him tonight; the old wound began bleeding once again. I never thought I would see him again after all that has done to ruin my life."

Showing concern for dear friend and boss, she sees the hatred in his face and replies by saying, "I can see that you're upset. Can I ask what Malcolm did to you to make you so mad?"

Sebastian calms down; his fangs become normal and so do his eyes. In a smooth and calm tone, he says, "Honestly, I don't know what came over me. I haven't been like that in decades. Malcolm betrayed a friend of mine named Hutch. For reasons I never understood, he was killed by the Horde. They were a Covenant of ruthless vampires that terrorized the East Coast from the forties throughout the seventies. Hutch was ratted out for the crimes he was committing against the Horde. As they were torturing him, I rescued Hutch. In the process, Malcolm was captured and then tortured. As a result, he was blinded because of Hutch's escape."

Jenessa rubs Sebastian's hands and says, "Now that you have calmed down, let's go back into the house and see what Malcolm has deciphered for us."

Sebastian puts his arm around Jenessa's shoulders, smiles at her, and says, "Thanks, I needed that talk. It's a good feeling to know when I have problems that I can come and talk to you. I guess we can put each other in a better place and see the silver lining through the dark clouds."

Chapter 7

Once back inside, Edmund signals for Sebastian to come over to the table. As Malcolm deciphers the map, Genie writes everything down, arranging phrases and symbols to make sense. Edmund and Sebastian take the paper and begin trying to make sense of the information. Edmund smiles and says, "From what I'm reading, we have to find a key to open the doorway to the Book. There are quests that must be performed and achieved in order to get these objects for the key."

Everyone sits around the table in amazement at what Edmund just said. Malcolm continues deciphering the map and says, "To further add to Edmund's comments, you will need to find three people of certain mythical entities. Once you find them, you must obtain a key from them in order to lead you to the Book. You need to find these people: Shiloh, Sable, and Van Gogh. You can find Shiloh in Salem, Massachusetts, and Sable will be down south in Florida. She's a member of the biker gang Lycos. Lastly, Van Gogh, probably the worst out of the bunch, resides in Las Vegas: Sin City. It's unknown what these people are or what they could be."

No one makes a sound; everyone looks at one another. Eventually, all eyes turn to Sebastian. He drops his head, looks over the notes, raises his head, and says, "I guess it's up to me to make the decision on what we are going to do. Well, the answer is obvious. We must find these keys, so the question is now: Who is going?"

Edmund speaks up first, "Well, count me in on this mission."

Jensessa speaks up next, "Count me in; I need to get away for a while."

Genie replies, "Jenessa, what are you saying? You have a lot going on right now. What about the store and all of Estelle's business affairs that need to be taken care of?"

Jenessa turns around and says, "I understand what you are saying, Auntie, but I need to get out of this town for a while. This will give me chance to clear my head as well. While I'm gone, you can run the show. I may be needed on this quest, so I'm in, like I said."

Jai Li replies, "What about me? Do I go, or do I stay here?"

Sebastian rubs his chin and says, "I'm not sure Jai; we may need some people to stay so it won't look so suspicious that all of us are gone. Marcella and Adam will stay behind to run Priceless. Edmund, you may need to stay just in case the Committee calls an urgent meeting."

Edmund understands Sebastian's concern over the loyalty and well-being of his friends. Persia looks around the table and says, "No one asked me if I wanted to go. I want to help find the Book too."

Sebastian heads to the kitchen, turns, and comments with a laugh by saying, "Persia, I didn't ask because I didn't think you wanted to go. If you want to come along with us, that is fine with me; but that's between you and Genie."

Malcolm puts his hands on the table, stands up, and says, "I hear you making plans, but there is one thing you've forgotten about. During the deciphering, it was mentioned that the people could be anything, meaning that anyone could be a vampire, a howler, or possibly a witch."

Edmund puts both hands on his hips, and in a semi aggressive tone, he says, "So what you're saying is we may have to tangle with howlers or witches and possibly vampires in order to get these keys. Sebastian, are you sure that is the right thing to do?"

Sebastian walks back to the table and with confidence in his voice, he says, "Regardless, even if we don't succeed, we can say we made an effort to retrieve the Book. The only thing I've got left to say is I'm not making anyone come on this quest. In case we all don't come back, I'm not bringing back any grief over losing any of you on my conscience."

Unseen and unknown to any of the participants inside the house, they are being watched by some deceiving eyes. The watcher pulls out his phone and makes a call. "Hey, I'm still doing surveillance at Jenessa's, and from what I can see, it looks like they may have found a way to decipher the map. They have some old looking man inside with them. What do you want me to do now?"

The voice on the other end of the phone responds by saying, "Just keep your eyes on the house, monitor who is inside, and keep me informed on what you see."

The watcher hangs up his phone and then dips back into the shadows behind some bushes. Unnoticed by him, he's being watched by Jamal who tries to stay out of the light also. Eventually, Jenessa's friends begin to leave and head to their respected homes to bring a close to this shocking evening.

Jamal continues to wait in the bushes. After all the cars are gone, he sees an opportunity to slip in and talk to Jenessa alone. He runs in the darkness, trying not to be seen. Once Jamal reaches the front porch, he turns to survey the area. As the watcher of the house sees Jamal standing on the porch, he calls Coach Deren. "Coach, Jamal is here at Jenessa's house about to go in. What do you want me to do?"

The coach replies, "I'm sending Andrei over there now to help you bring Jamal to me. Your job is to not let him leave that house."

Greg, the watcher, replies back to the coach and hangs up. He watches the house very closely. As Jamal knocks on the door, he continues to scan the area and tries to sniff out his fellow howler brothers. Persia comes to the door and says, "Who is it?"

Jamal responds, "It's me, Jamal. Persia can I come in and see Jenessa? It's very important."

She unlocks the door, opens it, and Jamal comes in. Suddenly, Jenessa comes in the room with a concerned look on her face and says, "What's up Jamal; you want to see me?"

He turns, looks at Jenessa, and says, "You're being watched."

"By whom? Who is outside watching us?" replies Jenessa in an angered voice.

Jamal starts peeping through the blinds to see if he spots anyone. He calms himself down, sits on the couch, and starts telling them what's going on. "Adrian and Coach Deren have formed an alliance in an effort to find the Book of Spells. Adrian said you are the key toward finding the Book, so we were supposed to be watching the house and reporting who we see come and go. I didn't want to get involved in this matter. I'm sworn by the pack not to warn you, but you are my girl, and I couldn't let any harm come to you or your family."

Jenessa sits on the couch in shock over what Jamal has told her. Not knowing how to respond, she walks over to the fireplace and says, "Why is Adrian trying so hard to get under my skin; what does he want from me? I am not the key; there is just some prophecy that says I'm supposed to be able to save the world. To be honest, I can't even save myself. One thing I'm not getting is what is this pack you are sworn by?"

Jamal's eyes get really big as he realizes now that he must tell Jenessa the ultimate secret. This vital information could destroy people of his kind, yet at this very moment, he feels the time is right to tell her. He stands and asks, "Is there anywhere we can go so that I can show you something in private?"

Genie doesn't hesitate and replies first by saying, "If you're going to show Jenessa anything, we're going to see it also."

"Very well, just don't say I didn't warn you," replies Jamal with a smile on his face.

Jenessa turns toward Jamal nonchalantly and says, "What is it you have to show me? We can go to the basement."

All of them start walking toward the basement. Once downstairs, Jamal walks out to the opening of the room and says, "Ladies, don't be afraid of what you're about to see. I'd rather show you than tell you."

With that said, Jamal begins taking off his clothes, down to his underwear, and suddenly, he kneels on all fours. He drops his head and lets out a loud growl; Jenessa's eyes get really big, and Genie and Persia are speechless. Slowly, Jamal raises his head, and his eyes are fire red. Hair has started covering his body, and his face has started forming into a wolf. As the girls watch, Jamal goes through the transformation into a howler. They see the fangs and claws begin to grow longer. His legs bend backwards, and bones are breaking. He howls and growls in pain during this process. Soon all of this comes to an end, and he is a howler. Jenessa is completely lost for words at what she just witnessed. She gets a grip on reality and says, "Jamal, how did this happen to you? How long have you been a howler?"

He can't speak, but she can telepathically link with him, and he responds by saying, "I've been a howler for a couple of months now; this happened after your grandmother died."

Just as quickly as his body changed into a howler, he changes back to Jamal with no clothes on. Genie throws a blanket over him until he puts his clothes back on. The ladies leave the basement to give Jamal some privacy to get dressed, and he comes into the kitchen when he's done. He warns Jenessa to be careful because the howlers from his pack are out there watching. Jamal grabs Jenessa by the hands and says, "I've got to go, but I'll be in touch in the next couple of days. Let Sebastian know what's going on so you guys will be safe. I'll go more into details about me later. Take care of yourself."

Jenessa's emotions are running high; she looks into Jamal's eyes and says, "Thanks, for looking out for me. We appreciate the heads up. The main thing is you be careful and watch your back. Make sure you call me in a couple of days, too."

They both look at each other, and he makes the first move toward her. They hug, and then they start to kiss. Genie and Persia both start to smile and Jamal heads to the back door and slips outside into the darkness. Jenessa shuts the door, walks throughout the house, and closes all the blinds so the watcher can't see them.

Jamal heads to his car parked on the back side of the neighborhood. Once Jamal reaches the car, he looks around, and without warning, he gets hit over the head and falls to the ground. The two attackers pick up

Jamal's unconscious body, put him in the back seat of car, and head to Coach Deren's house.

Haven-Crest has been quiet for the last couple of days, but all good things must come to an end. There is unrest with so many people hell bent on finding and solving the clues for the location of the Book of Spells. Since her encounter with a vampire that she can't remember, Det. Karen MacRae has been having a lot of scary nights. The nightmares are becoming more intense, yet Det. MacRae doesn't know whom she can talk to about this situation.

She lies across her bed to catch a quick nap before heading back on duty; as she sleeps, she dreams about the night her friend Amy Christian disappeared from the college. She sees the security guard at his desk, she walks past him to Amy's office, and she sees the map that was found at the college. Suddenly, she hears a noise and tells them she'll check it out. She gets her flashlight and walks slowly down the hallways, shining the light throughout the empty room searching for the noise she heard. Thinking that it was the wind, she drops her guard, and suddenly, she sees a dark figure at the end of the hallway. She flashes the light but sees nothing there. Without hesitation, the dark figure grabs her from behind with his arm across her throat. Unable to make a sound, she feels like a rag doll being lifted off her feet. Without a word being said, she feels his breath on her neck. As Karen's heart begins to race in her chest, she realizes that she could die. She makes an effort to fight back; suddenly, he sinks his vampire fangs into the side of her neck and begins to suck her blood out. Detective MacRae wakes up in a cold sweat; she gets out of the bed and goes in the bathroom to wash her face. To her surprise, she sees scratches on her neck and her imagination begins to run wild. She runs back into her bedroom and gets her gun; she slowly walks through the house with her flashlight, checking all the rooms for a would-be intruder. After about twenty minutes, she finds nothing, so she goes back into the bathroom, stares at herself in the mirror, opens the cabinet, and takes two prescription pills for her anxiety. She puts a Band-Aid on the scratches on her neck. Then she heads out the door to work.

Across town at Haven-Crest Memorial hospital, Doctor Marion Burton, the chief head surgeon, walks to his office to check over some paperwork on a resident there. As he opens the folder on one of his patients, suddenly, there's a knock at the door. He yells, "Come in."

Once the door opens, Dr. Burton focuses his attention on the person coming inside his office. Once inside, Dr. Kareem Jensyn walks over to the desk and says, "Good morning, Dr. Burton, and how are you today? I'm glad to be coming in for my second interview. I'm really looking forward to hopefully becoming a resident physician here with the world renowned Dr. Burton."

Dr. Burton laughs, shakes his head, and replies, "Dr. Jensyn, I called you back for this meeting to offer you a position at this hospital. Your reputation carries you well; I can tell you are the kind of person who will fit in nicely at this hospital. I will give you a couple of days to make your decision, not to rush you."

"Dr. Burton, you know I'm flattered and overwhelmed that you actually want to hire me. I know I can do a great job here at this hospital," replies Dr. Jensyn.

They shake hands, and Dr. Burton smiles. He is happy to have a capable, young doctor to help him treat patients at the hospital. Dr. Jensyn sits in the chair and asks, "So, when do you want me to start?"

Before Dr. Burton can answer, suddenly, there's an emergency at the hospital, and sirens and instructions are coming over the PA system. Dr. Burton stands, and with a concerned look on his face, he turns and says, "How about right now? I could use your help, and from the way it sounds, it may be a bad wreck."

As the ambulance attendants start bringing in the victims of an apparent car wreck, the victims are yelling in agony from the pain of the injuries they sustained. Once in the emergency room, both doctors pull the curtains back to see what trauma they are facing; it looks like the victim sustained multiple injuries, and blood is all over the patient. The scent is strong in the air. Dr. Jensyn says, "This one looks to be in bad shape. I'll take care of this patient, and you get the other one."

Dr. Burton pulls back the curtain and steps over to the other victim. Dr. Jensyn takes out his stethoscope to check the heart rate. It is very faint. The curtain flies open, and Head Nurse Allison comes in to assist the doctor. She says, "How is the patient? What is your diagnosis?"

Dr. Jensyn stares at the victim lying on the table. As he examines the injuries and looks at the blood gushing from the cut and scars on the body, Nurse Allison breaks his concentration again and says, "Dr. Jensyn, excuse me, we're losing the patient. What is your diagnosis so we can try to save this victim?"

Dr. Jensyn focuses his attention on Nurse Allison. He checks the vital signs of the victim, and he answers her by saying, "The heart rate is very faint. From the look of all this blood loss, we may need to give him a transfusion and jump starts his heart. Go ahead and administer an IV to get fluids flowing."

Nurse Allison yells, "Orderly, bring in the defibrillator now. Someone start compression on this man."

Everything is moving at a fast pace with nurses, orderlies, and Dr. Jensyn working to save a person's life. Suddenly, the heart monitor goes flat line; Dr. Jensyn reaches for the electrodes and yells, "Give me two hundred volts and clear."

Everyone in the room can hear the electric current run through the electrodes to the victim's chest. Dr. Jensyn stands back and checks the heart monitor. They get a very faint heartbeat; he rubs the electrodes together again and says, "Go to four hundred and clear."

The patient's body bucks from the electricity; then there is a pause of silence, and suddenly, the heart rate starts to climb. Dr. Jensyn rubs his brow, continues to examine the victim, and then after about five minutes, he says,

"Nurse Allison, after further examination of the victim, I believe that he has some broken ribs and a collapsed lung. I advise to wrap them for right now, and get him stabilized so he can get some rest."

Nurse Allison is impressed at the work Dr. Jensyn has done on his first day on the job. She says, "Nice work. Good to have you on this shift."

With all the nurses and both doctors helping to treat the victims, the emergency room is very busy for a while.

Nicolette walks out of her office and heads over to the research team as they are breaking the code on the map. Donna Gill sits at her computer working out a program to break the encryption on the code. Suddenly, she yells out, "Yes, I got it! Don't you mess up on me now? Once this program executes, we should be able to break the encryption. The code that it is written in is very old, but it can be broken with the right combination of hacking techniques."

Nicolette smiles and nonchalantly says, "Donna, I hope you have good news for me. I'm not in the mood for excuses right now."

Donna doesn't respond. She just keeps typing to break the encryption, and then with a loud cheer, she says, "Nicolette, I do believe I have done it. I have cracked the code!"

The deciphered code runs across the matrix computer screen. As Nicolette reads the messages, Erika writes them down. Without warning, Adrian comes into the room with his charismatic charm. He says, "Hello ladies, and how are you today?"

Nicolette stares him up and down and then says, "We're doing really well now that Donna has broken the code on the map. Once Amy deciphers the code and gives us our instructions on what we must do, we will be in business. Now, what can I do for you, Adrian?"

Adrian gives Nicolette a cheap smile and says, "You look as if you have no faith in me; I have been allying our team to make it stronger. I've enlisted a dear friend's assistance to help with any unseen obstacles we may encounter. My friend Coach Deren is the leader of a group of young howlers."

Nicolette raises one eyebrow and responds very nonchalantly, "Adrian, you never cease to amaze me. Just when I think you can't get any more stupid, you prove me right. Why on Earth do you want to involve our mortal enemy on this mission? Now, we have to watch our back for other parties and the howlers trying to get the Book. You may ask what they want to gain. It's probably the ability to kill off all vampires or enslave all vampires to the howlers. Now, your brother Sebastian is the smarter of you two; he would have handled this situation more professionally, and that is why my boss is very intrigued with him."

Adrian responds with boiling anger toward Nicolette. He does a blur movement, grabs her by the throat, and slams her against the wall. With his fangs extended and his eyes golden black, he says, "No one disrespects me like that and expects to live. Nicolette, I will rip out your throat and kill you without hesitation regardless of whomever you work for or are in allegiance to. Remember, little sexy vampire, I am a covenant king, and it would be hard for you to kill me."

As Adrian squeezes a little tighter on her throat to prove his point, without warning, Erika yells, "Adrian, don't hurt her!"

Adrian gives her a devious look, releases the chokehold on her throat and his face goes back to normal. He says nothing as Erika comes running over to check on Nicolette. She stares at Adrian and says, "What are you trying to prove, that you are the big dog in this group? We are supposed to be working together, not you against us."

Adrian gives Erika a nonchalant smirk and says, "I understand what you are saying, but no one disrespects me and treats me like I'm trash. You may be Antoine's flunky, but that doesn't give you the right to treat anyone like crap."

After about five minutes, the marks on Nicolette's neck disappear. Donna hands Erika a couple of pages of notes. She looks them over and says, "Everyone, we may need to hear what Donna has found out; the information seems to be very important. It says there are three individuals who have to be found in order to retrieve the keys they possess in the process of finding the Book. We need to find these people: Vangogh, Sable, and Shiloh. One resides in Las Vegas, another in Florida, and the last one is in Salem, Massachusetts. One more thing about the Book is to be careful of what desires one may wish for because they could come back to make one regret his or her choices."

Someone's phone begins to ring, and all of them begin checking their phones. Adrian realizes that it's his phone and answers, "Hello. Do what? I'm on my way. Keep him until I get there."

Adrian hangs up, turns to his female partners, and says, "Ladies, I have to leave for right now, but I'll be back later."

Adrian gets his coat and keys and then heads to the door. Once he leaves, Nicolette calls her boss and informs him of their discovery. She says, "Sir, good evening. I hope I'm not bothering you. I'm calling to let you know that we've broken the code on the map, so I'm about to make preparations for us to start tracking down the keys. Once I've completed the plans, I'll be in touch."

Her boss answers by saying, "That's the kind of information I enjoy hearing, and yes, keep me informed on the progression of the team."

After that comment, he hangs up. She turns to Erika and says, "Now that Adrian is gone, Erika, let me clarify this situation about what you did. First of all, you didn't have to beg and plead for my life; I was not afraid to die by the hands of Adrian. Next time, if I'm in a predicament like that, just let me die as a hero."

Everyone in the room says nothing. They just stare at Erika. She looks around the room, shakes her head, and replies, "Nicolette, why do you act like that? You used to be a very caring person, but now you are a bitch since Antoine promoted you."

Nicolette walks out of the room as though she has an attitude. Erika shakes her head; everyone walks over and commends her on standing up to Nicolette.

Greg and Andrei return to Coach Deren's house with the captured Jamal. They bring him in and sit him in the chair. He is still unconscious, and they tie him up with some wolfsbane dipped ropes to keep him weak so he won't get away. As the coach watches the guys carry out his orders, he wonders what Jamal said to them and what they are planning to do. Suddenly, Jamal starts to awaken. Focusing his eyes and trying to think to stop his head from hurting, he says, "Where am I? Why have I been brought here? Who knocked me out?"

Coach Deren walks over to Jamal, grabs him by the jaw, and says, "Why did you break the law and go to Jenessa's house? Adrian is on the way, so just relax. The hearing will begin in a few minutes."

With that said, the coach turns and walks back upstairs to his office while they wait for Adrian to get there. Adrian races over to Coach Deren's house to handle the problem that has arisen. He gets out of the car and comes in the house. He can hear Jamal struggling because he has been tied up. He comes into the room and immediately says, "What the hell is going on, coach? Please bring me up to speed about the things that happened tonight."

Coach Deren walks over to Jamal, grabs his head, and holds it up so he can see his eyes. With his anger fueling his rage, Coach Deren says, "Jamal, why did you do this to us? Why did you warn Jenessa about us watching her? Now she knows about us working with Adrian in efforts to find the Book. Sebastian will probably set a trap or be on guard to stop us. You are one of my prized howlers, a very rare one to say in the least. Why did you turn your back on the pack? What are you looking to gain out of all this? Is it asylum with Sebastian and his clan of vampires and witches? Do you know what we do to traitors of the pack?"

With disgust in his eyes, Jamal raises his head and yells at Coach Deren, "I don't have to answer you. I just can't believe that you honestly think you're going to get the Book from Sebastian. They are much smarter and cleverer at treasure hunting than you jackasses."

Adrian laughs at Jamal, shakes his head, and says, "My young pup, I wouldn't go around spreading false accusations like that because they could become very harmful to you. Now, coach, what do you think we should do to our new recruit? How do you howlers handle traitors?"

Jamal feels that the situation is about to take a turn for the worst as Coach Deren responds with frustration in his voice, "He has been tied down with ropes dipped in wolfsbane that should keep him weakened. Now, we have to know how far to torture Mr. Carmichaels being that he is the district attorney's son. Oh yes, I do have some forms of punishment for him. How about ten lashes with the bull rope dipped in wolfsbane to start off?"

Jamal, realizing that he is in grave danger, he makes no plea for his life. Adrian walks over to Jamal, grabs him by the face, and says, "You never really told us what you said to Jenessa; did you tell her we were watching the house to keep an eye on the whole family and crew for information? Well, since the cat has your tongue, I know another way to get what I want from you and in the process, get rid of you."

Nervously, Jamal sits weakened from the wolfsbane. He is unable to break free, and there is no help in sight, so he just endures the pain until he sees an opportunity to make a getaway. Without warning, Adrian comes up from behind with fangs extended and eyes all golden black. With reckless abandon, he bites Jamal on the bottom of the neck and releases vampire venom in his system, which is deadly to howlers. He doesn't give Jamal a full dose, but it is enough to take down an elephant. Adrian unties the ropes and then steps back to admire his dirty work. Jamal falls to the floor in excruciating pain, unable to transform into a howler, he understands that this is his opportunity to live, so he jumps through the den window and makes a run for it through the woods behind Coach Deren's house. Both men are surprised at the incredible feat that Jamal has undertaken in order to survive the torture that has been inflected upon him.

Once outside with only sheer will and determination, Jamal knows that he must use every ounce of energy to outrun the people whom he once called friends to make sure they don't capture him. In the distance, he hears a loud howl and knows that the coach has called in reinforcements to capture him. Jamal runs faster than ever before to avoid capture. Since he's familiar with the area, he knows where to hide to make sure he doesn't get caught. With the vampire venom in blood, his heartbeat is racing, and the only place he may be able to survive is at Jenessa's. He tries again to transform. Jamal knows that in howler form, his chances of survival become greater, plus he can get there faster. He puts his hands on the ground and concentrates, and this time, slowly he begins changing into a howler.

Fur begins to grow, his face and fingers change, and he bends down on all fours. Even though the process is slow, he changes in time before the other howlers can catch him. Jamal dashes through the woods at full speed, trying his best to elude his pursuers. He sees familiar landmarks and takes a quick route to Jenessa's house. Jamal sees he's in the clear; he reaches the opening that should bring him toward the house. Suddenly, he looks back thinking he hears something, and to his surprise, he sees two howlers running up behind him. He turns, and there's Coach Deren standing in between him and the house. The two howlers in the back wait for their signal to attack; Jamal knows this is his last chance at survival. The coach makes the first move by rushing toward Jamal. He does the same and rushes toward the coach, and the objective is seeing who will outsmart the other. The coach lunges in an attempt to hit him high, but Jamal slides under him and keeps running toward Jenessa's house. As Jamal gets closer to the house, he begins howling with hopes of getting Jenessa's or someone's attention. The two howlers make their move to try to stop him from reaching the porch; one goes low and the other jumps on the porch. They start to fight, and with all the commotion on the porch, the front light comes on. Jenessa steps out, sees the fighting, and chants a spell. A lightning flash runs the two howlers away. She stands on the ground in horror at what she sees: a bloody, injured, and barely alive wolf, but instantly, the wolf changes into … Jamal. Jenessa begins yelling in distress over what has happened to her very close friend.

Chapter 8

As Jenessa yells, Genie comes running out on the porch to see what's going on. She is shocked at the horror and damages that have been inflected upon Jamal. Now, he's unconscious, and they are not sure what to do. Jenessa starts to get hysterical about her close friend. Persia comes to the door and says, "What's going on out here? Why are you yelling?"

Persia turns around and sees Jamal lying on the ground. Genie pulls herself together, goes into the house, and comes back out with a blanket to wrap up Jamal. She turns and says in a calm voice, "Girls, we need to get him in the house so we can check out his wounds and see how badly he is hurt. Let's be gentle with him."

As they examine the injuries to Jamal, they come to the conclusion that they may need a spell to get him up so they can gently bring him inside. Genie starts reciting a chant, "Scars of the flesh, wounds of the body, and the blood that runs, let us bring this weary soul in to be checked for injuries that were inflicted by morons."

Slowly, Jamal's body begins to rise up. Persia and Jenessa quickly grab his body, and they proceed to lift him up and bring him inside to the couch in the living room. Jenessa comes out of the room with her clothes all bloody and says, "I think we need to call Sebastian and Edmund; they need to see what has happened to Jamal. Maybe they can help him. Where's my phone?"

Jenessa gets her phone to call Sebastian; it rings, and he picks up and says, "What's up, Jenessa? What's wrong?"

In a frantic tone, she responds, "Jamal has been hurt really badly; he was attacked by some howlers. Can you and Edmund come check him out? He has a lot of scars, and blood is everywhere. He has two vampire bite marks on his neck; it looks like some yellowish ooze is coming out."

Sebastian realizes that he must calm Jenessa down, so he replies with a relaxed voice, "Jenessa, take a deep breath and get a bowl of cold water, some towels, and alcohol. I'll be there in a few minutes."

Sebastian hangs up, thinks about what Jenessa said during their conversation, and calls for Edmund, who quickly comes running into the room. He says, "What's the matter? Why are you yelling?"

With an uncertain look on his face, Sebastian starts to put the pieces of the puzzle together; he realizes that howlers attacked a high school kid for whatever reason. Also a vampire has bitten him, and there is a pack of howlers in Haven-Crest. Sebastian shakes out of the trance and says to Edmund, "We have to go over to Jenessa's house; the boy named Jamal has been attacked by some howlers, and he has been bitten by a vampire. We need to leave right away to see if we can help. Get Malcolm; he may be of some use on this case."

Sebastian and Edmund get the bags they need for this mission. They run out of the house to get Malcolm and head over to Jenessa's. Sebastian calls Marcella and tells her they are on the way over to Jenessa's to check on Jamal. Even though the drive to Jenessa's takes only a few minutes, it seems like an eternity. She gets the items needed to help Jamal and begins wash the dirt off his face. She and Genie look at the bite marks and examine the yellowish ooze coming out of his neck. Genie is unsure about what she sees and wonders what it possibly could be. She turns to Jenessa and says, "Honey, I'm not sure about this. It looks like some kind of venom, and those are definitely vampire bites. He may be having a reaction to the venom in his system. I have heard of howlers getting bitten by vampires, but not too many of them survive to tell the tale, either. We'll just have to wait and see what Edmund and Sebastian have to say about this."

Jenessa listens to her aunt as she gives her a rough estimate of what she sees. Jenessa is hoping that is not the case for her special friend as she continues to apply the cold compress to Jamal's forehead. Suddenly, they hear tires squealing. They assume that it is Sebastian's car, but it is Jai Li instead. She knocks, comes in, and immediately goes into shock at what she sees. Jai walks to the couch very slowly in utter amazement. With tears in her eyes, she turns to her best friend, Jenessa, and says, "Jen, is he dead? What happened to him? Who did this?"

Unsure about what to say or how to respond, Jenessa musters the strength and says, "Some howlers attacked him, and he has a vampire bite on his neck. Sebastian and Edmund are on the way over."

Jai wipes the tear that runs down her cheek and replies, "I know; they called me to meet them here. Are you alright, and is there anything I can do to help?"

Jenessa reaches out, hugs her best friend, and whispers, "Naw, I'm just glad that you're here with me. Hey, did anyone call Chrisha? You guys know she hates to be the last one to find stuff out. Someone call and let her know what's going on."

Persia sees some headlights shining through the blinds and turns to everyone and says, "I see a car coming; it may be Sebastian."

The girls stay at Jamal's side keeping check on him, and suddenly, there's a knock at the door. As Genie opens it, she smiles once she sees Edmund. She responds politely by saying, "Come in, come on in, we've been waiting for you guys."

Edmund, Sebastian, and Malcolm come inside and instantaneously, they see the damage that has been inflicted on Jamal. They all rush over to him and begin examining his wounds. Edmund picks up Jamal off the couch and heads toward a bedroom. Malcolm says in a panicking voice, "Has the boy regained consciousness since you brought him inside? How long has he been out? We have to act fast because the vampire venom in his system can cause a lot of damage. We need to check and see if we have the herbal ingredients to stop this process. Bring me a yarrow flower, white willow bark, rosemary, sage and the most important ingredient: lo mai (sweet rice)."

Genie looks at Malcolm with utter amazement that he knows about those types of herbs. She then hurries into the kitchen to see if those ingredients are there. Persia comes into the kitchen also, and they start searching through the cupboards and canisters; they soon begin finding the needed ingredients. Persia gets the yarrow flower and the sage, Genie locates the white willow bark and rosemary, but neither of them can find the lo mai. Jenessa thinks about it, rubs her forehead, and then suddenly, she stands up and says, "I think I saw some at Grandma's Herbal Store. I'll go get it, and I'll right be back in a flash. Malcolm, is Jamal going to be alright?"

Malcolm rubs his forehead to wipe away the sweat, looks Jenessa in her hazel green eyes, and says, "If we don't get it really soon, we won't have to worry about Jamal ever again because by then, it'll be too late to save him."

Everyone goes silent; Sebastian comes out of the room with a sorrowful look on his face and says, "We have to hurry. Jamal's starting to get worse. His injuries are not healing as fast as normal; I think the venom in his system is slowing down the process."

Jenessa reaches for her purse, car keys, and jacket and then heads for the door. Persia jumps up and yells, "Hey, wait for me."

Malcolm frowns, realizing the situation is calling for drastic measures, and reminds them before they leave, "You need to hurry because this procedure has to be done before the sun sets."

Jenesa pulls back her jacket sleeve, looks down at her watch, and says, "It's three now; the sun goes down at five thirty. Let's go, Persia."

Since it is of the utmost importance in this quest to find and bring back some lo mai for Jamal, they leave with haste to get the objective and get back as quickly as possible. As Jai Li thinks about what Malcolm just said, a veil of confusion drapes over her face, so she walks over to Malcolm and says, "Excuse me, sir; can I ask a question? Why do they have to be back before the sun goes down? What will happen to Jamal if they are not back here in time?"

As calm as a summer rain, Malcolm reaches for Jai's hand with a scary look on his face and replies, "My dear, Jamal will transform into what he is and never turn back into a human again. He will remain a howler forever, so that is why they need to be back before the sun goes down. I heard the weather report, and there is supposed to be a full moon tonight."

Her stunned reaction is what Malcolm expected. Jai is unsure about how to respond to Malcolm, though she turns, scratches her head, and replies nonchalantly, "I thought it was a myth that if a howler gets bitten by a vampire, he will remain in howler form and never turn back."

Malcolm signals for Jai Li to have a seat so they can finish their conversation. He takes a sip of wine out of a champagne glass, takes a deep breath, and says, "Young lady, the story I've told you is true; I witnessed it myself long ago. I met a man named Miguel Reinhart, an English scholar and nobleman, and he had a dark secret: he was a howler. This was back during my vampire days of conquests; eventually, we became friends and terrorized the east coast until we began killing the members of a gang called the Horde. They hunted us down to an abandoned shack. They thought they had surrounded us, but I managed to get away. Miguel didn't; he was captured. Their leader then tortured Miguel to get him to reveal where other howlers existed. He refused to betray his pack to the Horde, so he was bitten by the vampire leader. They let him go for some unknown reason I never understood. A few days later, there was a full moon. As usual, Miguel turned into a howler, but this time he was more aggressive and more vicious when he attacked. When the sun began to rise, I noticed that Miguel became very agitated. His eyes turned yellow, and without warning, he got in an attack position to kill me. He growled and showed his fangs as though he was ready to kill. He pounced, and I blurred out of the way; he just jumped out the window and kept on running through the woods. I have not seen or heard from him since that night. I have heard of a lot of tales on how to cure a howler from a vampire bite."

Jai Li reaches for Malcolm's glass of wine to take a drink after hearing that story. She takes a big gulp, wipes her mouth off, and says, "So, if

Jenessa and Persia don't get back in time, that same thing will probably happen to Jamal."

Malcolm raises his eyebrow with a smirking grin on his face and replies, "Yes, I'm sure it will.

Since Jai Li is very optimistic and always eager to learn, she asks Malcolm some more questions. Her questions just come blurting out, "How long have you been a vampire? Who turned you, and how long have you known Sebastian and Edmund?"

Malcolm smiles and answers back, "Wow, little one, you do ask a lot of questions. Well, let me see; where do I begin?"

Out of their eyesight, Sebastian monitors Malcolm and Jai Li's conversation. He fixes a drink and heads back in the room to help Edmund with Jamal. Edmund watches while Jamal's bones begin breaking out of joint and transforming into the howler form of a wolf. He continues to yell during this process; the pain he's enduring seems unbearable, but with Edmund's help plus some sips of dark whiskey, he's holding up. Edmund looks at Sebastian with his concerned green eyes and says, "This doesn't look good. He's changing faster than I expected. The alcohol is helping to slow it down, but the sunset is coming very soon. I just hope that the girls make it back in time."

Sebastian doesn't reply; he just stares out the window with his mind full of concern for Jenessa and with hopes that she finds the lo mai to save the life of guy she so dearly cares for. Then he slowly turns, walks over to Jamal, and helps support his head while Edmund gives him some whiskey to cut down on the unbearable pain.

Because they are really pressed for time to retrieve the lo mai, Jenessa speeds through town to get to the herbal store. While on the way to the shop, Persia watches her cousin with a careful eye, making sure she's okay. Persia breaks Jenessa's concentration by saying, "I hope we find this lo mai stuff so that Jamal will be alright. I'm still in shock that he's a howler. I didn't see that one coming; did you?"

Not trying to ignore her cousin Persia, Jenessa's thoughts drift back to her house and Jamal; she hopes and prays that he will not change before they return. She quickly snaps back to reality and focuses on Persia. She smiles and says, "That was a shocker to me also. From what I've read, howlers are blood lined, so someone in his family tree had the gene. Could it be his mom, or could it have been his father; who knows? Our goal is to get the herb and get back to the house as fast as possible. After that, maybe Malcolm can answer some questions I have."

With that said, Jenessa makes a right turn that puts them right in front of the store. They jump out of the car. Jenessa unlocks the door, and they head inside the store. They both look around, trying to find the lo mai. Persia speaks first, "Jenessa, I don't see the stuff. I guess we need to split up; I'll take the back, and you handle the front. Yell if you see anything."

Jenessa nods her head and starts searching first behind the counter while Persia heads to the back of the store. She walks into the storeroom where all the extra supplies are stacked in boxes on shelves and racks. She pulls the boxes down so she can take a peek inside to see if she can spot the lo mai. Persia reaches up high over her head for a somewhat of an odd-shaped box that is stacked in between some other boxes. Relentless in her effort to get the odd box, she reaches for the broom to knock it down. She swings hard, and suddenly, all the boxes on top come crashing down on her. She sees the odd box lying in front of her. Jenessa hears the crash of boxes, and with concern for her cousin, she yells, "Persia are you alright? Did you get hurt?"

Persia moves the boxes, wipes the dust off of herself, and replies back to Jenessa, "I'm okay; I just got knocked down by these old dusty boxes. You might want to come check out what I found on this shelf."

Jenessa sees an unusual box behind some other boxes. Hoping that it's the box she's looking for, she moves the front two boxes and pulls out the hidden box. She opens the mysterious box, and low and behold to her surprise, it's the lo mai she's looking for. She picks up the small box and starts walking to the back to check on Persia. Suddenly, there's a loud BOOM and CRASH inside the store. Glass has been shattered all over the floor, and parts of the ceiling have come down. Dust and smoke are hovering all around. Jenessa moves some rubble out of the way and continues to head toward the back. While coughing from the dust and smoke, Jenessa yells, "Persia, Persia, are you alright? Can you hear me?"

There is no reply, only total silence, and now Jenessa's emotions are about to go from high to off the chart. She stumbles to the back of the store looking for Persia. With all the boxes lying everywhere, it is hard to see her through the cloudy room. Jenessa sets her backpack on the floor, stuffs the lo mai box inside, and proceeds to move boxes to find Persia. After she moves about two boxes, she hears a noise from the front of the store. Jenessa stops and goes up front hoping that someone saw what happened and called for help. Through the dust and smoke, Jenessa sees a figure standing in the doorway. As she continues to walk around in the rubble, she says to the person in the front of the store, "Did you hear what happened? It sounds like an explosion. I'm not sure what caused it. Can you call 911; I think my cousin may be hurt?"

At first, there's only silence from the person standing in the doorway. Then all of a sudden, she hears laughter. Jenessa's is confused about what seems to be going on with this person until he begins to speak by saying, "Jenessa, don't worry; the sheriff will be here soon enough to see about Persia. This is just a show of power to get your attention to let you know that I'm coming at you for revenge. I know this attack caught you off guard, but it is to let you I'm still coming for you."

As Jenessa begins to gain her wits and senses, she recognizes the voice of the stranger standing in from of her. Once the dust settles, she sees his face and her burning hatred for him begins to show. Before she can say anything to him, she feels that there is something odd about him. Now that her powers are maturing, she waves her hands, and all the cloudy dust is gone. Jenessa stares down the person standing in front of her, and with hate in her heart, she says, "What the hell do you want, Camden? I don't have time for any of your crap right now. I can sense a dark force within you. What have you done to yourself? Camden, tell me you haven't fooling been around with Necro magic; are you crazy?"

Before Camden can answer, he claps his hands together, and an impact knocks Jenessa to the ground. She can feel the dark force from within Camden along with the rage and hate he has for her. Jenessa moves very slowly and stands up; then she reacts quickly and summons a holding spell to pin him down so she can help Persia and they can get away. The holding spell tosses Camden up against the wall and immobilizes him there. Jenessa runs back to the storage room to help Persia; she begins moving boxes trying to get to her. She sees that Persia has some smaller cuts and a big gash on her forehead. Jenessa moves the last box off of Persia and then turns her over to try to wake her up. As she looks down at her, she sees something about Persia she has not seen before. Persia's true features are exposed, and the deep gash has started to disappear from her forehead. Now, her suspicions are raised, and her thoughts begin to run wild about what's going on with Persia. She knows witches can't heal that fast, no matter what type of spell they use.

As Camden tries to break the holding spell that Jenessa has cast upon him, he calls on his dark forces of magic; Jazmine summons negative energy from the beyond to break the holding spell. Jenessa gets Persia up on her feet, and they slowly start making their way from the storage area to the front of the demolished store. Camden, still trapped to the wall in his prison, yells and threatens Jenessa by saying, "You may have me trapped at the moment, but I am going to get free, so remember, Jenessa, this is not over. If I can't get to you, then I will get to the people that you care dearly about."

Jenessa doesn't respond to Camden's threats; she just continues to hurry out of the store with Persia and rushes to the car. Once she puts her in and buckles the seatbelt, she hurries to get in and drives away. As she pulls off, she sees Sheriff Michaels' car pull up to the store in her rearview mirror. She doesn't stop; she has a deadline to try to reach, and time is the major factor. It's now 5:10, and the sun sets at 5:27. As she begins to speed through town, Persia starts to regain consciousness. Attempting to focus her eyes, she rubs her head, turns to Jenessa, and says, "What happened; why are we speeding? Everything is so cloudy. What happened to the store? Was there an earthquake?"

Jenessa stares at her cousin, making sure that she's okay, and then she replies with a lot of answers that need to be explained, "Persia, are you okay? The boxes fell on top of you and knocked you out. You were yelling about something you had found; what was it? No, there wasn't an earthquake but something even worse. We need to hurry and get back because we have to have a team meeting."

Persia sits in the front seat, rubs her head, and tries to remember what happened. Then suddenly it comes to her, and she blurts out, "I saw an odd black box stacked on the shelf, and I knocked it down with a broom. That was when the boxes fell on me, but before the earthquake, I reached out, got the box, and put it in my bag."

With that said, Persia reaches down into her backpack and pulls out the black box. Jenessa's eyes get big, and curiosity gets the best of them. Persia looks at Jenessa and says, "Jen, we need to open this box. It could be some important stuff Auntie had hidden at the store."

"Well, just hold on. We'll be home in a few minutes, and we can open it then. I've got a question to ask you: What are you? I don't think you are a witch. When you were injured, some things I saw just have me a little confused," replies Jenessa.

Persia is unsure about how to answer Jenessa. Should she continue to lie, or should she just go ahead and tell the truth to her cousin? She turns to Jenessa with teary eyes and says, "Jen, first, what did you see when I was unconscious?"

Jenessa feels that Persia is stalling with the answer to her question, so she focuses on getting home as fast as she can. She replies by saying, "I saw a deep gash on your forehead, and like a wound on vampire, it disappeared very quickly, but to be honest, I saw something else that aroused my curiosity: Your eyes had a purplish color, and suddenly, they turned light brown. Why is that?"

Now, Persia's blood pressure has shot through the roof with the evidence that Jenessa has brought to her attention. She knows she can't evade the questions by not answering her or eluding the facts about what she is, so she simply just drops her head and tells Jenessa the truth by saying, "Jen, with what I'm about to say, understand that I never meant to lie or deceive anybody. It's just that I didn't know how to open up to you. I wanted to tell you my secret that night when we told Chrisha what we were, but I was afraid you guys wouldn't want me around if I did. A long time ago before I turned eighteen, I was attacked by a vampire. Somehow I didn't turn, but my mom cast a spell on me to keep me from becoming a monster. The vampire that bit me was a boy I fell in love with. I didn't know he was a vampire. The town I lived in was small, and the people hated mythical creatures, so when the murders started happening, the Covenant I was in began hunting down howlers and vampires and destroying them. I was in love with this boy named Ethan Dakota who was very charming, but I was unaware that he was a vampire. I trusted him; he's one of the reasons I came back to Haven-Crest. I heard through the grapevine that he was here with Adrian."

Jenessa looks down at the clock on the dashboard and realizes that they have twelve minutes before it's too late for Jamal. She gives Persia a pissed off look and says, "Regardless of the fact that you thought that you couldn't trust us, I opened up and told you personal stuff about myself and my friends. So, what are you? Half witch or half vampire?"

Ashamed by what she confessed to Jenessa, Persia replies, "I'm a vampire, but for whatever reason, I have some witch powers. My vampire ability is that I can see visions by touching blood, and my eyes are a violet color; I wear contacts to hide my eye color. I drink blood, but I don't go around biting and killing innocent people."

Jenessa slams on brakes outside the house, and they jump out of the car and start running for the front door. Genie hears the car doors shut and heads for the door. Suddenly, Jenessa and Persia bust in through the door, and they are yelling, "We found it; we've got the lo mai. Persia found a black box inside the storeroom."

Edmund gets the lo mai and proceeds to the kitchen to mix the final ingredient for the antidote for Jamal. Once he liquefies it into a serum, he heads back to the room with a couple of minutes to spare and gives it to Jamal to drink. After about twenty minutes, Edmund and Sebastian come out of the room, and Sebastian makes the announcement, "He's resting. We've got him stable, and I think he's going to be alright. We worked on cleaning up his wounds and healing any internal injuries that he suffered tonight, so what's this I heard about a black box?"

Chapter 9

As the sheriff and Agent Ambrose arrive at the demolished herbal store, the sheriff sees Jenessa's car drive just out of sight. He picks up his radio and calls in for backup, "This is the sheriff; I need a fire truck and some more deputies over here at Estelle's shop. It looks like an earthquake hit it."

Once out of range, Jenessa's holding spell releases Camden. He sees the sheriff outside and looks around for a getaway so he won't have to answer a lot of questions. He runs out of the back, unnoticed by anyone; he uses his black magic to cloak him so he can make it to his car and drive away.

The sheriff and Agent Ambrose get out of the squad car and walk slowly to the condemned building. Agent Ambrose looks at the sheriff and says, "I think we need to move inside very slowly because it still could tumble down on top of us. Let's just be extremely careful."

The sheriff nods his head. They both pull out flashlights and their guns and proceed to move in really cautiously through the ruins of the store. With dust and smoke still hovering around the ruins, they realize that it's hard to see anything. Agent Ambrose yells, "Is there anyone here? This is the sheriff's department and Agent Ambrose."

They continue to comb through the wreckage for any survivors, hoping that no one is inside the store. They head toward the storage room of the store, and there they see many boxes tossed around on the floor. The sheriff says, "I don't get it. This is the only store that has been turned into rubble. No other store has damage, so the questions I need answered are: What happened here, and who did this? I know someone who can answer those questions and many more. I saw Jenessa Craig's car driving off in the distance. She's our only person of interest in this matter; hopefully, she can shed some light on this situation. Once we get through here, we'll ride by her house and talk to her."

Suddenly, they hear the sirens from the fire trucks as they come up the street. Once they arrive and get out, Harold Maynard, the fire chief, comes over to the sheriff and asks, "Ross, what the hell is going on here? I don't see any fires out here. Why is this the only building that has been turned to shambles while none of the other ones have any damage?"

Agent Ambrose walks through the doorway and sees something on the floor. She kneels down and spots a set of footprints in the dust on the floor. She stands and sees an unusual outline on the wall. She touches the spot, and after further investigation, she notices that it is the outline of a man. Agent Ambrose walks back to the door and signals for the guys to come in and check out her findings. As the two gentlemen come inside and give Agent Ambrose their undivided attention, she shares her concerns by saying, "I've found some strange evidence that seems very odd in this scenario, like a set of footprints by this wall in the dust. I also found an outline of a man, which looks like he may have been trapped on the wall. From my observations, it looks like there could have been a fight of some sort."

Chief Maynard rubs his face to wipe away some of the smoke and soot that are still floating in the air. He replies by saying, "There is nothing in this town that amazes me anymore with all the mythical creatures roaming around causing all these deaths and attacks. We're just simply here to be their food and targets for them. I can guarantee you that this is a mythical confrontation that went bad."

Before any assumptions can be made, the sheriff makes the call about what needs to be done. He reviews the evidence that was presented to them by Agent Ambrose, walks outside, and tells the deputy, "Get Sam over here to take pictures of the condition of the store, and I'll go over to Jenessa's house to check in with her."

The sheriff gets interrupted by a call from Deputy Carter, "Sheriff, this is Carter; come back."

The sheriff responds, "Hey, Carter, what's going on?"

In a frantic voice, he replies, "You need to get here ASAP. There was another body found at Academic Trail. The news team is here, and people are starting to gather; we're trying to hold them back."

The sheriff answers back, "We're on the way."

He turns and yells, "Ewing, finish up this investigation while the rest of us go over to the trail and see what's going on at that crime scene."

They get in their squad cars to leave, and Deputy Ewing heads back into the store to search for more clues. Chief Maynard and his firefighter assist the deputy with his investigation by making sure that nothing at the scene might cause any type of fire.

Camden pulls into his driveway, gets out of the car, and goes into the house. Alden and Seth are at the table talking to their ally, the Lady in White, about news that they have discovered. Seth notices Camden's smoky odor and dusty clothes. He stands and follows him to the back room and says, "Son, what happened to you and where have you been? You look like you've been in a fight?

Filled with rage, anger, and revenge, Camden looks at his father and says, "I've been somewhere that you two seem to have forgotten. I was getting revenge for Jazmine. I attacked Jenessa and demolished her grandmother's herbal store, and, yes, I'm mad as hell because she turned the tables on me and got away."

In utter shock, Seth realizes that his son Camden is now out of control. He listens to him rant about revenge and trying to hurt someone. He knows he hasn't taught him about the side effects of revenge, and he wonders who has. He shifts his focus to Camden's reaction by saying, "Son, what are you doing? Why are you going rogue by attacking Jenessa? You know that her witchcraft is powerful, so why waste your efforts in causing trouble to get us noticed by the sheriff here? Just keep everything straight according to the plan we have been working on. Alexia has gathered some information about our competition breaking the codes on the map. We have to stick together in order to attain the Book. I wish you had come to me because what you've done is so dangerous; joining your soul with Jaz will make you submit to the dark side."

Camden replies to his father with anger in his voice, "Dad, I hear what you're saying. I'll work with you as you say, yet when my opportunity comes, I'm getting revenge as I swore to Jazmine that I would."

Seth reaches to touch his son on the shoulder, even though his powers may be gone, he can sense the dark force gaining power within his son. Seth turns and heads back into the kitchen where Alden and Alexia are. Once he comes back and has a seat, Alexia says, "Seth, is everything alright? Is your son still with us? I've come up with a way for us to get some sort of an advantage without having to do a lot of digging and investigating. I say we kidnap Jenessa's friend Chrisha and hold her hostage. That should put us in the forefront to make all the demands we want for her safe return back to Jenessa."

With a grin on his face, Seth replies, "He's fine; he just has to be shown the big picture. I have to agree; that sounds like a good idea. We need to find the right opportunity to grab her. After we kidnap her, do you really think that Jenessa and Sebastian will give us what we want in exchange for her to be returned unharmed?"

Alexia smiles at her partners and replies, "I know my brother, and I see he has developed compassion for these kids, so that will be his weakness. We can stack the odds in our favor to get what we want and more."

Before Agent Ambrose and the sheriff can make it to the crime scene, some townspeople and the news reporters have gathered, and the deputies have marked off the area with yellow caution tape. Reverend Carl Wardrett has arrived. He is greeted by some of his patrons from the church and walks over to greet them by saying, "The news is here. This is our opportunity to inform the town about what's going on with all these murders. People are unaware of what has been happening. God has sent me as his messenger to deliver the truth so that everyone can be aware of the wolf in sheep's clothing."

Suddenly, Jewel Walker from the Channel 2 News team walks over to the gathering with Reverend Wardrett. She points for the cameraman to start filming. She holds the microphone up by says, "Good evening, Channel 2 viewers; this is Jewel Walker, and I'm here in Haven-Crest at the Academic Trail. The sheriff's department and detectives have been called out to investigate a possible murder. A body was found by some joggers, and the local sheriff's department was called in. Right now, the body is covered up until the sheriff, Agent Ambrose, and Detective MacRae arrive to investigate the crime scene. Some of the eyewitnesses informed me that they've heard that more unexplained deaths have been happening around Haven-Crest over the last couple of weeks. I have the Reverend Carl Wardrett, pastor of the Greater Life of God Baptist Church here in Haven-Crest, here with me. Good afternoon. I'm glad I could interview you for our viewers. My first question is: Can you shed some light on these accusations about these mysterious and unexplained deaths?"

Reverend Wardrett smiles at the camera; he speaks very openly and honestly by saying, "Jewel, thank you for letting me have a moment to speak the truth to our viewers. Let me open up by saying there have been a lot of mysterious and unexplained occurrences that we, as townspeople, don't know anything about. Now, Jewel, these are only rumors, so I don't know how true they are, but I was told that a homeless man was found presumably dead from an apparent or possible animal attack. There was also a girl who went missing a couple of weeks ago. A body was found deep in the Black Hills. The cause of death was never released, and her identity still remains a secret. Now, viewers, I'm not saying that the sheriff's department is covering up vital information from the public, but we want to know exactly what is going on. We need to talk to the mayor; he's the one who needs to answer all of our questions."

As the cameraman turns the camera back to Jewel, she responds to the audience by saying, "In closing, I see the sheriff and Agent Ambrose have arrived, so I'll see if I can get a statement from Sheriff Michaels."

Jewel and the cameraman start walking toward the sheriff, but the sheriff continues to walk in the direction of the caution tapes. As soon as

Jewel gets close enough, she yells, "Sheriff Michaels, may I have a word with you to answer these simple questions: What's going on here in Haven-Crest? Are there bodies and people disappearing, and if so, why is this being covered up from the public?"

The sheriff stops, turns with anger in his eyes, and responds to Jewel Walker by saying, "Jewel, let me set the record straight; there are no cover ups, no incidences of withholding evidence, or mysterious disappearances being withheld from the public. Whoever you are getting your information from needs to stop speculating and assuming he or she knows what's going on. Now, quote me on that. Excuse me, I have work to do."

The sheriff ducks under the yellow caution tape and heads to the dead body on the ground that's been covered by a white sheet. He puts on some white gloves and slowly pulls the sheet back; the victim's face is very bloody, and he doesn't recognize her. Then, the sheriff raises the sheet to determine the cause of her death. Blood is all over her clothes. He turns to the first responder Deputy Liam Carter with a look of anguish in his eyes, and he says, "From your initial examination, what would you say is the cause of death? With so much blood all over her, it's hard to tell until we get her to the morgue."

He kneels down close to the sheriff and very softly whispers, "I believe she was attacked, but this was not an ordinary attack. She wasn't mauled; this looks like a message being sent to someone to get that person's attention."

The sheriff reaches for the victim to move her hair out of her face; then, he turns her head to the left and examines her neck for marks. He sees a lot of scratches and deep scars, and leans over toward the deputy and says, "If this is a message for someone, I wonder who did this and what that individual was trying to say. These attacks are beginning to get out of control; there are innocent victims who are paying the price for a monster to try to instill fear in us normal folks."

The deputy simply nods his head. The sheriff stands, and he sees Reverend Wardrett in the distance with his deacons; the sheriff makes a beeline to him to confront him about the comments he made to the news. He gets closer to the reverend and says with hostility in eyes, "What do you think you're doing? Why would you put false actuations in the media like that to stir up the residents of Haven-Crest? I believe you're looking to start trouble with these claims of alleged disappearances. You know the best thing for you to do is keep your mouth shut."

Reverend Wardrett smiles at Sheriff Michaels with a nonchalant grin on his face and grabs the sheriff by the arm and says, "Ross, let me tell you one thing: You don't scare me. Your threats mean nothing to me. I have the right to voice my opinion, and God has given me a message to deliver to the residents of Haven-Crest. My advice to you is to let the Committee know I'm coming, and I'm going to show you how to rid this town of supernatural and mythical creatures. They are the ones who break the law and need to be vanquished from this town forever."

Sheriff Michaels looks the reverend up and down, shocked at the response he just received. He hesitates, but he says, "What do you know about the Committee? Listen to me, and take heed to this warning: Don't go messing with a hornet's nest and expecting not to get stung."

With that being said, the sheriff walks away with Agent Ambrose. Once they get a few feet away, she looks at the sheriff with concern on her face, and she asks, "Do you think he was bluffing about knowing about the Committee? What are going to do now; do we alert the rest of the Committee?"

The sheriff shakes his head in disgust while he stares at the reverend. He turns, looks at Agent Ambrose, pulls out his cell phone, and responds to her while dialing by saying, "Yeah, I'm calling the mayor as we speak. They all need to know that a terrible storm named Reverend Carl Wardrett is coming."

The mayor picks up and says, "Hey, Ross, I heard that there was another body found down on the trail. Does it look like an animal attack?"

"Yes, sir, some joggers found one, a young black female, probably in her mid-twenties. I believe she may have been here a couple of days because she's starting to decompose. It looks like it could have been a howler attack. She has no vampire marks that I could see, but Celester is on the way to pick her up, so an autopsy can be done to find the cause of death. However, the nature of this call is for you to call an emergency meeting; I see a storm brewing. The good reverend is starting trouble, and he made a reference that he knows about the Committee. This type of situation could really expose the Committee and what we stand for in this town," replies the sheriff.

There's a pause by the sheriff, and the mayor speaks up and says, "I agree with you, Ross; the good reverend could cause a lot of trouble because he is well respected in the community, and a lot of the residents would eventually start believing his false prophecies. I'll notify the others, and as soon as you get the crime scene secured, get to the hall as fast as you can."

The mayor and the sheriff both hang up, and the sheriff and Agent Ambrose head back over to the deceased body. Agent Ambrose pulls the victim's blouse over to one side, and they notice bite marks from a vampire. They look at each other and make no comment as Agent Ambrose pulls the blouse back up. They say nothing to each other, and suddenly, Celester walks up and says, "Good evening, everybody, so what do we have here? How have you been, sheriff, and how about you, Monica? You been doing okay? From your initial observation, what would you rule as the cause of death?"

Agent Ambrose hands Celester some gloves. He puts them on, and Agent Ambrose pulls the curtain to cover the body from the public. Celester pulls back the sheet that has been draped over her, and his first reaction is, "Dang, she has a little kick to her. Agent Ambrose, go ahead and start the tape recorder so we can inspect the body before I take it to the morgue. I notice she has a lot of lacerations to her face and throat, so she must have put up a fight before she was killed. I see deep claw gashes across her belly, and her torso has a serve puncture wound with a lot of blood loss. She could have bled to death while trying to get away from her captors with the types of injuries she sustained. I'll give you my final analysis once I'm done with the autopsy."

Celester gives the nod to his orderlies to come and load the body onto the gurney to be loaded into the back of the van for transport. After the orderlies carefully load the lifeless body of the deceased young girl in the coroner's van, Celester shuts the doors, walks over to Sheriff Michaels, and says, "Come by the office later, and I'll be able to give you some information about the autopsy. Be careful out here; it's getting rough, even for the police."

The sheriff pats his friend Celester on the back and says, "I'll be okay; you just watch yourself. I have a few loose ends I need to tie up, and I'll see you later on."

Celester and his orderlies get in the van and head back to the morgue. By now, the news team and a lot of the people have left the crime scene. The sheriff and Agent Ambrose are unaware that they're being watched by someone who has a lot of answers as to what has happened to this innocent victim. Detective Macrae pulls up, gets out, and suddenly has a strange sense of perception. She turns and surveys the area, and she sees a young, hooded gentleman standing watching her with an icy glare. She hears someone say, "Detective Macrae, where have you been?"

She turns her head to see who called her. Once she turns back to look at the hooded individual, poof, he is gone like a puff of smoke. She looks around to see if her eyes and her mind are playing tricks on her, but the image is gone. She walks over to the crime scene, picks up a pair of gloves, and says, "What evidence have you guys gathered from the deceased body? Have the special units taken it back to the station?"

Deputy Carter, with his clipboard in hand, relays some information to her by saying, "The evidence that was found includes cuts, scars, and bite marks on her shoulder."

Detective Macrae turns as white as a sheet; she interrupts the deputy, "What did you just say? The victim had bite marks on her shoulder; did Celester say what caused her death?"

In light of her response and reaction to his comment, he looks down at his clipboard, raises his eyes, and replies to his superior while trying not to come off as being arrogant, "Ma'am, are you okay? No, he didn't say what the probable cause could have been. I know the sheriff and Agent Ambrose are going by the morgue later to check with him."

Detective Macrae pulls off her gloves and proceeds back to her car with so many unraveling thoughts running through her mind. She fears she's losing her mind, but she doesn't know who she can talk to. She wonders if her colleagues are thinking she is slowly starting to lose her grip on reality. She heads back to the office to investigate the evidence that was found.

In all honesty, Detective Macrae did see a hooded figure standing on the outskirts watching her. The hooded figure does a blur movement to leave the area to look for more trouble to get into. He knows that law enforcement will have to track him down, but with no evidence, they can't convict him of anything. Suddenly, a black Lexus SUV stops, the window comes down, and the lone figure inside the truck says to the hooded gentleman, "Good evening, Declan; do you need a ride? You need to get in because we need to talk."

Declan reaches for the handle to get inside the SUV. Once he is inside, the gentleman says to him, "I see you have been causing a lot of mischief and mayhem here in Haven-Crest. I applaud you on fulfilling my orders by leaving a trail of mysterious and unexplained deaths in this town. Law enforcement is completely baffled over trying to find any evidence to determine who or what committed the crimes. The reason for this meeting is for you to lay low for a while. From the information I've gathered, they're looking for you. I overheard the doctor I work for on the phone with another member of the Committee, so do the smart thing and come with me so you won't get captured. I'll hide you at my lake house for a while."

Declan stares out the window of the SUV; he slowly turns his head to give his alleged friend his attention. He replies by saying, "I understand what you're saying, but I enjoy playing cat and mouse with the sheriff and Agent Ambrose. They can't catch me; I'm one step ahead of them. I heard through the grapevine that the Committee wants me; Simon Ye and his enforcers have been patrolling the whole town looking for me."

The gentleman is starting to get agitated with Declan, and he responds with some hostility in his voice, "Look, I'm not letting my plans go down the crapper because you think you're better than everyone. Just follow the plan, get your belongings, and meet me here at 10:00 tonight."

Once they reach the Jameson Inn parking lot, Declan gets out and heads for his room to get his belongings. He is like other young vampires in that once they become arrogant, they feel as though they are invincible, and they usually end up making one too many mistakes. Declan is about to find out the hard way about being arrogant.

Declan blurs around the room stuffing clothes into his bag when he hears a sound outside the door. He stops, and suddenly, BOOM, the front door comes crashing down, and three men with guns filled with Pink Autumn come rushing inside. With all the disarray and confusion in the room, Declan can't regain his senses in order to get out before he gets shot. Simon Ye enters the room, and he yells, "Don't let him get out of the room; shoot anything dead that moves."

All of a sudden, shots begin to ring out inside the room. Declan still blurs around the room trying not to get shot. He blurs into the bathroom and locks the door. He pulls out his cell phone, but before he can dial, three shots are fired, and the bullets come right through the door into his back. Blood splatters out onto the floor, and Declan can feel the burning sensation inside his back that sets his body on fire with pain. Declan yells, though he knows he must get out of this room. He can hear Simon yell, "Come out, Declan; we don't want to hurt you. I know you've been shot, so come out so I can take the bullets out before they kill you."

Reaching for a towel to wipe away the blood from his mouth, he can feel himself getting weaker by the minute. He pulls up his shirt while standing in front of the mirror; he takes his fingers and inserts them into the bullet wounds to try to pull out the bullets. The Pink Autumn burns his finger at the slightest touch; he knows that he must get away now before it's too late. Declan takes a towel, wraps it around his hand, punches the window out, and narrowly escapes before Simon kicks the bathroom door in. Once inside, he realizes how Declan escaped, so Simon walks back into the other room with his three enforcers and says, "Declan got away, but he won't get far with those bullets inside him. Go and check everywhere and any place that looks suspicious for him."

The three enforcers leave the room and head into the night to locate and capture the rogue vampire. Simon makes a call to Doctor Barton; the phone rings, and the doctor picks up on the third ring and says, "Hey, Simon, what's up? Is everything alright?"

Simon sighs and replies, "I'm calling to warn you to be on the lookout for Declan. We tried to capture him, but he got away, but not before we managed to put three dipped bullets in him. Just in case he may come by for a little patch up, keep your eyes open and call me."

"Sure, I'm here at the hospital now doing some paperwork as we speak. I'll make rounds to see if he came in, and I'll call you back," replies Doctor Barton.

The doctor gets up and proceeds to make rounds through the emergency room ward. When he sees his new doctor on call, Doctor Jensyn, he stops and asks, "You've been working through the emergency rooms; by chance have you seen a young teenager come in tonight with gunshot wounds? I have some important people looking for him, so if he does show up, call me pronto."

Doctor Jensyn nods his head and says, "Sure sir, I will, but I haven't seen anything like that tonight. No young teenager came in with gunshot wounds. Why is he so important? You can trust me, sir."

Doctor Barton looks at his colleague, rubs his forehead, takes a deep breath, and says, "Don't worry yourself. Everything is alright; in due time, I'll tell you everything. If anything out of the ordinary comes up, call me."

Doctor Jensyn understands and doesn't push the issue of being informed about the important matter; Doctor Barton heads back to his rounds of the emergency room wards in search of Declan.

Chapter 10

Declan manages to get away from Simon Ye, but now they are combing the area with intentions of capturing him for the Committee. Declan blurs around the area staying one step ahead of the enforcers. His injuries make it hard to go far before he has to stop from the pain. His cell phone goes off; he stops and hides in a kid's tree house. He answers with pain in his voice by saying, "This is Declan."

The voice on the other end responds, "It's me. I heard you're on the run; Simon Ye is after you. Are you alright?"

Declan starts coughing up blood, and he begins moaning from the intense pain. He responds to the caller, "I've been shot with three bullets that have been dipped in Pink Autumn, and I'm in a lot of pain. The bullets feel like they are digging a hole inside my body. Right now, I'm in hiding in a treehouse over on Apple Street; I'm about two blocks from the hospital. What do I do now?"

There's a pause on the other end of the phone, and then the caller replies, "Try to make it to the parking garage, third level, section A, and look for my car. I'll go and unlock the door. Hide inside my car until I get off; I'll leave you something in the back to pull out the bullets and something for pain."

Declan attempts to maintain his strength with every ounce of blood he has left in his body and answers, "Okay, I'm on the way, and thanks for all your help."

As they both hang up, Declan realizes that he must make the ultimate sacrifice in order to reach the parking garage. He rises up to see if any of the enforcers are on the ground walking around. Declan rips the bottom of his shirt, places the fabric over the bullet hole, puts a piece of tree limb between his teeth, and reaches inside to pull out the bullet. He holds up amidst the pain, and to keep from yelling, he bites the piece of tree limb.

Out comes the first bullet, and he drops it on the floor. With his fingertips smoking and burning from touching the dipped bullet, Declan is starting to feel very lightheaded from the blood loss. He doesn't think he can do it again, so this is the opportunity to make a blur to the hospital. Declan blurs down the treehouse ladder, through the yard, and into a thick head of bushes; he sees a pair of headlights in the distance. As it slows down, he recognizes the driver of the van as one of the enforcers. The driver of the van surveys the area for a few minutes, and then he gradually pulls off very slowly down the street.

Declan blurs again; he goes around the corner and up the street past the post office. Declan is unaware that he is being followed by Simon Ye, who is trying to determine where he is going. He tries not to let the injured Declan get out of his sight and hopes that Declan will lead him to someone of great importance. All Simon has to do is follow the blood trail that Declan is leaving behind from his wounds. He follows him to the parking garage, third level, and then to section A. Simon's goal is to remain unnoticed by Declan. He spots Declan by some cars and wonders what he's looking for. Simon monitors Declan as he peeps through the different car windows as though he's looking for something. Declan falls down to his knees, and blood is spewing from his mouth. Simon sees this as an opportunity to learn who is playing the puppet master behind Declan's recent attacks in Haven-Crest. Suddenly, Declan sees the enforcers trying to sneak up on him, and he does the unthinkable. Declan blurs and jumps off the hood of truck onto the ceiling in the parking garage. Simon walks right underneath him. Simon looks around, and the enforcers search also, but no one sees him. As Declan can feel blood flowing from the bullet wounds and dripping through the ripped part of his shirt onto the floor, he hopes that no one sees the blood spots. To get his attention, Simon yells, "Declan, we know you're in here. Why don't you just come out and give yourself up? We're not going to hurt you. We want to take you to the Committee."

Without warning, the elevator doors open up, and all the attention is now focused on who may possibly be coming out of the elevator. Simon gives the cue to move in, but to their surprise, something blurs out of the elevator and remains unseen. It knocks out the light bulbs in some of the lights and catches the enforcers off guard. Through their initial reaction is to run, the enforcers stand up to the immediate danger that they cannot see. All that can be heard is slashing, flesh ripping, and blood splattering, and yelling from the victims. Simon understands that they are not alone; something came out of the elevator with the intention to kill whatever is in its path. In mere shock at what he has seen, Simon can't believe what he just witnessed. His three best enforcers were just ravaged like they were made out of paper. Only the lone light that swings back and forth provides some sort of visibility of what's going on. Once it swings back, Simon catches a glimpse of something hiding behind a car, but he can't make out what it is. He moves in closer for a peek. As he takes a step, the figure that killed his enforcers squats over their deceased bodies slurping blood and biting on their necks. Simon sees what appears to be really long white hair and a body dressed in white, though he can't see a face yet. Simon focuses his attention on this being in white. Once it has gotten enough blood to drink, the mysterious creature slowly turns around to face Simon. As the blood drips from its fingers and mouth, it looks at Simon with a deadly cold stare and a vicious growl, and it proceeds to walk toward Simon. With an aching sense of fear in his heart, he is unsure of whether to run or face the demon in all white. Simon tries to plea for his life by saying, "Why are you doing this? We've done nothing to you. There's going to be trouble if you try to kill me."

The killer in white responds by saying, "There is a reason why I'm doing this; there is a debt to be paid. You took away something that belonged to me, and I want to know why before I rip out your throat and drink your blood. Do you remember Fritz Marx; does that name ring a bell?"

"Y Y Yes, it does. He was a vampire who was captured and tortured at the request of the Committee," responds Simon with fear in his voice.

Simon holds on to his gun very tightly as terror overwhelms his senses. He can now see that the killer in white is a female. She stands in front of Simon and says, "I can smell your fear. What is so puzzling to me is that you can torture vampires when you are the enforcer, but when you are face to face with one by yourself, you're scared to death. Where is that big hunter who is not afraid of anything? I'm going to ask you two questions: For what reason was he tortured, and why did he have to die?"

Simon knows that no matter how he answers her question, he's most likely going to die, so he contemplates on exactly what information he must tell her in order to save his skin. He chooses the safest route possible and puts the blame on the Committee to save his own ass. He removes his helmet, wipes the sweat from his brow, and responds in a calm voice, "Fritz was tortured by me. I was ordered by the Committee to do it. My intentions were not to kill him but torture him enough to get information on how vampires are able to walk out into the sun and not burst into flames, and I also wanted to find out who the other members of the Clans in this area were. On top of it all, I wanted him to reveal any and all vampire secrets he could tell the Committee. However, his death was an accident. I told the guard to give me ten units of Foxglove, but he gave me one hundred units. Once I injected him, he had a seizure and died."

The Lady in White, unfazed by the remarks from Simon, looks at him with a fatal stare and doesn't respond. Then she walks behind him, blurs, puts her arm around his throat, and says in a hungry voice, "So, you were doing what you were instructed to do. I'm going to tell you a little about Fritz, the vampire; I came upon him back in 1925 when I was on a visit through Paris. Fritz was a very distinguished actor, world-renown and famous. During that time, he was an actor at Theatre de la Renaissance and performed in a lot of Shakespearean plays like Macbeth, Othello, and King Lear, but like many good actors, he had a dark side. He loved alcohol, gambling, and women. Fritz gambled away a lot of his fortune, and he owed big money to a French gangster named Pierre Alexandre. Fritz was in debt to him for ten thousand pounds, and during those times, that was considered to be a lot of money. I attended one of his performances and was quite smitten by Fritz's charms; we met after one of Fritz's superb shows, and he asked me out. While at dinner, Pierre's men found him and took him from the restaurant. It was unknown to everyone that I was a vampire. I followed them back to their hideout, and I saw them take him in and tie him up in the cellar. Suddenly, Pierre came in, and the torture process began. He ordered a guy to beat him up, and Fritz was punched in the face until his eyes were swollen shut. During the beating, Fritz yelled in pain. Then, they continued the torture to make an example out of him. Next, they placed his hands on a table and hit them with a metal hammer; they broke all his fingers. During the process, Fritz never told Pierre that he would give him the money he owed him, so Pierre continued the torture. This time they broke both arms and legs. I just watched in horror that normal people could resort to such violent acts toward each other, but we were considered to be monsters for things that we do. The last act that Pierre invoked to cause his death was they chained Fritz in a chair and tossed him in the river with his feet encased in cement. He sunk to the bottom of the river, and soon the bubbles stopped. Once everyone considered him dead, I dove into the river, broke the chains, and brought his body to the shore. I was so intrigued by him that I bit him to bring him back to get revenge on Pierre for what he did to him. He did come back as a vampire, and that next night, he killed all the members of Pierre's gang and methodically planned his last sweet revenge on Pierre. Since no one was able to tell the identity of the attacker, Pierre was in utter surprise when Fritz paid him a visit at his mansion. After that, I explained to Fritz all the details about being a vampire and offered him a place in my Red Clan. I still don't understand is why a non-violent vampire would get tortured and killed. I owe it to him to get revenge."

Simon speaks up quickly to save his soul by saying, "Ma'am, I can help you get revenge on the Committee, and I will tell you everything you want to know."

Intrigued by his plea, the Lady in White says, "I know you're trying to get on my good side, but all of that really won't help because my plan is in motion. Fritz must be avenged."

With a quick swipe at Simon's throat with her long claws, Simon's blood flows down his uniform. She begins biting on Simon's neck. Once all of his blood has been drained, she drops his soulless body onto the ground and blurs away before she is noticed.

Declan starts to climb down from the ceiling. He is bruised, bloodied, and wounded, and with so much blood loss, he can't believe that he's still alive. Once he climbs off the wall and reaches the floor, he collapses, but he remembers that he has to find his friend's car for the package he has left for him. Finally, he finds the car. As Declan opens the door to the black Lexus truck, he sees the black bag sitting the front seat. Declan begins to feel woozy, yet he manages to opens the bag and drink the two blood packs; replenishment and refreshment can be felt throughout his body. He reaches back into the bag and pulls out a pair of forceps. Slowly, he relaxes, reaches under the seat, and finds a bottle of Jack Daniels; he drinks a big gulp to cut out the pain, he grabs the forceps, and proceeds to pull out the bullets. After about fifteen minutes, the dipped bullets are extracted from his body. He takes a deep breath, and in a few minutes, he drifts off to sleep. After a couple of hours of peace and relaxation, he awakens just before daybreak. Unseen by some witnesses who have found the dead bodies, he exits the truck and blurs out of the parking garage.

Across town, Camden lies in his bed in a deep slumber; his dreams now are nightmares. The more subtle the dream, the more the desire for revenge corrupts the dream to become violent. Unnatural as some witches who practice witchcraft and suddenly start chanting to Black Necro, Camden dreams of Jenessa's death with a violent end to her life. He awakens with an indescribable hatred for Jenessa, and his thoughts are becoming harder to understand. He goes into the bathroom and washes his face, and when he stands up to wipe his face, he sees Jazmine in the mirror smiling. He wipes his face and then looks back into the mirror only to see himself once again. Camden goes back into his room, lights a candle, gets his Black Necro grimwar, and proceeds to chant to the spirits. Camden is unaware that the more he chants to make his powers greater, the more his soul becomes lost to the black realm. Seth feels the imbalance in the use of Black Necro. He awakens, worried about his son, and goes into his room to see what's going on. Once he reaches the door, he cracks it and peeks inside; what Seth sees is his son embracing the unholy union of the Black Nerco. What starts to happen now astonishes even Seth. The type of chanting Camden is doing starts to bring the dark spirits from hell into him. The end effect is tattoos that leave black connecting designs all over Camden's arms and back. He sees that his son is in immense pain, but before he can break the connection between the spirits, the chanting is over. As Camden collapses on the floor, Seth enters the room. He reaches down, picks his son up, and says, "Son, are you alright? What in the world are you doing, and what are all these marks on your body?"

As Camden begins to regain consciousness, he looks around the room, rubs his head, and says, "What happened; why am I on the floor? The last thing I remember is reading from my spell book. After that, everything went black."

"Son, this Black Nerco magic you're powering from is very dangerous. Can't you see the effects it has on you? Your soul is gradually being drawn to the dark side, and you're letting your sister Jaz embrace you with all this dark magic. Yes, it may feel good, but there a price to pay for this type of magic. Son, I want you to be careful, and I feel it may be too late," replies Seth as he holds his son in his arms.

Seth is fearful about the harmful effects of the dark magic his son is practicing; he knows the signs all too well. He knows what he must do to save his son's life before it's too late. He looks down at his son and says with concern in his heart, "Camden, don't worry. I'm here for you, and we'll get through this as a family. You need to sever your soul from Jazmine's; she's the link to all of this."

Camden says nothing, but he understands what his father is saying. He can feel that Jazmine's spirit has started to overwhelm him and make him do things he's not accustomed to, doing things like trying to hurt people out of revenge. After a few minutes, he gets up from the floor and gets into his bed for some long overdue rest on this cool October night.

The sunrise of a new day brings promise and hope for prosperity, yet in this situation, a lot of questions need to be answered. One in particular is what the ramifications of the destruction of the Herbal Store will be. Who caused it, and better yet, why? These are just a couple of the questions that come to the investigating mind of Sheriff Ross Michaels. As he fills up his car with gas, he knows he must start his initial investigation on the destruction of the store. Just as he hangs up the pump, he gets a call from Agent Ambrose and says, "Sheriff here, I'm on my way to pick you up so we can go talk to Jenessa. I'll be by there in a few minutes once I pay for this gas."

The sheriff hangs up and proceeds inside the store. Once inside, he heads to the coffee pot and pours two cups. Suddenly, he catches a whiff of some very fresh Dunkin Doughnuts; he immediately gets a half a dozen and head to the counter. Kris, the store manager, turns around and says, "Good morning, sheriff. How's it going today? I see you got some of them delicious and fresh doughnuts. How much gas did you get?"

Sheriff Michaels takes a sip of the hot coffee and says, "Hey, Kris. What's going on with you? I'm out early this morning; yeah, the doughnuts do smell fresh. You know I love doughnuts. I filled it up; I got sixty dollars' worth. Just credit it to my account. Kris, let me ask you something. Have you heard anything about what happened to the Herbal Store the other day?"

Kris turns his head and gives the sheriff a weird, frantic look and says, "The only thing I heard is that someone tried to break into the store, and the hex that Miss Estelle left on the store made it explode."

Sheriff Michaels starts to laugh; he shakes his head and replies, "Damn Kris, you are funny. I needed that to wake me up this morning. You still believe in hexes?"

"Sheriff, you don't want to mess with the hocus pocus. That stuff will mess you up," replies Kris.

The sheriff continues to laugh at Kris until tears begin coming out of his eyes. He stops laughing and says, "Kris, if you don't stop, I'm going to piss my pants. Let me get out of here and pick up Agent Ambrose. If you hear anything, let me know."

As the sheriff walks out of the store and gets in his car, he checks his phone for any missed calls and pulls out of the parking lot headed over to the Jameson Inn. After about a fifteen minute drive, the sheriff turns into the hotel parking lot and pulls around to the main entrance. Agent Ambrose comes out, gets in the car, and they pull off headed toward Jenessa's. Agent Ambrose picks up her coffee and says, "Umm, this is good and hot, so how are you this morning? Why are you smiling?"

The sheriff's mind is still focused on Kris, the store manager, and he begins to laugh again. The sheriff looks at her and says, "I'm thinking about what that crazy Kris from the store said to me. I asked him if he had heard anything about the herbal store collapse. He said he heard that someone tried to break in, but Estelle's hex blew up the store. This is the funny part: He asked me if I believed in hexes and cautioned me that hocus pocus could mess me up. I got some doughnuts too. This morning I thought we could go over and talk to Jenessa and see what she has to say about the store. Later, we could go by the crime scene at the trail and check that out."

"Hocus pocus? He still believes in that stuff? Well, for real in this part of the state, hocus pocus and voodoo still thrive really strong amongst these southern folks. Throughout my investigations, I've encountered people whose actions are tied to the fact that they honestly believe that it could possibly happen to them. Remember that belief is one of most powerful emotions of a human being," replies Agent Ambrose.

The sheriff has a distant look in his eyes as he ponders the comment from the agent; he knows that what she says is all true; the town of Haven-Crest has many different kinds of magical beliefs. A lot of types of magic are practiced, both good and evil. At the end of the day, beliefs are what give the power to corrupt people's lives and well-being. He turns to Agent Ambrose and says, "If I didn't believe in hocus pocus, I wouldn't believe in the supernatural things I've seen in this town over the years I've been on the police force. Now, Estelle was the nicest and most lovable person one could ever meet, but I've heard the stories on how she protected us from the supernatural entities that came through Haven-Crest over the years. She was a very powerful witch. One thing I respected about her was the fact that she always helped people in this town. She could have given them riches beyond their wildest dreams, but she helped them so they could get on their feet and take care of their kids."

"Throughout the places I've been in North Carolina, I heard her name mentioned before I even came to Haven-Crest. When I was in Asheville investigating a mauling attack that happened out on a farm back in the woods, I interviewed a hermit who knew a lot about Haven-Crest. He told me a little about Estelle being a member of the power of three; I know you know about this. Tell me the story about the Lamia," says Agent Ambrose.

The sheriff's blood pressure almost goes through the roof. With Agent Ambrose being an outsider, he wonders how she knows so much about Haven-Crest's folklore. There are only a very few people that know about the Lamia who tried to conquer the town. He decides that before he opens up to her, she needs to fess up about what she knows. The sheriff pulls the car into the Food Lion parking lot, cuts off the engine, and says to her, "Before we go to Jenessa's or do any investigating on any cases, what do you know about Haven-Crest? You seem to know a whole lot about the town and its history and personal demons. What do you really want?"

Cunning and deceptive as Agent Ambrose may appear to be, she knows if she tells the sheriff about her agenda, then her plan will be jeopardized. She does the honorable thing and says, "There are a lot of secrets I know about this town, but I will be honest with you. I've been tracking a presumed vampire, but I have no evidence that he is one. He's been killing people all across the State of North Carolina for years. Through some careful contacts that shall remain anonymous, I learned that howlers, vampires, and witches all branch out and eventually pick up residence in a particular town: Haven-Crest. The hermit told me that

Estelle and two other witches defeated the Lamia so she wouldn't destroy the town looking for the Book of Spells for Antione."

The sheriff gives Agent Ambrose an under eyed look, takes a deep breath, and says, "As we have gotten to know each other, I've felt that we've been totally honest from day one. What I'm about to say shall remain between us, and a lot of residents may not recall this. My father told me this when I was a kid. He was a member of the Committee then, and the town was under constant attack from the Lamia. The Lamia was killing and wreaking havoc on the people of Haven-Crest while looking for the Book. At that time, Estelle was a member of the Committee, so she proposed a way to stop all the turmoil. She and two other powerful witches from Salem banded together to cast a series of spells that would hold the Lamia in a tomb of eternal sleep. From what I can recall, it was said that as long as Estelle held the spell in place, the Lamia would remain there. Now that Estelle is gone, it's just a matter of time before she awakens from her tomb of confinement. I think it's time we bring Jenessa into the Committee to help protect the town. I'm sure Estelle has trained her in the ways of her lineage about being a witch. Her mother was a witch, but she didn't take the responsibility seriously, and she moved away. When she came back, she was pregnant. My main concern now is: When is the Lamia going to wake up and start an uprising in Haven-Crest?"

Sitting in the car in shock holding her coffee, Agent Ambrose's mind wanders as she contemplates the story she just heard from the sheriff. She nonchalantly responds by saying, "If this is true, then we may be in a world of trouble. After we ask her about the store collapse, we need to see if we can recruit her for the Committee. I wonder if anyone ever thought to ask Estelle where the body is buried or where her tomb is located."

The sheriff starts the car and begins to slowly pull out of the parking lot. He looks in the rear-view mirror, turns the police radio back on, and says, "I don't know if any of the members know where she is located, but as a child, I heard that she was entombed in a far corner of the town. It is rumored that she is in Snow Hill. If she is, there may not be a headstone. One would have to know how to find her. It would probably be like finding a needle in a haystack."

To give the sheriff a vote of confidence, Agent Ambrose says, "Well, it has been a month since Estelle has passed away, and we've been doing a great job so far as protecting these good people of Haven-Crest. Let's hope that she's still in her tomb and we can get backup assistance before the next war starts."

Chapter 11

The objective is to now find out who or what did the damage to the store and also see if they can convince Jenessa to join the Committee. As they prepare to talk to Jenessa, they pull up in front of her house. The sheriff and Agent Ambrose get out and head to the front porch. They ring the doorbell, and suddenly a voice says, "Coming. Who is it?"

The sheriff looks at Agent Ambrose and responds, "It's Sheriff Michaels and Agent Ambrose; we're here to talk to Jenessa if she's home."

Slowly, the front door opens up, and Genie steps from behind the door and says, "Hey, sheriff, how are you guys doing? Come on in; yeah, Jenessa is here, but she may still be asleep."

Agent Ambrose comes in first, and then the sheriff steps in the house and shuts the door. Genie says, "Excuse my manners. Would you guys like some coffee? Now, being that I'm her last living blood relative, why are you here?"

Agent Ambrose turns to Sheriff Michaels, and he replies, "Thank you for the coffee. The reason we stopped by is because, as I'm sure you know, there was some damage done to Estelle's store, and when we arrived on the scene, I saw Jenessa's car just going out of sight. The fire chief put in his investigation that the cause of the explosion was a gas leak so residents in the area would not suspect anything supernatural. While Estelle was on the Committee, she protected the town from any mythical entities that tried to destroy Haven-Crest for the Book. The other thing we want to talk to her about is possibly joining the Committee. We know that Jenessa comes from a lineage of witches, like you Genie, but…."

Before the sheriff can finish his statement, Jenessa comes in the room and interrupts by saying, "I think I need to be the one who can answer that question. Let me start by saying that I didn't see anything at the store. I wasn't even in the area at the time, so you must have just seen a vehicle that looked like my car going out of sight, so what is this other thing you want to talk to me about, sheriff?"

Agent Ambrose intervenes by saying, "Jenessa, we know you're still young, and this may be too much to ask of you; however, we are extending an invitation for you to join a group of people who take the interest of the people first by protecting them from mythical and supernatural entities. Your grandmother was a member of the Committee. She protected the town for many years, but now that she is gone, a horrible problem may have arisen: the legend of the Lamia's return."

"What the hell is a Lamia? What in the world is the Committee? What do they do? Grandma never told me anything about a Committee," replies Jenessa with some hostility in her voice as she tries to get some answers from the sheriff.

"Jenessa, first of all, calm down and let us explain; your grandmother saw that the Lamia was attacking the innocent people of this town by following orders from a monster named Antoine. He had her looking for a Book of Spells that was supposed to be hidden in Haven-Crest. As the Lamia was killing mostly kids, Estelle formed the Power of Three, an alliance of the three most powerful witches in Haven-Crest, and they cast a powerful spell that required all of them to perform specific magic, and they weakened the Lamia enough to put her in an eternal sleep. Over time, the other two witches met their demise by way of a vampire and a howler. Now that Estelle's gone, we fear the Lamia may awaken and start a reign of terror in Haven-Crest."

Genie chimes in the conversation by saying, "Sheriff, I've always thought that Lamias were only folklore. I never heard of them being in Haven-Crest. I remember hearing that they are immortal, and it is very hard to kill them. When I moved to California back in the mid-forties, I hooked up with a coven of witches, and I met a Lamia who was little girl. She was terrorizing the community by attacking residents and drinking their blood for eternal youth. The family that was being terrorized by this Lamia came to the coven for help, and two witches were killed by the Lamia for trying to interfere with its agenda. Sheriff, you stated that it took three of Haven-Crest's most powerful witches to put it in an eternal sleep, so what can Jenessa do by herself? I don't think she's ready yet for the task you're asking her to do."

Sheriff Michaels knows he must rationalize with Genie to get her to understand their concern for the town. The Sheriff reaches in his backpack, pulls out his laptop, sits it on the table, and says, "What I'm about to show you shall remain just between the people in this room; no one else has ever seen this very private and personal information that I'm sharing.

Back when witches who escaped the Salem witch trials traveled far and wide, some migrated here but remained unnoticed for a long time until a witch named Althea came to Haven-Crest looking for Estelle and Roman. Unexplained occurrences were happening throughout the town, and people were becoming afraid. That's when the Committee was formed. When Althea came looking for the Book, she brought the first vampire by the name of Lars Grayson, and he attacked and killed many people in this town. The Committee sought him out and allied with Estelle and Roman to join, so they became the protectors; they were the ones who got rid of Althea and Lars but not before they turned some teenagers into vampires. At that time, Mayor Sterling Kane's children went missing and were never heard from again. I know that vampires and howlers exist in this town and are causing the majority of all the deaths and murders. Over a long period of time, my uncle was the historian, and he kept records of tragedies and disappearances in this town. Now, my son Xavier has that task of being the town historian."

They all look over the slides on the laptop of certain family lineages, sightings, and unexplained cases. Jenessa sits back in her chair and says, "So, besides being the sheriff, you keep track of the entire phenomenon that goes on in Haven-Crest. Okay, since you're putting your cards on the table, I was there at the store when the collapse happened. I was there looking for some of grandma's spell books and some important papers that I needed. I don't know if I'm ready to be the town's savior; yeah, I am a witch, but I'm not as powerful as Grandma or Aunt Genie."

Genie walks over to Jenessa, grabs her hand, and says, "I want you to know that you are a very powerful young witch; you are more powerful than your grandmother and I ever were. You just haven't reached your potential yet; hopefully, with my help, you will; until the day comes when I feel that you are ready, I will be the Haven-Crest protector."

Persia reacts first. She yells, "Momma, what are you doing? Are you sure that you want to do this? What if the legend is true about the Lamia and she does become resurrected, then what?"

Genie walks over to the center of the room and says, "I believe it's my destiny to help my sister to prove to some that I'm not all bad. I'm doing this so no innocent people have to be the victims of something they don't understand."

Persia doesn't reply. She walks out of the room to the front porch, and the sheriff replies, "Genie, we appreciate all of your help in this matter, and we will keep you informed on the membership once we bring it to the Committee."

Suddenly, the sheriff and Agent Ambrose both receive texts on their phones at the same time. Agent Ambrose says, "Speak of the devil, and he will appear; we've got an emergency meeting to go to. We'll bring up the important matter about you joining, and we'll let you know later on what the verdict is."

Agent Ambrose and the sheriff both get up and leave Jenessa's house, and Genie walks out on the porch to try to reason with Persia. She sits beside her only daughter, puts her arm around her neck, and says, "Why are you upset? What I'm doing is helping the town, and this will assist us in learning the information that we seek from this town. Also, it will put us in a better light with Jenessa if she sees me as someone she can trust."

Persia responds to her comment very uncooperatively by saying, "Mom, why are you going through the hassle of trying to win over some of these people? What we need to do is stick to the plan, get what we came for, and leave before we get discovered."

At that very moment, Jenessa comes out on the porch with a black bag in her hands and says, "Is everything alright? Persia, don't worry. Your mom is the right person to be the savior. I'm not focused enough to do it; I know I'm not ready. We haven't opened the bag to see what Grandma had inside."

Jenessa opens the black bag and frowns as she pulls out a black bottle with white dust inside. Genie responds, "Do you know what that is? Let me see that bottle; it looks like some Phoenix's ashes. If my memory serves me, this used to make a Lamia weak. Now, why would Stell have something as important as this inside her storage room? We need to put this up for safekeeping."

Persia looks at her mother, and Jenessa looks back in the black bag. She sees a note, opens it, and then reads it out loud, "The content inside this bottle contains the Phoenix ashes that were used to subdue and contain a Lamia named Hayden, and her body lies buried in a cemetery in Cedar Grove. Hayden is very dangerous; if she awakens from her tomb, salt is another element that can weaken her."

Jenessa takes the bottle, puts it back into the black bag, stands up, and heads into the house to put it away. Genie and Persia come inside the house behind her. Once inside, Persia has questions about the note that was found, "So, what are we going to do now? Do we just wait and see if the Lamia wakes up, or do we try to find her?"

"This is a situation that witches handle. We are the ones who put her down, and we are the ones who must keep her from rising," replies Genie.

Jenessa reaches for her phone that's on the counter and starts to call Sebastian, but she gets interrupted by Genie, "Are you calling Sebastian? Why? Don't take this the wrong way, but we are witches, the mortal enemies of vampires and howlers. We are superior and more powerful than any of them. I have nothing against Sebastian or Edmund, but think about this, Jenessa: Why was Estelle a member of the Committee? You know they hate vampires and howlers."

As Jenessa's blood begins to boil at the thought of her aunt going against the only people who ever tried to help her understand what she truly is, she looks at Genie with an angry face and says, "Why would you even think like that? We are all a team, and you should not be trying to start a fire between us and them; we just look out for each other. If they found out this information, they would call to let us know what was going on. Anyway, I wasn't calling Sebastian; I was calling Jamal."

Neither Genie nor Persia says a word; they just walk out of the room. Jenessa calls Jamal, the phone rings, and he says, "Hey Jenessa, what's up?"

"Hey Jamal, I called to see if you were busy. I called to let you know I was coming over to talk," replies Jenessa.

"Okay, I'm doing alright. Yeah, come on over; I'm at home," replies Jamal.

Then they both hang up. Suddenly, he receives a text from Sebastian about coming over at nine for an important meeting. She replies, "Yes." Genie, Persia, Chrisha, and Jamal all receive the same text from Sebastian. Genie comes into the room and says, "We can let them know about the information we received from the sheriff tonight at the meeting, so where are you going?"

"Over to Jamal's for a little while; I'll be back," replies Jenessa.

Jenessa gets her keys and heads to the door. She pulls out of the driveway and heads up the street. Ten minutes later, a black Lexus pulls up in front of the house. A tall gentleman gets out and heads to the front door. He knocks, and Persia says, "Who is it?"

In a calm reply, he says, "It's me, Syngyn; we need to talk."

The door opens, and Syngyn comes inside. Persia smiles at Syngyn and says, "What brings you to this neck of the woods? How long have you been in Haven-Crest?"

"It's good to see you too, Persia. Where is Genie? We need to talk about something I just heard. My protégé informed me of an age-old folklore tale about a Lamia; I thought they were extinct. I heard that one exists here in Haven-Crest and that it took three powerful witches to put her down for a long nap until now. Through the grapevine, I'm hearing that now you and your niece will be Haven-Crest's new saviors," replies Syngyn.

With a huffy attitude, Genie replies, "Syngyn, why are you here? Yeah, you heard right; we are going to help keep the town from getting attacked by a Lamia. What kind of information have you found out about the Committee; have you infiltrated them yet? I might be getting on the board pretty soon, so I'll keep you informed."

Syngyn's reaction changes to hostile; he gets snippy to get his point across to Genie by saying, "Look, you don't have to patronize me. We've got a deal. If either of you try to screw me over or double cross me, remember this: I will kill the both of you without hesitation, so don't play games."

Both Genie and Persia say nothing; they just look at each other, and Persia replies, "It's time for you to go. Like my mother said, we'll be in touch."

Syngyn obeys Persia's request and heads for the door. He turns and gives the ladies an evil face and heads out the door to his car. Slowly, he drives down the street until he's out of sight.

Once Jenessa gets to Jamal's new location, she gets out, surveys the area to make sure she wasn't followed, and then heads inside. She has stopped on the way to pick up something for Jamal to eat. Since the attack, Jamal has been MIA until Sebastian decides their next move. Once inside, Jamal comes in the room with his shirt off, showing off his ripped body. Jenessa sits on the couch, and they begin to eat. Jamal looks at Jenessa and says, "I'm so glad you're here. I have been so bored being here by myself with no one to talk to, but I know this is the way to keep me hidden from the pack so that I won't get killed. Thanks for cloaking the area so that the other howlers can't sense my scent out here. Jenessa, can I be totally honest? I really miss you; I know I was a jackass back then, but you can see I have matured. I heard how worried you were about me while I was hurt. Honestly, my feelings for you have gotten even stronger."

Flattered by what Jamal has said, Jenessa simply blushes; she looks into Jamal's eyes and sees how sincere he is. She wonders why Jamal is suddenly so open and honest about his feelings for her. Since he has been honest with her, Jenessa confesses to Jamal by saying, "As you know, we've been through a lot. We've known each other since elementary school up until now. I can't sit here and say to your face that I don't still have strong feelings for you. You are my first love and the only guy to ever have my heart. You were the only guy I gave myself to body and soul. Once upon a time, I thought we were soul mates. I'm assuming that love and fate have given us a second opportunity to find out and see."

Jamal sets down the cup of ice tea and decides to throw caution to the wind. He turns to Jenessa, reaches for her hands, and pulls her toward him very slowly; then he leans in for a passionate kiss. Jenessa gives Jamal a sexy, alluring look with her beautiful green eyes. They both begin breathing very heavily and are holding and squeezing each other tightly. They pause, looking into each other eyes, and proceed to take the innocent moment to another level. Jamal begins to pull Jenessa's shirt over her stomach, but she stops him and says, "Wait, Jamal; we need to stop. Don't think I don't enjoy this magical moment with you, but I don't want to rush into another relationship so quickly. With all of this revenge in my heart I have for Camden for what his family did to me, I don't want you to be the rebound guy. Yes, I want you back in my life, but let's just take things slow until all of this is over because I do still love you, Jamal. Please keep this warm, hot body of yours on ice until that special day comes when we can pick up where we left off."

"I respect how you feel, and I understand what you're saying. I don't want to rush getting back into your life all over again. No matter how long it takes, I will always be here for you," replies Jamal.

Suddenly, Jenessa's phone rings, and she reaches for her purse on the table and pulls it out. She answers and says, "Hey Sebastian, I got your text earlier. I'm over at Jamal's house right now."

"Jenessa, we need to talk; it's very important. Edmund has gone to the Committee for an emergency meeting. Come to my house and bring Jamal with you because you two are the only ones I can trust," replies Sebastian.

They hang up, and Jenessa turns to Jamal and says, "Jamal, how about putting on a shirt? We have to go see Sebastian right now."

Jamal grabs a tee shirt and his keys. As he locks the door to the cottage, he turns and surveys the area with his keen howler senses. Jenessa gets into the car, and they drive away headed to Sebastian's house.

Once Edmund reaches the town hall, he goes into the usual meeting room; to his surprise, he feels all eyes on him. Edmund sits down, and the meeting begins. Mayor Dobson stands and says, "Good evening, everyone. I called this important meeting because through some of my confidential contacts, it was brought to my attention that our enforcer Simon Ye and his guards were killed in the underground parking deck. From the footage caught on the surveillance cameras, they were under attack by some strange unseen force. From the video, one can see them being killed, but who or what did it is not shown. From their last transmission, they were following the young vampire Delcan through town. Now that Simon is gone, what do we do for an enforcer?"

"With the different contacts and informants that we have out in Haven-Crest, we should be able to be more discreet than Simon was. I heard of a vampire hunter named Syngyn who will come and kill any vampire or howler that needs to be taken care of. The problem is there's no way to contact the hunter. He contacts you through sources he has," replies Doctor Barton.

Edmund says nothing. He just sits and watches everyone. The tension begins to get thick amongst the other members. Karen, the District Attorney of Haven-Crest, turns to Edmund and says, "Edmund, you're mighty quiet tonight. Is everything alright? What do you think about this Syngyn; you ever heard of him?"

Even though his curiosity has now awakened, Edmund tries not let it show. He smiles and replies, "Karen, I'm okay. I'm just finding it hard understand why there are so many attacks happening in Haven-Crest. Are there any new people we may need to check out? Being at Priceless, I get a chance to see different faces that may come through town. I haven't seen anyone new lately, but I'll check with my staff."

The mayor says, "Is there any more new business?" Dr. Barton raises his hand and says, "I want to address the members of the board. As most of you know, my health has been a major issue over the past few years. I want the Committee to know I've been a faithful and devoted member since I stepped in when my father passed away. I've been searching for the right person to assume my position on this board, and I think I've found him in my colleague, the new doctor at the hospital Kadeem Jensyn; I feel that he would be a great addition to the group."

"Well, we'll take that into consideration; I've heard good things about the care he shows the patients at the hospital. Some pressing issues were brought to my attention by the sheriff, and I feel that this is something we all definitely need to check into," replies the mayor.

The sheriff speaks up next by saying, "Agent Ambrose and I went to talk to Jenessa Craig about joining the Committee, but she declined the offer. However, Genie Fredrick, Estelle's sister, is willing to become the protector of Haven-Crest. She's a powerful witch. The big question is: Can we trust her? As long as Estelle had been living here, she never said anything about having a sister. I find that very odd for some reason. How about we put her on probation for a while until she earns our trust; anyone disagree?"

Edmund sees this opportunity to help out someone he seems to be smitten by; he speaks first by saying, "I agree with you, sheriff, that's a good idea. I know I haven't been a member on the Committee as long as the rest of you, but putting new members on probation is a good way to make sure they are the right fit for this type of organization."

The sheriff replies, "Okay that settles it then. I'll inform Genie that she's on a trial basis for right now, and her first mission is to locate the burial place of the Lamia. Since Estelle was the last member of the power of three, we definitely need someone to step in and fill that void. Due to the fact that we are out an enforcer, I'll get the deputies to beef up security around the town."

The next order of business before this committee is…."

Before the mayor can inform the other members, there's a hard knock at the metal door. The entire body of members goes silent, and they all begin to look at one another. Agent Ambrose pulls out her gun, and the guard says, "Who is it?"

The voice on the other side of the door replies, "Son, it's the good reverend; can you please let me in? I have some important business to discuss."

As all the members remain silent, suddenly, Judge Simmons replies, "Yes, guards open the door; let's see what the good reverend has to say."

The guards comply with the judge by opening the metal door, and the Reverend Wardrett enters the room and grabs everyone's attention by saying, "Good evening, everyone. I came by your little clubhouse meeting to see what's going on with the affairs of the town. A lot of the people in this town are unaware of what goes on behind these closed doors. I don't want to cause ripples in the water, but it's time citizens of this town were informed about what's behind all these cover ups of the incidents of these so-called murders or animal attacks that get broadcasted to the news and residents of Haven-Crest. I'm going to let you in on a secret. I know what the Committee does; you hunt down vampires and howlers. I just want all of you to know that I'm watching everything, and if you don't want trouble, you don't mess with me."

Judge Simmons stands up with anger in her eyes from the threat Reverend Wardrett has just made, and with an angry voice, she replies, "Reverend, don't come here throwing around false accusations about some kids' bedtime stories about vampires and howlers. I saw your interview with Jewel Walker, and believe me, you don't want to stir up the hornets' nest because in the end, you will get stung. You're not a prophet for the people; you are an instigator merely looking to start trouble. No, we've got our eyes on you. Now, you've had your say, so it's time for you to leave."

The guards walk over to Reverend Wardrett so he can be escorted out of the town hall. He goes quietly and calmly without any trouble. Once he leaves, Fire Chief Maynard speaks up first by saying, "What the hell was that? Is this so-called prophet trying to intimidate us? We need to keep a closer eye on him. I smell trouble with a capital "T." With all this gloom hovering over Haven-Crest and all the murders and mayhem going on, now we have to deal with the reverend?"

District Attorney Karen replies, "Calm down, Harold, the reverend is just trying to send smoke signals to see what secrets he can get from us. Let's just use our heads and be rational. Calmer heads can prevail in this situation."

Judge Simmons hits the gavel and dismisses the meeting. As the members leave to head back to their homes, Sheriff Michaels and Agent

Ambrose get into the squad car, and the sheriff reaches for his phone to call Genie, but before he does, Agent Ambrose says, "Before you call Genie, did you notice how Edmund was all for Genie becoming a member. That's kind of suspicious to me. What does he know? My spider sense is starting to tingle about him. What do you know about Edmund Martin?"

"Look, before you jump the gun, I've known Edmund Martin for many years; he has always helped the people in Haven-Crest by loaning money to deserving families or donating to different charities in the town. If he is a supernatural creature, then what is he: a howler or a vampire? Don't make me laugh, Monica," replies the sheriff.

Agent Ambrose turns and looks out of the window. Feeling that her point did not reach the sheriff, she says nothing. She decides to just change the subject and says, "Go ahead and call Genie so she can get started searching for the Lamia. I want to say that I'm sorry for insinuating that Edmund could be up to something no good."

Sheriff Michaels looks at her but doesn't comment further. Agent Ambrose feels she needs to clarify her comment by saying, "I didn't take it the wrong way; I just got the feeling Edmund may be keeping a dark secret. I'll take your word for it that he's a devoted member, so go ahead and call Genie and give her the good news."

Sheriff Michaels smiles and dials Genie's number. She picks up, and he informs her that she will be on a probationary status for a while and that her first assignment is to locate the Lamia that may have awakened.

Chapter 12

As the sun sets on the cool autumn evening, inside the now quiet office of Nicolette, her current acquisition, Donna Gill, and her highly trained computer hackers are going over some key finds since they broke into some supposedly impenetrable databanks to receive vital information. Donna works vigorously hacking different airlines and bank account transfers to determine when Sebastian and his Clan will make their departure to retrieve the clues to find the Book of Spells. Amy Christian comes into the computer lab, takes a seat, and says, "Donna, have you found anything interesting while you have been hacking tonight? Can I be honest with you? All of this is still hard for me to grasp. I would never have guessed in a million years that vampires really do exist."

Nonchalantly, Donna raises her head from behind the flat screen computer monitors, looks at Amy, and replies, "I agree. I'm still in awe at what I've seen, but one question comes to mind: Once they are done with us, are they going to kill us or really pay us? Do we band together, or will it be every woman for herself?"

"That's a good question, but I think if they planned on killing us, they would have killed us already once we deciphered the map for them. There may be a purpose for keeping us around, especially since we are experts in our fields of study," replies Amy.

Andre, one of Adrian's most trusted friends, comes into the lab, smiles at the ladies, and proceeds to walk over to the computer station. The ladies both look in awe at him as they admire the aura of seduction of vampire essence in Andre. He smiles and says, "Good evening, ladies; how are you doing? I came over to ease the speculation about what's going to happen to you guys. I see that you're intrigued about the tradition of vampirism. Let me be the first to say that it's true what they say: It is both a gift and a curse. The immortality is the fascinating aspect of the whole ordeal. Most people have a difficult time imaging being able to live forever and never growing old. Then, a vampire must embrace the truth about what he or she has become: a monster, a killing machine that needs to feed on human blood to survive. Vampires adapt to the new beginnings in life either by staying good or becoming very evil like me. I kill, and I take what I want. Adrian showed me the way to be true to myself and not be denied of anything that is forthcoming. Is this what you ladies desire to become?"

After that show of humbleness, the ladies are speechless and in sheer shock from what they've just heard. The puzzling question to them is if they should ask Andre to turn them into vampires. They both are hesitant, but Donna speaks first, "Andre, how long have you been a vampire? Do you know who bit you; do you regret being a vampire?"

Andre pauses and smiles as he sits on the table, and then he replies, "Well, ladies, let me just say it's been a helluva journey. I became a creature of the night in the year of 1915 during World War I. I was enlisted in the United States Marines, and originally, I'm from Elizabeth, New Jersey. I only enlisted to follow my big brother, Raymond, who was already stationed overseas in Europe. Once the war started, I was sent off to boot camp in Kentucky; after that, I was ready for Europe. Once the Marine aircraft carrier landed on the naval boat, instead of smelling the salt water, all I could smell was death and blood in the air. The squad I was in was a four man detail, and we did most of the recon missions to observe the enemies' camp for surprise attacks. On this night, it was extremely cold, and we were monitoring a small POW camp outside of Romania. On this particular recon detail, we sensed that something was wrong. We saw them torturing some POWs they had captured from the US Army. I noticed a solider on patrol, and instead of signaling for backup, I tried to take him down myself. What a big mistake that was. My first thought was to do a sneak attack, but suddenly, it was like he could sense me in the tall overgrowth of trees. Just like a blowing wind, the next thing I knew was that he was right on top of me as though he was trying to kill me. He knocked the gun out of my hands. I then pulled out my knife, and I stabbed him repeatedly to get him off of me. Even though I saw his blood spill out, he never stop coming at me; I caught a glimpse of his eyes through the moonlight, and they were golden-black. Then I noticed that he had fangs and was howling like an animal. I could feel the gashes he was giving me with his long fingernails. Also, I could see my blood starting to spill through my uniform. The smell of blood was in the air. I was getting weak from the blood loss, and it began to get harder to fight him off of me. Before I knew it, he overtook me, grabbed me by my head, and pushed my head to the side, exposing my neck. The next thing I felt were his sharp fangs going into my neck, and then there was a burning sensation like I've never felt before, as though my whole body was on fire. I saw him step back from me once he bit me. The pain I felt will forever be indescribable, and the surge of the toxic vampire venom running through my body and the misery I felt from this unknown attack was sheer agony. After about I guess what was fifteen minutes or more, I collapsed in the cold, wet ground. I felt as though I was dying and was unable to speak or move my body from this apparent attack. The vampire began speaking in some Romanian accent I couldn't understand, but I was able to interpret the dialect. He was saying that he was giving me a terrible curse for invading their country and killing the innocent villagers due to this war. He did a blur and vanished into the dark, cold night. I managed to stumble back to the outpost before I died from an apparent attack of some kind. The report file stated the cause of death was an animal attack while on patrol, and three days later, I awoke in a coffin on an aircraft carrier coming back to the United States with a strong hunger for blood that I had to fill. On the flight, I killed everyone on the plane except for the pilot, and once we landed, he was the last one to die by my hands. I respect this curse that was placed upon me. I thought I could handle this hunger for blood, but I was wrong. I've killed a lot of innocent people and ripped away towns during my rampages. I finally migrated to Miami back in the mid-1920s. My goal was to blend in with my new surroundings. It worked for a while, but I couldn't control the hunger, and the killings started again. Then I met Adrian, and he mentored me so that I could understand what I had become and helped me to adjust to the situation of vampirism."

Both ladies are fascinated at the story Andre just told them and want to ask a hundred questions. Andre is overwhelmed and not sure what to say. Donna shakes her head while Amy just remains speechless. As curiosity killed the cat, Donna asks, "Is it hard adapting to new cultures and modern technology, being that you're from the early 1900s? Actually, how old are you?"

Andre smiles at the ladies and replies, "You're not going to believe me when I tell you. I'm one hundred and sixteen years old, but I don't look a day over twenty-two. We, as vampires, no matter what our ages may be, adapt very quickly to change and our surroundings."

Amy embraces the questions and adds to the conversation by saying, "The immortality doesn't bother you? Knowing that you'll never age, have kids, or die doesn't at least concern you? You may have a legacy in the underworld, but what about the people you once knew, the family that you had, and having someone to share that with? I find it hard to understand or grasp the concept of being immortal."

Andre smiles at Amy and replies, "Over time, you will learn to adapt, and since society is always ever changing, the immortality will eventually become all natural to you. As you get used to watching the people you know live, love, and die around you; yet the aspect of them not living forever becomes a way of life, and they are soon only distant memories to you."

Donna becomes enlightened by the mere thought of becoming immortal; she sees this as an opportunity to fulfill her desire to become one of the chosen few. Amy starts to feel like this conversation is progressing in the wrong direction as she realizes that Donna has become very serious about becoming immortal. Andre takes his hand and moves Donna's hair out her face. He leans over and says, "Before you take the next step, Donna, make sure this is what you want, because there's no turning back once the commencement begins. Now, I see your devotion to this cause, but...."

Before Andre can finish his in-depth conversation with Donna, Adrian comes in the lab, overhears a lot of the conversations, and then comments, "Well, well, well, don't let me interrupt. I find it very intriguing that someone of your superior intellect would find that a childhood folktale about vampires and howlers could possibly be true. Donna, I'm like my dearest friend in that I see your eagerness to become one of us, but remember this: Once you enter this kingdom, the only way out is death. Are you sure this is what you want? Many have wanted the same vindication, but once they learned of the sacrifice for their survival, they immediately chose death. Honestly, you may thrive in this kingdom but only with the right guidance to steer you down the path of immortality."

After Adrian makes such a convincing statement, Donna is just so overwhelmed. She smiles and says, "Adrian, you don't have to ask me twice; I'm all in. Just let me tie up some loose ends in my personal life, and then I'm all yours."

Adrian cuts his eyes at Amy; he sees the way she looks at him. As she turns her head, Adrian does a blur movement, and he's standing right next to her. When she turns around to see him right next to her, she yells, "Whoa, where did you come from? That always catches me off guard. What can I do for you?"

With a smile on his face, he replies, "Why do you look at me with an unpleasant glare? You look at me with hatred in your eyes. What have I done to you to make you look at me that way? I offer you immortality at no price, and I offer you a place in my Clan. Some mortals would jump at the gifts I offer but not you. I don't get it."

Amy tilts her head back as she looks up at Adrian, and in a calm manner, she replies, "First, let me say I appreciate the offer you have bestowed upon me. I'm sorry, but I must decline. Adrian, I just don't feel my purpose in life is to live forever; I want to get married, have a family, go visiting different places, and grow old and die with my husband. To be honest, you defy the purpose of life. Being that you were created by the devil himself, you kill to satisfy a hunger in order to survive, and I'm a Christian woman of faith."

Adrian can feel his blood start to boil, but he figures that a rational mind can prevail in this conversation. He replies, "Those are strong words coming from you, Amy, though I learned over the years that my purpose in life is to feed on the blood of the humans. Once I learned to adapt over the centuries, being immortal has given me the sense of power because no matter what I do, I can never die."

Amy shakes her head and doesn't reply. Adrian backs off and respects her wishes. Then he walks back over to Donna and Andre so they can finish their conversation.

As the meeting at the town hall is now over, Edmund races to the mansion to inform the group on the different aspects from the meeting. He knows that Sebastian has called the important meeting with the clan and other close friends of theirs. After what was discussed, he knows this is a call for alarm. With the Committee starting to regroup its defenses as well as personnel with new members, Edmund realizes that time is of the essence. He pulls his car into the driveway and gets out and heads into the house. He is greeted by Adam at the door. Edmund does a blur movement and quickly stands by the big bay window. Adam comes into the room and says, "Sir, is everything alright? You have a really concerned look on your face?"

Edmund turns to his dear old friend and replies, "Adam, life as we know it is about to change. All different types of vicious creatures have come here to Haven-Crest and committed numerous crimes and murders and literally posed a threat to these innocent people who have done nothing to hurt anyone. From what some of the members said in the meeting, they are looking to get Syngyn, the vampire hunter, involved to hunt all the supernaturals so they can be killed."

Adam's eyes get really big, but before he can reply, Sebastian comes into the room. All he has heard is the ending of the conversation, and he quickly replies, "What's going on, Edmund? You look very stressed. Let's have a drink to relax you before we talk about whatever it is that has you very agitated."

Adam gets the bottle of very expensive bourbon and pours out three drinks. They all drink up and place the glasses on the serving tray. In a more relaxed tone and mood, Edmund takes a seat on the couch and begins saying, "Sebastian, like I was telling Adam, the Committee is about to shake this town up. There was a murder of Simon Ye, their enforcer, and some of his guards in the hospital parking garage. They believe that a Lady in White with white hair killed Simon. Now their goal is to hire Syngyn, the vampire hunter, to rid Haven-Crest of all the supernatural creatures that exist here. From the way they are plotting and scheming, they mean business, and that could spell trouble for us and the howlers. Now, on a lighter side of all this, I second the nomination for Genie to become the new Haven-Crest witch."

Sebastian stands and walks over to the fireplace as though he's in a deep thought. He turns from the fireplace and says to Edmund, "Edmund, before I respond to that comment, I want to say that I respect Genie and don't think I'm trying to cast ill-fated words against her character, but there is something about her I just can't seem to figure out. She came in town right before a lot of these unexplained strange events began happening. I know that you're smitten by her, but let's not drop our guard and lose our focus on the matters at hand. I still believe that Genie may be up to something."

As Edmund listens to the voice of reason from his closest friend, he ponders the idea that Sebastian could be right, but his heart tells him differently. Edmund simply smiles and replies, "Sebastian, you may be right in your assumption of Genie, so I'll keep my eyes open. What's going on with your meeting tonight?"

Before Sebastian can answer, he gets interrupted by Marcella, and she breaks the serious tension between the three friends by saying, "My God, why do you guys look so serious? I came early for this meeting of yours, Sebastian, so what's going on? I picked up Malcolm as you requested."

Again, Sebastian tries to inform his friends of the reason for the meeting, but before he can get started again, Jenessa, Jamal, and Jai Li all come in at the same time, and Jenessa says, "I see the gang's all here; hey, where are Aunt Genie, Persia, and Chrisha?"

Edmund replies, "Did anyone call them?

Jenessa pulls out her phone and calls Persia. After four rings, the voicemail comes on, so she leaves a message. Suddenly, there's a knock, so Adam turns and heads to the door. Once there, he opens it, and Persia and Genie come inside. Persia says, "Please, don't tell me we are the last ones to get here. Well, we made it; let's get this meeting started."

Jai Li surveys the room with a quick glance. As she notices that Chrisha has not arrived yet, she begins to get really worried about their dear friend. Sebastian gets everyone's attention, and then there's a knock at the door. Suddenly, Chrisha comes in, and the meeting begins. Edmund stands and says, "Hey, let me have your attention. We called you all here tonight to discuss some urgent information that Sebastian and I felt we needed to share. First, the Committee has lost its enforcer, Simon Ye, and now they are hell bent on trying to find the hunter, Syngyn. For those who do not know or have never heard of him, Syngyn is a vampire, and he also hunts down and kills supernatural creatures for a living. The Committee is in the process of hiring him for that purpose, so we must be very careful and watch our backs. They are still on the hunt to find Declan, so I'm just warning everyone. I also want to let you all know that I nominated Genie for the Committee as the new protector of Haven-Crest. She will be put on probationary status for right now; congrats to her."

Everyone turns to Genie and starts to congratulate her on joining the Committee. She smiles at everyone and says, "Thanks everyone; this means a lot coming from all my friends and family. I want to say thank you to my very special friend Edmund. Thanks for believing in me and giving me chance to help out. Well, enough with the mushy stuff; let's get on with the meeting."

Sebastian stands and takes the floor. He takes a deep breath and says, "Let me start by saying that a few weeks ago, we, as a group, deciphered the map and discovered that some of us will leave for the quest of finding the keys for the Book of Spells. Like I said then, I don't know what to expect on this journey. Some of us may return, and some may not. So, this is the last time I am going to ask who is going with me on the quest. Now, I have six airline tickets, and I really need five people to accompany me to find a great treasure."

No one says a word. Everyone looks around at each other, and Jenessa speaks up first, "Everyone, I know I'm the obvious choice, so count me in, Sebastian."

Jamal raises his hand and says, "I'm in. If we are going to find a howler biker gang, I'm sure I'm going to be needed."

Persia looks at her mother, and then she stands and says, "Momma, I know you may not be all for me going, but I think it will do me good to go. I need to do some soul searching, so count me in."

Genie doesn't reply but simply reaches out and hugs her daughter. Malcolm raises his hand and says, "I'm in because I know I can be helpful with any matters of traditions and cultures we may run into on this journey."

Jai Li laughs and blurts out, "What about me? No one wants me to come along. Trust me, I won't be any trouble, and I could use the change of scenery."

"Okay, okay everyone. I see we have our six people for the trip, so we leave at noon tomorrow. Now, Edmund and Genie will still be our eyes and ears as far as the Committee is concerned. Marcella and Adam will run Priceless while we're gone. Chrisha, my dear, help out where you can and stay out of trouble," replies Sebastian.

Genie feels this is the time to make a statement to everyone about Sebastian's agenda. While people are talking and celebrating about going on the trip, Genie says, "Can I say something to everyone? First, let me say that I appreciate everything that my special friend Edmund has done for me. To be honest, I didn't realize that this clan was so close to family and friends; it means a lot that we have a strong bond like that. I just want to say to all of those who are on the quest: Be careful, and, all six of you, return home safely."

They all smile and start hugging; slowly, Edmund makes his way over to Genie, reaches for her hand, and they proceed to go out on the balcony. They get to the rail and are standing under the stars and the moonlight. While looking into Genie eyes, Edmund says, "You really didn't have to say all that about me. You know I would've done anything to help you out. You are the right person to be the protector of Haven-Crest. I have never seen a witch as beautiful as you, Genie."

Emotions start to run high, and Genie sees the sincerity in Edmund's eyes. They move in very slowly toward each other. Their eyes being to sparkle, and they kiss while everyone in the inside watches the attraction between the two friends. Persia smiles at her mom, and she says, "Girls, since this is our last night before we go on the journey, I say we should have a girls' night out and go to the new club The Foxhole in downtown Raleigh. I heard that it be jumping off. What do you think?"

Jenessa, Chrisha, and Jai Li look at each other; they all laugh and agree that it's a good idea. Jenessa speaks first, "Persia, you just want to twerk at some boys before we go on the trip, right? What time are we going to leave?"

The four really close friends all begin to laugh, and Jai Li replies, "I say we should make an entrance about midnight, roll in, and have all the guys checking us out and all the girls jealous of us."

They all start cheering and getting revved up for the girls' night out. Sebastian doesn't say anything; he heads into his study. Jamal notices and decides to follows behind. Once Jamal comes into the study, he sees Sebastian sitting at his computer entering some kind of information. Sebastian sees Jamal enter the room, and he stops what he's doing and says, "Can I help you, Jamal? What's on your mind?"

Unsure of what to say, Jamal replies, "Sebastian, I came in to offer my sincere thanks for all that you did for me when I got injured. We don't know a lot about each other, but we share something in common with Jenessa:

her utmost friendship. She's big on friendship. She's really close to you, and she sees the good in you that most people don't. I see the kindness and loyalty you extend to members of your clan; I want to offer my loyalty to you and join the Grey Clan as my home also."

"Jamal, I appreciate that compliment; I would've helped anyone in that situation. Loyalty and friendship are some of the basics I look for in people. Jenessa has shown me true loyalty. She has been through a lot, so I'm returning the favor. Jamal, excuse me for being straight to the point, but is there a real reason you came in my study to talk to me?" replies Sebastian.

Jamal hesitates but figures that if anyone can answer his questions, it is Sebastian, so he asks, "Throughout all the travels you've been on, what do you know about howlers? There are still a lot of things about howlers I don't know, and I was hoping that you could possibly shed some light on this situation."

Sebastian turns around in his chair and gives Jamal his undivided attention, rubs his chin, and replies, "Where do I begin? I've met different types of howlers throughout my travels across the world. The relevant thing you may want to know is how you became a howler. From what I understood, being a howler is passed through the genes, so technically, someone in your family tree passed the gene down to you. Either your mother or your father is a howler. You are a howler, so you can't turn anyone else. You're stronger than a Lycanos, but when they bite someone, they pass on the Lycanos trait. The bite from a master vampire is often fatal to a howler, though the antidote is the blood from a rare vampire-howler hybrid. From what I have witnessed, you have red fur when you turn, which means that you're an alpha, so you're supposed to be the leader of your own pack. Some howlers are evil, and some are good. The question you want to ask yourself is: What are you? Also, to be in this clan, you have to know where your loyalty and commitment lie."

"Sebastian, I appreciate all the insight you've provided me on some aspects of being a howler. I would be loyal to you and would give my life to support and uphold the honor of this clan," replies Jamal.

Flattered by his remarks, Sebastian replies, "Jamal, it would be an honor to have such a reliable person like you in the clan. I see you can be trustworthy, and I feel you would be the right person to be chosen, so I offer you a membership position. I see your heart is in the right place, but let me see what the rest of the team thinks; I'm sure they all will agree, especially Jenessa."

Chapter 13

As the girls get ready for their night out, they are all at Jenessa's house trying on different outfits and matching different colors with combinations that make them look hot and sexy for girls' night. Persia comes out of the bathroom and says, "The way we are looking tonight, we are going to be fierce. It was really nice of Sebastian to let us borrow the black Mercedes. I don't want to sound so sentimental, but this will be last time we hang out for a while, so let's have a good time; alright, ladies?"

They all start cheering and continue to finish getting ready. Jenessa goes down to the kitchen, and she gets four champagne glasses and a bottle of Henriot champagne. Once everyone comes downstairs to the kitchen, Jenessa has poured four glasses of champagne, and the close friends stand around the table while Jenessa makes a toast, "Ladies, here is a toast to everlasting friendship, the love I have for all of you, and sisterhood as each of you are like a sister to me."

They all touch glasses and drink the champagne. With emotions running high, Jai Li smiles at her best friend and says, "Jenessa, that was a very deep toast; I never knew that you felt that way about us. I want you to know that I love you so much, and no matter what life may bring us or whatever we choose to do, we will always be sisters."

Jenessa smiles at Jai Li with tears in her eyes; she reaches out and hugs her best friend. Chrisha walks in on the sentimental moment, stands back, and says, "So, what's up with the hugs and tears? I guess I'm not involved in this, or is it because I'm not supernatural like everyone else?"

Jenessa turns to Chrisha, looks her in the eyes, and says, "Don't say that. You know we have all been friends since elementary school, so don't trip now. I hate that you're not going with us on the quest, but you get to hang out and chill at Priceless, go out on the town, and go shopping with

Marcella; you better enjoy that. You know that we're going to be calling and sending you videos."

After being reassured of a sisterly bond between friends, Chrisha feels more at ease. Jai Li comes over and hugs Chrisha, and all share some good laughs. Unseen by them, Persia watches with a burning jealousy in her heart over the emotions between the three friends. After another thirty minutes of getting dressed and putting on the finishing touches since the girls planning on it being a night to remember, they leave and head for The Foxhole. While in the black Mercedes headed to Raleigh, the girls laugh and sing to different songs on the radio. With a forty-five minute ride to the club, they will arrive at about 11:55. As the girls pull up to the red carpet at the front door of the club, the valet comes over to the shiny, sparkling black Mercedes to open the doors. As soon as the girls get out, they start to feel like celebrities. They see a lot of people in line trying to get inside of the club. They all walk up to the bouncers, and Persia says to one of the guys, "I need admission for four please."

The bouncer looks at Persia and says, "The back of the line is that way."

Persia sees this as an opportunity to use her power of persuasion on the bouncer, so she lowers her glasses on her nose, looks the bouncer in his eyes and says, "Excuse me, like I said before, my friends and I want to get in the club, and we're not going to the end of the line either."

Her charm works to compel the bouncer. He nods his head and lets the girls through the ropes to get inside the club. Loud music is blasting from inside. Once they go inside, they see all the partygoers having a good time dancing and drinking. They make their way over to the VIP section that has been roped off. Jai Li compels the bouncer to help them get a table, and a bottle of Grey Goose Vodka is brought over to them. As the girls all start dancing at the table, Chrisha says, "This place is nice; let's go down to the dance floor and check out some guys."

They nod their heads and proceed to the dance floor. Once they reach the dance area, suddenly the Dj starts talking over the music, and the partygoers all start yelling and make a Soul Train line. The lights go down, and the Dj starts to play "Crazy in Love" by Beyonce. The stomping and yelling make the club vibrates. Jenessa looks at her friends and sees everyone is having a good time. They clap and dance as the people make their way down the Soul Train line. It is unnoticed by the girls that they are being watched. The hooded young man makes his way through the crowd. Persia and Chrisha dance together, and then Jai Li and Jenessa dance together. Once they get done, they head back to their VIP table, though they get stopped by a couple of guys. The tall guy says, "Excuse me, ladies; I hate to bother you, but we just had to come over and meet you. I don't want to sound too bold, but you girls are very sexy. By the way, I'm Justin, and these guys are Stan, Phil, and Rodney. We're all seniors at NC State University. Where are you girls from?"

Flattered by what the guys are saying, Jai Li responds first, "Hey Justin. I'm Jai Li, and these are my best friends, Persia, Chrisha, and Jenessa. We're from Haven-Crest, and we're here for girls' night out. So, I'm assuming that you guys want to hang out?"

The guys look around at each other, and Stan speaks up, "To be honest, that was the game plan. Can we buy you girl's drinks?"

Chrisha interrupts by being bold and replies, "Sure, you college boys can buy us sexy girls a drink. You guys are welcome to come to the VIP table with us."

The guys all smile and head over to the VIP section, but on the way, the stranger who is watching the girls sees this opportunity to make his move. As he follows in the shadows throughout the club, everyone takes a seat. The drinks come to the table, and they all take shots and chasers. They play a few drinking games, and the girls are having a good time. Then Chrisha stands and says, "Excuse me, everybody; I have to go to the bathroom."

As Chrisha makes her way through the friends to get out, Jai Li says, "Hold up. I'm coming with you."

The two friends make their way through the crowd to the bathroom. They use the facilities, and as they both touch up their makeup, Chrisha smiles and jokes with Jai Li and adjusts her skirt while looking in the mirror. Suddenly, Chrisha sees her reflection in the mirror start to disfigure, and the reflection changes into Jazmine Crenshall. Chrisha's eyes become really big as she becomes frightened; she knows that Jazmine is dead. As the ghostly image hoovers in the reflection, Chrisha becomes too afraid to yell, and Jazmine says, "Chrisha, are you so afraid that you can't call for help? Just beware that we're coming for you. Tell Jenessa that my revenge is imminent. Because of her, this happened to me."

Instantly, the vision vanishes. Chrisha tries to regain her composure before she heads out of the bathroom. Unknown to everyone, as a result of the trauma and near-death experience she sustained due to the gunshot to the neck, she has gained an extraordinary sense: the sense of perception. The definition of perception is the ability to notice or discern things that escape the notice of the human eye. Having made the decision to keep this a secret from everyone, Chrisha endures the ghostly visions. She comes out of the bathroom and heads back over to her friends. Jenessa notices the change in her friend. Once Chrisha takes her seat, Jenessa leans over and says, "Are you alright? You look like you've seen a ghost."

"You can kind of say that I have. We have to talk later, but right now, let's enjoy the rest of the night," replies Chrisha.

They start pairing off and dancing with the college guys. As Chrisha takes a couple more sips of her drink to shake the vision out of her head about Jazmine, the mysterious hooded gentleman makes his way past the bouncer up to her. Once she sets the champagne glass on the table and raises her eyes, she immediately goes into shock over what she sees. Alden Crenshall is standing at the end of the table. He looks at Chrisha and says,

"Hey Chrisha, I know you're surprised to see me. I came by to warn you to be careful because Camden is out to get you. I've been following you trying to make sure that you're okay. I have to go, but like I said, be safe."

As Alden turns to walk away, Chrisha stands up and walks toward Alden, reaches out and grabs his arm, and says, "This must be the Crenshall's night because I just saw your sister in the bathroom. I saw her ghost in the mirror, and yes, I can see dead people. What's wrong with you? Why did you come warn me about your brother?"

"When did all this occur? I didn't know you were clairvoyant or have the perception to see something unique. The reason I warned you is because ahh… well, I care about you and don't want to see Jazmine and Camden hurt you or your friends. My advice to you is to leave here real soon. I overheard him saying that he was coming here tonight," replies Alden.

Chrisha pulls Alden closer to her. They begin to hug, and then Chrisha gives him a soft kiss on the lips and says, "I appreciate you looking out for me, and I care about you too. You be safe, and I'll be in touch with you soon."

Alden makes a dash around the table and heads for the door but not before Jenessa see the hooded gentleman leave. She heads back over to the table to talk to Chrisha when suddenly she notices a loud commotion coming from another table in VIP area. She sees two guys and about six party girls hanging out at the table drinking tequila shots and being very loud. They are beginning to draw a lot of attention due to the girls yelling from the excitement they are feeling. As the Dj plays a slow song to tone down the mood of the club, Persia and Rodney walk back to the table, but as they do, she hears a familiar voice she has not heard in many centuries. Persia focuses her attention throughout the club, and she hears the voice once again. As Persia turns her head, she catches a glimpse of someone she recognizes; she takes a closer look to make sure it's him. Suddenly, her blood begins to boil. Her anger comes to the surface, her true face is exposed, and the vampire is out for revenge. Jenessa and Jai Li see Persia expose her vampire nature to all the unsuspecting innocent people inside the club. They know her intentions are not pleasant; her true conviction is to kill the gentleman in VIP. Persia blurs over to the table with her golden-black eyes and her fangs out, but before the familiar gentleman can speak, she blurs, grabs him by the throat, and then slams him against the walk. With hostility in her voice, she says, "My, my, my, what do we have here? After all these centuries of running and hiding from me, who would have ever thought that I would finally catch you here in Raleigh of all places? Nathan, I could just rip your heart right out of your damn chest in front of all these people."

"Now, now, Persia calm down, you don't want to do that. Do you really want to kill an innocent man in front of all these witnesses? Wait and let me tell you something. You think I did you wrong, but I did care about you. I did what I did because I wanted us to be immortal together. After I bit you, that notion just flew out of the window, especially when I realized that you wanted to rip my head off," replies Nathan.

As Nathan tries to talk Persia down, she doesn't release her grip; it only gets tighter on his throat. Jenessa and Jai Li run up and try to pry Persia's hands away from Nathan's neck. Jenessa tries to talk some sense into her by saying, "Persia, don't do this. A lot of people are staring at us right now. They see you are a vampire, and pretty soon, the police will be here asking a lot of questions. If you won't let him go for yourself, well then, do it for me. Trust me; you'll get your revenge at a later time."

Slowly, Persia begins to release her grip on Nathan's throat but not slowly enough to stop Nathan from taking advantage of the situation. To send a message to Persia, he does a blur and grabs her arm and throws her across some tables. As Persia crashes into the tables onto the floor in VIP, she realizes that she must take full control of this mayhem. Jenessa steps in to help her cousin; she utters a holding spell, and suddenly things begin to get out of hand. Nathan, realizing that he is in grave danger and that retaliation is his key to surviving to see another day, looks for an opportunity to make a run for safety. Jai Li and Chrisha try to calm down the partygoers and control the chaos so they can leave the club. What happens next is just like the scene out of a horror movie. To escape, Nathan attempts to blend into the crowd of people as they try to run for safety. Once Nathan realizes that Persia and her friends have no intention of letting him leave, he takes matters into his own hands and begins killing people by ripping out their throats as they try to get out of the club. As Jenessa sees his eyes turn golden-black and his claws extend out, she knows they must figure out a solution very quickly in order to stop the bloodshed. The girls make their move to try to stop Nathan, but he outsmarts them by creating a diversion. Nathan grabs an innocent young girl. She yells, and he waits for the girls to confront him. Persia, Jenessa, and Jai Li stand in front of

Nathan and the young hostage. Everyone is wondering who is going to make the first move. Nathan decides this is a bargaining opportunity, so he says; "Now, ladies, I have to applaud your effort in trying to keep me from escaping, but I really have an appointment that I'm running late for. I know I didn't have to be this dramatic, but I needed to get your attention. Let's not make this anymore horrible than it has to be. I will let this innocent young lady go if you let me leave; no harm will come to her, I promise."

Jenessa replies eagerly with hopes of saving the life of the innocent young girl. She says, "Nathan, we don't want any more people to get hurt, especially her, so let her go, and we'll let you go unharmed."

"Hell no, Jenessa, I've been tracing this no-good vampire for over a century to get my revenge. If we let him go, I may never get my revenge on him. Let's think about this before we let him go," replies Persia who is being very uncooperative.

Before Jenessa can reply to Persia, Nathan does the unthinkable; he moves in very close to the young girl's neck, smiles at Jenessa, and says, "Ladies, time is ticking away, and you're going to have to make a decision on what you're going to do. Will it be save her or try to kill me? Better yet, let me do that for you."

As the girls watch in suspense at the horrific events that are unfolding, they all are silent, as if frozen in their tracks, and Nathan's actions seem to move in slow motion. He bites into the victim's neck to drink some of her blood, though with reckless intent, he draws his hand back. With his claws out and with a blur, he strikes the young, innocent girl across the throat, literally ripping it apart. Blood splatters everywhere, and her lifeless body collapses to the floor. What puzzles everyone is the not-so-concerned look on Nathan's face, and in disgust, the girls just stare at the now dead body. With the distraction now evident, Nathan makes his getaway to live another day to cause despair and heartache to someone innocent. Now that Nathan is gone, the girls know they will have to answer questions from the police about what happened in this girl's untimely demise. Persia becomes very angry, and without hesitation, she relates her feelings to Jenessa by saying, "Look at what you've done. It is your entire fault that she's dead. I told you to let me finish Nathan off, but doing things the Jenessa way caused all of this."

"Persia, why are you blaming Jenessa? She chose what she thought was the best way to handle this situation; I would have made the same call she did. You really need to back off! It's not our fault you have a century old grudge against Nathan," replies Jai Li.

Jenessa kneels down to the young girl's body and whispers something with an unconvincing smile. She holds onto her hand, tracing circles in her palm, and searches for something to say. Jenessa looks around at her friends with tears in her eyes. As those tears begin to run down her face, she says, "This shouldn't have happened to her, and she did nothing to deserve this. She was just at the wrong place at the wrong time and was killed by a murderer who didn't even know her name."

"I can relate to her situation because I was killed like that, but someone gave me another chance. We can't play God and turn her into something she may never be able to cope with or understand. It's just tragic that this happened. The lesson we learned is that some vampires are like a bad apples; they may look good, but they are rotten to the core," replies Chrisha.

"The best thing we can do now is just get the hell out of here before we get blamed for something we didn't do. I can hear the police sirens coming. Let's see if there is a door in the back so we can go," replies Persia.

They get their purses and head to the back of the club, hoping to find the exit. Persia finds a locked door, and suddenly, there's a loud crash and the door is open. They make a beeline to the Mercedes to head back to Haven-Crest. As they pull around the front of the club, driving very slowly, they see the police and ambulance already on the scene. As Jenessa drives, no words are spoken all the way home. It is unseen by the close friends that they're being watched by Alden as he blends into the crowd of people standing and staring as the police investigate the crime scene. He watches the girls drive out of sight, knowing that what he did will create severe consequences from Camden.

Back in Haven-Crest, Celister works in his office on some reports that have to be turned in to the mayor. The top priority right now is the murder of Simon Ye, a Committee enforcer who was recently killed. Celister looks over notes, reviews the photos that were taken at the crime scene, and documents evidence that was found also. Suddenly, there's a knock at the door. Celister goes to check it out and is stunned to see Det. Karen Macrae on his security camera. He opens the door and says, "Hey, Karen, how are you doing tonight? Is everything alright? You don't look so good; come on in and get out of this cold weather."

Before Det. Macrae can reply, she comes in out of the cold February night. She takes off her coat, sits down in the chair, and says, "Celister, how's it going, old friend? I stopped by to talk you about this Simon Ye case and some other things if you've got the time."

"Karen, we've been friends for a long time, so if there is anything you need, you know you can come to me. To be honest, you look a mess; what's the matter?" replies Celister.

Det. Macrae, realizing that her problem is not getting better, only worse, understands that something has to be done. The nightmares are becoming more real, and now she has visions of certain people. She inhales a deep breath, takes a drink of the coffee, and says to her friend, "Celister, I don't know where to begin. Let's talk business first. What was the cause of death for the victim Simon Ye? I was given this case by the Mayor, so if you know anything, bring me up to speed."

"Well, first let me say that the information I'm about to give cannot be put into your investigation report. This is just between you and me. Take a look at these pictures of Simon Ye; whoever committed this murderous act on him knew what he or she was doing. He has very deep lacerations to his throat, and tissues, muscles and tendons are literally ripped out by something very sharp. He died in the next couple of minutes after he was attacked. What, I'm about to say may send you for a loop. This was done by a vampire, better yet, by a vampire who knows how to attack its victim and kill very quickly," replies Celister.

As Det. Macrae just stares at the pictures of Simon Ye, her mind runs away as she contemplates the comments Celister just made. Her thoughts start to play her nightmare in her mind, and she begins to see the vision of that vampire. Det. Macrae drops her cup of coffee on the floor and turns as white as a sheet.

"Are you alright, Karen?" asks Celister as he looks at his friend with great concern.

Det. Macrae turns to Celister. He gets a towel and starts cleaning up the spilled coffee, and she responds with a dazed look on her face, "I've seen a vampire, and I do believe that he did something to me. Ever since my friend Amy Christian disappeared, I've been having these terrible nightmares, and they are so real that when I wake up, sometimes I have cuts and scratches on my body. I believe that a vampire bit me because I can't remember anything after I left Amy's office to look for the security guard that night. When I came to, the guard was lying next to me on the floor dead. Since then, I've been having these terrible nightmares about a guy; I can't see his face, but I feel him breathing on my neck. The terror that he makes me feel is horrible, and I wake up feeling very disturbed and afraid. People on the force look at me like I'm losing my mind, and I really feel like I am. Lord, what do I do?"

Celister reaches out for Det. Macrae's hands to give her strength. He looks her in the eyes and says, "Karen, don't think that you are in this battle alone. Listen to me; you're not losing your mind. What your subconscious is warning you about is the certain dangers we face as humans. I agree that something did happen to you. As far as what, I can't answer that, but I can put your mind at ease by saying that Haven-Crest does have vampires, howlers, and witches. Before you even think about asking me who the vampires are, I don't know, but I've investigated many recent crime scenes, and the way some people are killed is due to blood loss or trauma to the throat. I have to cover that up so the residents of Haven-Crest won't get in an uproar and start a riot or war here."

Det. Macrae widens her eyes, stunned, and in complete shock over what Celister just told her. Her initial response is to overreact, but she analyzes the information, and a lot of stuff starts to make sense. The majority of the attacks and murders were not animal but simply supernatural. She feels she is on the right track, so she asks, "Now, my questions are: Who ordered the deception, and why is the town so hell-bend on keeping mythical creatures a secret?"

"Well, what may look like a deception to you is helping to save the whole town from these monsters. There are good people who oversee the communities and residents of Haven-Crest. A trustworthy group of people protects the well-being of those in the town. The Committee was established for the purpose of bringing order to this town and preventing chaos. The Committee members' seats of office are passed down through family lineage. The mayor, sheriff, DA, fire-chief, resident doctor, and principal are direct descendants of the original Committee that was created to protect the town back in the 1800s. They are the ones who want Haven-Crest to be relieved of supernatural creatures, which is a good thing. Don't judge them until you understand what they are striving for in the town."

Det. Macrae shakes her head. After tonight, she now believes that there is a reason she has been having these powerful nightmares, which they are trying to tell her something; maybe the message is where Amy is being held captive or who bit her. She stands and hugs her friends and says, "Celister, thanks for the talk and the history lesson about Haven-Crest. I feel more at ease now. You've shed some light on a situation that could have driven me crazy, but now I know where I can come and talk to a dear friend to help keep the monsters at bay. Oh yeah, can I see Simon Ye's body to hopefully close out my case?"

Celister and Det. Macrae both head to the morgue. Once inside, they go to the mortuary's cold chamber. Celister pulls out the drawer with the dead body draped in a white sheet. He pulls back the sheet to display Simon's body and show the injuries and scars. Det. Macrae gets closer to examine the injuries to his neck. She touches the wounds, and suddenly gets a vision. She sees a Lady in White, she sees the attack that led to his death, and she snaps out of her trance and realizes it was just a vision. Celister reaches for her arm to hold her up, and he says, "Karen, are you alright; what happened?"

She pulls herself together and replies, "I saw what happened to him, and I saw who killed him. It looked a like a lady dressed in all white; also, she had long white hair. She ripped out his throat and killed his guards too because blood was everywhere. I can assume she was a vampire, but I couldn't see her face."

"Now do you believe me when I say that vampires really do exist here in Haven-Crest?" replies Celister.

Det. Macrae says nothing; she closes her folder, grabs her purse, and heads for the door to go to her car. Once inside her car, she realizes that after this night, she will never be the same again.

Chapter 14

As soon as the girls pull up in the driveway, they are met outside by Sebastian. He is standing with his arms folded, and he's very upset. Word travels fast in the vampire community, so Sebastian already knows about what happened. Now he wants to hear the girls' side of the story, especially from Jenessa. As they get out of the Mercedes, Sebastian says, "What the hell happened tonight? I heard you ladies were in the club fighting. Anyone want to explain why? Now, there's a murder, and we're leaving in about twelve hours."

"It's not what you think, Sebastian. Nathan Dakota was there. We tried to capture him for Persia, but he began killing innocent people, and he killed the young girl he held hostage. We never meant for any of that to happen," replies Jenessa.

With a confused look on his face, Sebastian responds, "That's the stuff I warn you about that could happen. As innocent as the evening was meant to be, tragedy doesn't exempt anyone. We have to use the right judgments in situations like this in the future. Now explain this for me: Why were you trying to capture Nathan for Persia?"

"Let me answer this. Years ago, that scum Nathan used me, and then he did something evil to me; I always swore I would get my revenge. I attacked him first. The girls were trying to get me to let him go, but revenge and hatred caused me to underestimate him. He took advantage of the situation and killed a lot of people for nothing," explains Persia.

Sebastian looks at the girls as they come in the mansion. By the way they walk past him; he knows they are feeling remorse over the young girl's death. The girls enter the study, and he notices how strange Chrisha looks. Sebastian sits in the chair and says, "Okay, ladies, I hope you have packed for the trip tomorrow. We leave for the airport at ten sharp, so, girls, chop-chop; time waits for no one. Chrisha, could I have a word with you please?"

As the rest of the girls head out to do their packing, Chrisha takes a seat to talk to Sebastian. Sebastian focuses his attention on her and says, "Chrisha, is everything alright? You look like you've been spooked; tell me what happened."

"First of all, let me say that I appreciate everything you've done for me and my family. There's no way I could ever say thank you enough for that. I know I stick out like a sore thumb since I'm the only human person in this Clan, but I enjoy being around everybody. Now, the reason I look so spooked is because ever since my accidental shooting, I have special powers. I never told anyone that I was technically pronounced dead for five minutes, but by some grace of God, I was revived. On that fateful night, I awoke as a new person; to be honest, I came back with a sixth sense. Like in that movie, I can see and communicate with dead people, and tonight at the club, I saw Jazmine Crenshall in the girls' bathroom mirror. She scared me to death, and she gave me a message for Jenessa, which was that she was going to get revenge for what happened to her. I'm so worried about Jenessa; just make sure nothing happens to her, Sebastian. I'm worried about the situation with Camden and his family, and Alden told me at the club that Camden is after Jenessa. I have a bad feeling that they intend to really hurt Jenessa," replies Chrisha.

"You haven't told anyone about this sixth sense? I would tell them; remember that they all told you what they are and what they have become. Be honest with them; they will still love you no matter what. You and your family don't owe me anything. I did everything out of loyalty, and I appreciate all the respect you all have shown to me and my Clan. Don't worry about the Crenshalls. I've got someone keeping an eye on them; overall, they are the least of our problems. There is something I want you to do for me. You can't tell anyone about this, and you should only report to me; I want you to monitor Genie and Edmund. I don't trust Genie, and I definitely don't trust Persia. There's more to them than meets the eye. Don't tell Marcella or Adam about what you're doing, and if you need anything, let me know. I just feel like Genie has a motive and that it's not a good one. As far Persia, there is something strange about her; what is it? Persia gives me a vibe that she's up to something too. I don't trust her. That's why I'm glad she's going along also so I can keep an eye on her. I don't want you to get the idea that I'm not happy for Edmund because I feel he deserves a woman who cares about him, but I think Genie is not the right one for him," comments Sebastian.

Chrisha sits back on the sofa, takes a deep breath, and replies, "Truth be told, I always felt something was fishy when Persia and Genie came to Haven-Crest after all that time. I agree that you that we can't trust either one of them, so I'll keep an eye on Genie while you're gone."

It puts Sebastian's mind at ease knowing that Chrisha will be his eyes and ears while he is away. He has a haunting feeling that something terrible is about to happen and he won't be there to do anything to help, which worries him. Chrisha leaves the mansion headed for home. Once she gets outside, she hears something stirring around in the bushes. She yells, "Who's there? I can hear you. You better say something before ….."

Before she can finish her sentence, something grabs her, and there's total silence. Her keys hit the ground. There's no sign of an apparent attack, and sadly, Chrisha has vanished.

As the cold night goes on, the rain starts to come down very steadily, and in the Haven-Crest cemetery, many of the tombstones project scary images. Suddenly, a dark shadow emerges from behind a sacred cross tombstone in the drenching rain. As the downpour continues, the lone figure stands in front of one particular tombstone. A cold, wet hand reaches out and rubs the cold stone. The individual kneels right in front of the tombstone to pay respect to the late memory of a cherished love one. With the steady rain still coming down, there is a feeling of remorse and loss. A voice sends shivers through the rain like thunder as it says, "Dear brother, I knew I would find you here tonight. You probably come here every year to pay your respect to your dear and beloved father. You were always the sentimental one, the one he loved so much, the one who he idealized and wished to be like him, and the only one who couldn't accept that he was gone and never coming back. If he were still alive, I would kill him myself; that's how much hate I have for him."

"He never did anything to hurt you, only to help you, but you despise him with such hatred. You always felt that you were the outcast, but you weren't. You began running with the bad crowd, so you can't be mad at him for what you did. There are not enough apologies in the world that could make me forgive you. You are my family, so that's why I haven't killed you already. No matter how many times you deceive me, plot against me, or even try to kill me, you are still my family, dear Adrian," replies Sebastian.

Adrian walks up closer to his older brother, who is kneeling in front of their parents' tombstone, and says, "You're such a fool, an immortal, supernatural creature who has so much emotion toward sentimental dates. Me, I've shut off my emotions; I don't have human feelings. I do what I want and don't worry about the repercussions for my actions. You need to do the same, brother, and cut it off. Stop trying to save the world and finding ways to turn yourself back into a human."

As anger starts to boil inside Sebastian, he realizes that Adrian only wants to provoke him into a fight, so Sebastian slowly stands, faces his brother, and says, "Let me ask you a question. Why do you want the book?

For what reasons have you allied with the howlers? I just want to know your motive; what is it you are trying to accomplish out of finding the book. Truth be told, a moron like you can always ally with the wrong crowd, but that doesn't mean that you're going to find the book."

Furious as Adrian's temper has become, without warning, he blurs, grabs Sebastian and slams him against a tombstone with the intent of hurting his older brother. As the rain continues to come down very steadily on the faces of Adrian and Sebastian, the goal of Adrian is to invoke fear in his brother over what he's capable of doing to anyone and everybody. One hand is grasped tightly around Sebastian's neck, and with the other hand, he pulls out a crystal knife. With the most devilish grin on his face, he says, "Dear brother, you probably know what this is; by chance, you may not be able to see it due to the cold rain tonight. It is a crystal knife that has been forged with our only true weakness: Foxglove. Now, if I stab you in the heart, it won't kill you, but only make you comatose until I desire to pull the knife out of your chest. I have one for you and one for our unpredictable younger sister. I think I need to be the ultimate vampire for a while."

As Adrian moves his arm to stab Sebastian, Sebastian looks up at his brother with the most devastated expression on his face. Sebastian realizes that deep down in Adrian's black heart, he really intends to stab him for revenge. Adrian's arm moves as if in slow motion. At the last possible moment, Adrian's neck gets snapped, and he collapses into the muddy puddle onto the ground. Suddenly, the knife falls, and Sebastian raises his eyes up to his savior. To his surprise, he sees Alexia. She smiles at her brother and says, "Sebastian, are you damn crazy? I know you weren't going to let that jackass stab you in the heart with that knife. Were you just trying to lay some kind of trap for our dastardly, corrupt brother?"

Sebastian bends down and picks up the crystal knife, looks at it, looks at his sister, and then replies, "First, let me say thanks for snapping his neck; he needed that. Next, I'm surprised that you even remember what today is, but it's good to see you, Alexia. Even with all the plotting, planning, and people picking sides, we're still family. Let me ask you something; why did you side with Seth Crenshall, the former warlock from England, to try to find the book."

Alexia picks up her umbrella and reaches into Adrian's coat to get the second knife out of his pocket. She examines the knife and says, "This rain has really messed up my hair; better give my hairdresser a call. Why are you all in my business, Sebastian? If everyone is teaming up and choosing sides, then why not me? I'm always looking for the best deal for me, and Seth Crenshall presented the best deal. Being that I'm an opportunist, I couldn't just walk away from this partnership."

"Why? What was the partnership? What do you want to gain by getting the book? Alexia, since you've been back, you have been causing a lot of obvious killings that have gotten the attention of the Committee. Why? Was this a part of your partnership with Seth? I know you've committed two murders, and I'm pretty sure that more bodies will be discovered as the police continue their investigation of the unexplained deaths in Haven-Crest. I know you killed Simon Ye, the Committee enforcer, plus a couple of his guards, and I know you killed Estelle Craig. Why? I know you did this for that damn Seth Crenshall, but he's going to get what's due to him. I'm going to tell you now that you may want to look over your shoulder, the reason being that Jenessa knows that you killed her grandmother, Estelle, and she wants revenge, witch style," replies Sebastian.

"Your friend, the little witch, better know what she's doing. Doesn't she know that we can't be killed and that we are direct vampires of magic? Yes, I killed Estelle. The old witch had to die for what she did to the Crenshall's; I owed it to her for killing Jazmine. An eye for an eye, so we can call it even, dear brother," comments Alexia.

Sebastian doesn't reply. He looks at his sister and knows that her heart is just as black as Adrian's. They ally themselves for selfish reasons and kill for pleasure to show power over the weak. As Sebastian walks away in the rain, he says to his sister, "It was good to see you, Alexia; we need to have another family get together real soon, and good luck on finding the book."

Alexia wipes away the rain from her face, smiles, and heads in the opposite direction, leaving Adrian still lying on the rainy, wet ground with his neck broken.

Chrisha begins to come to and realizes very quickly that she's not at Sebastian's mansion anymore. She sees that her hands have been tied, and her feet are tied up also. She has been gagged so she can't make too much noise. As Chrisha raises her head to get a glimpse at her abductor, he looks up in the rearview mirror and sees her head. The abductor smiles and says, "I see you have woken up, Chrisha. First, I want to apologize for the abrupt kidnapping. I know I startled you when I grabbed you, but to be honest, I know you wouldn't have come if I asked you nicely, now would you?"

Chrisha lies in the back seat listening to her abductor, trying to see if she recognizes his voice. Unable to raise herself up, she looks at the headlights from the passing cars. As the light shines through the windshield, she sees his face, and immediately, her fear level rises. In total shock from grasping the concept of whom her captor really is: Camden, she tries not to let her fear overwhelm her moral judgment. Before she can say anything, she sees a familiar vision from the night club respond to her,

"Chrisha, I told you that we were coming for you. You need not be afraid; you're just a pawn. We need Jenessa for the big prize."

"Jazmine, what is the matter with you? Why are you doing all of this? Is it for that stupid book? Are all you guys crazy? What is this book supposed to do, grant any wish you want? I don't understand why people are killing and kidnapping to get the edge in finding this so-called book," replies Chrisha.

As the car comes to a stop, Chrisha realizes that her life is indeed in more danger than ever before. As the back door opens up, Chrisha looks up as Camden reaches in to pull her out. Once outside the car, Chrisha gets draped with a dark cover, but she sees Seth, Camden, and Alden all trying to rush her inside so no one will see her. Chrisha doesn't fight back; she goes along for right now to save her own life. Seth pulls back the cover, looks at her, and says, "No need for introductions. You know what's going on, so some advice to you is to cooperate and you won't get hurt. Failure to comply will result in injuries to you or your loved ones." Alden takes Chrisha down to the basement, ties her up, and says, "Chrisha, I want to say I'm sorry. I didn't mean for all of this to happen, especially to you. My family is going to the extreme in trying to find this book. You can put your fears to rest; nothing will happen to you while I've got your back. Regardless of what may happen in this stupid ordeal, my family won't hurt you."

Chrisha bats her big, brown eyes at Alden and says, "Alden, I know you're sincere about what you're saying. That means a lot, but your family members are really scary, and I have a deep, dark feeling that they are going to really hurt me or one of my closest friends."

They hug, look into each other's eyes, and then share a brief special kiss. Alden looks at Chrisha and says, "Let me go before I get you in trouble. I'll be back later to check on you; try to get some rest."

As Alden heads back up from the basement, he runs into Seth at the top of the stairs, and Seth says, "Be careful, son; don't let her get inside your head because she knows you care about her. Just watch what you say to her, and see what information you can get about Sebastian and his Clan."

"I'll see what I can do," replies Alden as he heads to his room.

Over at the Carmichaels, Jamal packs his bag for the quest. All day he has been wondering what he is going to tell his mother about him leaving town for a while. The thought of them finding the book races through his mind. What would be a wish he could ask for? Many different topics come to mind like being wealthy, being in the pros, or removing the howler's curse. Karen comes into the room unnoticed by Jamal; she catches him off guard by saying, "Jay, what are you doing? I thought we were going out for dinner tonight? You look like you're packing for a trip of some kind. Where are you going?"

Unsure about what to say, Jamal looks at his mother with doubt in his eyes, grabs her by the hand, and replies, "Mom, you're right; I'm packing for a trip. I have been thinking about how I should tell you this. I'm leaving for a while, but before you become hysterical and stuff, let me explain. I think I need to find myself and figure out who I am. I want to know what my purpose in life is before I head off to college. To be honest, I just need some time alone to see the world and to understand what it is to become a man. I won't get into any trouble, and I will be back home with you in a couple of months. Now, be safe while I'm gone, and don't get married either until I get back."

They both share a good laugh, hug each other, and Karen opens up to her son about her opinion by saying, "Son, I respect that you are a grown up young man. I understand that you want to know about life and find out who you are as a person, and I want you to know that I respect your decision to leave for a while. I'm just concerned, as most any parent of a child leaving the nest would be, but I know in my heart that whatever life has in store for you, you need to explore and embrace it. Now, let's go get some dinner before it gets too late. By the way, when are you leaving?"

Jamal sighs, and replies, "In the morning, Ma, about ten; my flight leaves at noon. I'm sorry it's so sudden, but it's important that I do this now. This opportunity may never come again, and I'll be disappointed with myself for not doing this. I hope you can understand."

With tears in her eyes, Karen sees her son turning into a grown man right before her eyes. She wipes away the tears and says, "I do, son; I really do."

Then, mother and son get into Karen's 2014 Cadillac Seville and head out to Priceless to get something to eat. As Karen begins backing the car out of the driveway, Jamal's senses become alerted. He takes a sniff and notices a strange odor in the air. He realizes that something is not right; his howler animal instincts feel the presence of another howler. Jamal reaches over, grabs the steering wheel, and says, "Wait a second, Mom."

Jamal gets out of the car, surveys the area with his animal instincts, and suddenly, he sees a pair of red eyes staring through the dense bushes at him. Unsure of what to do about the presence of another howler in the area, Jamal takes another sniff in the air, and without warning, a giant solid white howler comes in on Jamal's territory. The white howler knows that in order to make other howlers follow his lead, he must strike fear in all territories, starting with Jamal's, so without even waiting for a show of dominance on Jamal's behalf, the white howler rushes toward the car with

Karen and Jamal inside. As they see the white wolf rushing to the car, Karen starts yelling, "What the hell is that; is it a white big wolf?"

Before Jamal can answer his mother, there's a loud BANG as the white howler crashes into the side of the car. Glass and debris shatter inside the car, and the force from the impact knocks Karen unconscious. As Jamal looks in horror at his mother, his temper begins to flare, and his animal features start changing his appearance. Shocked by the aggressive attack launched by the white howler, Jamal feels his fangs extending and his fingernails growing longer. As a result of this methodical attack, he wants to protect his mother and himself from this intruder. Jamal opens the door and doesn't issue any sign of retaliation to the white howler. It stands about ten feet from the car, but Jamal makes no effort to attack the intruder. He just stares back at the white howler. At the blink of an eye, the white howler begins growling and snarling at Jamal as though it is ready for round two; then it is uncanny that it just leaps back into the bushes and is gone.

"Jamal, what are you doing? What going on? What happened?" replies Karen.

Jamal doesn't reply. He just keeps checking to make sure everything is alright. He gets back into the car and verifies that his mom is not hurt. He looks at his mom and says, "Are you okay; did you get hurt by the shattering glass? I don't see blood anywhere; do you want to go to the hospital?"

"My neck is just a little stiff. Other than that, I'm okay. Are you hurt? Why aren't you answering my question? What was that? It looked like a giant white wolf; I've never seen a white wolf before. We need to call Ross and let him know what happened. Let me call Dr. Burton just to check out my neck," replies Karen.

Jamal is unaware that Karen came to before he got back to the car; she saw his partial animal features and witnessed his claws and the wild facial features also. As Jamal drives to the hospital, he wonders who the white howler is and why it attacked him. He listens to his mom talk to Sheriff Michaels and agrees to meet them at the hospital. Jamal knows in his heart he's doing the right thing by mending broken fences with his Mom, the DA in Haven-Crest, before he leaves for the quest.

After their arrival at the hospital, they get out and head inside to see Dr. Burton. They both head to the front check-in desk, and the night duty nurse says, "Good evening, can I help you; are you hurt in any way?"

"We need to see Dr. Burton, please. Is he on call tonight?" replies Karen.

The front desk night nurse reaches for her phone and pages Dr. Burton. She hands Karen the clipboard with forms she needs to fill out, and Karen takes the papers and starts filling them out in the waiting area. About ten minutes later,

Dr. Burton comes in the waiting area to see Karen. He takes a seat and says, "Hey, Karen. What's going on; are you ill? Is everything alright?"

"We need to talk to you in private. You're not going to believe what happened to us tonight, Marion. I'm okay; I just have a few cuts and scratches on my face," replies Karen.

Dr. Burton pulls up a stool, gets the alcohol and some cotton balls, and begins to clean her wounds up. Jamal just stands in the back watching the doctor clean up his mother's injuries from the attack. Without them watching, Jamal sends Sebastian and Jenessa a text to inform them of what happened tonight. Dr. Burton gets Karen cleaned up, and then he says, "Now that you're cleaned up and relaxed, tell me what happened to you. How did you get these scratches?"

"Well, Marion, Jamal and I were heading out to dinner, but when we came out of the house and began to drive out of the driveway, Jamal noticed something in the yard. Let me tell you that this was the biggest damn white wolf I've ever seen in my life. Something I noticed was rather odd; it attacked as though it was trying to claim its territory, and it just rushed my car. Then Jamal got out, and suddenly, the wolf ran off. You can believe me when I say this was a premeditated attack," replies Karen.

As Dr. Burton sits in awe at what Karen has just told him, he knows that a meeting may be in order to inform the rest of the Committee about a possible giant howler on the loose. Suddenly, Sheriff Michaels and Agent Ambrose enter Dr. Burton's office. Sheriff Michaels looks at Karen's face and says, "What happened to you, Karen? Are you alright?"

"Yeah, I'm fine, but we need to call a meeting tonight; I think we have a howler on the loose in Haven-Crest. I saw one tonight, and, trust me, he was big as hell," replies Karen.

Sheriff Michaels pulls out his phone and begins sending texts to the other members. Jamal watches his mother and wonders what she meant by saying, "Call a meeting tonight." Jamal walks over to his mother and says, "Mom, are you sure you're alright? I'm going to call Jenessa to come pick me up, so I'll be alright. I'll talk to you when you get home."

Karen stands up, reaches out to hug her son, and replies, "Don't leave before I get back because I do want to see you before you take off tomorrow. Hopefully, this won't take long."

"Mom, let me ask you something; what is the Committee?" asks Jamal.

As if swallowing a rock, Karen, unsure about what to say to her son, looks around the room at the sheriff, Dr. Burton, and Agent Ambrose, but she plays it off by saying, "We'll talk about that later; let me go."

Karen and the rest of the members leave Dr. Burton's office headed to the meeting hall. Jamal pulls out his phone and calls Jenessa to come pick him up from the hospital. As Jamal waits for Jenessa, the attack from the white howler runs through his mind like a movie, and he can sense that something sinister and evil is coming.

At party central, the condo belonging to Adrian Kane in the upscale area of Haven-Crest, the associates of Adrian, including Nathan, Andre and Candice, are having a little feeding party. Innocent young girls and guys are the victims being fed upon by these vampires. With the music blasting from the speakers, people are dancing and having a good time. Without warning, the double doors fly open, and a very pissed off and wet vampire, whose golden black eyes and fangs are out, appears. Right now all Adrian sees is red. As he makes his way through the crowd of people over to his associates, Candice raises her head from draining some blood from a young victim's wrist and says, "Hey Adrian; what happened to you? You look like you've been through hell; are you alright?"

With the most despicable facial expression Adrian can come up with, he raises his face and says, "This has been one of the worst nights in history for me; first, I am soaking wet from this hellacious rain, and second, I attempted to comatose my brother, but I ended up getting my neck snapped by my God forsaken devilish witch sister, Alexia. To make this situation more devastating, one of my associates attacked the golden goose Jenessa and her friends at a shady night club, and a young girl at the club was killed. For what reason, why, would you attack and kill an innocent girl? By the way, where is Nathan?"

No one says a word; they all just continue to feast on the innocent victims at the party. Feeling that no one is showing him the proper attention he deserves, suddenly, Adrian shouts, "I'll be damned if I'm going to be ignored by my associates. Where the hell is Nathan?"

With the authority being shown by Adrian, Andre speaks up and says, "Nathan is in the game room. What has he done now?"

"Now, was that freaking hard to do? All I asked is for someone to speak up and keep me out of the dark. Andre, I appreciate you being loyal to me. As a reward, this is a token of my honor to you," comments Adrian.

With that said, Adrian spots out the sexiest young lady at the little party. He walks over to her, looks into her beautiful hazel eyes, and compels her by saying, "You will not yell; you will obey my every request. Nod if you understand my request."

The young girl obeys Adrian; she nods to comply with him. Adrian gives a devilish smile and says, "Go over to Andre and let him feed from your wrist. Let him enjoy the delicious nectar that runs through your veins."

She obeys the command that she has received; she turns and heads over to Andre, takes a seat on the couch next to him, holds out her wrist and says, "Adrian says I'm a present for you."

Andre reaches over, grabs her wrist, extends his fangs, reveals his black golden eyes, and proceeds to bite on her wrist. Andre stops before he drains her of all her blood. Adrian grabs a towel, dries off his face, and heads into the game room. Suddenly, the doors swing open, and being caught off guard by the blur into the room, quickly, Nathan jumps to his feet and tries to blur out of the room. However, he's met by a force stronger that his own, and the grasp around Nathan's neck feels like a vice grip by a pair of pliers. All he can feel is himself being thrown against the wall like a rag doll. Nathan soon sees the sheer anger in his eyes. Barely able to speak, he utters, "What have I done? Why are you doing this?"

Adrian just looks at Nathan straight in his face, eye to eye, and says, "Now, of all the places to go have a good time at, you and a couple of guys go to Raleigh, and then to top that off, you get into a fight with Jenessa. From what I was told, it was over a girl named Persia. There were witnesses, and a couple of people, including a young girl, got killed tonight. Why? You need to explain all of this to me."

Adrian releases his grip from around Nathan's neck so he can explain himself. Nathan clears his throat and says, "Yeah, I was at the club, and I know I took things a bit too far, but it was three to one against me getting out alive. I had to make sure I survived by any means necessary. Now, the girl, Persia Fredrick, is related to Jenessa; she's her cousin; her mother, Genie, is Estelle's sister. I met them in a village in Black Diamond, Florida. I was still traveling with a young clan of vampires, and we were passing through. At that time, I still did not fully understood what I had transitioned into, and I was still learning to control the hunger and lust of being a vampire. Once we came to this village, we were smitten by the beauty of the women who resided there, and they were intrigued by us since we were newcomers to their town. After about a month, I met an innocent but very beautiful young witch named Persia, and we became very close. After a few weeks, we fell in love. I realized I wanted her to be with me forever, yet I made the biggest mistake in my life. This time in history was after the witch trials from Salem that had witches on the run and migrating to different states to start new covenants and alliances. Unknown to a lot of people, the witch lineage that runs in Jenessa's family tree is very powerful. Estelle was a very powerful and respected witch, but Genie's magic wasn't as powerful due to the fact that their father had an affair with another woman, and they kidnapped the baby once she had it to keep the secret from getting out. That's one of the reasons why Genie and Estelle weren't that close. During my time with Persia, I learned many witch secrets. Persia told me that when she turned eighteen, she was going to transcend into a powerful coven of witches to protect the area plus the village. We were told of an old wise tale about a transcending witch being able to channel all this power, but in the same instance, someone had to be sacrificed for the ritual. A dying witch's spirit would be needed in the transformation, and her essence would help make the young witch very powerful. Persia had a conscience, and she didn't want to sacrifice a witch for more power. Her first intention was to run away, but I convinced her to let me help her in ways she could never imagine. A couple of days before her eighteenth birthday, I revealed to her the way I was going to help her. I showed and told her I was a vampire, and she overreacted as I figured she would. She threatened to reveal me to the elders of the village, so to shut her up, I bit her and turned her into a vampire, which immediately stopped her clock so she couldn't transcend. I took her to her house and fled, and I've been on the run from her and her mother ever since until tonight. If she's here with her mother, then that means that they are up to something that is no good. That means someone's in danger and is going to die."

Adrian pours a drink, rubs his chin, and downs the shot in the glass. He reaches and pats Nathan on the shoulder and says, "I wonder if my dear brother knows this about Persia and her mother, Genie. Rumor has it she's taken a fancy to Edmund; I hear they're getting very close."

Both evil vampires laugh at the sarcastic joke, and they head out of the room back to the feasting party to have their fill of some innocent blood from the crowd that has gathered.

On that note, Edmund has come over Genie's, and they're both sitting on the couch sipping on some wine and looking into each other eyes. Genie has slipped into a sexy lounging gown. Edmund sits and admires her beauty by saying, "Genie, you are a very beautiful witch; it has been a long time since I felt this way about a woman. I just find you so amazing, and I enjoy spending time with you."

Genie smiles at the comments made by Edmund; she takes a sip of the wine and replies by saying, "Edmund, I don't know what it is about you. It has been a long time since I've felt this way about any man. Of all the men in the world, I fall for a vampire, a witch's mortal enemy, but times have changed; you can fall for anyone now, no matter what they are. You've asked me so many questions about myself, but tell me something about you. Did you have family, and when did you become a vampire?"

Edmund blushes. He also takes a big gulp of the wine, chuckles, and says, "What do you want to know? Well, I'm from a town called Northport near Washington, DC. It was a very small town and one of those places where everybody knew everybody else. My parents owned the only market in the town, so they definitely knew everyone. I was born in 1894 and was the only child, so I grew up working in the family business until my parents got murdered. I was working late that night on the payroll; my parents left, but my mother forgot her purse. They came back into the store, and someone or something followed them. All I heard was a big commotion and my mom yelling. By the time I came from out of the office, all I saw was a pool of blood and their throats ripped out. I knew no one would believe me if I told them what I thought I saw. As I stood there watching, a creature devoured my parents' bodies as well as their souls. I can't forget its face; a vampire killed them. As I stood there frozen in fear and unable to move, I watched the creature drink their blood. I knew that the creature was going to kill me, but it didn't; it turned, saw me, and blurred away. Once the police came to investigate the crime scene, there were so many questions, so I lied and said that two masked men robbed and killed them. I was unaware that my folks had a big insurance policy and had made some big investments. When I turned in the policies, I became very rich. I still lived in Northport and eventually married my high school sweetheart, Angela Jensen, and we had two children: a daughter, Carla, and a son, Justin. I thought I was the luckiest man on Earth to have a family that happy. I loved my wife, my kids, and all the people who knew me. I went on a business trip to Georgia; it was in Marietta. After the meeting, I went sightseeing in the town and got lost. Little did I know I was being followed, but later I came to know the extent of the danger I was in. Suddenly, I came to a clearing in the woods, and I was immediately surprised by what was following me. I heard a loud growl, and on cue, a pack of howlers come into the clearing. Quickly, I grabbed a broken tree limb to use as a club to try to fight off the pack. I realized that it was either going to help me or get me killed. The leader of the pack slowly began moving to me while the other two started circling in opposite directions, waiting for their opportunity to strike. I thought if I took out the leader first before he could make his initial attack on me, maybe then the other two may retreat to save themselves. I swung the club with all my might, and WHAM, the leader went down; however, the second part of my plan didn't go as planned. The other two attacked. I swung the club to hit the one on the right, but it hit the back of my thigh. Then I went down, and they both jumped me. As they were biting and trying effortlessly to rip out my throat, suddenly, they both stopped and quickly ran away. I was lying half mauled on the ground and still bleeding, and at a distance, I saw a figure walking toward me. He leaned over top of me and said I was dying from the attack and he was going to help me survive. He warned me that when I awakened, I would never be the same and would look at life in a whole new light. Then I blacked out and could feel myself drifting away, and I felt his fangs dig into my neck. Once he released the venom into my system, it felt like I was on fire. I died, but I awakened three days later in a hotel room. That's when I met the figure in the woods, and it was Sebastian. I hated him for what he did to me, but I accepted the fact that he saved my life. The consequence is that I would have to leave my family due to what I had become. I called my family to let them know that I was alright, and I would be home in a couple of days. To my surprise, when I returned home, a vampire had attacked and killed my family. My wife had her throat ripped out, and so did Carla. Amazingly, my son survived, but he was very weak from the attack. I made the decision to save his life by biting him and making him my first vampire, but once he resurrected in three days and I explained to him that in order to save him I had to kill him to make him immortal, he hated me for not trying to save his mother and sister. He also hated me for not being there to protect them. He retaliated and blurred away, and I never heard from him again; Sebastian and I looked for him for years, but we never found him."

Genie looks at Edmund and says, "Wow, I would never have thought that about you. You really must miss him; I'm amazed that you haven't found him by now."

Edmund sets his glass back on the table, looks at Genie, smiles, and says, "I know sometimes I stare, but I can't help it because you're so beautiful. Your beauty just draws me to you like a moth to a flame."

Genie begins to blush, but she sees this opportunity to take this relationship to the next level and does the unthinkable. She raises her sexy gown and saddles Edmund on the couch. With his eyes exploring all of her clothed body, he looks her deep in her eyes, and they say nothing. Rather, they let actions speak instead of words. Genie leans close to Edmund's lips. She gives him a sexy look with her gorgeous brown eyes. They both give into their desires. She starts unbuttoning Edmund's shirt and digging her manicured nails into his chest, putting long scratches on his skin. As the blood runs down, she proceeds to lick it. He responds by caressing her sensuous thighs. Their emotions are running high and blood pressures are rushing through the roof. Edmund's vampire features begin to become exposed to Genie. She stops and proceeds to rub the golden black veins under his eyes. Edmund turns away, and Genie says, "Please don't turn that magnificent face from me. I have fallen for the man you are, not the vampire you have become."

Edmund turns and faces Genie with his fangs extended out, and they begin kissing once again. This time it's more intense as Edmund gives in to his sexual urges and rips open Genie's gown to expose her naked body.

He caresses her body from head to toe; Genie pushes him over on the couch, snatches off his belt, and pops the button on his pants, and all the fun begins. Unknown to Edmund, while Genie is digging her fingernails into his chest, they are laced with Foxglove. After they finish and Edmund begins putting on his clothes, he suddenly starts to feel ill. He's unsure why, but he doesn't press the issue. They see a breaking news special on the TV, and Edmund says, "Genie, can you turn the TV up, please?"

Genie reaches for the remote, turns up the volume, and the announcer says, "This is Jewel Walker with Channel 2 News here in Haven-Crest at the Memorial Hospital; last night I brought you an exclusive breaking news story at ten about the two mountain climbers who went missing about a week ago. Luckily, they were found alive, or I should say barely alive due to some of the injuries they sustained. What I've learned from one of the ambulance attendants is that the gentlemen has been mauled and has a lot of injuries, and the female is in fair condition with injuries also. They have been braving the elements while they were lost in the wilderness. Their names are being held by the police until their immediate family members have been notified. Once I get more information about this case, I will relay it on to the viewers. Now, back to Joshua and Ashley in the Channel 2 newsroom."

While everyone in the emergency room runs around in a frenzy, it is sheer chaos and pandemonium with police, doctors, and nurses trying to help the young victims with their injuries. Doctors Jensyn and Barton hurry to the emergency room to provide assistance. They check on the gentleman first. Dr. Barton pulls back the curtain, and they both come into the room. As both doctors look at the near death injuries of the victim, Doctor Jensyn speaks first, and ask two questions before he starts examining the patient, "Sir, do you know where you're at now? Do you know your name?"

The patient lies back on the table with his eyes rolled back into his head. Dr. Barton opens his shirt and puts the stethoscope on his chest to check his heartbeat. In a very low whisper, the patient says, "I'm in the hospital. I've been lost in the woods for a week trying to make it home. My name is Ryan Morrow. My girlfriend is Kimberly Sutton, and we were hiking and got lost."

"Ryan, if you can understand me, can you tell me what happened? If you don't have the strength, then we'll do it later. Right now, I'm going to start dressing some of your wounds so I can get you more comfortable," replies Dr. Jensyn.

Dr. Jensyn reaches over to the hospital tray to get some alcohol and cotton balls to start the cleanup. He gets a sterilized needle and starts stitching some of the wounds. Suddenly, Ryan's body begins to buck, and he starts shaking non-stop. Dr. Barton sees a wound that looks like it's already starting to heal. The bed continues to shake; the doctors believe Ryan maybe having muscle spasms or a seizure. Out of nowhere, Ryan lets out a loud growl, and his eyes turn a glowing red. Slowly, Ryan sits up in the bed. They both take a step back from the bed. The nurse across the hall screams in fear. The doctors look at one another, and Dr. Jensyn reaches for the scalpel off the tray to use for protection. Both doctors know what is going on, but neither intends to elaborate to the other. As Ryan gets up off the table, Dr. Barton realizes that something has to be done before matters get out of hand. The ladies are on the other side of the curtain yelling because Kimberly is doing the exact same thing and is trying to attack the nurses.

Ryan continues to growl at the doctors. Dr. Jensyn knows he needs to subdue the patient to get him under control before someone gets hurt. He makes a move, but Ryan knocks the scalpel out of his hand. Ryan then charges him and swings his claws deep into his lower neck. Blood spews out from the gash. Dr. Barton jumps in and tries to distract Ryan. Dr. Jensyn goes down, and Ryan knocks the tray with the supplies on it over.

Ryan says to both doctors, "He's coming, and you're all going to die. Be warned."

Ryan starts to attack Dr. Barton. As he is about to bite him, Dr. Jensyn jumps up and snaps his neck. Ryan's lifeless body hits the floor like a rock. Dr. Barton runs over to Dr. Jensyn to check on his status. To his surprise, he sees what he can't believe; he sees a lot of blood on Dr. Jensyn's neck and on his doctor's coat. Dr. Barton moves his hand and says, "Are you alright? You're lucky that guy didn't kill you. Let me examine your neck. What the hell…?"

Before Dr. Barton can say what he sees, Dr. Jensyn grabs him by the throat, slams him against the wall, and says, "Dr. Barton, you know a lot about what's going on, much more than you lead on. You saw that my neck has healed; now, realistically, you can put two and two together to figure out what I am. I'm a vampire. Excuse my manners, let me introduce myself; I'm Syngyn, the hunter."

Dr. Barton is speechless at this very moment, looking at Syngyn with his golden black eyes and his fangs extended. Dr. Barton is so afraid right now that he actually thinks he's about to die. He tries to reason with Syngyn for his life. He replies with anger in his voice, "Kareem or Syngyn, I'm in shock right now. I would never have guessed in a million years you were a vampire. You know you can't kill me. I thought we were friends; you know I'm an original member of the Committee, and you know I despise vampires. We need your services to help with some vampire issues of our own."

Dr. Barton begins to rub his throat once Syngyn releases him. With the nurses still yelling, Syngyn says, "Before we talk, let me take care of this. I'll be right back."

Syngyn blurs through the curtain to the next room. He confronts Kimberly with his vampire features exposed, and he says to her, "Why are you here? I'm going to give you a choice: Tell me who turned you into howlers, or I'll kill you like I did your boyfriend, Ryan."

Slowly, Kimberly starts converting back into her human form, but with the injuries she has endured, she's on the verge of passing out. Suddenly, Kimberly collapses on the floor, and both doctors rush to her aid and help get her to the bed. They both work to get her vital signs stable so they can ask her some questions. After about an hour of working her on her wounds and injuries, she is ready to answer some questions from the doctors. Syngyn asks the first set of questions, "How did you become a howler? Who bit Ryan and you?"

Kimberly clears her throat and replies, "Well, Ryan and I were going hiking in the woods, and we got lost. Our phones couldn't get a signal, so we scrambled around trying to find our way out of those woods. We saw something, moving and came to find out that it was a big white wolf. It attacked and bit us; after that, we thought we were dead, but when we awoke, we realized that we were not the same any more. Then we saw the wolf turn into a man. He instructed us on what we had to do; something I find very strange is that I can't remember what he looked like, but I do recall his name: Antoine. The message is; to tell Dr. Barton to inform the Committee that he is coming, and no one is going to survive."

Syngyn looks at Dr. Barton and says, "I've heard a lot about Antoine. He is supposed to be the one who created us all. I've also heard that he's one very vicious vampire when he can't get his way."

Dr. Barton knows things are now getting out of hand. He realizes that Haven-Crest is now becoming the home of all mythical creatures who are trying to take over. Now that he knows that all these months, he was used by Syngyn or Dr. Jensyn to learn what he could about the Committee. The burning question now is: What do we they do? Should they dance with the devil or lose all their lives to Satan himself?

"What are you going to do now? Are you going kill me? Please, I don't want to die; I can help you," replies Kimberly.

Syngyn rubs his chin, knowing that if she can't remember what Antoine looks like, then he must compel her to forget a lot of things he instructed them to do.

Dr. Barton intervenes in the conversation by saying, "Syngyn, I know you're not going to kill her. Even though she's a howler, she could still be of use to us. I need to alert the others about what we have here and definitely take her somewhere so she won't be seen."

Suddenly, Agent Ambrose and Sheriff Michaels come into the emergency room with their guns drawn looking for the earlier commotion. After some serious debriefing in Dr. Barton's office on the situation, Dr. Barton drops a bomb on the two of them by saying, "Now that I kind of let you in on the specifics, here comes the gut punch. My resident doctor is Syngyn the hunter. Dr. Kareem Jensyn is a vampire, and we have a howler that has been turned by some legendary vampire called Antoine who has taken residence in Haven-Crest."

They both go silent. Agent Ambrose immediately goes into shock at what she just heard, and she replies, "Did you just say Antoine is here in Haven-Crest? I've heard a lot of tales about him, including how ruthless he can be and also to how vicious he is. We may want to start patrolling the area where we found them to see if we can get any lead on him. Better we start now than to have him get the jump on us. If this guy here is Syngyn, why hasn't he revealed himself before now, and what is his motive? Is he going to help us kill the mythical creature problems or just create a whole new type of chaos?"

"This is definitely a Committee type of discussion here, so call the troops, and let's get our heads together to see what we've got to do. Now, what we need to do is get this girl out of here and to a safe haven," replies the sheriff.

The sheriff and Agent Ambrose head out first to get the squad car positioned at a door so they can sneak Kimberly out past the news reporters and hospital people. Dr. Barton heads to Jewel Walker from Channel 2 News to make a statement to the press. "Before I begin, let me say that the Town of Haven-Crest appreciates and thanks all the people who participated in the search for the two missing hikers. Their names have not been released to allow time for the families to be notified of the rescue. I'm sorry to inform everyone that due to injuries sustained in the ordeal, we lost one of the hikers. Their injuries and wounds were more severe and profound than we imagined, so the sole survivor will be transported to a rehab facility when her condition becomes more stable. Now, will there be any questions?"

Jewel Walker responds first, "Jewel Walker with Channel 2 News here; Dr. Barton, you spoke of one of the hikers dying from injuries sustained prior to being rescued. Can you speak on what those injuries were? What caused them to get lost in the first place, and with the modern technology we have today, shouldn't it have been easier to locate them?"

"Jewel, I can't release that information just yet until the coroner comes in and does the autopsy. The only thing I can say on that is some of the injuries were from hyperthermia and dehydration, but there were some other injuries. I can't say what the initial cause of death was. Now, I have to go prepare the paperwork, so the hospital administrators will answer the rest of the questions. You all have a good night," replies Dr. Barton.

Dr. Barton walks away and heads to his office. The sheriff and Agent Ambrose take Kimberly out through the side door to an undisclosed location.

Chapter 15

Nicolette sits in her office talking on the phone to her contacts in the field who probably can help her. She works feverishly to get a lead on Sebastian and his Clan. With her luck, she is not generating the results she sorely needs, so Nicolette becomes very distraught, angry, and unbearable. She soon comes to realize that she may need to consort with the true devil Adrian to help her. She comes out of her office and says, "Donna, I need my top notch hackers to get to work plugging into surveillance feeds all around town and checking any video cameras also. We need to find Sebastian and see where he's going."

With that said, Sean and Susan both get to use their expertise in the field of security surveillance to follow Nicolette's orders. Nicolette looks around and replies, "Where are Donna and Erika? Has anyone seen them today?"

Sean speaks up, "I haven't seen them; I don't think they have arrived yet."

Not far away at a local Dunkin Donuts, Erika and Donna sit at a cozy table having a very deep discussion. Erika says, "Donna, have you made your decision about becoming a vampire yet? Is there anything else you need to know or want me to explain to you?"

Donna takes a sip of her coffee, bites her donut, and replies, "Erika, I know what I want to do, but I'm having trouble accepting the fact that I'm going to become a killer who murders people for blood. My conscience is winning the battle of me doing the right thing; however, I do like that there are perks to being a vampire. For one, the immortality would be nice. I want to be the best computer expert known to mankind. Is anything wrong with that?"

Erika looks at her friend, smiles, and responds, "Don't look at it as being selfish, just as achieving a goal. I recall I didn't have a choice in the matter of becoming a vampire; it was for survival and revenge. About twenty years ago, before I left for the bright lights and big city, I grew up a small, poor town in Tennessee. My family consisted of me, my younger brother and sister, and my parents. My mom helped out at the local restaurant part-time. My father worked two jobs, and he would drink away what little money we had after paying bills. Then he would come home drunk and start fights with my mom, plus he would chase after loose women from the local liquor house. A few nights after I graduated from high school, he went out drinking with his friend Roger who was like an uncle to us. They returned later on drunk, and soon my parents got into a shouting match. My mom calmed my dad down, and he went to sleep. My folks thought that Roger had passed out drunk, but he waited until they were asleep and came into my room and raped my sister and me. The next day when we confronted our parents, they thought that we were lying about Roger, so nothing was ever done about the shameful ordeal. I never felt I could trust anyone after that night. My sister, on the other hand, came to terms with what happened in her own way; she started hanging out, drinking, and smoking pot with the older crowd. She started dating older men as a result of that experience. After I left town and went to college, my brother joined a gang; a couple of months later, he got killed in a drive-by from a rival gang. Two weeks after that, my mom took an overdose from having to have to deal with my father's addictions, and she died. My junior year in college was the turning point in my life. I met a guy, and I was in love for the first time. I got a call from my father that my sister had gone missing, and no one had seen her for about a week. I came home and helped the whole town look for her. During this time, a gypsy carnival was in town, and the local sheriff thought that she had run off with one of the workers. I went to the carnival hoping that I would find her, but the only thing I found was trouble in the worst way: death. I asked a couple of people if they had seen her. A woman told me to go see Nadya, the fortune teller, so I listened. I paid the fortune teller fifty dollars to help me. She told me what I didn't want to hear. She said my sister had been killed and that it had been done by a man she knew, plus she revealed where he had hidden her body. She grabbed my arm and warned me that she saw a dark figure following me, and this journey would be my last. I didn't take heed to the warning. I wanted closure, so I went to where the body was hidden. Nadya was right; she was dead, but the dark figure had followed me. As I was about to leave, someone grabbed me from behind and knocked me out. When I came to, I saw that my abductor was someone I knew: Roger. After everything else he did to us, now he had done the unthinkable, which was to murder my little sister. I yelled, but I knew no one could hear me. Roger was bragging about killing my sister. He pulled out his knife and told me that the demons weren't going to let him have peace until he killed both of us, so he stabbed me a couple of times really deep. I could feel the blood rushing out of me from the wounds; everything was getting black, and it was getting hard to stay conscious. I couldn't believe what I saw next. The form of a woman came up behind Roger; it was Nicolette, and she grabbed him and snapped his neck. She told me that the only way to save me was to bite me. Since I was only half conscious, I didn't realize she bit me and turned me into a vampire. I never turned back; I left Tennessee and haven't returned to this day. If this is what you want, do what you feel; trust me, you won't regret it."

Donna sits speechless staring at her friend and is unsure about what to say. Their conversation gets interrupted by a phone call from Nicolette. Ericka answers, "We're on our way now; we just ran out and got some coffee."

Erika hangs up, looks at Donna, and says, "Here's piece of advice; if you decide to become a vampire, make sure the person who turns you is someone you can share the link with unlike my situation. I'm grateful for Nicolette saving my life, but truth be told, I hate that bitch with a passion. If you want to, let me be the one who transitions you to immortality."

"Out of everyone I've met, you would be the only one I would consider turning me to a vampire and showing me the proper way of adjusting to blood," replies Donna.

They both get their purses and cups of coffee and head to Donna's car. After the long conversation with Erika, Donna realizes that her decision is pretty much made; the question now is: When will the day occur? Donna's thoughts of transitions fade away as she focuses on the security surveillance she needs to do when she returns.

The smell of bacon and eggs fills the air at the Crenshall's home. Alden has prepared breakfast for the girl he has become smitten with. He walks up to the basement door, unlocks it, and proceeds to bring Chrisha her breakfast inside. Alden notices that Chrisha is still sleeping, so he sets the food on the table and walks over to the cot. He kneels down and moves her hair out of her face. Chrisha blinks and yawns as she sees Alden and also smells the food. She jumps up and says, "God, I'm hungry, but first, I've got to pee. Where's the bathroom?"

Alden, being the perfect gentlemen, walks with Chrisha to the bathroom. He stands outside of the door while she uses the bathroom, and once they return back to the basement, Chrisha comments on her freshly prepared plate by saying, "Alden, that plate sure does smell good. To be honest, I've never had a guy cook for me or even bring me breakfast before; you're the first. I guess that makes you special. I'll bet you do this in England for all the girls to flatter them, but on a serious note, why have I been kidnapped? I don't pose a threat to anyone. I'm a normal girl; I have no powers, and I don't turn into anything."

Alden smiles at first but then quickly turns his facial expression serious and responds to what Chrisha said, "I'm glad you like it, and you're the first girl I've every cooked for. You can tell I'm shy around girls, although I find something special about you. I guess it's the honesty you show me. You're like a diamond in the rough; once it has been cleaned up, it becomes the most gorgeous thing one will ever see. Now, as far as why you, I don't know. All I can say is…they are obsessed with finding this Book and what it can do for them. I can tell you this: They are going to bargain your life for the Book. I hate to be the bearer of bad news, but you want me to be honest."

As Chrisha eats her breakfast, a few questions come to mind, and she says, "Damn, this French toast is good; let me be the first girl to tell you, Alden, that yes, you can cook. Since you are being straight up, let me ask you this. What happens if Sebastian and Jenessa don't find the Book? Then what happens to me?"

"Don't let that bother you; I've got your back. Nothing is going to happen to you if your friends don't find the Book. Relax, you're safe; you're just here as a bargaining chip," replies Alden.

Chrisha continues to eat, but her focus is now on Alden's emotions. Unknown to Alden, Chrisha has her own objective.

"Alden, the last thing I remember is being knocked out at Sebastian's, so where are my car, and my phone, and what about my parents? I'm sure they're worried sick about me. I hope you have all bases covered because my friends will notice I'm missing," says Chrisha.

Alden starts to look uncomfortable, but he looks at his sexy captive and replies, "Chrisha, I went back and brought your car here. I have your phone. Lastly, I texted your parents to let them know you're going to the beach with Jenessa and Jai Li, so pretty much I've covered all the bases at least for right now. Remember when you told me that you were normal? I know you're lying because we can see and speak to Jazmine, and she informed us that you can contact people in the hereafter. This was a gift you received after you were shot a while back. Let me ask you this: Why don't you join us? We could use someone with your talents; do any of your friends know about this?"

"Why do you want me to join your family? What do you have that my friends can't offer me? I like you a lot, Alden, but don't get it twisted; I will never go pick a guy over my friends and family," replies Chrisha.

Their conversation gets interrupted by Seth yelling for Alden. He stands, gets Chrisha's plate, and turns for the door. Chrisha stands and takes a step toward Alden. He turns to say something, but Chrisha grabs him and they kiss. Then, Alden says, "Wow, I needed that. I'll be back. Let me see what he wants."

"After what you did for me, you can have that and more," replies Chrisha.

Alden smiles, walks out of the basement, locks the door, and heads upstairs to see Seth. At the top of the stairs, Seth stands with his arms folded, and his first reply to Alden is "Where the hell have you been? I know you were down in the basement with that damn girl. I know you really like her, son, but listen to me; she is our insurance policy in case things go wrong, so don't get too close to her. Leave your emotions at the door when you go in to see her."

"Dad, I know what I'm doing; I've got this," replies Alden.

As the sun begins to rise on a new day, some may believe that this is the turning point for a new tomorrow. A case in point is Det. Macrae. She wakes from a horrible dream all sweaty and out of breath. She sits up in her bed and takes a deep breath; she gets up out of the bed and heads to the bathroom. She sighs, sits down to use the toilet, and takes her hands and covers her face. Suddenly, she hears a crash from the other room. She becomes startled, her heart begins to race, and she knows she's inside the apartment alone; could it be a burglar trying to break in? She pulls up her pants and reaches for her gun on the counter. She yells once, "Who is it? You'd better leave now. I'm a police officer, and I will shoot."

As Det. Macrae moves ever so slowly toward the door and reaches for the doorknob, suddenly the door begins to shake as if someone is trying to enter the bathroom. She jumps back, becomes scared to death, and breathes very heavily. Then she releases the safety on the gun, aims it at the door, and says, "Whoever is out there, you better get the hell out of my apartment before I shoot your ass, and this is my final warning."

The door goes, BOOM really heard, she fires the gun, and the bullet goes through the door. She doesn't make a sound as she opens the door and steps out of the bathroom pointing the gun in both directions, making sure the coast is clear. She sees nothing but a bullet hole in the wall. She moves slowly to the kitchen, looks around, and gets out her flashlight. She shines it around the kitchen and living room, but she sees nothing. Det. Macrae soon believes that she's losing her mind and seeing and hearing things again. She lays her gun on the counter, pours a glass of water, and out the corner of her eye, she sees a dark shadow run behind the couch. Det. Macrae hears a soft laugh; she gets the flashlight and her gun and walks toward the couch. She takes a deep breath, shines the flashlight over to the couch, and to her surprise, she sees nothing. Before she can relax, Det. Macrae hears a knock at her door. She sticks her gun in the holster and proceeds to open the door. As the door opens, Det. Macrae sees Sheriff Michaels and Agent Ambrose standing there. Noticing the confused and disoriented look on her face, Sheriff Michaels responds first, "Karen, are you alright? What in the world happened to you? Do you need medical attention?"

"Let's get her inside and see what's wrong?" replies Agent Ambrose.

They step inside of Det. Macrae's apartment to check on her condition. She has a dazed and blank expression on her face. They get her to sit on the couch; Agent Ambrose gets her a bottle of water out of the fridge. Sheriff Michaels kneels down and asks Det. Macrae, "Karen, what's wrong? You seem like you've seen a ghost. We're here because someone reported they heard gunfire in the building. We checked your neighbors' apartment and found a bullet in the wall. Upon further investigation, we determined that the gunfire came from your apartment. Tell me, Karen, what happened? Did someone try to break into your apartment?"

Det. Macrae takes the bottle of water, takes a drink, and in a very calm manner, replies, "Ross, I'm not going to lie to you. I consider you to be a good friend and a great sheriff. As God is my witness, I think I'm losing my mind; I'm hearing voices and seeing things that aren't there. When I went to the bathroom, it sounded like someone was trying to break into my apartment. I went by procedure and shouted that I was a cop. I got no response, so I began walking through the apartment, checking all the rooms. When I came into the kitchen to get a drink, I saw something run behind the couch, and I heard a child laughing. I investigated, and I didn't see anything. I swear I saw a child run past me. I reacted, and my gun went off through the door. Ross, what's wrong with me; honestly, am I losing my damn mind?"

"Just as you stated, Karen, I'm your friend, and I have heard a lot of rumors pertaining to how you've been acting and looking lately. Talk to me; are you alright? I've heard you look out of your element and that you're not the top detective you were a couple of months ago," replies Sheriff Michaels.

Agent Ambrose comments, "Karen, you can trust us, and you'll be surprised by what we know that could probably help you."

Det. Macrae takes a deep breath, knowing in her heart that she can trust Sheriff Michaels and possibly Agent Ambrose. She opens up by saying, "Okay, all of this paranoia started probably a couple of months back after the librarian from Haven-Crest University was kidnapped; she is my friend Amy. Well, after that injury I sustained at the college, I began seeing these images. I would wake up in a cold sweat from one of the most horrifying dreams I ever had. They were so intense that I would wake up with cuts and scars on my body from them. Now, I'm too afraid to go to sleep because of fear of being killed by something that I may see in my dreams. That's why I've been looking and acting so edgy lately; I know my work performance has been spotty lately, but I have good reason. After a long talk with Celister, I never realized that vampires and howlers really existed, especially in Haven-Crest. I do believe that I was bitten by some vampire because some of the visions I have are of vampires."

Agent Ambrose reaches out to rub Det. Macrae's hands and replies with comforting words, "I believe you, and trust me; I know it's an uneasy feeling to have and that the world we live in can be so harsh and evil, but remember that you're not in this fight alone. You do have friends who will be there to see you through this ordeal. As an SBI Agent of the State, if an officer fires a weapon, then there's an investigation into the reason why and what the circumstances were pertaining to the incident. To keep IAD from launching an investigation, we'll say it was an attempted burglary, and you fired a shot and missed. Hopefully, that won't result in suspending you for firing your weapon. I think the right thing to do now is bring you to the Committee so you can tell them what you've told us because it could be the break we need in capturing the vampires here in Haven-Crest."

"I agree with you, Monica, so that's the excuse we'll use to everyone else. Karen, get some clothes; you can come stay with me at my house until we get to meet with the Committee," replies Sheriff Michaels.

At that very moment, Sheriff Michaels receives a phone call. He steps out of the room to answer, so Agent Ambrose helps Det. Macrae pack some clothes. In a few minutes, Sheriff Michaels comes back in and says, "I've already taken care of the shooting incident. Deputy Ewing will handle the break-in investigation and do the report. We may need to stop by Xavier's house because he said he has some vital information he needs to share with us tonight, so we'll stop by there on the way to my house. Are you girls ready to go?"

Det. Macrae grabs her coat, and they head to the door. So that they will not be seen, they head out through the back door. As Agent Ambrose drives around the front of the apartment building, they see that the Channel 2 News has arrived, and Jewel Walker is making her report.

"Good evening, everyone. This is Jewel Walker with the Channel 2 News here at the condo apartments on the upper side of Haven-Crest. From the 911 dispatcher, we heard that a shot was fired in one of the condo units. One of the officers on the scene told us that there was an apparent attempted break-in, but after the shot was fired, the alleged suspect escaped. The residents are a little uneasy that the suspect got away, but the officer stated that they were going to beef up security around the area with hopes of catching him. The suspect is described as a young black male with a light-skinned complexion about six feet tall; weight is probably about a hundred and twenty pounds. Viewers, he's considered to be armed and dangerous. Hopefully, once he's captured, the residents can sleep easier. This is Jewel Walker with the Channel 2 News; back to the newsroom."

As midmorning draws near, the limo pulls up to Sebastian's house for the departure to the airport so the Clan can leave on a flight to Boston. As cars begin arriving at Sebastian's, everyone commences to mingle and talk amongst themselves as they put their luggage in the limo. Jenessa, Jai Li, and Jamal arrive together. Marcella and Malcolm arrive next, and Persia and Genie arrive last. As Adam puts the luggage in the trunk, Sebastian comes out and says, "I'm glad everyone is here early so we can say our good-byes to everybody and get to the airport on time. Once again, let me say this is the day of reckoning for us. Hopefully with us setting forth to accomplish this quest in obtaining the Book, we can achieve our ultimate goal of defeating the evil that could possibly destroy the world as we know it. Everyone has instructions to follow, so we can go unnoticed by the townspeople and make a quick return. Anyone have anything to add? Wait, has anyone seen or heard from Chrisha today?"

Everyone looks around at each other, and Edmund speaks up, "The only thing I have to add is be careful and be safe. No one is above the Clan; you all work as a team. Now, on with the Committee news. Dr. Jensyn is joining the group and also Det. Macrae. From what I was told, she was bitten by a vampire and survived, but after that, she has had terrifying dreams and sees visions she can't explain. Genie and I have a meeting later on today, so I'll call you tonight and give you the details."

Jenessa replies to Sebastian's question, "You're right; I tried texting her, but she hasn't replied to me yet. I bet she probably didn't set her clock and has overslept."

"Don't worry about Chrisha, Jensessa. I'll go by her house on my way back to Priceless and check on her," replies Marcella.

Everyone starts hugging and saying their farewells, and they begin to load up the limo. Persia looks at her mother, and Genie blows her a kiss. She watches the limo pull out the driveway and head to the RDU airport. The ride is sort of quiet. Sebastian notices that everyone is keeping to their own thoughts and being silent. He breaks the ice by saying, "Ladies and gentlemen, let me say that I see the look of fear on your faces. I can understand how you feel, but understand that we are saving humanity. If we fail, then we are all lost. We are not alone; we have each other for strength, courage, and faith. I promise you that I will not let anything harm any one of you."

"Sebastian, I trust you, and I know that everyone in this car feels the same as I do. Don't worry, we won't let you down; we want to fulfill this quest as much as you do. As for myself, I can't see always being a howler; I want to go back to being a basketball star. Through whatever we encounter, we are with you one hundred percent, so our first destination is Boston in search of a witch named Shiloh," replies Jamal.

"I've checked some of Grandma's journals to see if I can find anything on Shiloh's whereabouts. From what I've read, she may reside in Danvers, Massachusetts. At the time when Grandma wrote in her journal, it was called Salem Village. Whose to say in this present day that witches are not still outlawed in that town. I suggest we be very careful in how we search for Shiloh," responds Jenessa.

Sebastian nods his head as he agrees with Jenessa. Within the few minutes, the limo driver pulls up in front of the Terminal 1 dropoff zone. Everyone gets out of the car and walks to the trunk to retrieve luggage before they start heading inside. Sebastian talks to the limo driver and then joins the group. They head to the ticket counter to print their plane tickets. After gathering all the information they need, they proceed to security to go through the metal detectors. After getting their bags and luggage checked by security, they head to the gate to board the flight to Boston. Once they are on the plane, the stewardess directs them to their seats. Sebastian, Jenessa, and Jamal sit together, and right across from them Persia, Malcolm, and Jai Li sit together. As the plane heads down the runway gathering speed for the takeoff into the heavenly skies, Jenessa becomes a little tense as she reacts to her ears popping, making it a little hard to hear. As the plane levels out at a height of 30,000 feet, Sebastian surveys the aircraft looking at the various people from different areas going to destinations unknown. Jenessa puts her hands over her ears to release some of the cabin pressure and Sebastian looks at her and says, "Are you okay? I'm assuming this is your first time on a plane. From the way you're holding your ears, I would guess they are popping."

Jenessa makes a frowning face at Sebastian; she gets closer to him and replies, "I can hardly hear what you're saying because my ears are popping; it's good I can read lips though. How long before we land in Boston? Give me a second to concentrate and stop my ears from popping. I want to talk to you."

Sebastian smiles at Jenessa. Being that she's sitting in the middle, she can pretty much go unseen as she does a little magic. Magically, the popping has stopped, and Sebastian leans over to Jenessa and says, "Now, I can respond so you can hear me. The flight is probably two and a half hours long; we should be there about two, and I have a limo waiting to pick us up once we land. I've had Adam make reservations for the Marriott for us while we're here, so what do you want to ask me?"

Jamal leans over so he can hear the conversation; Jenessa calmly looks at Sebastian and says, "Sebastian, do you remember when we had a talk about your past a while back when I asked what you went through and how you felt when you became a vampire? Who helped you to become the vampire you are now?"

As Sebastian looks out the window at the clouds, the question rings like a bell in his memory. Sebastian's mind wanders to the past to bring up an old wound that has been buried for many decades. He turns, smiles at Jenessa, and says, "Where do I begin? In 1891, I was still adapting to the adjustment of being a vampire, and at that time, I was still fresh and very reckless with my killings. I met this gentleman from New York who tried to teach me the real aspects of being a vampire. His method was to take what he wanted and act like no one could stop him. Everyone was our prey, no one mattered, and every life was mine for the taking. My advisor's name was Hutch; he was a bully, but he showed me that vampires were above the law and normal human laws don't apply to us. He showed me that strength concurs over weakness. Hutch taught me that being a vampire was a very hard adjustment at first due to having to understand that we are dead, but we're still alive. Our senses and emotions are much enhanced, like an animal, and lastly, he said that the hunger would be the one thing that could make or break a vampire. He taught me to understand the hunger and learn how to cut it on and off like a light switch. Hutch taught me that a vampire's personality would either be violent or very tempted. Though feelings, emotions, and anger are all amplified, vampires have to learn to control them. I never understood why, but Hutch taught me all of that. I was glad he did in the end."

Jenessa and Jamal are both intrigued at the story Sebastian is telling them. Before they can ask questions and without hesitation, Sebastian keeps on talking, "As I was a rookie, or green as some vampires called it, it was a lot to engulf at one time. Hutch took me to a witch to get a spell coin; a spell coin is a coin that a witch puts the daylight spell on so you can walk in the daylight without bursting into flames. Afterwards, Hutch melted the coin down, and I had it tattooed into my skin. The tattoo is how I'm able to walk out into the sun. Also, he taught me about the blur movement so I could learn how to move very fast in short distances without tiring myself out. I enjoyed understanding about the enhanced senses and sight; vampires can see and hear what is happening miles away. The touch was very hard to adjust to. It took practice not to be so aggressive that you hurt your victim. The taste and smell go hand-and-hand. Your taste for food comes and goes; you'll still be able to eat regular food, but the taste is different. Now, the taste for blood is hard to describe, though it coexists with the hunger. The hunger and taste for blood are what keep vampires on edge because we have to satisfy them in order to survive. If someone gets hurt or we see blood, our true faces are shown, and our golden black eyes glow, and our fangs extend out. Our fangs are hollow with very small holes on the end, which release vampire venom that is used to create other vampires. Once we open a wound on a victim, we then choose whether to create or just kill. If one is created, then he or she goes through a transformation phase into a vampire."

Jamal interrupts and says, "Sebastian, tell us more about the transformation phase."

"Now, with the information I'm telling you, you have to understand that I'm breaking one of the vampires' laws. We don't tell a lot about how you become a vampire to outsiders, especially to howlers, but you are sworn members of my Clan, so I guess this isn't breaking the law. Well, the transformation phase normally lasts for forty-eight to seventy-two hours. During the transformation, the vampire venom passes through the body and can cause a harmful burning sensation. Once the venom is part of the body, the transformation is complete. Then, the fangs develop, and the eyes change color. Being I was a rook, I didn't have an advisor like Hutch in the early beginnings to help guide me, but what I didn't know was that Hutch had enemies that meant to kill him and whomever else was allied with him. What happened is that he killed a vampire leader's son; Hutch was a vampire assassin who worked for money to assassinate rival vampires for the Co-op. There was a bounty on his head, and he was lying low for a while. Someone saw me with Hutch and a couple of weeks later, I was jumped and kidnapped by Avery to be questioned. I was tortured for three days non-stop; I thought they were going to kill me. They poured Pink Autumn that burned my throat in my mouth. They beat me with a whip dipped in Pink Autumn, which left cuts on my back, and worst of all, they tied my hands and put a bag over my face that had been dipped in Pink Autumn. After all that torture I went through, I never gave Hutch up to them. I was so weak; it was hard for me to stay conscious because I needed some blood to replenish my injured body. They were only giving me drops to keep me alive, but the third day, I got a mind link from Hutch that he was coming. He kept his word and rescued me, yet he killed Avery and his gang, which put another bounty on our heads by the Co-op."

Jenessa jumps in by saying, "Wait, wait; you're moving too fast. What is a Co-op?"

"The Co-op is a vampire coven or as humans called it, a gang of vampires. They are as bad as the Horde but more organized. Well, we stayed on the run for a couple of months. Hutch was still training me, and I had progressed as a vampire. I met Edmund and Malcolm, and I turned them to join our Clan. Hutch went to see a contact of his about a hook-up at the local blood bank, but he was set up by Malcolm who was a member of Julian's Clan. Avery's brother Julian killed Hutch out of revenge for his brother. Later, we found out he was ratted out by Malcolm, and they were after me. We managed to escape, and I left New York and moved down South for a while. I felt that with what I had learned from Hutch, I could now better myself as a vampire. As the saying goes, knowledge is power, and it was then I saw many beautiful things as I had learned to embrace my surroundings," replies Sebastian.

"Wow, Sebastian, who would have guessed that the guy sitting over with Jai Li and Persia is capable of betraying his Clan like that. Friendship and loyalty are two things that I judge people on. Once you've demonstrated and shown me those traits, then I feel I can trust you," replies Jamal.

Jenessa smiles at Jamal for what he just said. She realizes that he's now fitting in with the Clan. On a personal level, Jenessa sees that the trust and connection they both shared at one time are now starting to build back between them. Jai Li is intrigued to be sitting with Malcolm and is always interested in hearing stories, so she asks Malcolm, "If we find the Book, besides getting your sight back, what is one thing that you want over anything else from the Book?"

Malcolm turns to Jai Li, and even though he can't see her, he focuses his attention on her soft voice. Malcolm doesn't hesitate in his reply as he tells Jai Li, "I have desires just like everyone on this quest. Some may not be seen, although you can anticipate the obvious from some of us. I will be honest with you; yes, I want my sight back so I can see all the beautiful things as well as people whom I haven't had the chance to see yet. The wish I would like to have granted would be to become human once again so that I could enjoy the pleasures of growing old, having children, and finding true love with a woman. That might sound old-fashioned, but it's my dream. What about you, Jai Li?"

"Now, Malcolm that was sweet; I would never have thought you felt that way about becoming human once again. Since I'm still new at being a vampire, I want to stay this way for a while. I enjoy the power and invulnerability I have attained since joining the Clan. My wish would be to bring back Kirk, my old boyfriend, and make him a vampire so we could live together forever," replies Jai Li.

Persia laughs and comments, "Well, you know that won't happen because Sebastian would probably kill Kirk all over again for what he did to the Clan. Okay, you guys and all this sentimental wishing, how about being pleased with what you have become instead of wishing about what could happen? Have you thought about what if we don't find the cursed Book? I have heard about this myth for centuries, and no one has ever found it. Truthfully speaking, I think it doesn't exist, but that is just me thinking with some rational theory."

Jai Li's initial reaction is to immediately go postal, however, since they are 30, 000 feet in the air, a calmer head prevails, but she has to prove her point. Her fangs extend, her eyes turn golden black, her voice gets deeper, and Jai Li says, "Persia, why are you acting like an ignorant moron? What the hell is the matter with you? Look, you don't want to start something that your butt can't finish."

As Malcolm tries to defuse the situation before it gets out of hand, he says, "Ladies, ladies, you need to calm down. Jai, I can sense you've released the vampire. You need to relax and revert back before someone sees you."

Persia, not wanting to let Jai Li outdo her, retaliates by saying, "Who you calling an ignorant moron? I've taken enough of your crap, and trust me when I say you don't want to mess with me. My advice to you is to shut the hell up, and leave me alone."

Sebastian and Jenessa hear the conversation becoming heightened and the angry tones of their voices. Sebastian stands and says very loudly, "Ladies, ENOUGH!"

Everyone in the first class section becomes quiet, and they all turn and look at Sebastian. He sits down, and everyone goes back to what they were doing. Jenessa gets up, kneels down beside Jai Li, and says, "What's going on over here? Why are you two arguing?"

Jai Li answers to her best-friend, "It's your cousin; and she's over here trying to start some crap with her smart mouth."

"Jenn, talk to your little friend here. She may be a little vamp, but remember, I'm an old vamp. Trust me; I'm the wrong one to be barking at," replies Persia.

Jenessa comments in a hushed manner to her cousin and her best-friend, "Look, both of you need to calm down; this is not the place for this kind of stuff. We'll talk about this later. Be mindful that people are watching you, and don't expose what we are here on this plane."

The captain makes an announcement over the speaker, "This is Captain Warren. The seatbelt light has been turned on to avoid injury as we are about to experience some turbulence. Please have a seat until otherwise authorized by me or one of the stewardesses to move freely on the plane. Hopefully, we'll fly right through the turbulence and still be on time for our arrival in Boston. Thank you."

Jenessa sits back in her seat; she looks at Sebastian and how he watches Persia. He takes a deep breath and says, "What's wrong with Persia? She seems a tad aggressive toward Jai Li. Have you noticed how funny she's been acting since we left Haven-Crest? I'm not trying to start a conflict about Persia, but I've got my eyes on her."

"She's my cousin; I'll talk to her when we get to the Marriott, so let's not jump the gun on Persia," replies Sebastian.

About twenty minutes later, the flight makes it through the turbulence and safely arrives at the Boston airport. They exit the plane to meet the limo driver who will take them to the hotel. As they walk through the terminal, Sebastian watches and monitors everyone as they ride the escalator. Since he is a telepath, he listens to people's thoughts to make sure he stays one step ahead of his enemies. He makes eye contact with some of the people as he walks by, but suddenly something alerts his senses; he looks around to see what's setting him off. Sebastian can't make out anyone he knows or who it may be. He spots the limo driver, and once they get outside, he surveys the terminal one more time before they depart. Jenessa notices the concern on his face and says, "Sebastian, what's the matter? Is everything alright?"

"Don't worry; everything's alright. I was just checking out something before we leave to make sure we're not being followed," replies Sebastian.

As they all load up into the limo and start heading down the street, Sebastian notices a man with a long black cloak walking out into the street and watching them drive away. Sebastian realizes that a telepath is monitoring them, so they have to be really careful. They head toward the Marriott to check in.

Back in Haven-Crest as the night begins to take form and the rain continues to come down, two figures run through the woods in pursuit of an unfamiliar animal in the area. The animal that is being chased is mythical and has a plan of its own to set up the followers into a trap. One of the follower's stops, takes a deep breath, and lets out a loud "HOOWL" into the woods. Quickly, there is a return howl through the woods. The two chasers continue to follow the animal in question, thinking that they may have the animal cornered, but to their surprise, they are the captives of the chased animal. They run out into a clearing, and as both try to be totally quiet, they look around for the animal. One of the guys takes a sniff into the air to see if he can catch a smell of the animal. Very softly, he responds, "I can't catch his scent; it's like it just vanished. I don't even see any tracks. Follow me and be very careful."

Suddenly, three howlers ease out of the woods into the clearing. The woods are quiet, and all that can be heard is the sound of rain coming down and crumbing leaves behind the bushes. One of the guys starts to move slowly toward the bushes followed by one of the howlers, but before they can get close enough to check, without any warning, a big white howler jumps out and attacks the howler. With lots of snarling and growling, the gentleman start to move slowly out of the way, and the white howler rushes the single howler. The howler puts up a good retaliation fight, but it's not enough for the blood thirsty white howler as it goes for the neck and rips it out with its very sharp fangs. The man tries to run but to no accord; he doesn't get far before the white howler pounces on him and knocks him down. The only means of survival is to attack back, so the man slowly starts to change. His facial features begin transitioning into a howler. His fingers turn into claws, and hair begins growing all over his body. The other two howlers join the fight. They attack the white howler first, and the lone man climbs up and watches from up a tree. The animals are generating growling, snarling, and howling from the fighting due to the biting and ripping of flesh. Unbeknownst to the others, the last howler starts to sneak slowly behind to attack the white howler. Blood thirsty, the white howler fights off the other two howlers to their deaths. As blood drops off its chin, the white howler has ripped out both of the howlers' throats. Now, the body count has risen to three. With just one left, the white howler realizes this is a sure kill, but the last howler does the unthinkable; it bows down to the white howler, and the man in the tree jumps down in amazement at what he just witnessed. The white howler lets out a really loud howl and growls at the last howler. The white howler rises up quickly and precisely swings its sharp claws and then hits the last howler across the throat. As the blood splatters and runs all over the ground, slowly the last howler begins changing back to human form, and the lone gentleman stands alone against the ravenous white howler. The white howler has made no effort to attack the lone gentlemen and just walks away. Miraculously, he starts to convert back to human form. Slowly, the human features begin to show, and during this process, Adrian stares in utter shock at what he sees. The white howler now is a man and begins to talk very nonchalantly by saying, "Adrian, we finally meet. It a pleasure to meet you, I've heard a lot about you over the centuries. Let me say that your name carries high respect. You've killed a lot of people over the vast time you've been a vampire, and I'm quite impressed by your accomplishments. By looking at the reaction on your face, I can see that you're speechless by what you have seen. Before we go any further, let me introduce myself; I'm Antoine. You've probably heard a lot about me; good and bad, but do believe what you've heard? Adrian, I killed your friends for a reason, and that is because I have plans for you myself. We are going to gain the upper hand in this quest. I'm going to need the kind of person you are with your unique abilities."

As Antoine tries to convince Adrian to join in a partnership with him, Adrian thinks he can get the odds in his favor by trying to out hustle the hustler, so Adrian proposes a deal with the devil himself. He says, "I'm confused; I always heard that you were a vampire, but after what I just witnessed, how is that you're able to turn into a howler? Are you a Varcolac? I never knew one actually existed. As far as rumors, I've heard about you. I've heard that you don't like for anyone to see what you look like or should I say live to tell what you look like. How do I know that you won't kill me now that I know what you look like? I now know why you keep your appearance a secret. You do you know who you can be mistaken for, don't you? Enough about that, let me ask a question. What's in it for me if I decide to help you?"

"Ha-ha-ha, Adrian, besides being a killer, you didn't tell me you were a comedian with jokes. I am the last of my kind; technically I'm a hybrid, but Varcolac is what my kind is called. I'll let you in on a secret. Once I take over Haven-Crest, I will reveal information that will tear Haven-Crest into rubble. Back to the matters at hand, I never said that I would give you anything; maybe letting you live would be a reward enough for you. However, if you show me the initiative I'm looking for, we could strike some kind of deal," replies Antoine.

Thinking of a cleaver reply, Adrian says, "Before I commit to this deal, I need to know one thing. What is the partnership between you and Nicolette? I don't want to start any kind of confusion between you and her, so I will report directly to you with any and all information we uncover."

Antoine starts to laugh, realizing that he can't trust Adrian because he will try to double-cross him some way, somehow, so Antoine only gives him a little information by saying, "My, my, my, are you ready to move her out of her position to become my number one guard? Let's just say that if you are my number one, you need to be on top of everything. I shouldn't be the one who finds out that your brother is in Boston as we speak, getting a big head start on finding some clues that can lead him to the Book. On that note, either she's not doing her job or she has a motive herself. In all aspects, she has to go; I know it may sound harsh considering all that she's done for me over the centuries, but one thing I don't tolerate is betrayal. It's time to think of an alibi for your friends. I'm pretty sure the sheriff is going to come and ask questions about them being missing," replies Antoine.

To make sure that doesn't happen with Adrian, Antoine blurs over and grabs Adrian. He slams him against a tree and then compels him not to tell anyone about their meeting in the woods or that he's the white howler. He orders him to kill Nicolette, to assume her position within as lead of the Clan, and to depose of the dead bodies of his friends. Adrian begins doing what he has been told to do. He follows orders from Antoine and pulls out his cellphone and calls for Andre to bring the Clan to help him. Just like a whisper of wind, Antoine is gone. Adrian shakes his head and wonders what happened to his friend Coach Deren, and he sees that some of his pack of howlers lie dead on the ground. The blood continues to run from the dead bodies onto the ground as Adrian tries to remember what could have happened here.

Possibly four miles away buried deep in the woods is a family mausoleum in an area so quiet that all one can hear is the sound of crickets and an owl. However, on this night, the dead remain restless. Inside this area of Haven-Crest, there are many family secrets and what some people would call curses. For this particular family, the Nichols, evil and despair have followed them for many decades. No one in the town never knew why, but many speculated about the reason. The rumor goes that a descendant of the Nichols, his name was Oscar, was suffering through hard times. He felt that all hope was lost, and his faith in God had diminished. His faith was gone because his pregnant wife had passed away giving birth to their son. He hated God, and one evening while drinking some homemade wine, he offered his soul to the devil for riches and a wife. After that night, he only received a curse for all his trouble. A couple of days later, a runway woman named Sarah came knocking at his door. She needed refuge from her horrible past. Oscar felt sorrow for the fallen young runaway, so he took her in, and a couple of months later, they were married. Deep down in his heart, he knew that something wasn't right. His crops had withered, his animals grew sick and began dying, and his wife Sarah had become pregnant. Oscar felt he was being paid back for renouncing his faith in God. Instead of praying for forgiveness with hopes of receiving His blessing, under the advice of Sarah, he went to see a witch named Hazel. Unknown to Oscar, she was a friend of Sarah's, and she only complied with the curse that had been put on him. Nine months later, Sarah had twins, Langston and Logan, whom everyone thought were wonderful boys until they began doing devilish things to the town. Kids went missing, and buildings were being set on fire. Oscar was in total shock at what had been happening. Before he could send the boys away, a mob captured and killed them. Eventually, after the scandal, he and Sarah moved away to the next town, which was Haven-Crest. After that, Sarah became pregnant again, and this time she had a daughter, Hayden, who was evil just like her brothers. She had an encounter with a vampire, was bitten, and turned into one. Legend has it that she was the first child in Haven-Crest history to become one, and Hayden began terrorizing Haven-Crest, killing adults and kids for a few months. Oscar tried to kill her for all the evil she had done but he was unsuccessful due to Sarah killing him in her allegiance with the devil. Sarah tried to help young Hayden adjust to the hunger for blood, but at a young age, it's harder for a child to come to terms. Sarah would meet her fate by Hayden's actions. All this turmoil caught the attention of the Committee, so the Power of Three was formed. Estelle and two other powerful witches put a spell on Hayden to put her in an eternal sleep so she couldn't hurt or kill any more innocent victims. Estelle was the anchor to the spell, but now that she's dead, the spell has been broken, and Hayden is free to roam the town of Haven-Crest to quench her appetite for blood. With that being told, the earth inside the tomb begins to rumble, open up, and set forth a child monster. Unleashed as her young, dirty hand breaks through the ground, she continues to push through until she is free from her prison. With a strong appetite for blood, she knows she has to feed the urge by going to town, so she leaves the mausoleum and hurries through the night in search for blood.

Chapter 16

As nightfall approaches, the gloomy, cold rain continues to come down. Two pairs of prying eyes observe the cottage that sits in the woods. The prying eyes belong to Syngyn and Declan, who have been waiting for the right opportunity to strike the unsuspecting off-duty guards. They notice one guard making rounds outside, and they refrain from killing him. They overhear him calling in to Slam Dunk Pizza for a delivery to be brought out to the cottage. Syngyn thinks of a counter plan to be more effective in this kidnapping plot. A devious idea spawns inside of Syngyn's mind; the more diabolical it is, the more body counts may rise in the process. Syngyn wipes the water off his face and fills Declan in by saying, "I've got a way for us to get inside to get the young wolf Kim. We need to head to back to the main road and wait for the delivery guy to bring the pizza."

With that said, the two abductors head back through the woods to set up a trap for the unsuspecting victim. Inside the cottage, there are two off-duty officers, Brooks and Maye, and both are being entertained by watching the basketball game. Kim sits on the couch and checks her Facebook account. She is looking at pictures of herself and Ryan and wishing that he was still here. Her heart feels heavy with all the grief of losing her fiancé of three years, and she wonders how this happened to them. Officer Brooks sees the sadness on Kim's face and how she's accepting the realization that Ryan is gone. Officer Brooks looks away from the basketball game and says, "Are you alright? I see that you're sad. I can relate to what you're going through because I've been there. I lost my wife to a carjacking that went bad and she was killed. I was devastated, and it took me a long time to get over it, but with the grace of God, I pulled through, and you can too. It's going to be rough at first, but trust me; you're going to make it. Do you have any kids?"

As Kim wipes away the tears, she understands that Officer Brooks is trying to help her feel better, so she sniffles and says, "Thanks, I really needed to hear those comforting words, but I just can't believe he's gone. Ryan was a good guy, and to make things worse, he had just proposed to me. I really loved him, and what keeps on bothering me is wondering, "Who did this to us and why? Yeah, I have two daughters by my first husband; Ryan and I were talking about being a family and living happily ever after."

"I don't know what happened to you out in the woods, but it must have been horrible to not be able to remember anything that happened. I read the file, and it just said that you and your boyfriend were acting like wild animals and attacked some hospital staff. Can you tell us what really happened at the hospital?" asks Officer Brooks.

Kim pulls her hair out of her face, sits back on the couch, and says, "To be honest, I don't remember anything that happened at the hospital. Everything is so foggy, but I do remember bits and pieces; one thing that is so puzzling is I remember changing into a howler."

Both officers are stunned by what Kim just told them. They can't believe it, and their initial thought is, "She's high on some kind of drug." Officer Maye takes the first shot at her by saying, "Kim, you mean to tell us that when a full moon comes during the month, you turn into a howler? The only thing I have to say is that seeing is believing; prove it to me."

As the bright headlights shine down the path to the cottage, the unsuspecting driver is unaware that something deadly is about to happen to him. Due to all the heavy rain, the delivery guy drives slowly down the path. He spots a disabled vehicle with the flashers on, so he stops to see if can be of assistance. He pulls up beside the black SUV, rolls down his window, and asks, "Are you alright? Do you need some help or maybe a ride?"

The driver's side window comes down, and Syngyn replies, "I sure could use some help, I don't know why, but it just cut off. With all this rain, it picked a cold night to just shut down on me."

The delivery guy jumps out of his car and checks under the hood. He checks the battery cables and a few other things under the hood. He signals for Syngyn to start the motor. Once it cranks up, the delivery driver walks to the side of the truck and says, "Hey, I think your battery cable was loose, but you should be good now. I have got to go."

"I appreciate all your help, so how much do I owe you for all the trouble I caused you tonight?" replies Syngyn.

The delivery driver shakes his head, and before he can respond, suddenly something blurs by him and attracts his attention. As he turns his head and exposes his neck, quickly and precisely, Syngyn grabs him by the throat. He raises the delivery driver off the ground as he pleads for his life not to end this way. Syngyn smiles and says, "Why do you want to stop the inevitable? Your destiny has already been determined: death. Don't you want to die with some sense of honor? I plan on making this very quick so you won't suffer; you may not even feel the pain. I'm going to tell you what I am; I am an instrument of death, a vampire."

The delivery driver just cries and begs for his life, waiting for some sort of remorse on Syngyn's part to let him go free. He asks, "If you are an instrument of death, then why choose me? I have nothing to do with whatever you're doing. Please, just let me go free. I won't say anything to anybody."

Syngyn starts think that this plan was a bad idea, so he begins to lower his arm as if to let him go, but there's a blur made by Declan as he bites the innocent delivery driver and kills him. Syngyn releases his grip on his throat and lets the lifeless body drop to the ground. After the blood in the body has drained, Declan stands with blood dripping off his chin and says, "Why did you hesitate in killing him? Did you feel remorse with him begging for his life, or did you just have a change of heart? I did what I had to do, now let's get the wolf girl."

Syngyn doesn't reply. He simply watches Declan switch clothes with the deceased driver and so he can deliver the pizza to the cottage. As Syngyn picks up the dead body and puts it in the back of the SUV, Declan gets in the car and heads down the path to the cottage to deliver the pizza. As Syngyn follows Declan to the cottage to make sure he follows the plan accordingly, he starts to see that he must get more control over his actions. Declan grabs the pizzas from out of the bag and proceeds to the front door. As he knocks, Officer Brooks gets up from watching the game and says, "Hey, I got it since no one wants to get the door. I believe it's my turn to pay for the pizzas anyway."

Officer Brooks opens the door and then turns his back to check out the score. Once he turns around, Officer Brooks says, "Hey buddy, how's it going on this rainy night? Where's Gary at tonight? He's the normal guy who comes out here. Come on in and get out of the rain while I get your money straight. How much do I owe you?"

Declan slowly walks over the entrance way into the house. Once inside, he looks around the room and spots Kim. She takes a sniff in the air and notices something odd as she looks at Declan. She stands up, and suddenly her features begin the change; the howler inside of her is now trying to get out. Kim starts to growl and snarl at Declan, who watches in awe at Kim and says, "Hey, what's wrong with her? What is she doing?"

Officer Maye steps in and says, "Kim, what's going on? Why are you changing?"

In a growling voice, she tries to tell them what's going on before she fully transforms into a howler. Her features are coming very fast, and the pain is becoming very intense, but she says, "Something has triggered my aggression and is unleashing me into a howler. I noticed an unfamiliar scent when the pizza guy came inside that can mean only one thing…He's a vampire."

All three of the officers turn and look at Declan, and before they can say anything, he blurs and grabs Det. Shelton by the throat and raises him off the floor. With his fangs out, golden black eyes shining, and Det. Shelton dangling and unable to speak, Declan says to everyone, "Don't anyone make a move, or this cop will get his neck snapped like a twig. First, I want the cop who opened the door to invite my friend inside."

Officer Brooks looks around at everyone and slowly walks toward the front door. He opens the door and says, "Please come in out of the rain, whoever you are."

Syngyn slowly comes inside the cottage to make his presence known and says, "Now, officers, I'm going to offer you a onetime only deal. If you give me the girl, I won't kill you, but if you decide not to, then we've got a problem. I will give you a minute to decide."

Officer Maye's police instinct takes over, and he tries to rush Syngyn. Despite his heroic attempt, Syngyn grabs him by the neck also. As he looks into his face, Syngyn says, "Well, Officer Maye, you must want to die. Your feeble attempt to rush me to knock me off guard came to no success. Now, on my accord, this is what course of action I will take."

Without another word being said, Syngyn takes matters into his own hands. As Officer Maye dangles by his throat, he feels the pressure as Syngyn tightens his grip; a choice must be made of whether to bite the officer or just snap his neck. To prove his point, Syngyn snaps Officer Maye's neck, killing him instantly. He then looks at Kim and says, "Now, one of your protectors is dead. As for the two remaining, their lives are in your hands. You can go with us peacefully, or we can do this the hard way, and they die trying to protect you from us; the choice is yours."

Kim turns and looks at Officer Brooks and Det. Shelton, realizing that she does not want two innocent souls' deaths on her conscience. If she kills one of the vampires, then the other officer dies, so she makes the ultimate sacrifice by slowly changing back to human form. Officer Brooks hands her a blanket to cover herself up. She drapes it around her body and says to Syngyn, "What do you want with me? What could I possibly do to help you? I still haven't learned to control the animal inside of me."

"Sweetie, you just don't know how valuable you are to me as well as some of my partners. Trust me when I say that I won't hurt you; I am going to help you," replies Syngyn.

Declan begins to get confused because he doesn't understand all the compassion and promises Syngyn is making. Angrily, he responds to Syngyn, "What the hell is this? What's wrong with you? Where's the vicious killer, Syngyn, the man I admired when I first met you? Who is this easygoing, deal making, nice guy here? If he's not here, well then, I'm out of here."

Syngyn becomes enraged at Declan's comment, and to show him that the vicious killer is still present, he does the unthinkable; he blurs across the room to Officer Brooks, bites him, and rips out his throat. As a sign of dominance with Officer Brooks' blood dripping off of his chin and hands, Syngyn looks at Det. Shelton, who is still dangling in Declan's grip. Sensing his death is coming rapidly, Det. Shelton makes a plea for his life by saying, "Please, don't kill me. I have a family, and I haven't done anything to you. Can you let me go, and I won't say anything about what happened here?"

Syngyn is merciless and ignores Det. Shelton's pleas for survival. As Declan releases his grip, Det. Shelton thinks that his life has been spared, but Syngyn blurs over and extinguishes all hope for his survival. To give a quick death so he doesn't suffer, Syngyn rips his throat out. Det. Shelton's lifeless body falls to the floor. With no remorse in his heart, Syngyn walks over to Kim and says, "Now, with all the preliminaries out of the way, we can get down to business. Kim, get some clothes so you can come with us; I have some important people I want you to meet."

Nervously, Kim moves very slowly, thinking that Syngyn may kill her now that her bodyguards are dead. She replies, "Where are we going? Are you planning to kill me or sacrifice me for some stupid ritual? Before I put on any clothes, I want to know what's going to happen to me."

Kim starts to pack up some clothes. Instead of responding to her questions, Syngyn blurs over to her and injects her with a small vile of aconite to knock her out. Once she is unconscious, Syngyn instructs Declan to pick her up and put her in the SUV. Syngyn drags all the bodies together, and as they head out of the cottage, he sets it on fire. Within minutes, the cottage is a raging fire. As Syngyn and Declan head toward town, Syngyn looks in the backseat and says, "Now, we have our bargaining chip. We can go to the Committee and strike a deal with them. Trust me, after all the planning I've endured, you can bet that this is going to be a night to remember."

In Boston, Sebastian stares out the window looking at the gloomy skies. He wonders what plan of action they are going to need while looking for Shiloh. He scrolls through his phone looking for his contact Andree Cardan. Once he finds the phone number, he calls him for some assistance. Andree picks up and says, "Well, I don't believe it; this can't be Sebastian Kane calling me. My God, what wind blew you in to Boston?"

Sebastian laughs and responds, "Andree, my friend, you're right; it has been a long time since I've seen you. I'm in Boston because I need your help, plus you are the only person I trust. Can you come to my hotel room at the Marriott?"

"Sure, Sebastian, you know I've got your back. I'll be there within an hour," replies Andree.

Both hang up, and Sebastian heads out of the room to the continental breakfast. There he sees Jai Li eating some fruit. Sebastian gets a cup of coffee and joins her at the table. He says, "Good morning, Jai. Did you sleep well? I see you're taking advantage of the free food."

Jai Li laughs and replies, "No, my bed is terrible. Don't get me wrong though; the rooms are really nice. It's just that the beds here are very uncomfortable, so I decided to come down and eat breakfast. I left Persia upstairs still sleeping. I just can't get over how she was acting on the plane. What's her problem?"

"I just can't put my finger on it, but I know she and Genie are up to something no good. We will just have to watch her. I don't want to say anything to Jenessa about this because that's her cousin, and I assume they are real close since she saved her life during the Herbal Store explosion. Well, we all just need to be alert and monitor her so we won't get caught with our pants down," replies Sebastian.

They both continue to talk and eat breakfast while they wait for the others to come down. Jenessa, Jamal, and Malcolm come down next; they all take seats and enjoy the breakfast with the rest of the gang. As they sit around eating and conversing, Malcolm begins the history lesson by saying, "Everyone, let me say that we all have to focus on our main objective of finding Shiloh. I think we should stay together until we can get a good lead as to her whereabouts so no one gets lost. We should ask around first and try to get some of the townspeople to help us out."

Jamal speaks up first and says, "I agree with Malcolm; we should all stick together. This is a big city to get lost in. Where do we start first? Are there any clues to go on?"

Malcolm sips his coffee and replies, "I think we should start at a club I remember called The Skull and Bones near downtown Ipswich. I remember that a lot of witches used it as a meeting place when they were running from the hunters and the Puritans of the church."

Suddenly, Persia comes from her room and joins the Clan. She grabs some food and says, "Sorry for being so late. I slept like a rock; the jet lag must have really knocked me out. So, what's the plan for today?"

Jenessa replies by saying, "We're about to leave for a club called The Skull and Bones, and hopefully, someone will be able to give us some info about where to find her."

After they all finish eating, they leave and load up in the Tahoe rental headed to Ipswich. The GPS is set leading to the right area, but they don't see any Skull and Bones club. They see what looks like a retirement home, so Sebastian, Jenessa, Jamal, and Malcolm get out and head to the front door. They are met by a rowdy security guard; he stops them by saying, "Excuse me, people; visiting hours are not until noon and not any earlier, so you will need to leave and come back at the appropriate time."

Jenessa walks up to the security guard with the intention of trying to get him to understand by saying, "Sir, we've come a long way to visit my dear aunt. I understand that visiting hours are not until noon, but would you please bend the rules so I might be able to see my aunt before noon?"

The security guard seems to be getting annoyed by Jenessa's attempt to plea for a break, so to show her that he's the boss, he decides to become nasty by saying, "Look, I've told you the rules, and I don't give nobody no breaks. So just do like the sign says, VISITING HOURS ARE AT NOON! You can read, can't you? Now, you and all of your relatives here can just skip down the yellow brick road until noon."

"One thing I can't stand is an ignorant security guard. Now you don't have to be mean or nasty to patrons. My friend was being nice to you by asking to see her aunt, but now I'm going to do this the hard way," replies Sebastian.

Sebastian blurs by everyone and grabs the security guard by the throat, raises him in the air, stares at him with his calm green eyes, and he says, "Now that I have your attention, I'm going to compel you forget all about us coming by to visit here, so just bend the rules and let us go visit a patient inside."

The mean security guard complies with Sebastian. Once Sebastian releases his grip on his throat, he hands everyone a badge to get inside the building. Sebastian opens the front door, and all proceed to the front desk. They meet Claire, the receptionist, and she says, "Good morning. My name is Claire. Did that lazy security guard out there give you a hard time?"

"Good Morning, Claire, my name is Jenessa Craig, and we're here to hopefully find a lady named Shiloh. Yes, the security guard was rather rude I would say, but after a little persuasion, he let us in. I know that may sound kind of odd, but it's really important that we find her," replies Jenessa.

Claire checks through the resident log on the computer and successfully she finds a Shiloh in the database. She pulls out a notepad and writes the name down, and she sees that something is very odd, "Yes, we do have a Shiloh here in Room 8, a Shiloh Mills. What's very strange is that she hasn't had a visitor in about a year ago. The last visitor she had was a lady named Estelle Craig. Is she any relation to you?"

Jenessa's first reaction is to be shocked and stunned what she has just overheard. She responds slowly by saying, "Yes, she is; that's my grandma. I didn't know she came to see her. Can we please see her if it's possible?"

"I don't know. I don't want to get into any trouble behind this," replies Claire.

Sebastian steps up to the front desk and compels her with his soft green eyes by says, "Claire, trust me when I say we won't cause any trouble. Please, just allow us to see Shiloh. You won't remember us even coming in to talk to Shiloh, and you will act just like it's a normal day as usual."

Claire does what Sebastian says and reaches under the front desk for the remote button for the door. Once she opens it, they all go down the hall to Room 8. Sebastian knocks on her door, and Shiloh says, "Come in. I've been expecting all of you. Come and have a seat."

They all come in and take seats around the bed. Shiloh sits up in her bed and looks around the room, so Sebastian breaks the ice and says, "Shiloh, we came a long way to have a few minutes of your time with hopes of you being able to help us out. When you said you've been expecting us, can I assume you know who and what we are?"

"Yes, I do. I felt your vibes when you all walked up to the door, and in answer to your other question, I have the information as well as what you are searching for," responds Shiloh.

Jenessa is still puzzled that Estelle came to visit her a year ago. Before she can ask her question, Shiloh reaches out and holds her hands. Jenessa asks, "Shiloh, you know who I am, so let me ask you why my grandma came to visit you last year."

Shiloh smiles and replies, "My dear Jenessa, your grandmother told me about you, that you are the prophecy, and that you are the key to finding the Book of Spells. She was going to do her best to keep you hidden from those who mean to do you harm and train you to embrace and develop all your powers. When we were young witches still in Salem, Lazarus told of a child who was going to be our savior, but he couldn't pinpoint when the prophecy would happen. We just prayed and took precautions until the glorious day when we could come out of hiding and solidify our true lineage. Until that joyous day came, we continued to practice and form covens that would protect us from human and mythical creatures. When the word got out, a possible hybrid-dymphyre howler; witches, and evil vampires began looking for you centuries ago. Lazarus was killed by a notorious vampire named Antoine; he was determined to find out about the prophecy at any cost. Many witches paid the price as he was killing them in his search for you. Whatever you do, make sure you stay with Jamal and Sebastian because they are the keys to your survival. When Estelle came to see me, she told me to keep a charm that forges into a big key to a cave that contains the Book. Before I give you that charm, you must know this: When I left Salem with Estelle and Roman, I was a young, naïve witch. I believed that the whole world thought that the church leaders wanted to kill us; we witches went through a lot then trying to avoid detection and hide so Constable William Hayes and Minister James Bayley wouldn't prosecute all witches and sentence them to death. I began dabbling with a dark magic called Black Necro. I was consumed by its dark power and evil presence, but Estelle saved me from creating further harm on innocent people. I told Estelle I was going to train you on a spell that will aid in your quest. I know there are others who seek the map also, but this spell will show you a way to stay a step ahead of them. Always remember that the dark magic can consume you, so don't let a witch convince you otherwise. I have a journal that may be of use to you to guide you over time to enhance your powers to the fullest."

Jenessa doesn't respond to Shiloh, but Shiloh turns her attention to Sebastian, reaches out to hold his hands, and says, "Now, Sebastian, you are an important piece to this puzzle. Everyone has his or her own intentions, but yours has been a burning desire for many years. Ask yourself this: If you do find the Book, then what is your request from it? You know by reviving the dead that there are consequences that must be paid and that there isn't any guarantee that the person who existed before will be the same person when he or she comes back. I will tell you what I see in your future. You are going to unravel an ultimate secret that will change everything in your Clan. Some advice to you is that I can see all the hatred inside your heart. You need to come to terms with what you are and the things you've done in your past. The positive attitude you've chosen means that you're on the road to doing the right thing. Now, could everyone leave so I can talk to Jenessa by myself?"

Everyone follows her request and leaves the room. Shiloh reaches for her cane, gets out of her bed, and slowly walks over to the dresser. She opens one of the drawers, pulls out a small treasure chest, and sets it on top of the dresser. Jenessa, being curious, gets up and comes over to the dresser with Shiloh. Shiloh takes a golden key from around her neck and hands it to Jenessa. Jenessa takes the key, studies its exquisite designs, opens up the treasure chest, and looks at the souvenirs inside. She takes out a scroll, rosary beads, and a witch's journal. Suddenly, Shiloh takes the chest and taps the bottom of it with her hand. Then she slides down the bottom of the chest to reveal a hidden compartment that contains the charm to the key. It has been hidden there for many years and has gone unnoticed. Shiloh takes out the charm and hands it to Jenessa. As she reaches out to take it, Jenessa feels a warm sensation all over her body. She takes a necklace from her neck, and Shiloh slides on the charm and puts the chain back around her neck. Shiloh says, "Whatever you do, do not take this charm from around your neck; for one, it's cursed so no vampire or howler can remove it. The wearer has to be someone pure in heart and mind. The scroll is the spell you need to help you on your quest. You need to read it, study it, and remember it because you don't use it until you're in a predicament where you have no other choice. This is the one spell that will save your life and the lives of your friends as well."

Overwhelmed by everything she just witnessed with Shiloh, Jenessa looks Shiloh in her eyes and says, "Shiloh, I can never be able to repay you for everything that you have done for me and my friends. I wish we could have met under more pleasant circumstances because I have so many questions and really no one to talk to. My main questions are: Why am I the prophecy, and what difference am I going to make on this quest? I feel like I'm going to let them down because I haven't been practicing my witchcraft that long. If the truth be told, I believe if I had been a better witch, I could have saved my grandmother's life the day she was killed by Alexia."

"Don't beat yourself up thinking like that. Instead, tell yourself that you did the right thing by trying to save her, and just remember she accepted the fact that it was her time. She lived a long and prosperous life, and everyone in Haven-Crest loved her for being the special person that she was. What you've learned will be enough to help your friends find the Book, so go now and...." Shiloh gets interrupted.

Suddenly, they hear a loud CRASH from outside the room, and a lot of yelling in the hallway. Jenessa goes running to the door. She turns to Shiloh and says, "Stay here, and don't come out until I come back."

As soon as she opens the door, she sees a lot of smoke and dust, and through the commotion, she can see Camden standing at the end of the hallway. She sees that he's not the guy she was in love with months ago; he has become her worst nightmare. Camden sees Jenessa and says, "Jenessa, if you don't want your friends to get killed, you need to give me the deciphered map you have in your possession and tell me what the witch told you."

With smoke and dust crowding the hallways and residents' rooms, Sebastian can barely see Camden standing at the end of the hall. When he turns and sees Jenessa coming out of Shiloh's room, he blurs over to her and says, "What are you doing? You are not going down that hallway or giving him anything. How in the hell did he find us? See if you can stall him while I check on the others to make sure they are alright."

Jenessa nods her head and Sebastian blurs over to Malcolm and Jai Li. Both seem to be okay. They are just a little shaken up. As they get themselves together, he then blurs over to Jamal and Persia. Jamal has been knocked out, so Persia picks him up and blurs outside. As Jenessa steps out into the hallway, Camden sees her and responds in a very angry tone, "Jenessa, don't take me as a joke because right now I am not in the mood. Are you going to give me the charm, or do I have to take it by force?"

"Camden, your weak-minded threats don't bother me, and all this destruction and carnage you caused doesn't make you an all-powerful wizard. Your two-bit dime store magic is nothing but parlor hand tricks. Camden, do you want to see some real magic? Watch this," responds Jenessa.

At the last possible second, Alexia makes her presence known by stepping out in the open with Claire, the nurse from the front desk. Claire is screaming for her life, knowing that she may die at any moment; Alexia sees Jenessa and says, "Dear Jenessa, where's my brother? I know he's here somewhere. Sebastian, if you don't want this to get out of hand, you need to come out in the open."

Sebastian blurs back to stand beside Jenessa, and Alexia dangles the innocent nurse by her throat to hopefully get Sebastian to give in and give them what they want. Sebastian thinks he can reason with Alexia by saying, "What are you doing? Alexia, you don't want to kill that innocent nurse; she's done nothing to deserve your wrath, so why don't you just let her go?"

"Brother, Brother, there you go protecting these pathetic humans again, begging for their lives, and I ask you: Why? Why would someone as powerful as you, a vampire lord of his Clan and a ruthless berserker killer, beg for me to spare her life? Give me one reason why I should?" replies Alexia.

Sebastian takes a breath and looks at Alexia, but before he can answer her, she shows her older brother that she can take the initiative and kill innocence without a conscience or a care in the world for a human life. With the most despicable smirk on her face, Alexia pulls Claire's head back, extends her sharp fangs, and bites Claire's neck, draining all of her blood and killing her in seconds. Sebastian and Jenessa both stand in utter shock at what they just witnessed. Alexia just tosses Claire's lifeless body on the floor and looks at Jenessa and Sebastian with blood dripping off her chin and hands. She grins and says, "Ladies and gentlemen, that is how it's done with no guilt or thoughts of caring for humanity bothering my conscience. Dear brother, you can cut your humanity off and enjoy the taste of human blood once again. Regardless of what your newfound beliefs are now, you can't resist the aroma and the exquisite taste of blood."

Jenessa feels now is the time she needs to intervene, so she shuts her eyes, recites an incantation spell, and waves her hands. Suddenly,

Sebastian sees the phoenix glow unleash within her body and soul. Once Jenessa opens her eyes and swings her arms out, the force is so powerful that it knocks Camden through some glass windows that shatter on his way outside as he crashes to the ground. The force is so powerful that it gives him a slight concussion, and with the injuries he sustains, the blood comes gushing from a lot of the cuts to his face and body. When he really regains his composure, Sebastian and the Clan are long gone. After Jenessa knocks Camden outside, Alexia blurs over to her newfound partner to make sure he is unharmed and oversee his injuries. Like a wisp of wind, Alexia and the injured Camden make their departure before the situation really gets out of hand. After Jenessa and Sebastian realize that they are gone, Jenessa makes a beeline back into the building to check on Shiloh, but in the distance, there are sounds of police and fire truck sirens coming. Sebastian grabs Jenessa by the arm and says, "We've got to go; don't you hear the sirens coming? Where are you going? Jamal has been hurt, and we need to get out of here ASAP."

"I need to go check on Shiloh to make sure she's alright. Take Jamal and go. I'm coming right behind you," replies Jenessa.

Jai Li grabs Jamal, and Persia grabs Malcolm. They blur over to the Tahoe, load up, and are ready to go. Sebastian looks at Jenessa, and they blur inside to look for Shiloh. Once inside, they see nurses trying to help the residents outside in midst of all the chaos. They don't see Shiloh, so Sebastian blurs inside to her room and sees that there is debris in front of door keeping her trapped inside. Sebastian moves the debris and pulls the door open. Once inside, he sees Shiloh lying on the floor unresponsive. Sebastian blurs over to her, lifts her head, and rubs her white hair. Shiloh opens her eyes, and in a very low whisper, she says, "Sebastian, I think this may be the last dance at the ball for this old witch. It means so much to me that you came back to check on me, even though a higher power may be calling me home to join Him. One thing I do want to tell you is to keep your enemies close to you because you have one in your Clan. Give this to Jenessa, and tell her I hope this helps her on her journey to find what she is searching for."

Jenessa comes in the room and sees it's too late; Sebastian closes Shiloh's eyes and folds her arms across her chest. He stands and says, "I'm sorry; Shiloh had a heart attack, probably due to everything that just happened. You can't blame yourself; it wasn't your fault, and there's no way of telling if that was the real cause. She wanted me to give you this and said to tell you that she hopes this helps you on your journey. Jenessa, we have got to go now."

Sebastian gives Jenessa a brooch that was a gift from Shiloh, and he walks away. Jenessa kneels down just for a second and says, "I wish I could have gotten you out and hopefully saved your life. I want you know, Shiloh, I am going to make them pay. Camden and Alexia will pay for this, and you have my sworn oath on that."

Once Jenessa stands, Sebastian grabs her, and they blur right out of the window to join the rest of the Clan, leaving Shiloh for the rescuers to find her. As Sebastian and Jenessa join the rest of the Clan in the Tahoe, the mood is quiet; no one has anything to say until Jamal wakes up and says, "What happened; what did I miss?"

Malcolm turns and says to Jamal, "This is one day we won't ever forget. We may have won the battle, but we lost the war."

With a confused look on his face, Jamal just shakes his head and stares at Jenessa and sees that she is very upset. He sees a brooch she has clutched tightly in her hands. Sebastian breaks the ice and says, "Everybody, we'll get something to eat, and then we'll regroup in my room about our next move. Malcolm, I agree; we got the charm and another scroll to the map, but we lost a very nice person whom I love to call a friend today."

With that said, some of the Clan members' moods change, replaying the horrors of the events of the day only to bring out revenge that festers deep inside. One thing keeps ringing in Sebastian's mind: "How did they find us? What is the real reason why Alexia is helping Seth?" he wonders.

His thoughts come back when Jenessa says, "After the meeting, you and I need to have a talk."

Sebastian nods his head, knowing that the meeting will not go well.

Chapter 17

While Sebastian and Jenessa are in Boston, trouble is still brewing in Haven-Crest. With crime on the rise, the police department and the sheriff's department are on high alert. As people start taking all kinds of precautions to prevent themselves from becoming victims of the harsh reality of violence, Jewel Walker from the Channel 2 News makes a report to the viewers from the crime scene, "This is Jewel Walker from the Channel 2 News here in the Haven-Crest community this morning reporting yet another despicable act of violence. This morning, probably around two in the morning, some residents woke up to gunfire through the neighborhood. A few people we interviewed, who decided for their safety not to be named or videoed for TV, believe it was gang related. Two new rivals, both trying to solidify the area for their own turf, exchanged gunfire at one-another, leaving a lot of empty gun shells and shot out windows, and leaving two innocent people dead as a result. An 8-year-old boy and his elderly grandfather were both shot in their homes by stray bullets from the apparent gunfight. Their names will not be released until the families are notified. The community is speaking out for justice against the never ending battle of gang violence, and we have the Reverend Carl Wardrett here to give us a little insight on what's being done to stop such violence that takes the lives of innocent victims. Reverend Wardrett, the floor is yours," replies Jewel Walker.

"Good morning, Jewel and all the viewers of Channel 2 News; for some who don't know me, I'm the pastor, Reverend Carl Wardrett, and I came here to offer all my friends and fellow townspeople hope. I can't say that I will get rid of all the gangs overnight, but with time and effort, I will do so. It makes no sense that these good residents of Haven-Crest live in fear every day not knowing if they're going to live to see tomorrow. If the so-called protectors of Haven-Crest would get out and do what they're getting paid for, we would have this gang violence under control. The members of the Board of Officials who should be doing something about these attacks and missing persons are hiding details and information from us tax paying people of this town. Like I always say, it is time for a change to get new, fresh people on the political seats in this town; we need to vote for a new mayor, sheriff, and people in administration. Because these criminals insist on deceiving us, they are covering up issues that need to be brought out to the public. I'm here to make sure the people have a voice and a person in charge who has their best interest at heart, and I intend to make sure that certain issues are addressed and that help for the community is received. I have a supporter joining forces with me to make sure the laws are upheld and that the Committee's cover-up will stop. My supporter and I will end gang violence and stop all the unexplained deaths that have been plaguing Haven-Crest for years."

Jewel Walker takes the microphone from Reverend Wardrett, and she finishes her breaking news by saying, "Once again, if you're just tuning in, we are here investigating what appears to be a random act of gang violence, and two people are believed to have been murdered as a result. Once we get more information, we will pass it on to all the viewers in our later broadcast; this is Jewel Walker for Channel 2 News, back to Joshua and Ashley."

As Adrian arrives at the hideout, he realizes that finally his day of reckoning has come; so he heads inside to handle some long overdue business. Once he comes inside, his mood is nonchalant, and he speaks to Erika by saying, "Good morning, Erika; how are you today? Where is everybody? Is there any news on what my brother or sister may be up to? Where is Nicolette?"

Stunned by his courteous remarks and attempts to be nice, Erika responds very subtly by saying, "Everybody is checking surveillance cameras and all databases for anything out of the ordinary, and Nicolette is in her office waiting on an important call."

Adrian heads right to the door, gives an easy knock, and heads inside; he goes in and takes a seat. Nicolette leaves a voicemail, turns around in her chair, and says, "Adrian, you're up mighty early this morning. What can I do for you?"

"Nicolette, I know we haven't seen eye to eye. We've had a few disagreements, but overall, I think you've earned my respect. It takes a person with balls to stand up to me; I have much love for you, so I'm going to be a gentleman and tell you this instead of doing what I'm expected to do. To be honest, I've met Antoine, and he's not happy. You've been with him for decades, and he feels like you let him down by not doing your job. He found out himself that Sebastian is in Boston, and Alexia is hot on his trail. You haven't even gotten any clues to finding the contacts, so he wants me to kill you. However, I'm going to give you a choice instead; I can just rip out your heart and give you a merciless death that would be very honorable, or you can leave this organization and never look back. The choice is yours," replies Adrian with a devilish smirk on his face.

Nicolette becomes enraged; she stands and knocks all the office materials onto the floor. She begins changing. Her fangs extend, her eyes become golden-black, and now she's ready to attack. Adrian sits back in the chair watching Nicolette snarl and growl in anger. She looks at Adrian and says, "Who the hell do you think you are coming in my office and talking about giving me a choice and saying I haven't been doing my job for Antoine? I've given him all my blood, sweat, and tears for many decades. I have done things for him I didn't believe I could do. Now, I'm getting treated like I've betrayed Antoine, but I haven't; I've been loyal to him since he changed me. Since you will be in my position, remember this: If you've ever been loyal to anything or anyone, you need to be loyal to Antoine. Let me tell you this: I came from a rich family in Manhattan. I was born back in the1930s, and my father was a land developer and engineer who drew blueprints for a lot of builders of malls, amusement parks, and apartment buildings. I was spoiled because I could have anything I wanted. After high school, I went to college at Syracuse University, and I got my Master's Degree in Engineering. I wanted to be a land developer like my father, but my whole world changed in the summer of 1952. I went on spring break to London with three of my best friends. While enjoying the sights and indulging in the culture, I met a guy at a Lower England nightclub whom I found to be very intriguing, handsome, and mysterious. He bought me a drink, and we talked the night away. He told me that he was a part of a firm called the NGU Squad. Little did I know, that was just a front to what they really were; they were a cult that liked sacrificing and paying homage to the devil. My friends and I were invited to an underground club called The Ink Spot. All kinds of riffraff hung out there. We were very nervous, but I had to see that mysterious gentleman again. Our game plan was not to get separated, but after about an hour, all of that changed. They picked us off one by one, and I was last; even to this day, I honestly don't really know what happened. Undoubtedly, my drink was drugged, and I literally blacked out. When I came to, I was tied, gagged, and shackled to a table in some undisclosed room. All I remember seeing were six hooded figures standing by the table in a circle. As the ritual began, they all start chanting, "Ashes to ashes" and "Blood to blood," over and over. As the ceremony commenced, I was extremely frightened. The leader came up to the table with a very large knife; he cut the buttons off my shirt and marked my face and body with some sort of blood out of a bowl, and the next thing I felt was that knife cutting my chest open. He used no anesthesia, no pain killers, no nothing. I could feel my life just slipping away, and as everything started to go black, I saw the five hooded figures get their throats ripped out one by one. As I shifted my soft, blue eyes to my possible savior, to my horror, he pulled back his hood to reveal his face. I saw his fangs extend, and his eyes were golden-black. Out of all people, it was the handsome guy. I could feel the blood just rushing out of my body; my captor leaned over and said to me, "I can save you if you want to live and you desire me to do so, but you will be my confidant for all eternity." Since I wasn't ready to die, I feel I made the correct choice by saying, "Please save me. I don't want to die." He smiled, and after that, I believed I had died because I don't remember anything else until I woke up dressed in a beautiful gown at a mansion in England. I asked him what his name was, and he told me it was Antoine. Ever since that day, I've been loyal to Antoine for many years, so for you to come in here and tell me you're his new head of this Clan is downright disrespectful to me. You can tell Antoine I said to go to hell."

Adrian seems somewhat impressed by her actions; nevertheless, he has a job to do for his new boss, so he gives Nicolette one more look and ruthlessly, cold-heartedly, and without any type of hesitation, he blurs, grabs her by the throat, and slams her against the wall. He shows her no remorse; Adrian rips out her heart from her chest, and her lifeless body just falls to the floor in her office. With blood just dripping from his fingers, he turns and sees everyone in the office staring and watching in horror at what just transpired. Suddenly, the office door opens up, and a very distinguished gentleman comes inside and says, "Adrian, I applaud you for following my orders; you've passed the test and killed Nicolette. Now that task is done, let's get down to true business. I need you to send a team to Boston. I just heard through a good contact that an elderly living facility had an unexplained gas explosion, and there were three deaths. One of the casualties was an elderly woman named Shiloh Mills, and she died from an apparent heart attack. Adrian, send some loyal contacts to follow Sebastian and Alexia. For the next order of business, I have a new member to our cause; I have our witch to combat Jenessa. Being that Jenessa is the prophecy, I give you Medusa, the voodoo witch."

The room goes silent as everyone's eyes focus on Medusa. The air is thick, and as Medusa makes her entrance, she surveys the room by checking out everyone as she walks over to Antoine, his new partner in crime. Once she is standing by his side, she says to the crowd, "I know my appearance may startle some of you, but trust me; you have nothing to fear from me. I'm here to help out an old friend, so once I'm brought up to speed with what's going on, you can rest assured we'll be back in the hunt for the Book."

Adrian wonders to himself, "What is the sole purpose of Medusa being here, and what does she hope to gain by helping Antoine? Who else could be trusted to go with Andre to Boston? I guess it will be Nathan in case all hell breaks loose."

Adrian looks at Antoine and says, "Antoine, I'm going to send Andre and Nathan. Candice, you can stay with me and help me take care of some unfinished business here in Haven-Crest."

Candice doesn't reply to her fearless leader as she obeys his orders and keeps her attention focused on Medusa. Andre looks at Adrian and says, "As soon as we get packed, we'll head out to Boston to see if we can find them. What town are we heading to?"

"From some hacking, I found that Sebastian used a credit card at a Marriott hotel in Salem. I would say start there because they haven't checked out yet," replies Donna.

Andre and Nathan both get up and leave out the room to pack for the trip. Antoine seems very pleased at how Adrian has come in and taken the initiative to get the team organized. Antoine smiles and says, "Now, my strategy for us to seize control of this town and eliminate our rival clans is an old ploy, but it still works in this day and time. Candice, I want you to go to Priceless and monitor Marcella and Adam. Medusa, I want you to monitor those damn Crenshalls. Adrian, our goal is to find that Lamia before it starts killing everyone in Haven-Crest. I found the tomb where she had been held captive, but once Estelle was killed, the curse was broken and that devils spawn became unleashed to prey upon the innocent victims in this town."

Antoine grabs a bottle of blood and pours two glasses for a toast. Antoine takes one glass, holds it up, and says, "I propose a toast for an everlasting partnership; may we find the elusive Book first."

Adrian doesn't reply; he just taps glasses with Antoine. Outside the office, Donna looks at Amy and says, "Now that Nicolette is dead, I hope that Antoine honors the deal we had with her and doesn't kill us after all of this is over."

Amy gives Donna a worried look and replies, "From the look of things, this deal with Adrian doesn't stack up in our favor. God, if you don't hear any more of my prayers, please hear this one. I know what we're doing isn't right, but it's our only means of survival. I believe if they find the Book, life as we know it will go all to hell."

"Amen," replies Donna.

As the sun starts to set, the street lights come on, and about four blocks away, there are some teenage boys skateboarding in the park. Unknown to them, they are being watched by a pair of devious eyes. As the boys just keep on skating, the hunger is overwhelming. Hayden senses the sweet smell of their blood and realizes this is the opportunity to strike, so she blurs over to the unsuspecting skaters. They are caught off guard by the young girl, and they all wonder how she moved so fast. One of the boys asks, "Hey, little girl, how did you move so fast? Do you live around here? Why are you dressed like that?"

Hayden looks at all the boys and doesn't reply. Realizing that she has more than enough food to satisfy her hungry appetite, Hayden takes a deep breath, and slowly, her breathing becomes deeper and deeper. Hayden says, "I'm so hungry."

The boys are now getting concerned about the little girl. One of the boys gets brave enough to walk over to see what going on with her. By now, she knows that it's time to strike, so her vampire features come on in full display; her fangs come out, her eyes become golden-black, and her claws extend. Hayden growls and quickly begins swinging her claws to kill the unsuspecting boys. Before they can react to what is going on or try to get away, their lives are taken away from them. In a matter of minutes, Hayden has killed five young, innocent boys, and now, she stands over them with her bloody hands and face. With her child's mentality, she understands that playtime is over and it's time to move on, so she leaves, headed to somewhere safe.

Back in Boston, Alexia takes the injured Camden to a safe place to attend to his injuries. Once they enter the abandoned mansion, Camden awakens. Alexia bites her wrist and gives Camden some of her blood in order to heal him. In the back of his mind, Camden knows that if he were to die with vampire blood in his system, he would become one. He doesn't hesitate. He drinks the blood, and it starts to heal him more quickly than using witchcraft. Camden tries to sit up, but he can't; he realizes that his injuries are more serious than he first thought. With so many questions running through his mind, he looks at Alexia and says, "First, let me say thank you for rescuing me because if you hadn't, I'd probably be dead from these injuries. I didn't realize that Jenessa was that powerful; her magic cannot to be taken lightly. I see now that she didn't resist trying to hurt me, but our next encounter will be different. The Black Necro didn't fail me; it's just I need to summon more of its dark forces. I have to rely on Jazmine helping me next time. One thing I don't get is why Jamal was there with them. He's not a vampire or a witch."

"You witches can see everything, but you can't sense when another mythical creature is in your presence. I'm a vampire who can read minds, and I can sense that he's a howler, which stacks the odds in Sebastian's favor. However, unknown to him, he has a traitor in his Clan: that's how we were able to find them so easily here in Boston. Once Sebastian makes his next move, my contact will call us with the tip off," replies Alexia.

Camden shuts his eyes and concentrates to summon the dark energy needed to help heal his wounds. As his soul drifts in to a dark plane of death to find Jazmine, after about ten minutes, he finds her and says, "Jaz, what happened to my powers? Jenessa almost killed me today, and if it wasn't for Alexia, I may not have made it. I thought the sole purpose of me embracing the Black Necro was to make me more powerful than any witch. Is Jenessa truly that powerful, and do I stand a chance of defeating her?"

As Jazmine's soul hovers in front of her brother, she responds by saying, "Brother, why are you so worried? That was just a test, even though you may have failed, but trust me, we will get revenge. Next time you will see the full extent of the Black Necro. Just let your wounds heal so we can get ready for round two."

Alexia blurs out of the room to go get them something to eat. She gets in her car and heads out of the driveway. While on the way to town, she wonders what her dear brother may be thinking about the events that transpired today. With that very thought, on the other side of town, Sebastian and his Clan arrive back at the Marriott; the mood is not a pleasant one. As emotions run high, anger, sorrow, and fear fill the atmosphere inside the Tahoe with no one even recalling the devastation that happened at the nursing facility. Once Sebastian pulls into the parking spot, he cuts off the engine and says, "Let's go inside the restaurant and eat, and then we'll set a course of action for our next move."

As everyone exits the Tahoe headed to the Marriott's restaurant, their attitudes have become somewhat evasive because everyone is unsure about what the next move is and is anxious about the possibility of what may happen. After everyone places an order with the waitress, they all begin talking and sharing some laughs. Jamal sits beside Jenessa and starts soothing her thigh under the table with the hopes of changing her sour mood. As she looks at him and smiles, Jamal leans over and whispers, "Are you alright? You look like you are really pissed about something. Is there anything I can do?"

Jenessa looks at Jamal with her sexy green eyes and replies, "I appreciate you being so concerned about me, but I'm alright. We'll talk about what happened later on tonight. FYI, you know rubbing my thigh is one of my weak spots."

Jamal blushes as he smiles back at Jenessa, and Persia just watches the innocent seduction between Jenessa and Jamal. Persia feels that this is the right time to get some things out in the open, so she starts the controversy by saying, "If no one is really going say something, well, I guess I'll start the ball rolling. What the hell happened at the nursing home? That was a train wreck ready to happen, and what did that old woman say to you guys anyway? Is this an indication of the type of unorganized teamwork that we're going to be subject to, and if the old woman gave you some important information, why are you not sharing it with us?"

"Hold up, Persia; I don't know why you're trying to insinuate that I'm hiding something. Is there something you want to say to me? You've been acting very strange ever since we left Haven-Crest. I wonder why. Remember, you asked to come along; no one made you, so I'm warning you not to start any kind of scenes to draw attention to us. If you don't want to stay, then I'll send you back home. I share any and all information with my Clan if you really want to know. Shiloh told me that I have an enemy in my Clan. Ever since she made that statement to me, I've been wondering who it could be. Who would want to sabotage our mission, and who told Alexia where we would be at in Boston? I would have embraced the fact that they could have followed us, but Alexia made me believe that this was no coincidence. Since you want to stir the pot, by chance could the cheat possibly be you?" replies Sebastian.

The anger builds inside of Persia, and she just explodes with so much hatred in her reply, "Sebastian, let me say this to you: You were once a legendary killer, but somewhere along your journey, you lost your way and became this savior for the people who hate you for being what you are. Remember, no one controls Persia. I do what I want, and you want us to remain a secret and live in fear of what these humans think of or may do to us; let me show you what I am capable of doing."

Persia looks at Sebastian with a most devious glare. To prove her point, she notices the waitress coming to the table with their orders. Persia becomes impulsive and blurs over to the waitress, knocking the plates out of her hands and grabbing her by the throat. To show Sebastian that she has no conscience, she pulls back the head of the innocent mother of two kids and exposes her throat. Jenessa quickly stands and tries to reason with her cousin by saying, "Persia, what are you doing? Why do you want to kill this innocent woman, and what are you trying to prove to us? Just let her go, and we can talk all this frustration out. We are family, so there's nothing we can't work through."

"Jenessa, do you honestly believe that crap you're trying to sell to me? Do you know that I'm tired of all this talking and trying to compromise with me? How about you just deal with this on your conscience for a while," replies Persia.

As if in slow motion before anyone can blur over to stop her, Persia unleashes her fangs and her claws and literally sinks her fangs into the young woman's neck. Persia drinks her warm human blood, and with a swift stroke, she rips out her throat with her long claws and tosses the body to the floor with muscle tissues and skin all pulled back. With blood dripping from her mouth and hands, Persia understands now that there's no turning back, so she blurs right out of the room. Patrons are watching and wondering what just transpired at the table. Whispers begin all over the restaurant; Sebastian can hear the voices inside of his head. He knows he must compel the people inside the room before someone tries to leave. He sees some people using their phones to call 911, so Sebastian shuts his eyes to concentrate. Sweat starts to bead up on his forehead. Suddenly, everyone in the restaurant goes stiff, and Sebastian says, "Everyone within the sound of my voice, I want you to relax your mind; everything you just witnessed, you will forget, and you will not remember seeing the waitress either. Just go about eating and enjoying your dinner tonight."

Sebastian opens his eyes, and Jamal picks up the dead waitress and heads out the back. Everyone goes back to enjoying a normal night. Sebastian leaves some money on the table, and they all head upstairs to their rooms. Once inside the elevator, Jenessa says with panic in her voice, "I can't believe what just happened. What in the hell is going on here? We lost Shiloh today. Then my cousin Persia has just killed a waitress, and now who knows where she's gone? Can the night get any worse?"

Malcolm interrupts and replies, "Jenessa, please don't self-destruct. I know this has been a devastating day thus far, but always have faith that things can get a lot better. Just remember that you have us; we are here for you, and we love you."

"Thanks, Malcolm, I needed that. I love you guys also, and I know that we are going to make it through this," replies Jenessa.

Once the elevator reaches the fifth floor and the doors open, they all get out, and Sebastian says, "Let's go to my room for a minute. Can someone text Jamal for him to meet us there?"

Everyone heads into Sebastian's room, and he walks over to the bar for a drink. He pours some bourbon in a glass and drinks it all up. He turns to everyone and says, "I just don't know where to begin, but first things first: What happened at the home for the elderly was unexpected, and I didn't mean for Shiloh to have a heart attack because of it. We all could have gotten a lot of knowledge and help from her, especially Jenessa, but she told me that I was the key to the puzzle. I'm assuming that through me, our chances are better. Even though it may seem like I'm not hearing your questions and comments, please know that I am, loud and clear. What she told me about will unravel an ultimate secret; that secret and the hatred inside my heart fuel my desire to find the Book. I know I must come to terms with the terror and agony I've caused over the centuries, but I hear those voices begging me for mercy all the time. I conquered the hunger by not giving in to the vampire urges, and now, I'm helping all of you to be better people."

Everyone in the room goes speechless. After a few minutes, Jai Li speaks first, "Sebastian, let me say that no matter where you go, I'm right behind you with no questions asked. You haven't steered me wrong yet, and I'm positive everyone agrees with me when I say that."

"Thanks for that vote of confidence, so let's call it a night and get some rest. Tomorrow brings a new day, and we have a flight to Florida tomorrow afternoon. Good night to everybody," replies Sebastian.

As the Clan members all starts to head out of the room, Sebastian sees that morale has improved with the vote of confidence. It is showing on their faces after Jai Li made her comment about her leader. Everyone leaves except Jenessa, and Sebastian fixes another drink while Jenessa takes a seat on the couch. As Sebastian joins her, he takes a sip of the bourbon and says, "You and I do need to have a talk. There are some things that only you and I need to know. There are other things Shiloh told me while I was in the room with her in addition to there being a traitor in the Clan. She said there are going to be consequences if I revive the dead with the Book."

"We may need to check the journal that Shiloh gave you for more understanding of what it could mean. When I confronted Persia, I scanned her mind and found out she has been compelled. I'm pretty sure it was Alexia. That's how she knew where we were, but as for what she did to the waitress, I just can't understand why. What makes this situation even more unpleasant is that I can't break her compulsion that she has. I'm sorry; I will do everything in my power to free her and see that no harm comes to her. Tell me what's on your mind," replies Sebastian.

Jenessa gives him the look of a mad ass witch before she answers. Sebastian can see the anger in her face, but she calms down enough to say, "Sebastian, I appreciate everything you've done for me and my friends, but right here and now, I give you my solemn vow that I intend to kill Alexia. With every ounce of my powers, I promise you I will kill her. I don't want any ill feeling between us for that. I love you to death, and I know that there's a reason why you and I are so close. Alexia is the reason my grandma's not here. Shiloh had a heart attack at the retirement home due to Alexia's evildoing, and now we find out that she has compelled Persia into killing an innocent woman for some unknown purpose. Why haven't you killed them? She and Adrian make your life so miserable. I have seen how the things that matter to you end up becoming destroyed by their evil. They must pay for the things that they've done and the people they have hurt in the process."

"I can't be mad at you; I know you're only telling me the truth. Maybe after all these centuries, I think it's time for them to have that eternal sleep they so deserve. That's enough talk; we have a plane to catch tomorrow, so go enjoy yourself with Jamal and Jai Li. I need to give Edmund a call to see what's happening in Haven-Crest and with The Committee," replies Sebastian.

They both stand and hug, and both of them feel that something was accomplished during their talk. After Jenessa leaves the room, Sebastian picks up his cell phone and calls Edmund, but all he gets is his voicemail, so he leaves a message and hangs up.

Chapter 18

Although the day didn't go as smoothly as everyone hoped, eventually the evening gets a lot better. Jenessa finally makes it back to her room; she takes a shower and tries to get relaxed. Once she comes out of the shower, she slips into a sexy nightgown she brought along and comes out of her room to fix a glass of Jack Daniels. Suddenly, there's knock at the door. Jenesa takes a sip of the Jack and then proceeds to the door. She looks through the peephole and says, "It's late, Jamal. What do you want?"

"I thought we could have a little private time so we can talk. Can I come in?" replies Jamal.

Jenessa thinks about it for a second and still feels jetlagged from the flight. She unlocks the door, lets him in, and says, "I'm not going to be up late, so let's talk and have one drink. Then I'm off to bed."

Jamal comes in and sits on the couch. Jenessa, being a gracious hostess, pours him a glass of Jack Daniels also. Jenessa takes a seat beside Jamal on the sofa in her sexy gown. She takes her long, beautiful leg and props it under her other leg so she is turned sideways to face Jamal. He sips the Jack Daniels and says, "This is good. I see you're drinking this Jack straight with no chaser; you're being mighty brave. You may want to slow down and just sip on this stuff. I'd hate to see you with a hangover in the morning. I just want to talk to you about what Shiloh said to you because I saw how upset you were once you came back to the truck. I don't want to be the one who digs up old wounds. I just want to say that I'm glad you kicked Camden's ass today. I wonder how badly he got get hurt because Alexia blurred him out of there fast before anyone could check on his status. Your powers threw him through the window, and I'm sure the glass cut him up pretty badly. Honestly, since I've became a howler, I haven't really talked to anyone about this; I guess I'm just unsure how someone will react when I do. It's a lot to adjust to; being able to turn into a wolf is something I will undoubtedly never get over. Years ago, I wouldn't have relished the thought of becoming a supernatural creature. What's so unbelievable is that these are some of the stories we used to hear as children, but in all actuality, we do exist; some of us are good and some bad, but it is what it is though. Let me ask you: If you're this so-called prophecy, when does the foretold legend become true? I've seen some of your powers manifested. I saw the witchcraft unleashed from inside of you. I know you can really do some heavy damage with that, but what about your vampire and howler blood ties? By being part vampire, would you need blood to control the vampire hunger like Sebastian?"

Jenessa takes a big gulp of the Jack, wipes her mouth, and replies, "Honey, truth be told, I don't know what to expect anymore. Once I first found out I was a prophecy, I just couldn't wrap my head around the very concept of being a witch, much less a vampire or a howler, but after embracing the whole unnatural situation, seeing things that I honestly just couldn't believe were true, witnessing visions of people whom I've never met before, and seeing my dead mother for the first time really sent shockwaves through my mind. Without the help of Grandma and Sebastian, I would probably be in the cuckoo's nest by now. One thing I've learned is the power of control. Knowing that I have all this power scares me because of what I possibly could do to harm someone without really being aware of the consequences I may inflict. Oh yeah, let's not forget temptation; it's always present and makes the difference in being a good witch or being like Camden, who has given in and embraced by the dark side. Grandma told me that once my powers reach maturity, whomever I ally with will have the edge toward finding the Book. Shiloh gave me a journal and a spell in a scroll that is supposed be our secret weapon. I'm hoping that the journal can shed some light on my soul purpose of being the prophecy."

"Wow, I never knew that your life was that complicated. I thought being a howler was hard. Adapting is the principle key in this type of life-changing ordeal. From what I've witnessed, some type of event triggers the evolutionary change. Distress triggered the witch phase; I wonder what would trigger the howler or vampire phase. Being that a howler is an animal, I would bet my trust fund that it would take some sort of animal instinct or behavior to trigger the phase," replies Jamal.

Jenessa takes a big gulp and finishes off the glass of Jack, and the effects of the alcohol finally take hold. She looks at Jamal with a hunger in her eyes, and he begins to think that she may be a little tipsy or drunk. Jenessa says, "Jamal, I don't know if it's the alcohol or, like you said, my animal instincts starting to emerge, but I'm finding it very hard to control myself right now. My adrenaline level is rising because I can feel my heart beating very fast, plus your animal scent is so alluring that my body is heating up like an inferno. Something is urging me over to you on the couch, and I can't resist its power."

Jenessa pours another drink and heads back to the couch. No words are spoken as Jenessa sits down beside Jamal, gazes into his eyes, and gives him a soft kiss on the lips. As Jamal looks at her, his animal urges become aroused also. He holds her hand, and suddenly, Jamal senses the aura of the full moon being hidden behind the clouds. Slowly, they continue kissing and giving in to their desires. Jenessa rips open Jamal's shirt, dips her fingernails into his chest, and saddles him on the couch. As he starts kissing her neck, Jenessa throws her head back, and Jamal notices that her eyes have turned a golden yellow. They both start breathing heavily and growling at each other. Jamal unties her gown from the back and the glimmering satin fabric slides right off her naked body. Passion overwhelms them both, and they throw caution to the wind and let their animal instincts take over. As the alcohol runs its course and call of the wild has ended, they lie in each other's arms, holding onto the love that has brought them back together. Although the night of passion has ended, the new day starts a new chapter in their lives that has uncertain possibilities which they intend to face head on, letting nothing stop them.

As Edmund stands on the balcony looking out into the early morning sunrise, he hears the birds chirping, sees dew on the grass, and gets a nostalgic feeling that warms his ever so dead soul. "Majestic" is a word and a feeling that comes to his mind as he turns and looks over his shoulder at Genie as she lies in the bed still asleep, or so he thinks. He starts to wonder about Sebastian and the Clan away in Boston since he hasn't gotten any messages or phone calls from them. He walks back into the room and picks up his phone and he notices an unplayed voicemail, so he walks back out on the balcony and plays it. He listens to Sebastian's message; immediately, Edmund's eyes widen from the news he has just received. Edmund puts his hand on the rail and turns back to Genie, who is now awake and sitting up in the bed. She says, "Good morning, babe; what's wrong? You look like you've gotten some bad news? Is everything alright; was it Sebastian who called?"

With so many questions, Edmund doesn't know really know how to respond to Genie, so he feels telling her the truth instead of lying to her would be the noble thing to do. Edmund walks back into the room, sits on the bed, holds Genie's hands, and with sincerity in his eyes, says, "I was just listening to a voicemail that Sebastian left me on my phone, and it was a bad day for them. Somehow Alexia and Camden showed up, and there was a major fight between Camden and Jenessa with her almost killing

Camden. They met Shiloh and she gave them the charm, a journal, and a spell. However, during the melee, she had a heart attack and died before she could help them. Jenessa was heartbroken that she couldn't learn anything from her before her demise."

Genie's reaction is what Edmund expected; she is shocked, but he knows she is going to ask the ultimate question he really can't answer. Genie says, "So, how's Persia? Did Sebastian say anything about her? Please don't let anything happen to my baby. I've been trying to call her, and I haven't gotten her to pick up."

Edmund takes a deep breath and replies very easily by saying, "Persia didn't get hurt at the home for the elderly. Persia is okay; don't worry so much about her. She's a grown woman. Sebastian says he believes Persia lost her phone. When he calls back, I'll have him get her to call you."

Genie becomes at ease after Edmund assures her that Persia's alright. Edmund gives her a light kiss on the lips and says, "Let's go downstairs and get some breakfast."

Genie nods head, gets up, and puts her robe on to go downstairs. As they head downstairs, she says, "Honey, I'm going to fix you a breakfast you won't ever forget. I hope you like omelets."

"You know what they say; the way to a vampire's heart is with food and blood. Everything you need should be in the kitchen. I'll be there to help you in a few minutes. I've got to make a couple of calls first, so you can get started without me."

Genie smiles and heads into the kitchen while Edmund heads into his office. Once inside, he shuts the door and sits at his desk, realizing that he needs to talk to Sebastian to find out what really happened to Persia. Edmund calls, and Sebastian picks up and says, "Hey, Edmund, you got my message; let me just say that it's not going according to plan. We were infiltrated by Alexia. She somehow compelled Persia to get our whereabouts here in Boston, and they tried to stop us. Jenessa injured Camden, and they got away. In the process, we loss Shiloh along with any opportunity to find more information on the Book. Shiloh told me I was the link to this whole ordeal and said that I may want to reconsider raising the dead because that may not be a wise decision. After we went to dinner, Persia tried to call me out and killed an innocent waitress in the process before she blurred away. I compelled the whole room to forget what had happened. I've been trying to track Persia down, but Alexia has clouded her mind from my telepathy. Right now, I don't know where she is. Jenessa has been trying to do a locator spell to see if she can find her also. What's going on there?"

"Nothing much going on here. I have the meeting with the Committee in a little while, and I'm about to go by Priceless to checked on Adam and

Marcella. Other than that, everything has been sort of quiet except for five young boys getting murdered down at the skateboard park. From what was told, they had their throats ripped out and were drained of blood also. We may have a new vampire lurking around, or it could be Declan. I'll keep my eyes open. So, what's the game plan for the next destination?" replies Edmund.

Sebastian pauses and says, "Well, our flight leaves in a couple of hours headed to Key West to find a woman named Sable. Edmund, promise me one thing. Just be careful. I have a bad feeling that something is about to happen."

"Sebastian you're acting like a concerned parent. I promise you we'll be alright until you get back. Let's hope nothing happens with the next quest and that there are no more dead bodies. I'll talk to you when your flight lands," replies Edmund.

As Sebastian hangs up with Edmund, he just can't shake the unpleasant feeling that one get when sensing an eerie feeling about something. After talking with Sebastian, Edmund knows that hiding the fact that Persia is missing from Genie is going to have dire consequences when she finds out. While Edmund is in his office out of sight and out of mind, Genie calls Syngyn to bring him up to speed on the plan, "Hey, it's me. He's in the other room probably talking to Sebastian. Once we eat and run by Priceless, then we'll head for the meeting with The Committee at the courthouse. Just think, honey, we're about to open the eyes of The Committee and set Haven-Crest on fire; I think I hear him coming. Talk to you soon."

Genie hangs up her phone as Edmund walks into the kitchen. Not to seem so suspicious, Edmund says, "I hope I didn't interrupt an important conversation."

"No, it wasn't important; it was just Persia returning my phone call. She said she's having a good time in Boston and told me about the accident at the home for the elderly too. Enough about my mother-daughter talk. Let's eat before the food gets cold so we can go by Priceless before it's time for the meeting," replies Genie.

Edmund's vampire radar goes off as he realizes that Sebastian just informed him that Persia is missing, yet Genie told him that she just spoke to her on the phone. He sees a deception forming right before his eyes and wonders why Genie would lie to him; he begins to see through the clouds of deceit. Was Sebastian right all along? Do she and Persia have a motive, and are they working with The Committee? Trying not to let his emotions get the best of him, a thought rings in his head that she might betray him like that. Not to seem upset, Edmund plays along with her in an effort to find out more of what her plans are. He takes a bite of the breakfast omelet and says, "Genie, this is simply delicious. I've had some good breakfast omelets before, but damn, this is great. You are a really good cook, plus you are an amazing woman. I just can't help but be fascinated by your honesty, companionship, and love. Would you make an old vampire like me proud and be by my side as my wife? I know this may catch you a little off guard, but, Genie, I love you, and I hope you feel the same way about me."

Feeling stunned is Genie's initial reaction, and she is shocked that a noble man like Edmund has fallen love with a conniving, cold-hearted, and hateful witch like her. Genie looks in Edmund's soft, green eyes and says, "Edmund, I don't know what to say. I feel the same about you. Yes, I love you, but I can't help but wonder why you want to marry me. Don't get me wrong. I love spending time with you, and I've never met an incredible man such as you in my life. Any woman would be a fool not to marry a good man like you, Edmund, so I have to say yes."

Edmund leans over and gives Genie a spontaneous kiss. They continue to eat, and soon afterwards, they get dressed and head out to Priceless. After about a fifteen minute ride, they reach the restaurant. Before they get out to head inside, Genie says to Edmund, "I want you to know that you've made my day. I want the world to know that I'm engaged to the most special man in the world, and it doesn't hurt that he's sexy too. Are you going to let Adam and Marcella know that we're engaged?"

Edmund smiles at Genie, reaches for her hand, and replies, "It's not that I don't want to tell them, but I want to tell Sebastian first. What about you? Are you going to call Persia and inform her of the engagement?"

"I plan on calling her later on tonight to give her the happy news," replies Genie.

They get out and head inside Priceless. Once inside, they are greeted by Marcella. She sees the happy aura and says, "What's going on with you two? You both look mighty happy for a couple who's an hour late. Have you heard from Sebastian? What's going in Boston? Were they at that home for the elderly that blew up?"

Edmund replies, "Marcella, right now I'm in a great mood, and yes, I heard from him this morning. He left me a message and said that they were there when the nursing home exploded. One of the contacts died from a heart attack, but they did get the charm. He didn't go into a whole lot of detail, but I'll call him later. Anything interesting going on; where's Adam?"

Marcella continues to stare at Edmund and Genie. She says to Edmund, "We need to talk in private about some Priceless business. Genie, can you excuse us? Would you like a drink? Help yourself to anything. This will only take a minute."

Marcella and Edmund walk back toward Edmund's office and shut the door. Once inside, Marcella sits on Edmund's desk, and Edmund fixes a drink. He says, "What's going on? What's so important?"

Marcella shakes her head and replies, "Have you talked to Sebastian today, and have you been watching the news about the missing basketball coach? To top all that off, the cops found a couple of dead bodies in the woods this morning. I don't know what the hell is going on, but we need to be very careful until Sebastian gets back. Also, we have a more pressing matter that needs our attention now. Chrisha is missing. I went by her house after everyone left, and her mother said she received a text that she was going to the beach with Jenessa and Jai Li. That was two days ago, and I've been checking everywhere and have found nothing. Things are not adding up; it's like there are too many coincidences happening at the same time. You may want to let Sebastian know, but I'll keep my eyes open. One other thing: When you go back out, check out the woman in the blue jacket. She's been here the last two days, and she looks so familiar. I think she may be watching the place or looking for someone."

"I talked to Sebastian this morning, and he told me that Persia is missing. She's been compelled by Alexia, and she told them that they were headed to Boston and to the home for the elderly to find Shiloh. I haven't said anything to Genie about this; she would probably go off the deep end, so they are searching for her as we speak. Genie lied to me about talking to Persia. I think she may be up to something; I just don't know what yet. I woke up this morning with this weird feeling about something bad happening today. With these dead bodies and now Chrisha missing, what else can go wrong?" replies Edmund.

Edmund reaches for the remote and turns on the TV, and there's a breaking news alert already on, "This is Jewel Walker with the Channel 2 News here in Haven-Crest. We received an alert about ten minutes ago that some dead bodies have been discovered in the so-called Eerie Forest. Some fishermen walking through these woods right behind me found what could possibly be three bodies. From what we overheard, some wild animals may have killed them, but we really won't know until an autopsy report comes out. Right now, it's unclear who they are until authorities identify the bodies and their families get notified. This is just one in a long list of unexplained deaths that have been happening over the last few weeks, so residents, be aware of your surroundings, and be careful if you are out at night by yourself. I will bring you more updates once we receive further news; this is Jewel Walker with Channel 2 News, back to Josh and Ashley."

Edmund cuts off the TV, looks at Marcella, and says, "Things are not adding up. Five kids were mauled down by the skating park, three people are missing from the college, and now Chrisha is also missing. Could there be more howlers or vampires in the area that are causing all these deaths? After this meeting today, I think we really need to focus on what is going on in town. Just hold the fort until I get back."

Marcella nods her head, and they head back up front. Edmund surveys the room and spots the woman Marcella warned him about. She looks pretty harmless, so he just keeps walking. Edmund sees Genie at the bar having a drink. She turns to him and says, "What's wrong? You seem like you're stressed. How about a drink before we go over to the courthouse?"

Edmund doesn't put up a fight. He pours a glass of bourbon, takes a big gulp, and says, "I needed that. Genie, are you ready to go?"

She smiles at Edmund and says, "Yes, let's go. Marcella, don't worry about Edmund; I'll keep my eye on him."

Marcella smiles and replies, "Please do because right now my hands are full, and I could really use the help."

They all laugh, and Edmund and Genie head out to the courthouse. Once they get in the car, Genie asks, "Was everything alright with Marcella?"

"She needed me to sign some checks for the banks, and I had to approve the payroll for the employees. She also told me that the coach from the university is missing and two students also. I saw on the news that someone found three dead bodies in Eerie Forest. The town is beginning to become unraveled before our very eyes. What is so frustrating is I don't know the root cause. Could it be a pack of rogue howlers or a couple of vampires passing through trying to cause trouble?" replies Edmund.

Genie doesn't reply to Edmund. She reaches out and rubs his hand to offer her comfort and assurance that things are going to get better. They pull into the parking lot, get out, and head inside. As they walk down the lowly lit hallway, Edmund just can't shake that weird feeling he has been having all day. Edmund and Genie come in, and Karen says to Edmund, "Hey stranger, I haven't seen you around lately. Where have you been hiding? I see you got a girlfriend."

Edmund blushes, smiles, and replies, "It's good to see you too, Karen, and the answer to your question is we're friends with benefits."

Karen laughs, and Edmund takes his seat so the meeting can start. Mayor Dobson stands, takes the floor, and starts the meeting by saying, "Friends, we have a problem. Crime is escalating to an all-time high. I mean pretty much someone is dying every day in Haven-Crest. It's all over the news that we've had eight dead bodies recovered in the last seven days; that's too many. The town's in an uproar. What are we going to do? Something has to be done now to stop the murders. Are we closer to finding Syngyn, the hunter?"

Sheriff Michaels adds to the conversation by saying, "You're right, mayor; something has to be done. Who or whatever is killing the people here has to be stopped. My guys are out on patrol making sure that the residents are safe, but we can't be everywhere to see everything. Genie, have you been able to locate the Lamia? Someone called and reported that he saw a little girl in tattered clothes lurking around the neighborhood over on Chestnut Street a couple of days ago. That could have been what attacked the boys at the skate park. Celister hasn't given me the autopsy report yet on the bodies that were found in Eerie Forest, so we still do not know the cause of those deaths. On top of all that, we all know that the good Reverend Wardrett will be paying us a visit pretty soon because he lives for this type of attention. I was also told of a solid white wolf roaming the area. With so many trees being cut down now, wolves are basically looking for food. However, as long as I've been hunting and fishing, I've never seen a white wolf. From what I've read, they are supposed to be sacred."

The mood from some of the members of the Committee becomes intense, Genie answers Sheriff Michaels by saying, "Sheriff, I've been working on some spells to hopefully track her down so we can find her. The fact that she's a child makes it very hard to pinpoint her location."

Doctor Burton takes the floor, realizing that he has the answer to all their questions and problems, so he says, "Everyone, I told you a while back that I had intentions of giving up my seat on the board, but I want all of you to know that I've been convinced to stay. I mentioned that I have a new doctor working at the hospital, but the other day under extreme circumstances, I witnessed something that changed my view on mythical creatures. I now realize that they walk among us and appear to be normal people, which makes it even harder for us to identify them. When the two missing hikers were brought into the emergency room the other night to be checked out, little did I know that something had bitten them and turned them into howlers; they both changed, and I saw my resident colleague also change before my very eyes. What I'm trying to say is that Dr. Kareem Jensyn and Syngyn are the same person, so he's the vampire hunter we've been looking for. He told me that he has a big surprise for us, so I invited him to this meeting."

Immediately Edmund goes into shock. His eyes widen, and his breathing becomes very heavy. Karen notices that something is wrong with Edmund, so she leans over and says, "Edmund, are you alright? You look like you're about to get sick."

Edmund pulls himself together, turns to his friend, and responds by saying, "Karen, I'm okay. I think I ate something that didn't agree with my stomach. I hope it's not a virus. Don't worry; I'll be alright. Thanks for being concerned about an old man."

Karen smiles at her friend and turns her attention back to Dr. Barton. He continues to inform the Committee about Syngyn by saying, "Technically, Syngyn saved me and some of the nurses in the emergency room by killing one of the howlers: the male howler, Ryan. We managed to kidnap the female howler, Kim, with hopes of being able to understand the aspects of becoming a howler. Also, as an added bonus, we have a young vampire, Declan, in our possession to further interrogate."

Mayor Dobson and Judge Simmons both smile, and now some Committee members begin to embrace the concept that they have the upper hand in this eternal battle of survival. Dr. Barton finishes his points by saying, "The only way we're going to rid our town of those monsters and cold-blooded killers is to eliminate them before they eliminate us. Members, I present to you Syngyn, the hunter."

Syngyn makes his grand entrance. He comes out in a hooded robe with the hood draping down so no one can see his face. Syngyn walks to the front of the room and says, "Good evening, everyone, it's an honor to meet all of you and definitely a pleasure to be in your company. I heard that you require my services for ridding your town of mythical creatures, in particular some vampires. Yes, I am a vampire; however I'm not one by choice. I was more or less a victim of a heinous crime against nature. I was supposed to be killed by my captors, but by some unseen sympathy, I didn't journey through the tunnel of light into heaven; instead, I'm still stuck in hell. I'll return to that story very shortly, but let me change the subject for a moment. The gift I present to you is this: I have a female howler named Kimberly and a vampire named Declan."

A guard escorts the two mythical creatures into view for the Committee to see. All of the members' attention is focused on the young monsters that have been presented to them. Principal Maynard stands and says, "What is this? These are kids. What are going to do, torture them? I'm not going to have this on my conscience. I hate all aspects of the supernatural, but this is not right. Don't you all see that we are breaking the law by what we are doing? No matter what I say or how I feel, you're going to torture them to get what knowledge you can, but please do not kill them."

"Susan, are you out of your damn mind? I understand what you're saying, but consider this: With regard to these kids you're trying to protect, what happens if they corner you one night, drink your blood, and kill you? We have to protect ourselves as well as our families and the innocent people of Haven-Crest. I have no intention of killing them, but we may have to result to drastic measures to retrieve the information we need from them. Look at them; if they could get loose, they would probably rip our throats out as we speak. We've come too far to get sentimental over them.

Our ancestors didn't start this Committee for nothing, and I should not have to remind any of you that we have a purpose of protecting Haven-Crest from the supernatural and all other sorts of mythical creatures," replies Mayor Dobson.

Syngyn interrupts the conversation by saying, "Ladies and gentlemen, I brought you these two supernatural entities to answer a lot of questions you may have about us. Now, since they both are still new to our kind, they may be helpful to your cause or possibly be detrimental to your lives. I've given them some high doses of Pink Autumn and Aconite to keep them calm, so they won't cause any trouble. Also, they have been chained up just as an extra precaution."

Edmund feels that someone has to resume control of this situation before it gets out of hand. He turns and looks at Genie and says, "Wait, this is inhumane; we can't treat them like animals. What are we doing? Can't you all see that we're going about this the wrong way? We need to keep them tied up and interrogate them to get the information we need without torturing them. I know that it is imperative we find out who's responsible for all these killings around town. We need to reassure the residents that we, as the Committee, have complete control over all the negativity that has plagued us over the last nine months or so."

The other members begin mumbling amongst one another and nodding their heads in support of Edmund's comments. Edmund notices that Syngyn doesn't show any sign of support in his opinion, so to try to understand Syngyn's motive, Edmund says, "Syngyn, I'm not trying to say that your method is devious, but I'm just saying let's just take a different approach. First, let me say that I've heard a lot about you. Your name has rung loud through the vampire community, I'm sure, but since you're a vampire, why would you want to kill your own kind?"

Syngyn starts to laugh, and Edmund soon becomes pissed by his reaction. With his hood still covering his face, Sygyn turns and replies, "Edmund, you're very observant. Truth be told, I've never been asked that question, but my answer would be.... ahh, I would sum it up to "payback." Like I said earlier, I didn't ask to become a vampire; my transition was due to conditions forced on me by someone I looked up to and someone I admired, and the worst thing of all is that I loved that person with all my heart."

To anyone else in the room, those words do not make sense, but Edmund understands the message loudly and clearly. Now that his curiosity is sparked, Edmund tries to mind read to see who it might be, but somehow he can't. Genie stands up, walks over to Edmund, and says, "Honey, what are you doing? You need to stop before this gets out of hand."

Unknown to them, nosey Karen overhears the conversation and looks at Edmund and Genie. Karen now is starting to put the pieces to the puzzle together that something is not right. Before anyone can move or say anything, Declan starts to come to and becomes very aggressive and tries to break free. He turns to Syngyn and says, "Syngyn, what the hell am I doing chained to this chair? I thought we had a deal. Why did you just use me to help you kill all those people and now you turn me over to these self-righteous killers? For what reason? All of this to kill …."

Before he can finish his statement, Syngyn rips Declan's heart right out of his chest with his sharp claws. As blood drips from Syngyn's hands, Declan's head drops down. Syngyn turns to the Committee and says, "Well, sorry about that. I didn't mean to kill him, but I could not let him spoil my surprise. Don't worry; if I found him, surely I can get you another vampire, and we still have a howler."

Judge Simmons stands up in horror over what just took place. She says, "What in the hell is going on, Syngyn? Can you explain to me what the sole purpose of killing Declan was; what is your plan?"

Genie speaks up and says, "Wait, everyone, let's hear Syngyn out before we cast judgment on him."

Fire chief Maynard intervenes by commenting, "I agree with Karen. If we were going to interrogate them, why did you just kill our prisoner? So, what was he about to say? He mentioned that you were behind some of the murders that he was committing. Why? Maybe we should capture you and torture you for what you have done to the innocent people of Haven-Crest."

After Judge Simmons expresses her opinion, the other members begin questioning one another about his intentions in this situation. Syngyn just watches them bicker, seeing that his plan is being well orchestrated. Syngyn waits for his cue from his ally Genie, and she beings reciting a holding spell to keep the members in their seats. Unknown to everyone, Kim has started waking up. She hears all the bickering and wonders where she is and how she got there. Kim notices the shackles and realizes that she can't get loose. As she pulls the chains to slide her wrists free, to her surprise, she gets a rude awaking. Once she gets the shackles over her wrists, she gets a strong burning and sizzling reaction. She realizes that her only chance at freedom is to turn into a howler and do what it takes to get free from her captors so she can live to see another day. Suddenly and very slowly, she begins changing. The Committee hears her bones breaking, and they notice the physical changes up close and personal. The room goes silent. There is not one word or a peep from anyone; they just sit in amazement and horror at what they see. Kim goes down on her hands and knees. Her arms pop out of joint as well as her legs. Her fingers become sharp paws, and hair quickly sprouts out of her body. Syngyn moves out of the way. Once Kim transforms into a wolf, the Committee members start panicking, and the room becomes very much in disarray. Some of the ladies are yelling for protection from Kim.

Edmund feels that someone must take charge of this chaos and restore some order before it gets out of hand. He waves his hands and says, "Everyone, please settle down and remain calm. The more fear we show, the more her aggression toward us will increase, and she may be more likely to attack. Just remain calm and let me draw her attention so you can all get out without getting harmed, and hopefully, we can get her to relax."

Everyone becomes silent and listens to Edmund's orders as Syngyn just stands and watches what goes down. Edmund takes off his coat and begins to wave it at Kim to get her attention. Kim just continues to snarl and growl at Edmund. Suddenly, in a hurry to leave, Principal Maynard knocks over a chair, and the noise from the commotion attracts Kim's attention to her. With a quick look, Edmund sees Kim arch her body to rush and attack Principal Maynard. Edmund realizes he must make a choice: Should he save Principal Maynard and expose himself as a vampire or simply let the Kim attack and kill her? The obvious choice is made. Edmund blurs and knocks Principal Maynard out of the way, and Kim catches Edmund off balance and knocks him to the floor. With a quick twist of her body, Kim lunges at Edmund with her fangs drawn back and bites Edmund in his lower neck and in the process, she rips out some of his throat. He tries to get up, but he falls back onto the floor due to the amount of blood loss. Genie comes running over to see if she can help him with his injuries. Karen Carmichaels also comes over to offer her help to her fallen friend. Standing in shock, Agent Ambrose and Sheriff Michaels look at one another. Agent Ambrose puts her gun back into her holster, and she walks over to check on Kim's condition. During the lunge at Edmund, he managed to break one of her arms, and she somehow miraculously changed back to her original form. Agent Ambrose drapes her body with a blanket. The sheriff walks over to Mayor Dobson and says, "Is everyone alright? Is anyone severely hurt and in need of medical attention?"

Genie turns her head with tears in her eyes and replies, "Yes, it's Edmund. He needs a doctor. He's badly wounded by the howler bite. Dr. Barton, come on over here and check him out."

Dr. Barton gets up off the floor, picks up his medical bag, and slowly walks over to Edmund. Mayor Dobson stands up and says, "Hold on, Marion. Did anyone see how fast Edmund moved to save Susan Maynard from that howler girl? I hate to say this because he has been my friend for a very long time, but I believe that Edmund is a vampire; that's the only explanation I can think of to account for how fast he moved across the room to help her."

Syngyn sees this as the perfect opportunity to offer in his opinion. "Mayor Dobson, I think the term is called "blurred." That is what we vampires do to move very fast. Committee members, the facts and evidence are here before your very eyes. It's not hard to understand that you've been deceived by one of your most trusted members. He has been helping to hide the vampires' identities and actions so you won't capture and torture them. Once you get over the shock that you have been betrayed, you can put the pieces of the puzzle together and realize that if he's one, then there have to be more vampires besides him. Let's get him to confess now."

Sheriff Michaels turns to Agent Ambrose and says, "He's has a good point. All along we've been hunting and trying to locate vampires in Haven-Crest, yet we had one of those damn vampires right under our noses and didn't even know it. What do we do with him now?"

Judge Simmons stands and says, "We need to find out who the other vampires are besides him because they could be the ones who are causing all these killings."

The members agree with Judge Simmons and think they should torture the wounded Edmund for some information, but Genie now becomes appalled at how they are trying to torture Edmund. She says, "Why are you all acting like an angry mob trying to lynch him before you hear his side of the story? You need to let him speak."

Unknown to the members of the Committee, Syngyn has compelled some of the guards to follow his orders, so Syngyn interrupts by saying, "Wait, guards, stand Edmund up so I can ask him a couple of questions. Edmund Martin, why haven't you told anyone that you're a vampire? Now that your secret has been exposed, can I boldly say that Sebastian Kane, the rightful owner of Priceless, is also a vampire? After some intense investigating, I found out that he was the one who turned you into a monster, and you became a vampire because of him. I would guess that Marcella Jacobs and Adam Mercer are both vampires also. I think the Committee would like to know if you and your Covenant are responsible for the murders and killings in Haven-Crest over the past year or so."

As Edmund stands with the guards holding him up, he uses every ounce of strength he has left in his body to answer Syngyn. Edmund starts coughing up blood from his wounds and then takes a deep breath and replies, "Yes, you found me out, and yes, I'm a vampire. Like Fritz told you while you were torturing him, I can't reveal my Clan to you. There's no way I would do that to the people I care about. Tell me, Syngyn, why are you a vampire hunter? Why do you hunt down vampires for people who hate us for what we are? Vampires have come a long way since the early days of hunting and killing humans, but there are some vampires that still kill for the taste of human blood. As long as I've lived in this town, I've done nothing but try to protect Haven-Crest from any kind of mythical creatures that pose a threat."

Edmund coughs again, and more blood comes up. Syngyn walks over to him and replies very nonchalantly, "That was very insightful. It almost brought tears to my eyes to hear your words, but with all that having been said, let me explain this: I hunt vampires for one simple reason. I hate them because I became one not by my choice but by someone else's choice. For years, I've plotted my revenge. I needed the help of a cunning ally, someone to get close enough to give me the right opportunity to strike, so I sent my ace-in-the-hole, and SHAZAM, I'm here in Haven-Crest. The best thing of all is this individual is not going to see this one coming......Ain't that right, DAD? You're not going to believe this, but Genie, the woman you fell in love with, helped me do all of this to you."

Edmund goes into sudden shock. He looks around at Genie as he holds the towel around his throat to stop the blood flow from the howler bite. Genie sits there with a devious smirk on her face. Edmund finally realizes that Syngyn is his long lost son. As he watches Syngyn pull back the hood on his robe to expose his face, slowly and very methodically, Syngyn walks over to his long lost father. Syngyn stands eye to eye with Edmund, looking at him with a burning hatred in his cold heart, and quickly and without any hesitation, Syngyn sticks his sharp claws into Edmund's chest and pulls out his heart. It beats for a couple of seconds, and then Syngyn looks at Edmund and says, "Revenge is ever so sweet, and payback is a bitch, old man."

Edmund finally gets to go to heaven by following the white light to the tunnel into the hereafter. As the members of the Committee look around at one another and the questions remains: Where do they go from here? What's going to happen once Sebastian finds out his best friend, brother, and business partner was killed by his estranged vampire son, Justin, also known as Syngyn? This saga continues.......

Edwards Brothers Malloy
Thorofare, NJ USA
December 29, 2015